After the Kill

The kill had been strangely silent and created a momentary stillness before the noise of the city rushed in on him. The noise seemed to bring the night with it; everything around him turned the color of charcoal. Central Park was empty, abandoned. He clapped his hands and the black wolf trotted to his side. The wolf was panting slightly. Dane ran his hand down the side of the wolf's head. It came away covered with dirt and blood. He saw Lange's body, an unrecognizable lump in the center of the dark grove, no different from the rocks that lay strewn throughout the park. High above the trees, a row of lights came on in one of the apartments. They shone down like blind white eyes in the night sky . . .

PREDATORS

ERIC SAUTER

PUBLISHED BY POCKET BOOKS NEW YORK

This novel is a work of fiction. Names, characters, places and incidents are either the product of the author's imagination or are used fictitiously. Any resemblance to actual events or locales or persons, living or dead, is entirely coincidental.

Another *Original* publication of POCKET BOOKS

POCKET BOOKS, a division of Simon & Schuster, Inc.
1230 Avenue of the Americas, New York, N.Y. 10020

ISBN: 0-671-61719-2

First Pocket Books printing April 1987

10 9 8 7 6 5 4 3 2 1

POCKET and colophon are registered trademarks
of Simon & Schuster, Inc.

Printed in the U.S.A.

FOR BETH AND MOLLY

Acknowledgments

A lot of people helped with the creation of *Predators* and they deserve credit. My very special thanks to:

My agent, Adele Leone, for her suggestions, her faith, and her hard work. A writer couldn't ask for a better agent or friend.

My editors, Bill Grose and Paul McCarthy; Bill, for his support, his judgment, and his ideas; Paul, for his suggestions, his perseverance, and his attention to detail; they helped make *Predators* a better book.

My wife, Beth, for proofreading the manuscript every time I asked her to and for putting up with my lunatic behavior for the past year.

Denise Gess, for her ideas, her enthusiasm, and her friendship.

Dick Marek, for his interest in the book and his suggestions.

Marty Kurtz and Howard Levin of NYC Bureau of Animal Affairs, for giving generously of their time and answering all of my strange and obscure questions. They do a tremendous job with very limited resources. I hope I've done them justice.

Detective Kennedy of the Central Park Precinct, for showing me around and answering my questions about police procedure in the Central Park Precinct.

The behavior of the wolves in *Predators,* at least in the first section, is based primarily on the book by Barry Hannah Lopez, *Of Wolves and Men.* One incident in that section is modeled on an anecdote reported by Lopez.

Although Lopez tends toward the mystical in his writing, his book remains the best one on the subject. It is highly recommended for anyone interested in learning more about wolves. The illustrations alone make it fascinating; his insights make it invaluable.

As for the later behavior of the black wolf in *Predators,* anything is possible.

THE FIRST TIME Dane saw the black wolf, it saved his life. He'd been walking for days, traveling north along the base of the range, well below the hard green line of fir and spruce. The clear skies of the late Canadian autumn had been replaced by endless drifting clouds as flat and gray as the surface of an anvil. He kept moving, unable to slow down, and stopped only to sleep and to scavenge for whatever he could find to eat. A meal was usually a few handfuls of dried wrinkled blueberries left by the herds of deer and caribou on their way north to the relative safety of the Stikine. Even now, as winter closed in around him, Dane stayed clear of the plateau and the towns that were scattered along its western edge.

When the sun was a smudge of yellow fading behind the clouds, he crawled beneath the wide boughs of a fir and drifted off into a sleep that was as restless as his days. In the morning, he awoke to find several inches of snow on the ground. He crawled out from under the tree and stopped. Cut clean and deep in the new snow were the tracks of a wolf. Dane examined one paw print closely. It was as big as his own hand, the largest he'd ever seen. He followed the tracks to a spot several yards away where he made another discovery.

1

There, directly across from the place where he'd fallen asleep, the wolf had lain down to watch him. He felt around the wide, deep depression, crushed the packed snow between his fingers and brought it to his face. The snow gave off a sharp sour smell. Dane touched it to his forehead first, then rubbed the snow into his cheeks before stepping away.

The tracks led into the dense forest toward the mountains to the north and west. He retrieved his pack and rifle from beneath the tree and followed them. For the first time in months, he felt the tentative stirrings of emotion come alive inside him. The new feelings surprised him; he thought he had buried them forever. He picked up his pack and rifle and hurried along.

By midmorning, he had tracked the wolf more than ten miles. Once or twice he caught a distant glimpse of the animal, a black shape moving swiftly through the rugged landscape of the range. Occasionally, the wolf stopped to watch him from a promontory, curious but unafraid. Dane would blink and the wolf would be gone. Soon they moved out of the lowlands and climbed through sloping stands of evergreens and sharp clusters of imperial-blue granite.

In the late afternoon, while he traversed a wide rock-strewn gully, he came upon a freshly killed marmot. Very little of the animal had been eaten. Instead, it had been killed and abandoned, left like a warning for him to find.

Sometime later, he realized that the wolf had climbed into the cold, dry air of the high rocks. Dane stayed at the treeline, unable to go any higher. He was on the verge of complete exhaustion. At this rate, he thought, the wolf would outdistance him and leave him in the middle of an empty wilderness.

How far had the wolf gone? He had known wolves that traveled as much as sixty miles a day hunting for food. And he had seen a pair of wolves bring down a doe after running her for nearly twelve miles through deep snow without a break.

He stopped to rest against a rock covered with dark brown lichen. The anger that had driven him out of Minnesota and west across the Canadian prairie had turned to loneliness and desperation, and now, finally, it had beaten him. He felt no anger, no fear, only a bittersweet sense of inevitability. The wolf had led him to this and he had come willingly this time. That seemed like enough.

Dane started walking again, but without any urgency. There were still a few more hours of daylight. He would make the most of what he had left.

Up ahead, the mountain fell away to a dry, gravel-bottomed riverbed that twisted between clusters of aspen and birch toward what looked to be a larger canyon. He stopped for a moment and then entered the mouth of the vanished river.

The riverbed wound through tangled thickets of dead and broken trees and scrub growth and several large boulders that seemed to have fallen and shattered like timber. Dane climbed over the rocks and trees and stepped into the canyon. The river that had once flowed through it had run the length of the canyon and disappeared at some point further on that he could not see.

But what he could see was extraordinary. The canyon that lay between the high ridges was essentially hidden. Probably no one had ever seen it before, certainly no one had ever walked through it as he was walking through it now.

Trees and tall buffalo grass had taken over the riverbed. The grass grew in wide circular veins of faded brown and green that reached above his ankles and slapped against his legs. A birch grove, a sanctuary in the center of the riverbed, caught his attention and he made his way toward it. The grove stretched across the canyon to the foot of the mountains on both sides. Behind the trees, the riverbed was barren except for a small stream that meandered across the canyon. To the left, just beyond the stream, was a cluster of large boulders; to the right, a wide scree that stopped at the edge of the forest.

Dane dropped his pack on the ground and lay back with his head on the pack and the rifle beside him, and stared into the empty sky. A gust of wind blew through the canyon and a handful of dead leaves scattered over his face. No one would even hear it, he thought, and reached for the rifle.

Something stepped across the floor of the canyon in front of him. Dane sat up quickly.

The black wolf stood in the center of the canyon, an enormous creature as still as the rocks. Dane let the rifle fall quietly from his hand.

That was how it began.

Part I

WINTER

Chapter 1

DANE WAITED FOR the wolf pack to return. Mating was over, long before the last moon, and he had expected them sooner than this. He thought he saw one slip into the canyon several nights ago but now he wasn't so sure. It might have been an outsider, a lone wolf straying through the pack's territory. It could just as easily have been his imagination. The winter had put him on edge and now that it was coming to an end, he was anxious for the pack to be together again. Once the pups were born and weaned, the pack could begin the journey westward toward the plateau and the coast. By then it would be summer, the best of times.

Dane stood beside the cabin door and could smell the spring in the air. Snow still covered most of the canyon. But patches of greenish-gray lichen had begun to reappear on the newly exposed sections of granite that shone in the soft morning sun. Near the stream, new grass pushed itself up through the half-frozen ground. Far off, somewhere beyond the surrounding ring of mountains, he heard the ruffle of an avalanche and his mood darkened abruptly.

Why hadn't the wolves returned?

Dane worried like a new bride about the wolves of the canyon. One of them might eat infested meat and grow sick and weak from parasites. Another, even one of the hunters, could cut a tongue on a sliver of bone and bleed to death. Any one of the wolves could be crippled or killed while hunting; a broken rib might puncture a lung and the wolf would drown in its own blood. And there were worse things.

Dane kept a record of what he saw. He'd written in his journal:

"During the third winter moon, I traveled to the summer rendezvous point and found a set of four traps near the river, just beyond the little falls. They were rusted and the bait was frozen and old. I think they were left behind last fall because the trapper didn't feel like carrying them or forgot them. I sprang the two that were still set and removed the spring plates and threw all four of them in the deep part of the river."

Dane closed the door behind him. The aroma of wood-smoke and pine and the damp musty odor of the dirt floor beneath his feet enveloped him. The walls were made of logs cut from lodgepole pine and white spruce, and held together with plaster made of clay and gravel from the riverbed. The low ceiling, no more than a foot above his own head, consisted of several layers of pine boughs woven into a tight skein and covered with square chunks of sod and another layer of pine boughs for roof cover.

There was no window, only a small square frame cut in one wall that was shuttered tight now. When he opened it in early summer, he tacked up a tattered piece of cheesecloth to keep out the bugs. The door was built from several thick slabs of lowland maple and hung with heavy elkhide hinges. All in all, the cabin was no more than twenty feet square.

On the other end of the cabin, steam rose from a large black kettle that hung on a curved iron pole over a circular firepit. Smoke drifted up around the kettle in thin lazy lines toward a small round opening in the ceiling.

Stuffed into the corner next to the firepit was his bed, a sack mattress filled with a mixture of goose feathers and pine boughs and covered with several red, blue, and gray blankets. On the other side, a long double-plank shelf ran nearly the length of the cabin. The shelf held several half-empty bags of salt, sugar, beans, rice, and oatmeal, jars of honey from a hive near the mouth of the riverbed, and wild blackberry preserves, beeswax and rabbit gut for candles, more jars of dried herbs and goose grease for cooking, a wooden box of needles and thread, a whetstone and some knife oil, a handful of cooking utensils, and at the far end near the door, a hand-operated shotloader.

A square table and two rough-hewn chairs stood near the shuttered window. In the nearby corner was a small chest of drawers and above that a warped and pitted mirror of polished metal. On the table, a pair of candles burned in a holder fashioned from an old mule-deer antler. Candlelight, fragile and uncertain, fluttered around the cabin.

The cabin was well hidden in the birch grove. From the top of either ridge, it looked more like a lopsided pile of broken trees left over from a flood, and except for an occasional whiff of pale white smoke that drifted from the small covered opening in the roof, it was impossible to tell that anyone or anything lived there at all.

Dane sat at the table and wrote in a large journal. Each evening he brewed a pot of tea made from raspberry leaves and lemon grass and wrote in his journal. He wrote continuously, pausing only to take short sips of the sharp sweet tea. With his broad shoulders and thick arms curved around the notebook, it looked as if he were guarding some secret. His hair, long and dark with a faint aura of red, was chopped off bluntly at the shoulders and tucked into the neck of a heavy black wool shirt, one of the last traces of his old life that he had brought with him. He kept his beard trimmed with a pair of broken scissors that he'd bought in Dawson during his first year in the canyon.

He'd hiked into Dawson that first winter to buy what he thought he might need. Dawson smelled of gasoline and whiskey and everywhere he went people stared at him. He filled two crates with supplies and paid a pilot who was willing to drop it for him at a spot sixty miles north of the canyon. It took him two weeks to haul it back from the drop site.

"The winter was harder this season," he wrote. "It drove the herds south earlier than I expected. I hope we've seen the last of it. I'm still eating the dried venison haunch from last fall and getting pretty sick of it. I saw a pair of marmots sunning on the overhang but they were gone before I could get close enough. I wish I could have some duck eggs for breakfast.

"Sometime ago, I heard a plane, the first since the weather began to turn. It was some distance away and hard to place but it sounded like it was moving south. There have been so many planes and helicopters in the last two seasons that the pack hardly notices them anymore, but I hear every one of them.

"I have come so far and now it seems I haven't traveled far at all. The traps, the men in the planes. I'm afraid of what will happen next. I could move up north into the Yukon Territories but how far would I get? How long before we run out of land and time?"

He stopped writing and rested his head on his arms like a schoolboy and stared into the flames of the candles. When he shut his eyes, the image of the flame imprinted on his vision, first red, then orange, then yellow white, then faded completely to black.

Where were the wolves?

There were eight wolves in the pack now, including the pup that had been born last season. The yearling had survived and stayed with the pack instead of going off on his own or being driven off by one of the older males. He kept a certain distance from the rest of the wolves. In the social hierarchy of the pack, the pup was at the bottom. He would not reach sexual maturity for at least another season, perhaps longer, and was still learning how to hunt. The hunters, the black wolf and two of the females, sometimes brought food home in their bellies and regurgitated it for him so he could eat with the pack.

Because of his size and his skill as a hunter, the black wolf was the pack's dominant male. For a timber wolf, he was extraordinarily large, one hundred and sixty pounds. He stood over three feet high at the shoulder where the heavy muscles bunched up around the back of his neck.

He could run at nearly forty miles an hour and shatter the leg bone of a female moose with his jaw. Although he looked black, his coat was actually several different shades, from a dark burnished red coloration that swirled around the inside of his legs and belly to a thin, almost indistinguishable line of dark gray hairs on the underside of his tail. The long hairs that grew along his back and across his shoulders were a mixture of dark gray and black.

The black wolf's mate was a brownish-gray female who weighed only ninety pounds, closer to the normal weight for a Canadian timber wolf. It was early winter, three seasons before, when the black wolf brought her into the canyon. She gave birth to her first litter of pups the next spring. All three newborns died of pneumonia. The next season she did not conceive.

The two other females in the pack were both hunters and helped supply the pack with food. They hunted larger game together with the black wolf during good weather, especially in the fall and late spring when the herds of caribou and elk began moving to new feeding grounds.

The older female hunter was the pup's mother. She ran with a noticeable limp from a fractured right thigh bone that had set badly after the pack fought to bring down a bull elk the summer before. Her mate, the dominant male after the black wolf, was one of three other mature males in the pack.

The two other males assumed most of the responsibility for teaching the pup. During the hunt, they often took the pup with them and trailed behind the hunters while they made the kill.

The black wolf wasn't the pack's first dominant male. The old male was gone by the winter that the black wolf had brought the gray into the pack as his mate, the same winter that Dane had walked into the canyon alone to die.

"I watched the black and the gray mate this season," Dane wrote. "They ran through the rocks near the den for most of the day until I thought I would collapse just from watching. They were together a long time, which must be a good sign. The last pups she had died. I remember that she shoved them out of the den into the sunlight and lay down next to them. I think she expected them to suckle but they were half dead already. She kept pushing at them with her nose and whining. Finally, she just gave up. I buried them up on the ridge so nothing could get at them.

"The night after that, I had the dream again," he wrote and stopped. For a moment, he could not imagine writing about it but continued. "It was the same as the others. I was watching them mate. He climbed high on her back and I tried to get closer to see. But when I got closer, everything changed. Suddenly I was in his place, and when I looked down at myself, there was no difference between us at all. I had become the black wolf."

He'd had the dream more frequently than ever that winter. Each time, he would wake in the morning to find the hair on his stomach stiff and white with dried semen. The first time it happened, he felt guilty and confused. But that soon passed, and he came to accept it. Afterward, he clung to each memory as he would to an old lover.

Dane pushed himself away from the table and stood up. His hand was stiff from writing and he flexed it several times before picking up the notebook. He opened the top drawer of the small chest and placed it on top of the other four, one for each year he had lived in the canyon.

He closed the drawer and put on the heavy sheepskin vest that hung from a wooden peg near the door before he stepped outside. His feet slid a few inches on the packed snow in front of the door as he bent down to pick up a small wooden bucket. He stopped to gain his footing, then continued down the path to the stream.

At the water's edge, he threw his head back to look up at the sky, an immense black canopy that was strewn with a thousand stars like seeds scattered over an empty field. To the north, he could see the pulsating ripples of the aurora. Sometimes, they hung suspended in stillborn waves of blue and green before they swept across the horizon, pulling down deep red ribbons that churned up the heavens.

The path curved toward a small point that hooked out into the stream and formed an eddy. Except for a thin film that was sometimes there in the mornings, ice never formed there, even in the coldest part of winter. The water swirled constantly. It cut into the frozen bank and softened the ground beneath his feet.

Dane dipped the bucket into the freezing water and felt the cold bite into his hand. The hole had grown larger over the last few days and had come within a few inches of the center of the stream where the swift-moving water had finally worn through the ice, laying it open like a wound.

Dane filled the bucket only halfway and released it. He watched the bucket bob in the slow current, then stared into the shadowy darkness of the clearing on the other side of the stream. One of the shadows detached itself from the jumbled forest of boulders on the left and padded softly around the edge of the clearing. It was joined quickly by another.

Dane held his breath.

The black wolf and his mate turned their heads toward him and then trotted to the center of the clearing. More shadows slipped out of the rocks and surrounded the two wolves. Dane counted them quickly, four, then five, then eight, as three more wolves emerged from the trees on the right side of the clearing.

The black wolf approached one of the female hunters, holding his tail stiff and straight out. They circled one another slowly. The female rolled her head to the right, pulling back the corners of her mouth in a submissive grin. The black wolf laid his head across her shoulders and nuzzled the back of her neck. The other wolves paraded stiffly around each other as though in an elaborate dance. As the tension broke, they chased one another through the clearing, poking and pushing each other.

The black wolf stepped away from the others and raised his head. He began to howl. It was an oddly delicate sound that traveled along a ragged scale until it broke sharply and swooped back down to where it had begun. The others joined in and their voices blended together in rough harmony. Their howling grew louder until it filled the canyon, engulfing even its own echoes. Then, as abruptly as it began, the howling stopped. The black wolf broke from the pack and ran across the clearing toward Dane. He moved so swiftly that he seemed to glide over the riverbed.

Dane backed away from the water's edge. On the other side of the stream, the wolf stopped and lowered his huge head. In the starlight, his eyes were perfectly opaque. Dane shifted his weight and carefully put one hand on the ground next to his knee.

13

The black wolf bounded over the stream and stood a few feet from him. In the clearing the other wolves flowed silently together. They stood in a loose wedge formation with the two female hunters in front as they sometimes did just before a hunt.

Dane put his other hand on the ground. The wolf took several short steps forward and pulled back his muzzle, exposing the long sharp canine teeth. Dane dropped closer to the ground and turned his face upward toward the huge open jaws that were only a few feet away from him and moving closer. He could smell the the wolf's heavy scent. The animal's sharp acrid breath felt hot on his cheek.

The wolf's eyes were close and clearly visible, a circle of pale yellow with large black pupils. They seemed to freeze everything between them. Dane raised his eyes to meet the wolf's stare.

The wolf moved forward and sniffed the ground beneath Dane's body. Then he raised a heavy paw and placed it on Dane's shoulder. The wolf stepped over him and pressed down, forcing him flat on the ground. Dane felt the warmth from the wolf's body against his back and listened to the singsong whine that came from deep in the animal's throat.

Dane took a deep breath and rolled on his side. The wolf did not resist. Dane raised both hands and grabbed the heavy fur around the wolf's neck. His own throat was now exposed. On the other side of the stream, the rest of the pack waited impatiently.

The black wolf gently closed his jaws on Dane's open neck and released him. The whining grew louder. Dane shook the wolf's head and laughed.

The pack had come home at last.

Chapter 2

THERE WERE FOUR new hunters in the bar that night, probably waiting for a pilot. That was the only reason they came to the Lakehouse anymore, especially now that the bar at Big Bear was open. The bartender heard their plane land a little after seven, and since he knew it wasn't the mail plane—that wouldn't be in until Thursday and he wasn't expecting anything on it anyway—it had to be some new hunters trying to get a jump on the season. They came in a couple hours later.

You could always tell the beginners by their new boots, the bartender thought. Most of them piled off the plane looking like a mail-order catalog had thrown up all over them. The Velcro on their pockets ripped and snorted every time they dug for a dime.

New hunters liked to talk as if they were going to eat your leg. One of them always asked where he could get himself a handful of griz and the bartender wished to Christ they'd never made *Jeremiah Johnson*. He liked the movie but he just couldn't see anybody wanting to live in the goddamn mountains and take potshots at the local wildlife. The mountains in northern British Columbia hit about seven thousand feet and were colder than hell practically all year round. People went into the mountains all the time and died.

There was a fifth man with the group. He stood with his back to the room and stared indifferently at the bottles stacked across the back of the bar. He wasn't a local guide because the bartender knew all of them.

The bartender had been in Dawson a little over a year, and what he thought about it when he arrived was that he was getting closer to where the world had begun. What he thought about it now was that he was a long way from Youngstown, Ohio, and not getting closer to anything at all. He could pinpoint his location exactly, about three hundred and twenty miles south of the Yukon Territory and about eleven hundred and fifty miles north of the Seattle city limits. He was in British Columbia, right smack in the middle of the western Canadian wilderness. The knowledge didn't help him at all. His whole life felt like one big slide down the coccyx of the Cassiar Mountains that he could see from the back window of the bar. He figured that pretty soon he was going to shoot right off the ass end of the world entirely.

The Lakehouse was on the north shore of Lake Bedaux, seven miles from the main road that followed the eastern edge of the lake before peeling off in the direction of the Yukon Territory about two hundred miles further north. Dawson was on the western side of Bedaux, a sleepy little village of squat cinderblock houses and one-story frame shacks that hung on either side of the gravel highway like rags off a wire fence.

In summer, the temperatures reached into the nineties and the air was thick with blackflies and gnats and mosquitoes. The caribou and elk came down from the mountains to feed on the bunch grass and the high blue gamma that grew on the prairie. You could see them sometimes, drifting like clouds of smoke against the mountains far in the distance. Higher up, small herds of stone sheep made their agile way through the high ridges and the forests of spruce, jumping higher and higher, legs locked together like dancers, while the rocky ground fell away beneath them. Hunters came back and told stories of sheep jumping twenty-five feet across open ravines like kangaroos.

In the foothills, there were moose and wolverine, mountain elk and black bear. Most of the grizzly had fled further north into the Yukon as more people came into the country. There weren't just hunters anymore but geologists and mining engineers, too, and aerial seismographers who explored the country by plane and helicopter and soared high over summer fields of blue Jacob's ladder, buffalo berry, and the bright red and yellow explosions of Indian paintbrush, taking pictures of what lay underneath.

There were three lodges in Dawson and a twenty-five-hundred-foot airstrip that was the town's primary connection to the outside world. The mail came in on Thursdays. That gave people something to do over the weekend besides getting drunk and beating on one another.

The hunters stayed in town until the first serious snow began to fall in mid-October. A few always tried to wait it out until spring and lived to regret it. In December, the sky was like a piece of sheetmetal clamped over the town. By January, a frozen corpse or two would show up near the lake, usually with a bottle close at hand. In the dead heart of February, people would go crazy from drinking grain alcohol or antifreeze and fall into a gibbering coma a few feet from their front door.

If the snows were too deep or the game population too scarce, the predators would sometimes sneak into town. Garbage cans banged and clattered in the middle of the night and people kept their dogs and cats inside.

Once, so many years before that the event had grown into legend, the owner of the coffee shop shot a stray timber wolf that had followed the smell of garbage to the back of his restaurant. It took him two shots to kill the animal.

In the wolf's stomach, along with some of the garbage, they found the fresh remains of a cat and a woman's gold wedding band wrapped neatly in a ball of fur like an anniversary present.

Most of the time, the wolves stayed away from Dawson. Sometimes in the twilight, if the wind was right and you were listening, you might pick up the sound of distant howling. Someone might hear it and wonder just what it might sound like close up. Then they'd go back inside and lock the door.

A few probably had heard it close up, those who came into Dawson on their way to someplace else. They stayed one or two nights until they got the smell of the place and the people and then they were gone. The pilots would always talk about seeing some lunatic cutting up through a ravine into the Cassiar, avoiding the sound of the plane as if it were the voice of a god they didn't care to know.

But now the bartender had a new bunch of flatlanders to contend with and he hoped nobody decided to punch one of them out just on general principles which, like a lot of other things, he wished to Christ nobody had ever invented.

The fifth man nodded, not so much a motion as a slow downward shift of his eyes. There was something oddly familiar about him. The bartender had never seen him before, he was almost certain of that, but still there was something.

He had a thick wedge of a face, a soldier's face, angular and blunt. It was hard to figure his age but he wasn't that old. What little fat there was on him was visible only as a slight bulge beneath a squared-off chin. His hair was brown and cut short.

The bartender heard him say, "I'd like a whiskey," so he reached behind the bar and poured a shot from the bar bottle and set it in front of him. The man looked down at the glass and said, "I thought I ordered a whiskey."

The bartender remembered who the man reminded him of and kept his mouth shut. He swept the glass off the bar in one motion and dumped it into the stainless-steel sink. There was a bottle of Jameson's not two feet from his hand and he poured a new shot from it to the top of the glass so that the amber liquid lapped over the rim, and set it down in front of the man without comment.

The man took the shot down in two neat gulps and smiled at the bartender, a thin empty smile that stole across his face like a thief. It was just the way they looked.

They weren't like anybody else at all. Usually, they came in by themselves and even the pilots who would start a fight for a nickel avoided them. They didn't talk to anybody; there was nothing they wanted to talk about in the world. They were just waiting to get out there.

Killers, the bartender thought, they all looked the same.

Chapter 3

VAN OWEN WAS always quiet before a hunt. It seemed the natural order of things. He was shedding bits and pieces of acquired civilization as he drove himself back down the trail toward a primitive consciousness that ran through him like an underground river and that he was now bringing to the surface. The first thing he tried to lose was language; the next was himself.

Van Owen's face had changed very little over the years. His skin was tan and smooth except for the small white webbing of scar tissue from an infected wound near his left eye where he'd been caught by a half-dead cougar. His jaw was strong, chin hard and prominent, his eyes dark and curiously close together. He could concentrate his stare on someone until they felt as if they were being held at gunpoint.

The flight from New York to Vancouver had been long and boring. While they waited for the charter to take them north, the five hunters ate in an airport restaurant decorated with model planes that hung from the ceiling. Van Owen said very little during dinner and the four hunters seemed to know enough to leave him alone.

He took these hunting trips two or three times a year, whenever he could squeeze them into his schedule. There was usually a waiting list of members who wanted to hunt with him and who were willing to pay for it. Van Owen was a celebrity, he understood that, and waltzing this bunch of amateurs through the woods was just part of the job.

It was a two-hour flight from Vancouver to Dawson. For the first hour, the eight-seater Cessna Crusader was rocked by cross-winds as it flew up the coast mountains before the pilot took the short dog leg east toward the interior. Van Owen sat behind the other hunters in the rear of the small plane and looked out into the turbulent darkness.

He had read the files on the other four passengers before leaving New York. In addition to the application information that was recorded when they applied for membership, there were special files that were updated periodically as a matter of course when they joined the New York Sportsman's Society.

The Sportsman's Society was almost a century old and occupied two adjoining Gramercy Park townhouses designed by the French architect Antoine Claireaux in 1881. It was one of New York's few remaining gentleman's clubs and Van Owen had been its president for nearly six years. He was the only reason it survived.

When the chairman had asked him to take over the club, Van Owen discovered that the society had been in a process of quiet but steady dissolution for a long time. Membership had dwindled and the endowment fund had been depleted by bad loans and even worse investments. The one asset that kept the society from complete bankruptcy was the tax break provided by the designation of the townhouses as historical landmarks.

Although the club had changed somewhat over the years, the interior, especially the main room on the second floor, still retained most of its original splendor. There was the twelve-foot-tall black marble fireplace and the wide parquet floor with its inlaid map of the world, as it was thought to be in 1881, cut from rosewood and Madagascar teak. The high-vaulted ceiling was dominated by four enormous crystal chandeliers that could be raised and lowered by a set of pulleys in the main kitchen. Neptunes of hand-rubbed onyx complete with brass tritons sprouted from the walls every few feet and gave every new visitor the initial impression of being trapped inside a Grecian urn.

Van Owen had been a well-known hunter and adventurer in the Far East when he'd been introduced to the society's aging chairman. The chairman's son, a real estate broker from Southern California, handled the introduction; Van Owen had once taken him leopard hunting in Malaysia. There were the rumors, of course, stories of Van Owen's connection with some of Asia's less desirable elements. The chairman found the rumors intriguing and hired him on the spot.

When Van Owen took over, he kicked out the society's oldest members, who were living rent free in several furnished suites in one of the townhouses. The suites were replaced with health club facilities to attract a younger and more affluent membership. He built a shooting range in the basement and persuaded the board of directors to lease an apartment overlooking Central Park for him as a bonus. Van Owen kept files on the board of directors, too.

Unfortunately, the society required his presence to function, a fact of life that irritated him more and more. The newer members wanted their pictures taken with him at parties and they liked to parade him past their young wives. He learned that more than a few of the wives found their husbands as useless as he did.

Van Owen spent most of his time alone and slept with the members' wives when they were available, although usually never more than once. He scared most of them too much for a second time.

Lately he had become increasingly bogged down in the day-to-day management of the society. There was less time for him to hunt, fewer opportunities to lose himself in the dark intricacies of the kill. He sank inward toward what seemed to be a deep and abiding silence, getting ready for what he knew was coming. Already he could feel the first familiar signs; the pressure that burned just beneath his skin, a languid paralysis that stiffened him like the first intense moments of orgasm, the nightmares that took over when he was awake.

How much longer could he hold on? Another year? Two?

He could postpone it, divert it, but once the pressure reached the surface, he wouldn't be able to control the explosion. He could wait. It had happened before. He stayed alive by feeding on the memory.

Sometimes, when it got to be too much, he thought of taking one of his rifles and heading out alone into the city. It was in those moments that he realized just how bored he had actually become. He looked down at Central Park from his apartment and saw himself. He figured he could last a week down there before they caught him. How many could he take with him before the end? More than enough.

The flight smoothed out after the pilot turned east toward Dawson. One of the hunters, a chunky personal injury lawyer named Blackburn, interrupted Van Owen's thoughts. The lawyer was holding a tiny dictaphone in his hand, shaking it like a marimba.

"Is there someplace we can go when we get there?" he asked.

"Sure," Van Owen said, and closed his eyes.

"Like a bar," Blackburn added.

Where did he think he was headed? If Blackburn didn't watch himself, one of the locals would wind his clock for him. Van Owen might even let them.

"I could do with a bit of a drink myself," another of the hunters said. That would be Walker, the magazine editor.

"He says it's okay," Blackburn told the editor, relieving Van Owen of the need to answer.

"Super," Walker said enthusiastically.

Van Owen thought of the four the same way he thought of any animal he hunted. He made certain that he understood more about them than they would ever understand about him.

In the window seat directly behind the pilot, George Lange, a thin, monastic-looking stockbroker, gazed absently at the dark brown curtain that hung loosely in back of the cockpit. On his lap was an advance copy of next week's *Forbes*, open to an article on the most recent Wall Street trading scandal. Van Owen had seen Lange's picture on the article's first page with what he was certain was a strong condemnatory quote to go with it.

Since he had inherited his seat on the exchange from his father, not to mention half the firm that bore his name, Lange never felt compelled to cheat anyone except his own partners. He had that unique sense of moral blindness that comes only to those who have never really had to work for a living. Lange's current weakness was his third wife, a twenty-three-year-old ex–legal secretary. Lange's wives kept getting younger and younger and Van Owen wondered how he kept up with the latest one. Maybe he thought the hunt would help improve his virility.

Benjamin Walker sat next to Lange. He kept his long legs crossed at the ankles and his face at a jaunty pictorial angle as if he were waiting for a breeze to come by just at the right moment and ruffle his feathery white hair. Walker had been a war correspondent once and had never lost his sense of the dramatic pose.

On Walker's lap was a crossword puzzle from the *Times* of London. As he had gotten older, he had become an irritatingly aggressive Anglophile. Walker had lived for a year in London and had picked up a number of annoying habits along with a cricket bat that he claimed had belonged to the Prince of Wales. He kept it in an umbrella stand by his desk and took it out occasionally to swing in front of his visitors' astounded and baffled faces. Instead of saying good-bye, he hung up with a cheery "Righto!" A number of writers, not to mention editors, photographers, and illustrators, had entertained fantasies of beating Walker to death with his cricket bat after one "Righto!" too many.

Walker was also a homosexual, although few people knew it. He never acknowledged his sexual preference unless absolutely forced to, more out of what he thought of as an obligation to sensible English manners than anything else. At the moment, he was smitten with a tough-looking graphic designer who lived on the fringe of the East Village and enjoyed treating Walker badly. The worse he treated him, the more things Walker gave him. For his most recent escapade, showing up at the editor's apartment building at four o'clock one morning with two drunken leatherboys in tow, Walker had given him a pair of Graves chairs. If he kept it up, in another month or two he'd have a completely furnished apartment.

Behind Walker was Frank Blackburn. Blackburn spoke quietly into the dictaphone while glancing through the thick brief that was balanced on his chubby knees. The lawyer was nearly thirty pounds overweight and dressed like he'd seen every Stewart Granger jungle movie ever made. He was a successful personal injury lawyer who maintained a home near Westport for tax purposes but spent most of his time in New York away from his wife. In court, Blackburn attacked like a rat terrier and made certain that his clients rode into the courtroom on wheelchairs or, if he thought he could get away with it, on a gurney with an intravenous drip stuck prominently in a vein.

Blackburn believed in what he was doing, a highly advanced and specialized form of tribal vengeance. He had told Van Owen that he thought of himself as a knight and the courtroom as a jousting field. Other than that, Blackburn had no secrets, although his wife had one or two. She was having an affair with one of his associates and was probably going to divorce him within the year.

The other passenger was something of a mystery to Van Owen. Dr. Daniel Carroll was what he seemed to be, a successful surgeon and professor of medicine at Cornell Medical Center, a devoted husband, father of two children, generous with his friends and colleagues, honest and dignified. What the hell was he doing here?

"I always thought I should do it," he'd said when Van Owen asked him. Although he had never been a sportsman, Carroll's father had gone hunting every fall and winter until his death the year before. Carroll thought this was a good way to put his father's memory to rest. Van Owen had forgotten that the world was still capable of producing people as sincere and as foolish as Dr. Daniel Carroll.

The pilot pulled back the curtain and said they'd be landing in a few minutes. They descended rapidly, the thick clouds opening up to reveal the lighted blue path of the runway. The landing gear dropped with a metallic groan and the plane whipped past piles of snow and a quonset hut with a flashing red beacon.

At Big Bear, they took five separate rooms. Van Owen set his bag on the floor of his room and thought no more about it. Then he lifted the two aluminum gun cases onto the bed, knelt down in front of it, and opened the first case.

There were two rifles in the case. One, a worn Ruger 77 .7mm Magnum, a caliber the company no longer made. It had a purplish-blue barrel and a custom walnut stock with a thumb-size gouge near the breech that he had worn smooth from endless rubbing. The Ruger had a range of about five hundred yards and the heavy jacketed .7mm slug splattered on contact, taking out chunks of bone, tissue, and organs at random. Van Owen fitted a 3X9-power variable Redfield scope on the Ruger and carefully tightened it down.

The other rifle in the case was a .270-caliber Winchester, an old Model 70 that he had carried for years. With its straight-line trajectory, he could take out an animal at close to three hundred and fifty yards with very little damage, a clean kill.

In the other case, he carried a Freulich-Hanover 12-gauge shotgun that had been presented to him after a successful boar hunt in West Germany. The silver filigree on the barrel still shone.

From a fitted slot next to the shotgun, Van Owen removed a standard army-issue .45 automatic, checked to see if any of the clips had been damaged, and rammed one into place. He sighted down the heavy barrel, brushed a loose piece of white padding from it, spun around on one knee, his back pressed against the hard edge of the mattress, and pointed the gun at the center of the door, tightening his finger evenly on the trigger.

There was a hesitant knock. He lowered the gun slowly and pushed himself off the floor with his left hand.

"Hello?" a voice said.

He opened the door. Blackburn stood there with a look of dumb surprise on his face when he saw the gun.

"I was just wondering when we were going," he said, keeping his eyes locked on the gun.

"I'll let you know," Van Owen said, and closed the door.

The lawyer's mouth was moving as the door swung shut and Van Owen heard him say, "Sure," a few seconds after it cut him off.

Van Owen did a quick check of all three rifles, making certain that they hadn't been damaged in transit, then he laid them back in their cases. From his bag, he took out a black leather knife sheath and pulled the knife loose. The blade was six and a half inches long from the point to the handle; the top edge was heavily serrated and could cut through hide and all but the toughest cartilage. He'd had it made for him in Japan. It was constructed like a samurai sword, a layer of iron welded between two layers of steel and folded upon itself dozens of times to produce a single blade, a process that made it practically unbreakable. Even after weeks of use, it had an edge like a razor. He snapped the leather sheath on his belt and pushed it behind his back. Without looking, he slid the knife into the sheath.

They were waiting for him in the lobby. He picked up the keys to the rented car from the desk and ignored the clerk's questions about his plans. He told the other four to meet him out in front.

"But there's a perfectly good bar here," Walker said.

Van Owen ignored him as well. A few minutes later, they stood outside the front door. Like good little scouts, he thought, as they climbed obediently into the car.

Chapter 4

THE BARTENDER ASKED Van Owen if he was waiting for a pilot. It seemed like an eternity before he answered.

"His name is Harris," Van Owen said.

The bartender searched the room. "He's not here," he said. "I'll let you know when he comes in."

"How well do you know him?"

The bartender was going to say that he knew Harris well enough but realized he was being asked for an opinion. The bartender never gave opinions. You never knew when someone would show up later and make you eat it sideways. He took the easy way out.

"He's okay," he said, and moved down the bar toward a tray of dirty glasses. For some reason, he felt like a target. Van Owen's voice cut through the noise and stopped him in midstep.

"He's late," Van Owen said.

The bartender waited for whatever else was coming. When nothing more arrived, he glanced back quickly. But the hunter seemed only mildly disgusted and the bartender felt relieved. Disgust was a fact of life in Dawson and easy to handle. It was when they started shooting at you that things got dicey. Fucking bush pilots, the bartender thought as he slipped the dirty glasses into the gray lifeless water of the sink. They were almost as bad as the goddamn killers.

His concentration broken, Van Owen looked at Dr. Carroll, who stood next to him, carefully sipping a glass of schnapps. The doctor seemed calm, a little detached from his surroundings.

"Tell me again why you're here," he said. He made it sound as if he were resuming a conversation after being unexpectedly interrupted by a long-distance call. At first, Carroll seemed confused.

"I told you already," Carroll said. "Didn't I?" He bent his long body down toward Van Owen.

"Yeah," he said, and smiled at the halo of whiskey around the bottom of his empty glass. "In your father's memory, wasn't it?" Carroll nodded.

He laughed. "That was about the strangest bullshit I've heard in years. It sounds like *Mort d'Arthur.*"

To his surprise, Carroll laughed, too. "I suppose it does," he said. "Maybe it's just a convenient excuse."

"Have you ever shot anything?"

Carroll appeared to take the question seriously. "You mean outside of a patient or two?" he said with a straight face. He grinned quickly, then, like a window slamming shut, grew serious again. "No," he said, meeting Van Owen's gaze, "I've never shot anything in my life. Maybe a sparrow or something when I was a child. But nothing that ever really seemed alive."

Van Owen searched the doctor's face and found nothing but sincerity. That must do wonders for him at the hospital, he thought. Carroll's eyes were a bright blue and perfectly balanced on both sides of an aristocratic nose. His mouth curved down into an even-tempered line, an expression that inspired confidence, or, he thought, one that could deliver the bad news and make it sound like the best thing for everyone. No malpractice suits for kindly Dr. Carroll. The man didn't even realize he was halfway back to apeland just standing at this bar.

None of them did. He looked past Carroll to the others. Blackburn and Walker had their heads close together. They were watching a drunken Indian at the other end of the bar who kept clawing at his bloated pockmarked face. One of the Indian's eyes sagged lifelessly in its socket; the other bounced around like a loose deck chair. Blackburn was laughing to himself. Walker looked curious, as if he were considering the possibility of a feature story on one-eyed savages. Just beyond Walker, Lange, the stockbroker, stared into his drink. He was probably thinking about his wife.

"We aren't like real hunters, are we?" Carroll said, and Van Owen wondered if the doctor ever mistook his sense of dignity for courage. It was a common mistake, a kind of disease that infected anyone who thought there was some sort of nobility to dying. There wasn't. Some things lived, some things died. You worked to stay on the winning side. That was it. Van Owen wasn't about to get into any gee-whiz philosophical discussion with him.

"The idea is, I show you where to point the gun and you shoot whatever's at the end of it," he said, and squeezed out a smile. "Afterward, we'll take a picture of you and your trophy." And a year from now you can toss it out after one of your friends from the Sierra Club pukes all over it at a party.

"What do you get out of it?" Carroll asked him, not unkindly.

"I get to keep my job."

"It sounds easy."

"That's because it is," he said.

Blackburn popped out from behind Carroll, a clown's grin on his round face. "You guys ought to get a load of this Indian down here." When he got no response, he shrugged his shoulders. Fuck 'em, he thought. If they wanted to miss something as good as this, that was their tough luck. The Indian looked just like one of his clients—before the verdict. He laughed at his own joke. That was pretty good, before the verdict. He was going to have to remember that one for the office.

"What do you think of this place?" Walker asked Lange.

"What?" Lange said even though he'd heard the question quite clearly. He wished the editor would just go away. Something about Walker irritated him.

The simple fact was that *everything* about the editor irritated him.

"I said, what do you think of this place?" Walker repeated.

"I think it's super. It's just so, so—"

That was part of it, Lange thought. Walker had an opinion on everything and felt the need to share it. He expected to find the editor posting reviews of his latest bowel movement on the bathroom wall. Righto! Just super! Lange had no use for the press anyway, even when they quoted him. They asked pointless questions and they got everything wrong.

Lange had his firm and his two ex-wives; the first one lived in San Francisco with a strange Mexican woman and the second was still in the house in Greenwich. The current Mrs. Lange was a bit young even by his standards and worth every dime, but lately she'd been running through an awful lot of dimes.

Walker was still trying to think of the right word to describe his feelings.

"Primitive," Lange suggested.

"That's it!" Walker said. "Primitive!" He raised a glass. "Here's to the primitives." He tapped his glass against Lange's and took a long drink. "Are you nervous about tomorrow?" he asked. "Our first hunt and everything?"

"No," Lange said. Was he nervous? No, curious. A little anxious, maybe, but not enough to worry about. Unlike Walker, he kept his emotions to himself. It helped the business. People wanted their broker to have a personality of porcelain; they got solemn around money.

"Honestly?"

"Well," Lange said, hoping to end their conversation, "just a little. That's normal, isn't it?" Normal? What was normal? Was Walker normal? The things that his new wife did to him couldn't ever be called normal, he knew that. She had this *thing* she liked to strap on . . . my God, he got hard just thinking about it. She told him she liked to walk around town with it on sometimes. He pictured her strutting through Saks, talking to perfect strangers with that monstrosity stuck between her legs, talking to strange *men* as if everything were normal.

That's what you worried about when you were forty-nine years old and had a twenty-three-year-old wife who did things that you thought weren't even physically possible, things that made you feel as if your eardrums were about to burst. But what did she do while he was away? The thought made him uneasy. Exactly. He'd call her the minute they got back to the lodge.

"What are you drinking?" It was Walker again.

"Scotch," Lange said.

"You've hardly touched it."

"I don't drink much." People also liked their brokers sober, he thought, a little angry at being reminded of his limitations once again.

Walker drank Scotch, too, but Walker *drank* Scotch. He didn't piss around with it the way Lange did. But what could you expect from a broker? Or even the great white hunter with his one quick shot? He looked over at Van Owen but the hunter seemed to be ignoring all of them.

The bar had gotten loud and it reminded Walker of his war days. He loved the traveling. He loved not knowing precisely where he'd be in the next twenty-four hours. In those days, he'd open his eyes and find himself in a bar just like this one in some strange country with little brown people who smiled politely when they brought the drinks and then went out and slit each other's throats at night and stuck the heads up on sticks in front of the American hotel. He missed war the most. War was as common as rain. After a while, you couldn't tell one from another.

It didn't matter because you were flying through it. Nothing touched you, not the people, not the dying, not the stench, not even time. While everyone else was getting old out there in the jungle, Walker had found a way to glide past it. Even now, he traveled whenever he could, but it wasn't enough anymore. Nothing seemed enough anymore except for moments like these.

He gazed around the room, his heart pounding in his chest. Jack would love this, he thought. If Jack wasn't such a prickly bastard to begin with. The night he'd brought those two teenagers to the apartment, Walker had nearly thrown him out for good.

He was glad he hadn't but he'd told him never to do it again. Jack had told him that he'd do anything he goddamn well pleased and if he didn't like it he could find somebody else to suck off. The memory had a shrill sound to it. Jack's sulk lasted until he saw the chairs and then he wrote Walker a nice sweet letter blaming too many pills for his lunatic behavior.

Walker forgave him but it was going to be the last time. The boy was getting on his nerves. Let's face it, the boy was getting *old*. It was time to move on, time to travel. Besides, summer was coming and the park would open up again. Who knew what might happen?

Walker left Lange to his own thoughts and rejoined Blackburn. He liked the lawyer. At least he knew how to have a good time. Van Owen, the editor decided, was another story. He was still staring across the room as if none of them even existed. Well, Walker thought, to hell with him.

The pilot didn't come in until nearly eleven. He pushed open the door and scanned the bar for any strangers because they were probably his new hunting party. He wanted to find them before they found him because he wasn't in the mood at the moment, not for them or their guide and definitely not for any shit about where he'd been for the last hour or so.

For the last hour or so, he'd been flying through fog that was as black and oily as paint. There'd been a major foul-up in St. Regis, a dinky little burg on the Gulf of Alaska, one hundred and seventy-five miles up the coast. He had to drop off a rush order of trawler equipment and reluctantly accepted a check from one of the ship's grease-stained owners while the tight-lipped partner rummaged through the crates to make sure everything was there.

That wasn't the problem. There was supposed to be a package of photostats from a joint oceanographic survey team waiting for him at the airport. He was told they weren't due in Vancouver until the following week, which meant he could have picked them up, taken care of this little hunting trip, and then flown them into Vancouver at his leisure. He waited two hours for the stats. Then he got on the phone and found out that they weren't expecting him until next week and the documents hadn't even been processed, let alone collated and copied. Which meant that he was going to make another trip and add another hundred dollars or so in fuel bills, which meant basically that he was screwed six ways to Sunday and in no mood to take any crap from a bunch of flatlanders about why he wasn't there at precisely 2150 hours.

The bartender was looking his way, so he ducked along the wall and headed for the pilots' corner. Along the way, he grabbed a stray Molson off a table and chugged it. Somebody shouted something at him but he kept on going.

Another pilot, a crazed Irishman named Doyle, saw him coming and tossed a fresh one to him, splattering beer all around. He caught the bright green bottle by the neck and lifted it to his mouth, the cold foam running over his fingers and down his chin. Doyle put his arm over his shoulder and dragged him into the corner.

"You're a little late, Harris," Doyle said. "We'd about given up hope."

"Those assholes in Regis jerked my chain for two hours," Harris said, scanning furtively for another beer. "I've got to make another trip next week. I hope the fog thins by then."

"You must be joking," Doyle said. "It's worse than fucking Purgatory up there. You looking for something?"

"Another beer," Harris said. Doyle reached behind him and took one off the table. "One for each hand," he said. Harris ducked under the Irishman's arm and leaned against the battered wooden wall. He felt tired and worn out. Another hour and he wouldn't be able to stand up straight.

"Tough night?"

"Tough enough," Harris said. "I've got some new clients in here someplace. Unless they were bright enough to stay home."

"That'd be the bunch at the bar," Doyle said. "They've been here since I came in. They look a little green." He raised an eyebrow. "Come to think of it, so do you."

"Who's in charge?" Harris could think of at least four different guides he didn't want to see tonight. Or tomorrow morning.

"Which one do you hate the most?" Doyle asked. He enjoyed breaking bad news to people.

"All of them," Harris said. "Every last one of them." He couldn't think of a guide who didn't try to bust his balls about their guns or how much money they were making. If it wasn't

34

guns and money, it was how much pussy they were getting back in Vancouver. One day of that horseshit was enough to make him go berserk. Harris closed his eyes and rubbed one of the bottles against his cheek and waited for the worst.

"You're a lucky man, Harris," Doyle said. "It's a brand-new one."

"Shit," Harris said, and opened his eyes.

"It's tough being a working man these days, isn't it?" Doyle said. "Forced to break in these pissant newcomers. Why don't you give him to me? How much are you getting?"

"Three," Harris said, "plus fuel, supplies."

"Three!" Doyle said. "For how long?"

"Four days."

"Four fucking days!" Doyle roared. "I'll do them for two and a half and not have to work a day until July. Three! I should go over there and tell them what a shit-eating bastard you truly are." The Irishman grinned at Harris, his eyes wild with envy.

"Fuck 'em if they can't take a joke," Harris said.

Doyle slapped him hard on the back. "That's the spirit."

"You get a good look at him?"

"Who?" Doyle seemed positively mystified.

"The pissant newcomer," Harris said. He was trying to figure out just what he was going to have to deal with tonight. If it got to be too much, he was going to walk. Doyle was looking at him shrewdly and probably thinking the same thing. Harris decided that throwing his business away on the Irishman would be an act of gratuitous stupidity. Doyle was worse than a hyena. He'd suck the blood out of you with a straw.

"Oh, him," the Irishman said. "He didn't look all that tough to me."

Chapter 5

"HE'S HERE," the bartender said. He brought the news as soon as he saw Harris standing by the door.

"I saw him," Van Owen said.

Then why in the merry hell did I run over here like Paul Revere, the bartender thought. The answer was simple. He was afraid. It came to him as he watched Van Owen looking over at the corner where the pilot was trying unsuccessfully to remain hidden. Harris didn't know what he was getting into this time. The bartender thought about warning him. He entertained that notion for about six seconds. No sale, he thought, the boy's on his own.

The pilot was in no hurry to find his way over to the bar—which was not entirely unpredictable. Van Owen was new and would get jerked around just as long as he put up with it. He studied the pilot's face. Harris looked to be in his mid-thirties, a little thick, with the soft pudgy features of a beer drinker. Like most of the other pilots, he wore a dark blue down flight vest. There was a strip of silver duct tape across one shoulder. It stood out like a brand-new scar.

Pilots were fundamentally stupid when they were on the ground. He had never known one who proved that observation wrong. No matter what they did in the air, once they hit the landing zone their brains slid right out their ears. He supposed it was Vietnam. Most of them had been in the war and thought they were still heroes. Especially the chopper pilots. They figured the ground was going to kill them sooner or later, so what they did down there didn't count. They were superstitious bastards and he didn't like them at all.

But it was too late and there were too many people around for Van Owen to tear into Harris. He'd wait. There was plenty of time. They were going to be together for four days. He'd waited six months for a pilot once, before he finally caught up with him in a cheap motel room outside of Reno. The pilot's name was Rink, a beefy ex-navy flier from Tennessee. Rink was short and stocky and had arms like the front legs of a bulldog. The first time he went under, Van Owen propped him up against the closet door and punched his head until he fell over. Then he kicked him into the bathroom and hit him some more. He'd heard Rink lost an eye. Tough being a flyboy hero with only one eye.

Van Owen watched Harris push through the crowd of pilots and walk toward the bar. The pilot staggered a little as he made his way across the room. He had the same look as all the others. It was hard to explain it but it was like they were waiting to get hurt. The pilot stuck out his hand.

"Charlie Harris," he said. "I'm your pilot. You must be Van Owen."

He shook his hand once and let it fall. "You're late," he told him. He spoke the words quietly so that Harris had to lean over to hear. The pilot's breath smelled like beer. He listened to what Van Owen said and nodded his head slowly.

"I had some bad weather tonight," Harris said. "All the way from St. Regis." There was enough of an edge to his voice that Van Owen felt the first sharp pinch of adrenaline rush into his gut. The pilot jerked his thumb toward the ceiling. "You know where that is? It's way the hell up the coast, almost to Alaska. I couldn't see fifteen feet in front of my face." He held his hand up in front of Van Owen's face, jerking it back and forth as if he were trying to bring it into focus.

Harris dropped his hand and Van Owen wondered how much more of an explanation he was going to get. But that was it. The pilot clapped him once on the shoulder and slid up to the bar.

The bartender gave Harris another Molson and the pilot introduced himself to the other hunters. He leaned on his side against the bar so that they were forced to step forward to shake his hand. And they did, as if Harris had just come riding in off the plains with stories of shootouts and savages. They were as full of questions as ten-year-olds at a rodeo.

"What about the weather?" Lange asked.

"There's a line of snow squalls up north but I think we'll be all right," Harris said. "At least for the morning. That doesn't mean much around here. I've seen it snow in June."

"Where are we going?" Walker asked. He wondered about Van Owen but the hunter seemed uninterested in the entire conversation.

"Depends on what you want," Harris said. "South of the Wolverine River, it's okay, once you get off the plateau and into the hills. There's lot of stone sheep and elk. We can take a day and maybe look for some moose."

"I want to hear about griz," Blackburn said. He spoke with his teeth clenched, drawling his words. Walker exploded in hard little bullets of laughter.

Harris hated going after bear, especially when they were coming out of hibernation. They were hungry and skittish and unpredictable, and assholes like the one standing in front of him usually got their arms ripped off thinking they were Daniel Boone.

"Not many left," he said.

"I'll take one of the stragglers," Blackburn said stubbornly.

"I can't recommend it," Harris said. Please, he thought, let's stick to things that don't bite back.

But Blackburn wouldn't let it go. "I didn't come four thousand miles to shoot at a bunch of goddamn sheep."

"What exactly do you recommend?" Van Owen asked. The pilot turned around but Van Owen was staring at the floor.

"Everybody usually knows what they want before I get here," Harris said.

"I know what I want," Blackburn said, "and I don't want any sheep."

38

"I don't care," Carroll said. "Really."

"I'll take one of those sheep," Walker said. "I'm going to have it made into a coat."

"Super," Lange said, but the editor wasn't listening.

"I'm still waiting to hear your recommendations," Van Owen said. He raised his eyes and stared hard at the pilot.

He was feeling very light, almost as if he were floating. It was always that way. A calm settled around him, a sensation of emptiness waiting to be filled up. He remembered the way Rink had looked at him as he stood in the doorway of the motel room. Surprise gave way to confusion and then quickly to fear when Van Owen started to hit him. Rink kept yelling but he never said a word. He followed the pilot around that motel room like some kind of divine retribution.

The bartender heard Van Owen ask Harris for his recommendations. The bartender wondered how many stitches it was going to take to sew the pilot up when Van Owen got through with him tonight. Harris kept right on talking. The bartender moved in a little closer.

"I told you," Harris said. "It depends on what you're after." He took a long pull from his beer. "Do you know what you're after? Have you got that much figured out?"

For a second, Harris thought Van Owen was going to have an epileptic fit. He stood stiffly and seemed to vibrate with a sudden and unexplainable energy. His eyes became glassy and opaque. Harris realized that Van Owen was going to hit him and hit him hard. The realization left him dizzy. He steadied himself on the bar.

Magically, the bartender appeared in front of him. "Can I get you another Molson?"

"Sure," Harris said, trying hard to finish the one he had in front of him without pissing down his leg. He could feel Van Owen beside him at the bar, studying him. It was just like being watched by a snake.

The bartender reached beneath the counter for the bottle of Jameson's. "How about you?" he asked Van Owen. "One more?"

Van Owen heard the question from far away, and he let it pull him back from the edge. Sometimes when he forced himself to back away, it was like coming to the surface after a long glide underwater. Everything looked brand-new. It was like that now.

The bartender filled Van Owen's glass and smiled anxiously. "Why don't you take them up to Big Rider?" the bartender said to Harris.

"Any griz up there?" Blackburn said. The others were listening for the answer. For reasons he didn't understand, the danger had passed and Harris wondered if he had imagined it. Right now, Van Owen looked relaxed, maybe even bored. The change was more than a little unnerving.

"Is that what you want?" Harris asked. Van Owen only shrugged. "I'll give you something better than that." Harris looked at the bartender. "Think he'd be interested in hearing the story?"

The bartender pulled a rag from his apron and wiped down the bar. "What story is that?" he said sweetly.

"You know what story I'm talking about."

"I hear lots of stories. We got one for every day of the week around here."

"People have *seen* him," Harris said.

"Most people would swear they saw Jesus Christ for two bucks and a new hat," the bartender said.

"What story?" Carroll asked.

"It's worth about two pounds of horseshit in your lunch bucket," the bartender said, but it didn't have any effect. He didn't care anymore because he wasn't going to waste his time listening. Harris was going to end up with his throat cut one way or another. The bartender had saved his sorry ass once tonight and that was more than the son of a bitch would ever do for him.

"What's this story?" Walker asked, pushing between Blackburn and Carroll. Lange hung back behind him but with a look of mild interest on his face.

"There's a story around here about some guy who lives with a wolf pack—north of the Wolverine someplace. A couple of the pilots have seen him. At least that's what they say."

"What do you mean he lives with a pack of wolves?" Walker asked seriously.

"I mean he *lives* with them." He glanced at Van Owen. "He even hunts with the pack. One guy saw them run down an elk south of Tatlatui last spring." Harris felt he ought to add something personal to what he was saying. "I believe it."

"Does anyone know who he is?" Carroll asked.

Harris shook his head. "The first time I heard about it was two years ago but the story's been going around for longer than that."

"I still don't quite understand what you mean by he lives with these wolves," Walker said.

"I mean he's one of the pack," Harris said. "He's part fucking wolf."

No one said anything for a moment, then Lange spoke up.

"I've never heard of anybody living with wild animals," he said.

"Me, neither," Blackburn added. "It sounds like a pile of shit in your lunch bucket."

"That's not entirely true," Walker said. "There was the wolfboy of France. He grew up with a pack of wolves."

"I'll tell you something else," Harris said. "I heard he killed a couple people who tried to find him." Lange shook his head contemptuously.

"You're serious, aren't you?" Walker said.

"Absolutely," Harris said. "Ask anybody about it."

Blackburn started to howl. He got down in front of the pilot and raised his head toward the ceiling and howled. Lange quickly looked the other way and Walker put one hand over his mouth to control his laughter. Carroll tried to get the lawyer to stop but only ended up looking more embarrassed than before.

"Forget it," Harris said sullenly after Blackburn quieted down. He grabbed his beer off the bar and gulped half of it. Carroll quietly excused himself.

"Hey," Blackburn said, "where's he going?" His audience was deserting him. He was starting to get offended.

"To the bathroom, I think," Lange said.

Walker patted Harris on the back and told him it was okay. "It's a good story," the editor said with a sympathetic smile.

"Yeah," Blackburn said. "Screw grizzlies, I want the fucking wolfman."

"You believe me?" Harris asked the editor.

"Anything's possible," he said. "I don't think it matters. I told you, it's a great story." Blackburn whispered something to him and Walker laughed, that hard little laugh again.

Harris felt a sour taste rise up into his mouth. He felt like a fool.

"Have you ever seen him?" It was Van Owen. He'd nearly forgotten about the hunter.

Harris was silent.

"I asked you a question."

"Yeah," Harris said. He hunched his shoulders when he said it as if he expected a blow. "I saw something."

"Why don't you tell me about it," Van Owen said. He was serious. Harris saw it as the key to his survival.

"I saw him, this guy, standing with a pack of wolves," Harris said. "In one of the northern canyons." Van Owen stared at him with those snake eyes again. "I only saw him for a couple seconds," Harris said apologetically.

"That's all?" the hunter asked.

"That's all I needed," Harris said. "I saw something else, too." The pilot waited a few seconds and leaned closer. "There was a black wolf standing next to him," he said. "The biggest goddamn wolf I've ever seen."

"You sure about that?" Van Owen asked mildly.

"I seen wolves before," Harris said. "This one looked like it weighed two hundred pounds."

"Could you find the canyon again?" Van Owen asked.

"I doubt it," Harris said. "I don't even know how I found it in the first place. It's big country up there. You could fly around for weeks and never see the same tree twice."

"But you saw the wolf?"

"I did," Harris said with just a touch of pride.

"And the man?"

"They were there," Harris said. Christ, he thought, maybe the guy wants to go after both of them. The thought made him shiver and he pushed it out of his mind.

Van Owen nodded and turned his back on the pilot. It took

Harris a couple of minutes to realize that their conversation had come to an end and that somehow he had lived through it. The guy wasn't serious about finding the wolves, he just wanted to hear the story. The pilot ordered another beer, amazed at his own survival. It *was* a great story, he thought. Too bad it was the only one he knew.

Chapter 6

DANE WAS BORN near Copper Harbor in Michigan's Upper Peninsula, the son of a mining engineer who left the mining business on a whim and bought and lost, in slow succession, an appliance outlet, an auto-parts store, and finally, a drugstore. His mother, to compensate for the constant insecurity and her own loneliness, retreated into fiction. She sat by his bedside and read to him from Dickens and Thomas Hardy. She stayed with her books and never really moved much beyond the nineteenth century.

When he was nine, he ran away for the first time and stayed near a pond not more than a mile from his house. That day he watched a feral cat give birth to a batch of kittens. That night he slept on a hill above the marsh and listened to the screech owls while they hunted for water rats. The police found him the next morning and brought him home.

His father wanted to use the belt on him but his mother, wiser and more cruel, confined him to his room for a week. The second night of his confinement, Dane awoke suddenly from a dream that he was being shut up in a closet. The sheets were twisted around his small neck like a noose. After four long days, she relented.

By the time he was in his teens, Dane preferred a sleeping bag in the backyard to his own bed and spent his summer nights outdoors. His mother envied him, seeing in her only son the same kind of natural innocence that she found so attractive in her fictional heroes. He had no friends but didn't seem to care. During those summers, his father was often gone, sometimes for months, living out his own fantasies. "On business," his mother told him.

After high school, he went to work for the Fish and Game Department when they needed extra help. Most of the time, he lived on his own in the woods. He kept a journal of what he saw. His father had come home to stay, transformed somehow into a sick and sullen old man. His mother remained preoccupied with her books and rarely left the house. They were like strangers. Dane was often gone for weeks. When he returned, she would greet him at the door with a perfunctory kiss as if he'd only been to the store on an errand. His travels took him further and further away.

He hiked into northern Minnesota and beyond, slipping unnoticed across the border into Canada. Three years after he left school, Dane saw his first wolf.

It was November. He had hiked through Minnesota all the way to the North Dakota border and then turned northeast toward the small village of Champleau near Lower Red Lake, part of a series of shallow finger lakes that stretched one hundred and fifty miles into Ontario. He had been to the area the summer before and wanted to see it again.

There were no more than two hundred and fifty people living around Champleau, mostly stern-faced Norwegians who worked six days a week and went to church on Sunday, good Methodists that they were. Dane arrived in Champleau just before noon, bought supplies from the grocery store, and by sundown had pitched his narrow tent beside a small backwater at least twenty miles from the nearest human being. The place was open to the sun, bordered on one side by a wetland filled with the reedy stalks of dead cattails and on the other by a huge willow that hung twenty feet out over the backwater.

The next morning Dane strung several fishing lines from one of the overhanging limbs and by late afternoon had managed to catch several small white perch. He was climbing down the trunk with the fishline when he heard something moving through the marsh. He stopped to listen. It was probably nothing, he thought, just a raccoon getting a start on the night's hunting.

He pulled the hooks and strung a gill line through the fish and tied the line around the trunk of the willow. He left them there and went back to the tent for his fish knife. As he crawled out on his hands and knees, he saw the wolf.

The wolf stood halfway between the tent and the tree. The animal looked small, not that much larger than a dog. Dane remained perfectly still. The wolf cocked his head to one side and stared at him curiously.

After a few minutes, the wolf walked over to the tree and sniffed at the fish. Then he took the gill line in his teeth and pulled on it until it snapped and the string of fish fell to the ground. The wolf held one of the fish down with his paw and shredded it quickly, stripping off pieces of the raw white flesh with his sharp front teeth.

When he finished the fish, the wolf picked up the rest of the string and dragged them off into the woods behind the tent. Dane tried to follow but the wolf outran him. A few days later, he found a few feet of the fishing line but that was all.

For the next three weeks, Dane searched for the wolf. The weather grew colder and soon the backwater was layered with sheets of clear ice. Snow fell and hid everything under fresh white powder. Dane discovered new tracks around him almost every day but never saw the wolf.

Occasionally, he found evidence of a kill, a smear of blood on the snow, a tuft of hair caught on a broken branch, but never the wolf. He knew the animal was out there, just beyond the range of his vision, hiding from him.

As the weather got colder, his search grew more frantic and haphazard. He stumbled through the woods without direction, crisscrossing his old trails several times without realizing it. His search took on a will of its own and Dane submitted. He allowed himself to be taken by the wolf's mystery and didn't care if it never ended.

During the full moon, he hunted for the wolf at night and arrived back at camp at daybreak exhausted, everything in him gone except for the need to go on searching. He stalked the surrounding countryside, his heart pounding with a terrible joy that he did not understand. He lost himself in the darkness and the woods.

On the last night of the full moon, he startled a deer herd grazing on the dead grass beneath the snow in a large meadow. In the chalky white light the deer looked like ice statues. Then they ran, swinging across the meadow in a huge rippling shadow.

Dane knew he couldn't stay much longer. The air had turned bitter cold and he wasn't prepared for a winter camp. The backwater was frozen over and he had to chip through two inches of ice to make a hole for his drinking water. Snow fell nearly every day and piled in high drifts around the tent.

On his last morning, he folded the tent and stored it with his pack in the crotch of the willow. With the rest of the day left, he set out to look for the wolf one last time.

Heavy snow began to fall in the afternoon and Dane gave up. He had walked close to a dozen miles, working his way in a crooked circle back to the camp. There was no sign of the wolf. Dane sat down against the tree and stared out at the snow and empty backwater.

The wolf stepped onto the ice and stood watching him, just as he had that first day. The animal had grown since then. The fur along his tail and back seemed changed, darker, heavier. It bunched up around the wolf's shoulders like a cowl.

Dane walked slowly to the edge of the ice and dropped to his knees. The wolf continued to watch him but did not move. He was drunk with questions. Why had the wolf waited? Why had he come to him now? There was only silence. Dane felt suddenly engulfed by the animal's great indifference toward him.

As if in response, the wolf bowed his head once, a brief acknowledgment of Dane's presence in his world, and loped away across the backwater into the frozen marsh.

For Dane, it came like a blessing.

That night, the state police stopped him as he walked through the deserted streets of Champleau. When Dane told them his name, one of the troopers said they'd been looking for him for the last ten days. They drove him to the barracks so he could use the phone.

It didn't take very long. The phone number they gave him belonged to his mother's attorney, a man Dane had met only once. The attorney's voice was subdued. In the background, Dane heard the distorted sound of a television set. The attorney had some bad news for him.

His parents had been killed in an accident two weeks before. His mother was driving his father to Marquette when the car went off the road and hit a tree. The attorney was very concerned. There was some money from his mother's estate that had to be dealt with soon.

Dane had trouble remembering what his parents looked like. When he tried to bring them up from his memory, the only image he could recall was that of a man sitting up in bed, the sheets wrapped neatly across his sunken chest, staring empty-eyed at nothing; sitting in a straight-backed chair next to the bed, a woman holding a book, the pages creased and torn from so many readings.

They'd been holding off the funeral until they heard from him, the attorney said. When did he think he could get home? What a strange question. Dane wanted to tell him that he was already there.

After the funeral, Dane returned to Champleau and found work with the local game warden, a congenial man named Schmidt who hired him to set out salt licks, check permits in season, and keep track of the local game population. Schmidt read Dane's monthly game reports with genuine enthusiasm.

"I swear," Schmidt told him, "you ought to get yourself a job writing for one of those sportsman's magazines. You're better than any of them."

Schmidt looked the other way when he found out that Dane was living in an abandoned logging shack in the middle of one of the state preserves that were scattered throughout that corner of the state. He introduced Dane to Reiger, a retired hunter who scuttled around the woods with a gimpy leg and a wooden cane with a yellowed ivory dog's head that he liked to caress with the palm of his hand when he talked.

Reiger owned some land around one of the big lakes. He had a one-story log cabin that overlooked the water, with a tall wooden shed in back of it that he kept locked.

"What do you keep in there?" Dane finally asked him.

"Not a goddamn thing," Reiger said as if only a fool would ask such a question.

"Then why do you keep it locked?"

"Teenagers," Reiger said, and spit on the ground. "I don't want to come home some night and find a bunch of them fornicating in it."

It took awhile for Dane to understand that Reiger had become his friend. Dane brought him copies of his reports and they sat and talked for hours in the evening. The old man listened and smiled and grabbed Dane's knee like he was his only son. During the day, Dane followed the wolves of Champleau and learned everything he could about them. He had never felt so complete in his entire life. It lasted for two years.

The first new houses went up around Champleau in the spring. He and Reiger drove past the billboard that announced the opening of "Lake Country Estates." They stared at the red, white, and blue plastic flags that hung in front of the model homes above a banner that promised a free washer and drier to the first new buyers, and said nothing. A station wagon pulled up and two young children jumped out of the back. A man and a woman got out and looked at the house while the children scampered underneath the flags like they were at the circus.

"Get me the hell out of here," Reiger said.

On the porch that night, Dane asked him how they could just come in and build houses like that.

"Because they can," Reiger said at last. "That's just the way it's going to be."

After he left, Reiger phoned Schmidt and told him to come over for a few beers. While he waited for the game warden, he sat alone and wondered, and not for the first time, just how much trouble the boy might turn out to be.

By the fall, there were three new subdivisions around the lakes and there was talk about a new shopping center going in a few miles outside of town the next spring. During the day, the roads were clogged with construction crews in their pickups and flatbed trucks loaded with excavation equipment and stacks of new lumber.

Winter turned into a nightmare. The snow started in early November and seemed to fall without a letup until the middle of January, followed by a wave of bitter cold. When it finally broke, the forests around Champleau were littered with the dead bodies of deer. They were everywhere and looked like sheet-covered corpses under the snow.

The construction had destroyed some of the best feeding areas and the heavy snow had buried whatever natural food was left everywhere else. The animals were forced to feed on what they could scavenge. They stripped the bark from the trees and pawed at the ground for frozen roots. When that was gone, they climbed up the trees on their front legs to chew on the tough spiky pine boughs that made their mouths bleed and their stomachs swell. Soon, deer appeared in backyards and parking lots searching for whatever food they could find. The new homeowners shot them down in their driveways.

The wolves killed the deer in record numbers that winter, more than even they could eat, slaughtering them with a ravenous glee. They ran the sick animals into the ground, ripping open their necks and bellies, and then abandoned them, still half alive, to bleed to death or freeze. The coyotes and the foxes came after the wolves and feasted greedily on what they'd left behind. It was as if the destruction of the land around Champleau had unearthed an alien virus that infected everything.

Quietly, Schmidt asked a few hunters to meet him at Reiger's house. Something had to be done about the deer herd, the game warden told the men when the meeting began. The state had sanctioned a kill and authorized him to carry it out. He was paying fifteen dollars a head for bucks, twenty-five for does. Was that going to be in cash? one of them asked. Schmidt said it was and all of the men signed up. Reiger stood by the door and leaned on his dog's-head cane and looked hard at each man as they left.

The next Saturday morning, Reiger was sitting in a chair by

Dane's bed with his cane across his lap. Dane slept uneasily, tossing in the narrow bed. The sound of gunfire woke him up.

"I wanted to be the one to tell you," Reiger said. When he touched Dane's arm, his fingers were cold and smooth and felt like old wood. "Schmidt had to organize a kill," he said.

"Why?" Dane said.

"The state told him they had to thin out the herd," Reiger said. "Too many were dying. That's what they're doing right now. I wanted to be the one to tell you so you wouldn't go and do anything foolish."

"That's crazy," Dane said. "They can't do that." He got up and began to dress.

"They can and they are," Reiger said. "We can't do a goddamn thing. It just ain't our woods anymore."

"I can," Dane said.

"They'll throw you in jail," Reiger said. "If one of them doesn't shoot you first."

Dane dressed and listened to the guns. Most of it came from the direction of the meadow where he'd startled the deer herd two years before. He guessed that the hunters had forced the animals out into the open where it would be easier to kill them. If he could work his way to the top of the field, he could fire down at their backs and drive the hunters away.

"We need you around here," Reiger said quietly.

"What?"

"I said we need you around here." Reiger sighed. "I need you. We're going to have to protect this country. We can't do that if you're in trouble or all shot to hell. You should know that by now."

Dane jerked open the cabin door. "Listen to that," he yelled at Reiger. "They don't want to protect it. They're shooting everything that moves." The gunfire was sharp and rapid, like a string of firecrackers.

Reiger stood up and slammed his cane down hard across the bed. "They're thinning out the herd!" His voice was so loud that for a moment it blocked out everything else. "Shut the goddamn door," he said at last, and slowly settled both hands on the cane. Dane closed it and sat down on the floor.

"I'm sorry," Reiger said.

"Me too," Dane said. "What are we going to do?"

"I don't know," Reiger said. "Why don't we go worry about it over breakfast?"

The state brought in trucks and hauled off the deer that lay sprawled across the field. The snow melted underneath them and the ground was pitted with watery pink craters. Steam rose from the bodies and one of the hunters said it was so warm standing among them that it felt like a spring day.

Schmidt told Dane he wanted him to conduct a new survey of the area after the kill. "That way," he said, "we'll know where we stand."

By May, it was obvious to Dane that the kill had worked too well. The herd had been cut by one-third and the surviving deer fit the shrunken habitat. Predators were the problem now. The easy winter kills had increased the indigenous population and induced a heavy wave of spring births. Now, without the deer herd, there wouldn't be enough food to go around.

He told Schmidt that the kill had been too severe and that the only solution now was to prohibit any hunting around Champleau for at least two years so the herd could expand naturally. With enough time, he said, the balance between the predator and game populations would correct itself.

"You expect me to put a ban on hunting around here?" Schmidt said. "There's no way I can justify that."

"It's the only solution that makes sense," Dane said.

"What planet is it that you're living on?" Schmidt said.

The wolves of Champleau began to disappear. Dane thought at first that they had gone north into Canada, following their instinct that game was more plentiful somewhere else. But a two-week trip in late June showed no sign of any kind of movement out of the region. They had simply vanished. So had the other predators.

When he told Reiger about it, the old man seemed unconcerned. "There's some poaching going on, so you decide it's the end of the world. The wolves will come back."

"How can you be so sure?"

"They always have," Reiger said.

In the end, Dane stumbled on the answer. He was surveying a new section to the east of Champleau when a line of

Canadian thunderheads rolled over the trees. They broke open at noon and dumped a heavy windblown rain that turned the woods around him cold and dark in a matter of minutes. He crawled underneath a pine and lay on his back in the dry brown needles smelling of sweet resin, and fell asleep.

When he woke up, the rain had slowed to a steady drizzle. He walked for nearly an hour until he came to an old abandoned logging road that was only two overgrown ruts in the earth. The ruts were filled with water and the vegetation was crushed and bruised from recent use. Someone had driven a truck up the old road.

Dane followed the tire tracks until he came to a spot where the truck had pulled over and stopped. In the woods just off the road, he found the first trap.

Dane continued up the road and found five more traps spaced about half a mile apart. The last one was set in a deep hole. A coyote pup floated in six inches of cold muddy water. He reached down and felt for the trap. It was closed high up on the coyote's front leg. The pup had drowned.

He sprang each of the traps as he went, making sure he left no trace. Then he sat and waited for whoever had set them to return.

The truck was there the next morning, just after sunrise. He heard it coming slowly up the road, the engine racing as the driver shifted gears to get through the heavy mud. It reached the last trap. The driver stopped the truck and got out. Dane moved further back into the woods, away from the trap.

The driver found the pup and threw the small rubbery corpse into the bushes. He swore as he stuck his hand in the cold water to pull the trap off its stake and dragged it back to the truck.

"We set out six goddamn traps and only one of them had a thing in it," Schmidt said, and tossed the trap in the back of the truck. "We got one coyote pup, that's all. I don't believe it was the rain, either. Somebody came by and sprung those other traps."

The passenger rolled down his window and cleared his throat.

"If I had a dog as nervous as you, I'd take him out to the shed and shoot him myself," Reiger said.

"I'm telling you," Schmidt said. "Somebody sprung those other traps on us."

"I hope they had as much fun as I'm having right now," Reiger said.

Schmidt kicked the side of his truck. "You don't believe me."

"I'd rather we had this discussion over a cup of coffee," Reiger said. He turned on the radio but kept it low. "Why don't you go get the pup so we can get the hell out of here?"

Schmidt couldn't find the coyote anywhere. He looked around where he'd thrown it but it was gone. The whole thing was getting too spooky. He hustled back to the truck and climbed in the truck without saying a word. If Reiger wanted the goddamn pup, Schmidt thought to himself, he could go poke around for it himself. Him and his goddamn cane.

Dane cleared out the shack quickly. He packed what he thought he was going to need and left the rest for whoever wanted it. He loaded his rifle and stuck the extra boxes of shells in the outside pockets of his jacket so he could get at them. Fifteen minutes later, he was standing by the side of the two-lane road that ran into Champleau. Usually he walked. Today he was in a hurry.

A sugar beet farmer in a red pickup truck stopped and told him he could hop in back if he didn't mind riding with the dog, a big black Labrador that slept beside him all the way into town.

In Champleau, Dane waited in line at the bank. A few people recognized him and said good morning. He nodded. When he got to the teller, he handed her the worn green passbook and told her he was closing out his account. The teller smiled.

"You're not thinking about leaving us, are you?" she asked.

Dane shrugged. He wanted her to hurry.

"This is a lot of money," the teller said. "You sure you want to carry this much cash around?"

Dane told her yes.

"Okay," she said. She counted out the money carefully and told him to be extra careful with it.

Schmidt and Reiger were eating breakfast in the front booth of the coffee shop two blocks down, a spot they usually occupied until nine-thirty, which Schmidt had decided was a sensible time to start work for the state. Dane left the bank and walked up the street to the fish and game office, a square brick building with a wide parking lot that it shared with the propane dealer next door.

He stooped next to the front wheel of Schmidt's truck and cut a six-inch gash in the tire with his knife. Then he hiked three and a half miles through the woods to Reiger's cabin.

The front door to the cabin was unlocked and Dane pushed it open with the barrel of his rifle. The breeze was off the lake and carried with it the distant sound of an outboard. He stepped inside and closed the front door behind him.

Reiger liked to leave the shades down in the morning and the cabin was cool and dark. To the right was a big fieldstone fireplace. Reiger's old wooden desk sat in the rear of the room facing the backyard. Through the row of windows, Dane could see the shed. On the other side of the room was a gun case, an old oak wardrobe that Reiger had rebuilt.

Reiger kept an extra set of keys in the top drawer of the desk. It was locked. Dane smashed the front of the desk with the fireplace hatchet. In the drawer with the keys, he found a large brown accordion file filled with papers and emptied it on the splintered desktop.

He selected one letter and read it. It was from an attorney in Minneapolis. "I'm happy to report that because of what the Department of Environmental Resources refers to as a 'negative influence on animal habitat activity' in the Champleau area, they have decided not to challenge our application for development of the lake property. Mr. Schmidt's strong personal support of our position that the Champleau habitat was no longer large enough to support a game population of significant size and diversity plus the quick elimination of predator activity in the area . . ."

Dane threw the letter down and unlocked the gun case,

removing the heavy steel wire Reiger kept strung through the trigger guards. There was the old Remington that Reiger said he'd found in a Tucson gunshop, the big Powell that he used to hunt for elk in Alaska, and all the other guns that Reiger had told him about over the years. Dane took each rifle down and smashed them one by one on the fireplace and left the pieces strewn across the floor. He picked up the keys and headed for the shed.

The stench hit him the moment he unlocked the door. He stepped back from the smell. Flies poured out of the open door and covered his face and hands like dust. He brushed them off and looked inside.

The walls of the shed were covered with pelts. There seemed to be no order to them. Red fox hung next to coyote, layer after layer nailed haphazardly to the wall as high as he could reach. Scattered among the other pelts were the wolves of Champleau.

Reiger had dug a pit in the center of the floor. Flies swirled over the hole in a dense cloud. Dane pulled one of the pelts down from the wall and swept them out of his way. The bottom of the pit seemed to be alive. He looked down into it. Stubby white maggots churned through a lumpy soup of dirty red liquid and gleaming white bones. The smell was unbearable.

Dane ran out of the shed, holding his hand over his mouth to keep away the flies while he sucked in lungfuls of air. When he stepped back inside, he saw the picture. It hung on a nail next to the door, and the glass was covered with a greasy black film. The string snapped when he took it down. He wiped off the glass.

The photograph underneath was warped and streaked with waterstains but still clear. Reiger stood in the snow holding a dead wolf by the scruff of the neck with two hands. Spread out behind him on the snow were dozens more. The hunter had written across the bottom of the picture: "Record Wolf Kill, Red Bank, Montana, September 4, 1957."

Dane stared at the photograph until he heard Schmidt's truck pull in the driveway.

* * *

Schmidt hated being the one who had to go in the shed. The place smelled so bad that he wasn't going in there again without a comment.

"It's mighty convenient being an old man," he said. "And a cripple to boot." Reiger laughed and continued up the drive to the house. Schmidt figured this time he could just hold his breath and throw the traps through the door. He trundled down the path with the traps draped over both arms.

"What the hell is this?" he said when he saw the open lock. He elbowed the door open and pushed his way inside. Dane came out of the darkness and hit him in the throat. Schmidt fell to his hands and knees. The traps spilled over the dirt floor and slid into the pit. Dane kicked him in the side of the face. The blow broke Schmidt's jaw and knocked him backward through the open doorway. He lay motionless on the ground in front of the shed. Lacy rivulets of blood ran down his face and dripped onto the grass.

Reiger knew what had happened the moment he opened the front door. He kept an old service revolver hidden in the back closet and hurried across the room to get it. His cane caught on one of the broken rifles and he fell down hard on his right hip. He heard Dane cock the gun before he could turn over and come face-to-face with whatever the boy was going to do to him.

Dane tossed the picture on the floor. Reiger didn't bother to look at it.

"When I was your age," he said, "I used to kill the bastards like vermin."

Dane broke both his arms with the butt end of the rifle before the old man finally passed out from the pain.

Reiger woke to the smell of burning wood. He opened his eyes and saw that the shed was on fire. Oily smoke poured out of the door and rolled out across the lawn, enveloping him. He heard someone call his name but they seemed far away. Reiger didn't think they were going to make it in time to save the shed but maybe they could keep the fire away from the house. Next to him, Schmidt groaned and spit up blood and pieces of his teeth. Reiger tried to reach for him but he couldn't move his arms.

57

He raised his head again and looked for Dane but knew the boy would be miles away by now. Canada, Reiger thought, big country up there, easy to lose yourself. A good place to hide. That's where he'd go if he were on the run. One wall of the shed collapsed. Sparks and bits of ash rained down on both of them. Reiger tried to hold that thought but it slipped away, just as he felt himself being pulled back, out of reach of the fire and the black tongue of smoke that slithered over the grass and licked at his heels.

Chapter 7

DANE WOKE WITH the dream of Champleau still vivid in his mind. For one brief moment he was trapped in that suffocating shed with Reiger's face next to his, bloated and distorted by memory.

He staggered out of the cabin to escape what was left of the dream. The sky above him was black but the stars were not as bright as before. Beyond the ridge, the first pale streaks of sunlight lit up the horizon. Dane brought a handful of snow to his face and held it against his aching eyes. Later, he could lie out on the rocks on the top of the ridge and let the sun warm his neck and shoulders.

The cabin was cold. He had forgotten to bank the fire before falling asleep and all that remained were a few dull orange nuggets. Dane pushed the coals together and stacked several pieces of kindling around them and blew gently. The kindling smoked and crackled and caught fire. He added more kindling. When it started to burn, he laid a few large pieces of wood on the kindling and prodded the fire to keep it going. By the time the sun was up, it was hot enough for cooking.

For breakfast he ate more of the venison that he fried in a big cast-iron skillet until it was burned black. After eating, he put the leftover grease and scraps into a bowl for the gray wolf.

He couldn't shake the ghosts of Champleau. The dream came less often now; sometimes two or three full moons would go by without it. With each new season the memory dimmed until it was like an old ache, something that always surprised him a little when he found it was still with him. The first year had been the worst, when he would wake up nearly every morning shaking and crying, the stench of the shed all around him.

He dressed quickly and carried the bowl of greasy scraps across the stream. Most of the wolves were sprawled over the clearing to catch the early morning sun. The yearling saw him and stood up quickly, shaking himself off. The young wolf moved away from him, closer to the woods on the other side of the clearing. Two of the males were asleep in the middle of the riverbed. One of them raised his head and looked at Dane over his shoulder and went back to sleep. The third male slept soundly next to the two female hunters in the nearby rocks.

The black wolf was wide awake and waiting for Dane by the den, a large comfortable hole that the gray wolf had dug out between two boulders that leaned together in a rough arch. Dane bent down and shoved the bowl inside the den.

The black wolf sniffed curiously at the bowl. Dane laughed and pushed his head away. The wolf grabbed his wrist and tried to pull him away from the den. Dane refused to budge and the wolf soon grew tired of the game. He turned over on his back and stuck his legs in the air. Dane scratched the wolf's throat, pulling at the thick dark fur with his fingers.

Dane left the den and walked across the clearing toward the cliff, the black wolf trotting after him. The two females woke up and watched them. One of the hunters got up and shook herself. Dane stopped at the edge of the cliff. The black wolf stood next to him and sniffed the air.

When the black wolf had first joined the pack, the dominant male had been an old gray wolf. The old wolf was feeble with arthritis and there were traces of black blood in his scat. One day, Dane watched the old wolf go from animal to animal, nuzzling each one and rubbing against them with great affection. One by one, the wolves lay down, all except the black, who stood next to the old wolf, his head bowed in a last act of loyalty. The next morning the old wolf was gone. He had wandered off to die alone and the black wolf had taken his place.

Dane raised his eyes toward the mountains. When his time came, he thought, that was how he wanted to die.

Chapter 8

VAN OWEN WAS awake long before sunrise. For the next four days, he could work with little or no sleep at all, getting by on short meditations that he took whenever he could. He could close his eyes and relax instantly. His internal alarm would wake him within fifteen minutes. He trained himself to do it with the help of a young Thai girl named Diap. Van Owen had brought her with him from the mountain villages near the Burmese border. Their classroom had been a room next to the Chao Phrya River in Bangkok.

Van Owen would squat naked in the center of the matted floor and shut his eyes, letting his mind drift into semiconsciousness.

He was aware of everything around him, the dank smell of the river, the rustle of the straw mat beneath his feet, the rhythmic whump of the overhead fan, and the sensation of his own sweat as it ran down his neck and chest. Within minutes, his awareness would dissolve into an insignificant pinpoint of amber light.

Diap would circle around him holding a slender bamboo rod called a jaji. One end of the rod had been cut into a dozen petal-shaped blades, each one filed razor sharp. Van Owen had to wake himself just before she hit him with it.

It took two months to learn the technique properly and his back and chest still showed the scars. When his training was over for the day, Diap would kneel beside him and suck the blood from the wounds and spit it out on the mat, probing the tiny cuts with her tongue. Like all Thais, Diap was superstitious. She told Van Owen that his wounds had to be cleansed or the evil spirits that lived in the river would enter his body and devour his soul. Van Owen believed her.

After Diap finished with his wounds, she would reach between his legs and massage him to an erection with her small hands, then gently shove him back onto the mat and use her mouth on him. When he began to grow larger, she would spread her legs and touch herself until her whole body trembled from the strain. When she was ready at last, she would slide down on him with such force that he would climax instantly.

The hotel room at Big Bear was dark. Around the edge of the curtains, there was a thin corona of silvery-white light. Van Owen stood in the center of the room and lowered himself to the floor. He crouched on the balls of his feet, his forearms balanced lightly on each knee. He was transported back to that empty room. He could hear the sound of Diap as she glided over the mat and waited for the sharp sting of the bamboo. His fingers curled back like a shadow dancer until everything in the room was reduced to a small pinpoint of light.

Her face swam in front of his eyes and he reached out to touch her. His hands passed through her flesh. She was a watery image floating on the surface of the air, always there, always waiting.

The room grew brighter. Van Owen rose and stepped into the bathroom. After a quick shower, he dressed and laid out the Ruger and the Winchester.

He once asked a retired South Vietnamese captain, a man who interrogated prisoners of war, what he missed the most about his job.

"The surprised look in their eyes," the captain said with a laugh. "They think they are immune. They never think it can happen to them."

There were five on this trip. This morning Van Owen would start with the pilot.

* * *

Harris stood under the shower, hoping the hot water would wake him up. He hadn't had that much to drink last night but his head felt spongy. He had to fight down the bile that bubbled up from his stomach.

Harris knew what it was. It was Van Owen. The guy was genuinely scary. He thought about the way the hunter looked at him while he was telling that story about the wolves just to save his ass and his stomach twitched. What had he gotten himself into this time?

The pilot turned the hot water up a little higher and let it pound on the back of his neck. He wasn't ready for Van Owen. He doubted if he was ready for anything this morning except maybe another beer. Thank God he'd remembered to slip a couple bottles in his coat before the bartender kicked him out. He could kill both of them on the way to the airport.

Maybe he *should* get Doyle to take this trip off his hands, he thought. Keep a grand just for dealing with that spook last night and give Doyle the other two and wave bye-bye to both of them. Harris's stomach began to calm down. It was an idea worth considering.

The shower curtain flew open and Van Owen's face swam out of the steam toward him. He screamed and backed into the corner of the shower in terror. The face came closer. Harris banged his head against the white tile wall. Bright flashes of pain arced down the back of his skull. He slid to the bottom of the tub and landed hard. Hot water splashed over his legs and feet. Van Owen reached over and turned it off.

Harris was shaking so badly that he had to squeeze his hands together between his knees to keep them from dancing away from him. The pain in his head filled his eyes with tears. He held them shut and felt the tears run down his cheeks.

The hunter threw a towel at him. It landed in the tub.

"You're late," Van Owen said. "Hurry up."

Van Owen drove him to the airport at first light. At the turn by the lake, Harris could see the blue metal roof of the terminal building. Just beyond the terminal was the maintenance shed. His helicopter was parked in front of it.

A mechanic in a drab army parka and jeans stood by the engine flap with a cup of coffee in one hand and a big silver flashlight in the other. The pilot figured the mechanic had bad news for him. Why should he be any different this morning?

After the shower scene, Van Owen hadn't said a word to Harris. He acted as if the pilot wasn't even in the same car with him. Harris decided it was time to find out what the hell they were going to do. He had a flight plan to file and wanted to get all the garbage out of the way as quickly as he could. Maybe he still had time to think up another excuse. He had one worked out already. Sorry, he was going to tell him, but Canadian law says I don't have to work for a fucking asshole zombie and you're it. But Harris knew that wasn't going to happen, not with Van Owen.

"So," he said, his voice filled with empty cheerfulness, "you decide what we're going after today?"

"Wolves," Van Owen answered without taking his eyes off the road.

The mechanic had found a cracked gasket and they lost an hour while he replaced it. Once they were airborne, Harris crossed the Stikine and flew north toward the big open canyons that spread out from the plateau through the upper part of the Cassiar range like the ribs of a big fan. The auxiliary fuel tanks were full and the helicopter moved more slowly than usual.

The helicopter was a late model Hughes 650C that had been rigged to haul seismology equipment between the mainland and explorer ships in the Alaskan gulf. Because of the rough duty, the helicopters were rotated out of service twice a year and then sold.

Harris had torn out the steel casings on the cabin floor and had mounted four comfortable swivel chairs, one in each corner. He'd replaced the main cabin doors with a set of double panels, so he could open up the top panels and leave the bottom ones closed like a dutch door. On the other side, he ripped out the standard row of portholes and replaced them with two sliding windows. He put in a small auxiliary refrigerator and a gun rack, and covered the cabin floor with indoor-outdoor carpeting. Then he painted the whole thing jet black and cut in three big yellow accent stripes along the tail. Inside, the place was as comfortable as a den. From the outside, it looked like a gunship.

Of course, they needed a special permit to hunt wolves but that wasn't his problem. Van Owen either had one or he didn't and Harris didn't give a shit one way or the other.

All he had to do now was find the wolf pack for Van Owen to shoot at. That could take forever. Even if he got lucky, it could take awhile. The canyons were practically all alike up north and he couldn't even begin to remember where he'd seen the wolves.

It'd been over a year ago now. He'd been returning to Dawson, late as usual, and riding low over the canyons to make up time. The day had been overcast, his visibility was rotten, and he was jumpy from maneuvering around the updrafts that jerked the helicopter back and forth and threatened to throw it into the mountain every time he came down a ridge.

He remembered goosing the chopper down a canyon that was almost as wide as it was long, and that's when he saw the wolves. They stood in the middle of a dried riverbed, half a dozen or so right together, at least that's what it looked like. They didn't move when they saw him but that wasn't surprising. There was so much shit flying over BC these days that if you looked every time you'd need a neck brace to hold your head up. The wolves were used to it by now.

He slowed the chopper down and looked back at the pack. A man was standing with them. Harris was so surprised, he nearly lost it. The chopper wobbled, and by the time he got it straightened out, he was beyond them and it was too late to go back. But he knew he'd seen a man standing in the middle of that pack of wolves.

Now all he had to do was find them again. At the rate they were going and with the fuel they had left, Harris guessed he had another hour to do it. He hoped that was enough time. The snow squalls they were predicting had changed direction twice in the last forty-five minutes. This time they were moving right down on top of them.

A thought suddenly occurred to him. If it wasn't the same wolf pack, who would know? There were a lot of wolves in the canyons this time of the year. All he needed to do was find one of them, *any* one of them, and he was home free.

Van Owen rode next to him in the cockpit, separated from the others by a perforated plexiglass door. Blackburn and Walker were eager for the best view and grabbed the chairs by the door. The other two didn't seem to mind the window seats. Lange kept a tight grip on his rifle and ignored everyone else. Carroll opened his window a few inches and watched the scenery.

The lawyer and the editor drank coffee from a big silver thermos. The coffee was laced with whiskey. Blackburn had bribed the night clerk into selling him a bottle after they got back from the Lakehouse. He offered some to Lange. The broker declined. Carroll accepted half a cup and spit out his first sip. Blackburn grinned at the doctor and beat on his chest with a fat hairy fist. Carroll tried to respond but gave up. The noise of the blades made conversation impossible unless he yelled and Carroll didn't feel like wasting his time yelling at Blackburn.

They flew down one of the smaller canyons, level with the treeline. A few of the ridges were still snow-covered but most of them were clear. The exposed rock was gray blue and riddled with thick purple veins. Blackburn brought the rifle to his shoulder and swung it around, gazing through the sight at the blur of colors.

"It's fabulous!" Walker yelled at him. The lawyer nodded and kept his eye on the sight. It occurred to Blackburn that he'd never shot anything in his life. He thought about Harris's story and wondered what he'd do if he had a man on the other end of his sight. Blackburn squeezed the trigger. The cold metal clicked to a stop against the safety. It was an interesting sensation.

Carroll leaned over and asked Lange if he was all right.

"Of course," Lange yelled back. "What about you?"

"Okay," Carroll said. He wanted to talk to Lange suddenly, even if meant yelling back and forth, but the stockbroker had turned away. Carroll tapped on his knee. "Is it what you expected?" he asked when he got Lange's attention.

"What?"

"Is this what you expected?" Carroll said, opening his arms

to indicate the whole thing—the mountains, the helicopter, the people, the hunt, everything, God in his magnificent heaven, Carroll would have said, anything to draw Lange out, so that for once on this journey he could feel connected to another human being. He hadn't realized it before but the mountains unnerved him. There was a feeling of mercilessness there that was amazingly strong. He felt as though he were flying over his own tomb.

"I don't understand," Lange yelled back. "Tell me what you mean."

Carroll didn't think he could do that.

Harris found a landing site, one of the dozen or so throughout the territory that were jointly maintained by the different mining companies. The one they were on was typical. The engineers had blown off the top of a ridge and flattened out what was left. The edges of the site were marked with faded red flags. Down both sides of the ridge, hundreds of dead trees, knocked over by the blast, rotted on top of one another. Harris checked their fuel supply and drank a cup of Blackburn's coffee. He kicked the gravel with the toe of his boot while the big blades spun overhead.

Carroll stood next to Walker and the lawyer at the other end of the landing site. Walker gestured wildly, pummeling the air with his hands. Carroll moved out of the way as if he were afraid of catching the editor's enthusiasm. Lange stayed by himself in the helicopter.

Van Owen ducked under the rotating blades.

"You're lost," he said to Harris.

"I don't think so," Harris said. Van Owen seemed more amused than angered by his answer.

"Do you have any idea where they are?" Van Owen asked.

Harris threw his cup on the ground. It skittered across the gravel and disappeared over the edge close to where the three other hunters stood.

"I said I'd find them for you," Harris answered.

"I bet you will," Van Owen said.

But he'd better hurry. The wind was blowing hard off the northern range and pushing the dark line of snow clouds ahead of them.

* * *

Thirty minutes later, Harris suddenly realized he had crossed the northern end of the canyon where he'd seen the wolves. He slapped Van Owen on the shoulder.

"This is it," he yelled.

"You sure?" Van Owen yelled back.

Harris nodded. "I'll go back along the east ridge," he said. "See if you can spot them."

Harris swung the helicopter around and flew down the spine of the ridge, staying close to the treetops. If he spooked them, there was nothing he could do about it but at least it was better than diving down on them with his first pass. *If* they were still here.

Walker stuck his head in the cockpit.

"What's going on?" he asked. "Why are we turning?"

"Get ready," Van Owen yelled. "Tell the others."

"We found them?"

Van Owen took hold of Walker's shoulder.

"Just get ready."

Walker closed the plexiglass door. Harris pointed to a wide snowbank at the bottom of a dropoff in the middle of the canyon.

"There's a riverbed just beyond that," he said. Van Owen nodded and swung around in his seat. Harris leaned toward him, trying to see over his shoulder. He kept the helicopter as close to the top of the ridge as he could, surprised by his own growing excitement. Goddamn, he thought, I want them to be here.

Van Owen turned around. "They're down there," he said.

"All right!" Harris yelled, and banged on the window. "I'm going to look for a place to set her down on the other side of the ridge."

Van Owen shook his arm. "I don't want you to land," he said.

"What?" The pilot didn't understand. What did he mean, he didn't want to land?

"Don't land," Van Owen said. He put his mouth next to Harris's ear so the pilot could hear him. "Circle around and go up the west ridge. I want to come at them from the side near the rocks. You understand?" Harris shook his head. He still didn't know what Van Owen wanted to do.

Van Owen grabbed Harris by the chin and twisted his head so that they were face-to-face.

"We're going to take them from the air," he yelled.

Finally, Harris understood.

Dane heard the helicopter. He rolled over to watch, but it was moving too close to the treeline for him to see it clearly. They often flew along the ridges like that to keep away from the wind bursts that ripped through the canyons. The helicopter moved away and Dane turned on his back. The sound of the machine faded, once again leaving only the wind and the warmth of the fading sun on his face. The sky was clouding over rapidly. He'd have to go back down soon.

He let his mind wander. It was summer and there were new pups playing in the green fields of the Stikine. They rolled over him, nipping at his hands. From the branches of a nearby tree, a crow barked at them. The black wolf and the gray slept nearby. The rest of the pack ran toward them through the tall grass. In his mind, the dream was warm and alive.

He heard the helicopter again, but closer this time. Dane had to cover his eyes with his arm to see it. The helicopter turned sharply over the center of the canyon south of where he lay. It rolled awkwardly back and forth, then leveled off and flew in his direction along the ridge. Dane sat up on his elbows. Suddenly the helicopter surged up the ridge directly toward him. At the last moment, it broke away and soared over the riverbed and the wolves.

Van Owen told them they weren't going to have much time once the helicopter was in place. He held up a pair of fingers.

"Two minutes," he yelled. "That's all you're going to get."

Blackburn and Walker braced their rifles against the sides of the door. As the helicopter began its final run, Van Owen gave Walker the thumbs-up sign. The editor grinned back. Harris accelerated over the canyon and the force of it pushed Carroll against the back of his chair. Lange readied himself methodically. He took the cartridges from his jacket pocket and loaded them one by one into the gun.

Carroll tried to get his attention but the stockbroker only glared at him and continued loading the rifle. What in God's name am I doing here? Carroll thought. He looked around him. Walker and Blackburn were bent over in their seats, halfway out of the helicopter. Van Owen stood in the middle of the deck and leaned over them to see. He kept one hand on the ceiling as the helicopter straightened out along the side of the ridge.

Carroll dropped four shells into his rifle and pushed the window all the way open. Cold wind slapped his face. He steadied the rifle. I am going to do this, he thought.

They swept down the ridge, close to the trees. Carroll saw a wash of colors at first, dark greens, grays, wide patches of white. Then he saw the wolves, no more than six, maybe seven; it was hard to tell. They scattered in all directions across the riverbed.

Everyone started shooting at once. Lange stood up to get a better line of fire. He aimed carefully, making each one count. Blackburn and Walker were laughing and firing wildly, caught up in the noise and the excitement. The sound inside the helicopter was deafening. Carroll swung the rifle toward the rocks at the bottom of the ridge.

The two males were still asleep in the open and they were the first ones to die. One of them tried to get up and was knocked flat by the force of the bullet that ploughed into his neck. The other wolf was dead before he could raise his head. The yearling was next. He sprinted for the woods and was almost into the trees when Blackburn and Walker spotted him. Walker fired three quick shots. The first one missed but the second hit the wolf's right front leg and he went down, tumbling over onto his back. The third shot ripped through both lungs.

The other male stayed with the two female hunters. All three ran across the clearing almost directly below the helicopter. Harris swung it around. Lange had a clear shot and fired at one of the females. The bullet slammed into the wolf right behind the shoulders. She dropped and didn't move. Blackburn and Walker killed the other two wolves, the female and her mate, as they raced for the woods. They fell a few feet from where the yearling lay on his back, bleeding to death in the snow.

The gray wolf ran awkwardly through the rocks trying to

reach the safety of the birch grove. Lange saw her and cut off her escape. Harris turned the helicopter so it faced the rocks, giving all four hunters a clear field of fire. Bullets ricocheted off the boulders all around her. In desperation, she threw herself at one and tried to climb over it. A bullet shattered her spine. She fell over, paralysis spreading through her body. Her front legs twitched rapidly and scraped the dirt. Another bullet hit her in the side of the neck, then another and another. Blood and bits of fur splattered on the rocks.

Carroll emptied his rifle into the trees and closed his eyes. When he opened them again, the shooting was over.

Then Blackburn yelled, "My God, look at that one!"

Carroll looked out the window and saw an enormous black wolf running straight down the canyon for the cliff.

When the helicopter flew at him, Dane rolled over and slid down the rocks on his stomach, digging in with his hands and feet to stop his fall. He jumped to his feet and saw the helicopter turn over the riverbed. A man with a rifle leaned out the door and started shooting.

He knew it was too late even as he scrambled down the narrow twisted path to reach the canyon floor. Every few feet, he could see the helicopter as it hovered over the wolves. It had a gleaming black shell and three yellow stripes along the tail. Like some giant insect, it moved slowly back and forth across the canyon. He screamed at it but his voice was lost in the relentless chopping of the blades and the roar of the guns.

When he was closer to the canyon floor, the black wolf broke out of the rocks. Dane ran off the path and cut down the ridge at an angle toward the cliff. If he sees me, Dane thought, he might come to me. But the black wolf kept running.

Blackburn dropped the crosshairs in the middle of the wolf's back. The bastard was really going for it, he thought. He squeezed the trigger, feeling the tension give way. Van Owen slapped the rifle barrel aside and the shot went wild. He spun around in his seat.

"What the fuck are you doing?" Blackburn yelled. His face was sweaty with exertion and he was hyperventilating.

"It's mine!" Van Owen yelled back. He was holding the Winchester.

"Fuck you!" Blackburn yelled and swung the rifle at him. Before the lawyer could bring it around, Van Owen hit him on the side of the head with the Winchester and shoved him out of his chair. Walker was too surprised to do anything except stick his foot out to keep Blackburn from rolling headfirst into the wall.

Van Owen wound the strap of the Winchester over his arm and braced the barrel against the door. Harris turned the helicopter around and followed the wolf. Van Owen fixed his sight on the center of the wolf's back but didn't shoot. He wanted to see if the wolf was going to jump.

The black wolf didn't hesitate. He leaped off the cliff and dropped sixty feet to the plateau, sinking into the deep snow up to his shoulders. He struggled free and charged through the thick icy crust with agonizing slowness.

Van Owen steadied the rifle and pulled the trigger.

The storm hit ten minutes later, filling the canyon with thick clouds of snow. Van Owen and Walker dragged the bodies of the dead wolves out of the rocks and the nearby woods and piled them in the middle of the riverbed.

Blackburn stood by the helicopter and watched them work. He probed the side of his head gently, wincing when his stubby fingers found the tender spot. Carroll sat quietly inside the helicopter. Lange too. Blackburn thought they both looked a little shell-shocked. Out in the clearing, Walker squatted next to one of the wolves and poked at the animal's bloody muzzle with a stick. The editor wanted to see the wolf's teeth.

Harris hopped out of the cockpit and walked to where Van Owen stood watching Walker inspect his kill.

"We've got to move," Harris said. "Now."

Van Owen shook his head. He didn't seem particularly worried.

"You got any canister dye?" he said. "I want to mark it so

we can find them later." He looked around at the others. "The boys are going to want their souvenirs."

"No time," Harris said. "I just talked to Whitehorse. This shit is coming too fast. We got about five minutes to get our ass out ahead of it."

Blackburn stomped past them on his way to the cliff.

"What the fuck does he think he's doing?" Harris said. What the fuck was everybody doing? Fun was fun, but this was serious. Nobody seemed to understand that if they didn't get moving soon, they were going to end up as dead as the wolves.

"I'll find out," Walker volunteered. He stuck his hands in his pockets and wandered after Blackburn. Harris couldn't believe it. Walker was out for an afternoon *stroll* in the middle of a blizzard.

"What about the dye?" Van Owen asked again.

"Didn't you hear me?" Harris said.

"I heard you." It was the end of the discussion.

"Fine," Harris said, and walked back to the helicopter. He brought out a canister of red smoke dye and a black plastic tarp. "Here," he said, handing everything to Van Owen.

Van Owen grinned. "Looks like we missed him."

"Missed who?" Harris asked.

"The wolfman," Van Owen said.

"Shit," Harris said. He couldn't tell whether Van Owen was serious or not but he was tired of playing games. "You do what you want," he said. "I'm leaving in three minutes."

"Yes, sir," Van Owen said.

Walker caught up with Blackburn before the lawyer reached the cliff. "What are you doing?"

Blackburn pointed at Van Owen. "I want to see what that son of a bitch cheated me out of," he said. And if that didn't make him happy, Blackburn was going to slap a lawsuit on the bastard that would keep him in court for about the next two thousand years.

They reached the edge and looked down.

"I can't see very well," Walker said. He was starting to worry about the snow. Suddenly there seemed to be an awful lot of it.

"It isn't there," Blackburn said.

74

"What?"

"The wolf isn't there," he said. "Look." Walker followed Blackburn's finger but all he could see was white snow. Which, he supposed, was the point. If the wolf was down there, shouldn't he be able to see it? He leaned forward as far as he could but he still couldn't see anything, not even a vague outline. The wolf was gone.

Blackburn snorted. "Bwana fucked up."

Van Owen spread the tarp over the wolves and secured each corner with a heavy stone. He pulled the pin on the dye. The canister spun around on the ground, spewing a thick column of red smoke from one end.

"Hey, big shooter," Blackburn called to him. "You blew it."

"What's that?" Van Owen said.

"The wolf is gone," the lawyer said, and laughed. "You didn't get him."

"What do you mean gone?" Van Owen said, but he had already started for the cliff.

"I mean you missed him," Blackburn yelled. "He's gone."

Blackburn was right. Even through the snow, he could see it wasn't there anymore. There were some new tracks leading off toward the ridge and he followed them until they disappeared into the trees. No problem, he thought. A wounded animal wasn't hard to track, even in this snow. The whine of the helicopter engine startled him. Smoke from the canister billowed out in the wake of the big blades and turned the gravel at his feet red.

Blackburn and Walker were both climbing into the helicopter. Walker hesitated, then stepped away from the door and waved for him to hurry up. Harris throttled the engine and the helicopter lifted a few feet off the ground. Walker waved frantically at him.

There was nothing left for Van Owen to do. He walked slowly toward the helicopter. It never entered his mind to run.

The storm stalled over Dawson for nearly three days before it drifted westward, but by then the hunt was over. They all had to get back to their work, their wives, to whatever. Harris didn't care. He was just glad to see them go. After they took off, he drove straight to the Lakehouse for a drink. It was the middle of the morning and he didn't care, either. He couldn't have found the canyon again anyway, not after the storm. Nobody would ever find them now. There was a rough kind of justice in that. The snow had buried them, let them stay buried.

Part II

WINTER
ONE YEAR
LATER

Chapter 9

"YOU KNOW, DOYLE," Harris said, "you really are a cunt of misery sometimes."

Harris was drunk again, nothing unusual, maybe a bit further along this evening and feeling a lunatic edge creep into his voice. Anything to break the monotony.

Doyle glanced at Harris over his shoulder, his right eye locked in on the point of the pilot's chin.

"Piss off," Doyle said, and went back to his beer. He kept his head so low that he only had to tip the bottle back slightly to let the beer pour into his mouth. It saved extra motion. Harris thought it looked demented.

So did the bartender. He thought both of them ought to be locked away for at least six months, preferably in the same cage.

The bartender had heard stories about Doyle. Twice he'd wrecked his plane. Once he nearly drove it through the Dawson terminal. It was always a fateful balance, Doyle and booze, and now everything had tipped the wrong way. They said it was the fact that his wife had left him several months before that sent him over the edge.

She wasn't his real wife, only common-law after all this time, but she left him just the same. Somebody said it was for a real estate agent from Kamloops. That was the humiliating part if it was true. No wonder Doyle looked depressed; no wonder he tried to bust a sizable chunk out of the terminal when the manager told him he was eight weeks behind in filing his duplicate flight log. Doyle aimed the plane at the front of the terminal but tore half of his wing off instead. Sheared it off clean, just like using a pair of wire cutters. Then he spun the plane around and tried to fly it out again. They said there were five people hanging on to the remaining good wing screaming for him to stop when Doyle went skidding down the runway cackling like a madman.

The bartender caught Doyle's signal for another beer and placed another Molson in front of him. He sat it down gently on the bar as if Doyle were some sort of holy man and could not be disturbed. The truth was that just lately the bartender had been a little depressed himself. It was the same old winter lethargy, that inward turning that started when the wind shifted and the sunlight grew brittle and white. It made him sympathetic with anyone who shared his feelings, even if it was a weasel like Doyle.

The other reason he walked softly around Doyle was that the man tended toward violence whenever he was disturbed these days. The bartender needed a bar full of airplane like he needed frostbite. He looked at Harris sitting next to Doyle and wondered if it wasn't time to start thinking about getting out of Dawson before he became a permanent fixture like the two specimens in front of him.

Harris ordered another beer and turned around to look at the rest of the bar. It was full tonight. The weather showed signs of breaking and everybody seemed in good spirits. Except for Doyle, who was beginning to irritate him, and the guy sitting by himself at the corner table. Even from here, Harris could see that he wasn't having a good time. He'd only had one beer in the same time that Harris had had at least three.

Besides, he'd never seen somebody with skin that white. He must have been living in a cave all winter, Harris thought. The pilot nodded at him and smiled but the man only stared.

Christ, Harris thought, I wonder if I owe him money.

Dane felt like he was drowning, trailing pieces of his skin and flesh behind him, like lines of phosphorescence in a dark southern sea. The noise clung to him like the smell of smoke and beer. When he'd first stepped into the bar, he thought he was going to choke. A feeling of uncertainty overwhelmed him suddenly. The feeling was so strong that he almost turned and left, afraid that he couldn't go through with what he had been planning for a year.

All Dane could remember of the past year was the pain. It had taken nearly six months for the wolf to heal. The slug had passed through the heavy muscles along his right shoulder and out his chest. The wound was massive but clean, no bones splintered, no arteries shattered, only muscle damage, and that finally healed in time. Once the wolf regained his strength, there were months of slow, almost endless training.

The memory of the pain had pushed Dane forward into the bar. He'd closed the door behind him and shaken off his uncertainty. Through the haze, he'd seen the pilot.

Dane had spoken to the airport manager the day before and asked about the black helicopter with the three distinctive yellow stripes along the tail. There was only one like it in northern British Columbia, the manager said, and it belonged to a pilot named Harris.

"He lives in an alley," the manager said, as if that explained everything there was to know about Harris.

Dane nodded, almost afraid to move. He felt as if the nerves in his own body had become corroded somehow and were sending out false signals. In one hand, he held some keys. The hand began to ache suddenly.

The manager stood beside him in front of a long counter covered in bright salmon-colored Formica. One long strip in front had peeled away and the manager flicked the loose edge with his thumb.

"He drinks too much," he told Dane. "You ought to know that if you're thinking about hiring him." The manager waited for Dane to say something, and when he didn't, he added, "He's not as good as he used to be."

The manager walked him to the door. Outside, alongside a concrete pillar that was partially covered with dirty snow, a blue van sat idling. White clouds of exhaust spewed out and vanished in the wind.

"That your van?" the manager asked.

Dane nodded.

"I wouldn't leave it running like that in town," he said. "Somebody might borrow it for a day or two."

Dane got back into the van and drove around the lake toward Dawson. The ice had receded from the shoreline, leaving a dark ribbon all around the edge. By the time he got into town, Dane noticed that his hand no longer ached.

Harris decided that he didn't owe the man any money, that he probably didn't even know him, although it was getting difficult to see anything clearly inside the Lakehouse. The smoke was as thick as morning fog and it seemed to wrap itself around the noise of the bar. There was a new modern-looking jukebox in the corner near the bathroom with bright red flames shooting up both sides and a panoramic view of what looked like the surface of the planet Venus but was only a plastic sunset on the square back panel.

The jukebox had survived the winter without anyone putting his fist through it. The old one had been busted so often that by the time they tossed it in the lake two years ago, the front was as cracked and starred as the windshield of a quarry truck.

In a way, Harris missed the old machine. But then Harris had lost so much in his short life that he missed almost everything.

His life had taken a wrong turn in the last year or so, he thought; it had slipped just out of his grasp. His bookings were the same, maybe even a little better than last year, but every one seemed to leave him angry and dissatisfied. He drank too much and slept too little and lived like a stranger in his own skin.

Harris turned and looked around the room again. The man at the table hadn't moved. He was still staring at him. The pilot thought about walking up to him and asking him what his problem was but changed his mind. He was probably just one more lunatic who thought that Harris reminded him of his dead brother or something equally twisted, and besides, what was Harris going to do if the guy went after him with a linoleum knife? As if to answer his question, the man left the bar. One down, Harris thought, and turned back to Doyle.

The Irishman finished his beer and wiped a limp hand across his mouth. He looked at the pilot without smiling. Sometimes when he looked at Doyle, Harris saw himself a few years older, another drunk on a bar stool. The thought of it made him mad all over again.

"So, Doyle," Harris said, loud enough for the bartender to hear. "I hear your wife liked to suck strange cock. Is that true or what?"

Doyle grabbed the empty beer bottle by the neck and swung it at Harris's face.

The pilot ducked and the bottle flashed past his eye, missing his face by less than an inch. It slipped out of Doyle's hand and flew across the bar. The bartender saw the flash of green and heard the bottle smash against the wall. Doyle reached for another bottle but the bartender caught his arm. The Irishman swung his left hand around and clipped the bartender on the shoulder, just enough so that he lost his grip and stumbled against the back of the bar.

Harris didn't know quite what else to do, so he slapped Doyle across the back of the head and ducked under what he thought was going to be another roundhouse with an empty beer bottle. Instead, he fell face first off the stool. On the way down, he grabbed Doyle's leg and pulled him down with him. The bartender watched as they rolled around on the floor and reached underneath the bar for the eighteen-inch weighted pool cue he kept there.

The fighters immediately drew a half circle of spectators who cheered them on while they punched drunkenly at one another. The bartender made his way through the crowd, holding the pool cue close to his side and tapping it lightly against his thigh.

Doyle and Harris faced each other. Each one swayed gently to and fro, seemingly unable to move. Like an old engine, they had to be started up. They were pushed around the edge of the circle by the crowd, moving slowly, shuffling on heavy feet.

Doyle cocked his chin and wiped something from his eye. Harris stopped momentarily to watch and listen to the crowd. He wondered how he had managed to bring all this on himself with so little effort. The bartender moved cautiously along the edge of the spectators, stopping a few feet behind the Irishman. Doyle stepped back and the bartender swung the pool cue straight out from his shoulder. It caught Doyle at the back of his skull and knocked him off his feet. For a moment, he floated in midair and then settled in a heap on the floor. Everyone stared at him, stunned into silence, as if they'd just witnessed a minor miracle.

The bartender didn't waste any time. He grabbed Harris by the arm and spun him around, twisting his arm high up behind his back. Harris's shoulder quickly reached the breaking point. He stood on his tiptoes and yelled for him to let go. The bartender tucked the arm up a little bit higher and pushed the pilot through the crowd toward the door, whispering to him all the way across the bar.

"You pull this crap in my bar again," he said, surprised and maybe even a little frightened by his own anger, "and I'll rip the goddamn thing off." He held Harris against the wall and opened the door.

Harris peered around the edge of the doorframe. He wasn't quite sure what had happened but he knew he wasn't ready for this; it was colder than fuck out there.

"I don't want you coming in here for a while," the bartender said. "You understand?" Harris stared into the darkness. He was trying to look indignant.

"You understand me, Harris?" the bartender asked again.

"Sure." Harris chewed softly on his lip. The cold air numbed his skin. "Do you think I could have my coat first?" he asked.

Dane saw the pilot's house clearly. It was down a short alley lined with humps of gray snow that in the spring would turn back into trash cans. Piled next to the door were half a dozen black plastic garbage bags. Dane kicked the one nearest the door and the bottles inside clinked together. He stood beneath a single bulb that hung inside a wide metal shade that was rounded at the top like a skullcap. The only other light in the alley came from a street lamp that was around the corner and halfway down the street.

It wasn't really a street, only a dirt road that angled off the highway on the outskirts of Dawson, a dogleg that went straight past the alley for several hundred yards and then curved around an abandoned foundation and finally stopped in a pile of dirt and rocks and an empty field.

Dane took out his knife and smashed the overhead bulb with the handle. Pieces of glass exploded on his hand and sleeve. Without the bulb, the light from the street lamp was so soft that it seemed like daybreak in the alley.

Dane listened for any sound from the surrounding buildings but everything remained quiet. He waited a few more minutes just to be sure and went to work on the door.

Harris drove his car around the lake and made it past the post office building before he ran it off the road. The car fishtailed slightly on the ice-crusted road and drifted gradually to the right, then rolled into the narrow snow-filled ditch on the other side of the post office. The back wheels spewed snow and gravel in a high plume. The car sank into the snow and stalled. Harris opened the door and sprawled onto the road.

He lay on his back with his legs still draped across the front seat and opened his eyes. The stars rushed by overhead. They became thin lines of light that wavered across the black sky. Harris felt something back up in his throat. He jerked his legs off the seat, banging his shins hard against the wheel and pulled them free. He lay on his side for a moment and then climbed to his knees and threw up. It was like someone was trying to twist the muscles of his stomach into one big knot.

When it was over, he rested his head on the icy road and wiped the tears away from his eyes. The pain in his stomach subsided gradually. He got to his knees again, felt comfortable with that, and grabbed the edge of the door and pulled himself to his feet. He looked around at the car and the smear of steaming vomit on the ground next to it.

Jesus, he thought, get me home.

His apartment was almost a mile away. Harris fumbled around in the front seat for his gloves but couldn't find them. He slammed the car door shut and walked away. They could yell at him tomorrow. Right now, he wanted a warm bed and maybe one more cold beer just to cut through the taste in his mouth. He knelt down and ate a handful of snow, rubbing it around his face. The cold made him shiver.

Dawson was like a cemetery on a winter's night, silent, empty and gray, filled with shadows and pale light. There were few street lamps, most of them old and weak. Harris stayed on the side of the highway and walked with his head down. Occasionally, he stopped to spit out the sour taste that was still in his mouth.

Harris knew where he was by the landmarks, the big Shell station with the wide overhanging roof, the coffee shop and the bank across from one another at the corner where Dawson's main street met the highway, the streetlight over the intersection, the old stained-glass clock hanging above the bank entrance, broken long ago, the hands stopped permanently at 4:05. He crossed the highway to take a piss on the cornerstone of the bank. In the morning, he thought, they'd come out and find the date of 1921 covered with a thin yellowish glaze. When he finished, Harris zipped his pants and leaned with one bare hand against the cold rough brick and looked around.

Across the street someone stood in the shadows by the side of the coffee shop watching him. It sent a shock wave through him and he backed up against the wall of the bank. What was left in the pit of his stomach rolled several times. He slipped around the corner of the building and looked across the street again. Whoever it was stood there with his hands in his pockets facing the bank and staring at him. Harris knew that was what he was doing, he could feel it.

Harris stared back until the warmth of the alcohol still in his body started to calm him down. He leaned his head forward to try to see who it was but it was too dark.

"Hey," he yelled, but the figure didn't move. Harris started to giggle. He knew who it was after all.

"I see you, Doyle," Harris yelled but nothing happened. Doyle was trying to be cute. "You still want a fight, Doyle?" Harris stepped to the corner. "Come on, cocksucker, we can do it right now." When Doyle didn't come forward, he leaned off the curb and spat into the street. "Fuck you, Doyle, you chickenshit asshole," Harris yelled. He threw up his hands in disgust and walked back to the bank. At the edge of the building, he stopped and looked to see if Doyle was coming after him.

There was no one in front of the coffee shop. Harris looked hard but he couldn't see anyone. What is this? he thought. He checked up and down the street but it was deserted. What was Doyle doing, playing hide-and-seek?

The thought occurred to him suddenly that it might *not* have been Doyle at all. It could have been anybody. It could have been that lunatic he vaguely remembered seeing at the Lakehouse, the one with the linoleum knife. Harris giggled again. That was it, some lunatic was coming after him with a goddamn linoleum knife. Jesus, he thought, the laughter dying in his throat, just get me home. He staggered awkwardly up the highway toward the apartment, the distant streetlight like a homing beacon.

Dane lay on the ground beside the coffee shop and watched the pilot run. When his retreating figure dissolved into the darkness, Dane got to his feet. Harris would be at the apartment in minutes, so there wasn't much time left.

Harris was sweating when he reached the alley. He stopped long enough to look behind him to see if he was being followed but the road was empty. Harris stood in the stillness and listened for the sound of footsteps coming after him but the street was empty and quiet.

He sat down on one of the submerged garbage cans and relaxed. After a few minutes, he dug out his keys from the inside pocket of his jacket and walked to his apartment. He hummed a song to himself, something from when he was a teenager in Detroit. The bulb was out again over the door and he twisted around so he could see the key. He opened the door and slipped inside.

Something was waiting for him in the apartment. He saw it the moment he turned around and looked down the dark hallway. It was there, just a few feet ahead of him on the floor. The smell in the hallway was strong, a sharp wild smell that made him pull his head away. The shape on the floor began to move toward him. Harris felt his flesh crawl up the back of his skull and he bit his cheek to keep from screaming. Whatever the thing was in front of him, it wasn't human and it wouldn't stop moving.

Harris stood against the wall with tears in his eyes, his breath coming in quick agonizing rasps, trying somehow to press himself closer to it. He looked toward the half-closed door and tried to move closer but his legs wouldn't work. His whole body was stiff. His fingers were claws dug into the wall.

Without warning, the door opened slowly, letting in a pale shaft of light that rolled down the darkened hallway. Harris forced himself to look at whatever it was at the end of the hall. It was very difficult to see in the shadows. The shape moved again and he finally saw what had been waiting for him.

A large black wolf crouched on the floor ten feet away. Harris squeezed closer to the wall. The thing was enormous. The wolf stared up at him but Harris's brain registered only the wolf's size and the eyes. They held him there, freezing him in place. As the light crept over the wolf, he watched the eyes change color. At first, they were yellow, but then as the light shifted away, they turned cold and white. The wolf rose from the floor and crept forward slowly, padding silently down the hall, mouth open, teeth exposed. The animal seemed to float toward him.

Harris lunged desperately for the open doorway. He almost made it.

As he turned, Dane blocked his way. Harris screamed and shuffled backward into the hall. He screamed again when he saw the wolf advancing on him. He covered his face with both hands and slid along the wall toward the floor. He screamed all the way down. Dane clapped his hands together once. The wolf stopped.

Harris passed out. He fell over gently, collapsing like an empty suit of clothes, his head coming to rest on the floor no more than a few inches from where the black wolf waited.

Harris awoke suddenly. It was as if he'd been in a trance and someone had snapped their fingers and now he was awake again. Except that everything was dark, even with his eyes open. It was all so simple. The lights had gone out. In a minute or two, they'd be back on and then he was going to get himself another beer. Harris needed another beer. He'd been dreaming that there was a wolf in his house and that the animal had been stalking him. Jesus, the thing was big. The vividness of his memory was unnerving. That wasn't all. There was a guy who controlled the wolf, who could make the animal do anything he wanted to just by clapping his hands or something. It was bizarre but at least it was over. He was going to get that beer now.

Harris tried to stand up but he couldn't. His wrists and ankles were wired to the arms of the chair. The lights weren't out, either. He was blindfolded. Shadows played across his eyes through the black material.

Harris smelled it again, the same sharp wild smell that had been in the hallway. He dropped his head to his chest and shut his eyes tight. Even with the blindfold, he wanted to keep them closed. He didn't want to see what was out there because he already knew and he didn't want to open his eyes anymore, not ever again.

Dane looked around the room again. What kind of man lives like this? he thought. It was small and cramped and rundown. The walls had once been green but they were faded and streaked with dust. In one corner, part of the ceiling had broken away and a large piece of it hung loose, surrounded by concentric circles of brown waterstains. There was an old metal desk covered with papers that spilled over on the floor and a black file cabinet shoved at an angle against one wall; obviously the pilot's office.

The rest of the furniture, the two wooden chairs that didn't match, the green couch with piles of dry, crumbling foam beneath each sagging cushion, and the lamp that wobbled on a cracked pedestal base, was either broken or worn out. The whole room seemed to answer his question.

Scattered everywhere on the bare linoleum floor were more piles of magazines and newspapers. A metal wastebasket overflowed with bottles. The air in the room was warm and humid. Sweat made the skin on Harris's forehead glisten.

Dane sat facing the pilot in the other chair, a foot away from him. The wolf lay on the floor alongside the pilot's chair and stared intently up at Dane. He was waiting for whatever signal Dane might give him. Even now, Dane could see the wolf's alertness to every sound and movement. The animal's muscular shoulders were hunched up as if to ward off a blow, and the thick muscles of the wolf's forelegs twitched involuntarily. The wolf began to pant. Harris cocked his head toward the new sound.

Dane knew what the airport manager had told him about the pilot and that was all. Except that it was Harris who had flown the hunters into the canyon a year ago and that now the pilot was frightened and alone. Beyond that, Harris was a cipher.

Dane reached out and took hold of Harris's wrist and the pilot's body stiffened and jerked away. He tried to pull his hands away from the arms of the chair and Dane saw the flesh on the back of Harris's wrists swallow up the thin black wire. A few seconds later, a bright line of red began to fill in the tiny crevice.

"I need some information," Dane said quietly. He was afraid that Harris might start screaming again. The pilot strained harder against the wires. Both wrists were bleeding now and the blood seeped through Dane's fingers. He wiped them on his pants legs, taking the time to clean each finger separately, and waited.

"Where is it?" Harris asked. His mouth was dry and his voice cracked. The words caught in his throat.

"I want some information from you," Dane said again in the same quiet way.

"Where's the goddamn wolf?" Harris said, his voice breaking up as he spoke.

"Right beside you," Dane said.

"Keep it away from me."

Dane gripped one of Harris's wrists again, harder this time, and leaned forward so that his mouth was only a few inches away from the pilot's face.

"Listen to me," he said. "A year ago you flew a group of hunters into the mountains. I want their names. You can give them to me."

"What names?" Harris said. "What the hell are you talking about? I flew a lot of people into the mountains last year."

"I want the names of the men who killed my family," Dane

said, and the words sounded strange to him, as if he'd heard them for the first time and not been thinking them over and over for the past year.

But when he spoke them out loud, listened to the sound of them, everything became clear, all doubts erased, all fear gone; he was certain of what lay ahead, unconcerned how far it might take him, unafraid whether or not he would ever come back.

"We didn't kill anybody's family," Harris said, but there was an odd note in his voice, a quaver that shook him even as he was saying it. He remembered something. It fluttered and grew and then he remembered the wolves.

"Who are you?" Harris whispered. That was what he said. What he wanted but was too terrified to say was this: what in God's name are you going to do to me?

The names were in a manila folder that was stacked with many others in the bottom drawer of Harris's desk. The drawer had squeaked and rattled when Dane pulled it open. Inside were several pieces of paper, a copy of an invoice for three thousand dollars, and a stained and crumpled brochure from the New York Sportsman's Society. He read the brochure first, then the rest of the papers. That's where he found the names.

He couldn't connect them with the death of the canyon wolves. Lange, Walker, Blackburn, Carroll, Van Owen. They were strangers to him, sounds without meaning. He put the papers aside and looked through the brochure once again. The Sportsman's Society was larger than he thought. It had over three hundred members; it even had its own private hunting lodge. He folded the papers together and stuck them in the pocket of his coat.

"Is this what they paid you?" Dane asked. Harris still had the blindfold on and spoke without raising his head.

"I don't remember what they paid me," he said. He moved his hands and the wire bit into his wrist again. The sharp pain startled him.

"Three thousand dollars."

"Yeah," Harris said, remembering through the pain that it was a good price, even with all the crap. He wanted to smile at the memory but the fear returned like a wave and mingled with the pain. His smile stopped cold. Harris remembered something else.

"Van Owen's the one you want," he said.

"Why?"

"Because he's the one who wanted to go after the wolves," Harris said. "He even wanted to go after you."

Dane slapped his hand twice on his leg. The wolf stood up quickly, his head nearly level with the pilot's. If Dane looked closely, he could still see the small depression over the right shoulder where the bullet had gone in and the slightly larger one on the side of his chest where it emerged. It was a clean shot with little fragmentation but the slug had still missed the wolf's heart by less than a quarter of an inch.

Harris pushed the chair back with his toes and the wooden legs scraped loudly on the linoleum. At the unexpected noise, the wolf dropped, his long front legs stiff, head lowered almost to the floor. Dane slapped his hand against his leg and the wolf trotted to his side.

Dane knelt down and pulled back the thick fur around the scar on the wolf's shoulder, brushing aside the heavy black hairs and the darker gray ones underneath. The wolf remained still while Dane examined the scar, turning his head once and looking up at Dane with a calm curious gaze. The scar tissue was light pink in color, the flesh smooth. It was the same on the wolf's chest. During a long run, the wolf favored that side. Dane thought that it slowed him down.

"What's going on?" Harris asked anxiously.

Dane stood and looked down at the figure in the chair. He wanted to hate the pilot but what he felt now was closer to pity than hate. Harris was pathetic. He hadn't expected that.

"Who did the shooting?" he asked the pilot.

"All of them," Harris said quickly.

"Van Owen?"

"He got the one that ran over the cliff," Harris said. He remembered it now, the way the wolf ran toward the overhang and the way the cold air played across the back of his neck through the open door behind him as he swung the helicopter in the wolf's direction. He watched the wolf gain speed as it reached the edge and leaped into space, a cloud of snow and gravel falling behind the wolf as the animal fell. Then he saw the barrel of Van Owen's rifle jut from the door behind him. Van Owen steadied it against the side of the door and fired a single shot as the wolf began plowing through the thickly crusted snow.

"But you must have been there," Harris said. "You must have seen it."

Dane said nothing but moved around to the pilot's chair and stood behind it.

Harris whipped his head back and forth.

"Where are you?" he said. "What are you doing?" He was frantic. The chair rocked with each swing of his head. Dane put both hands on Harris's shoulders and the pilot gave a yelp. The wolf's ears picked up at the sound.

"What was he like?" Dane whispered.

Harris knew the answer already. It was as if it had been inside him for a year and had just now found a way out.

"What was he like?" Harris repeated. "Except for you, he was the scariest bastard I ever met in my life."

Dane bent down to unwrap the wire from each of Harris's ankles and to loosen the ones around his wrists just enough so that he could work himself free in the next few hours.

"What are you doing?" the pilot asked. For all Harris knew, the man was going to release him and *then* turn the wolf loose on his neck. But once the wires were off, nothing happened. The room was abnormally quiet. Harris couldn't even hear the wolf breathing. Tentatively he moved his right foot around in a half circle from the leg of the chair.

"Hey," Harris said. "Where are you?" He shook the chair, kicking it with his feet. "Hey, goddammit," he yelled, louder this time. "What's going on?" The room remained silent.

Harris tugged at the wires on his wrists but paused after a few seconds because of the pain. But they weren't as tight as before and it would take maybe an hour before he worked himself loose. Then he was going to find that cocksucker. He tugged again gently on the wires, trying to slowly pull them apart. There was a sudden draft of cold air in the room that came from the front hall. Harris stopped struggling with the wires. The man must have gone and left the front door open.

But what about the wolf? There would be no reason to leave the wolf behind, not if the man had decided not to kill him. But why did he just leave? Why did he make it easy for Harris to get loose?

Because he knows I'm not going to do anything, Harris thought, not now, not ever. The truth was, he was just too scared. It was the same with Van Owen. Harris felt the skin on his face turn hot against the cold air.

He raised his head, still shrouded in the blindfold, and screamed hoarsely into the empty room. It was as close as Harris ever got to a feeling of shame.

Dane and the black wolf were approaching the entrance to the alley when Harris cried out. The sound was too faint for Dane but the wolf heard it and turned sharply, his ears flattened against the side of his head. It was like a brief explosion and then silence.

Dane stopped a few feet from the wolf.

"What is it?" he said. Already his fingers had found the small silver whistle in his pocket. The empty street stretched away into darkness on either side of him.

The wolf stared at the end of the alley and waited. When nothing else happened, he padded to where Dane stood and together they walked up the street to where the van was parked.

Chapter 10

THE GIRL STOPPED beside the highway and watched the goshawk as it soared high above the wide Alberta prairie. The bird hovered overhead, caught on a current of warm spring air. The wind shifted and the hawk folded its wings in closer and went into a slow drifting dive.

Far in the west, against the gray and white rise of the Rocky Mountains, there was a flash, a reflection off the midmorning sun that was still only a small white ball in the east. The hawk pulled out of the dive and soared again, rising higher and higher in ever-widening circles over the empty fields that stretched out like a patchwork of brown and black.

Jenny watched the hawk fade into the sky and looked west down the highway. She knew he'd be coming for her. It might take him awhile now, but he'd come after her. She was about one hundred and fifty miles south of Calgary and had gotten a ride with a young rancher to just outside of Suffield, a nondescript smudge of gas stations, stockyards, and grain elevators in the middle of nowhere. She could still see them in the distance, thrust like stubby fingers into the bright blue sky.

She had an American fifty-dollar bill stuffed into the toe of her boots and another twenty-two and change in Canadian in the front pocket of her jeans. Everything else she had was in the green knapsack she carried slung over her shoulder:

another pair of jeans, a sweatshirt from the University of Calgary, a couple of turtleneck shirts, a ruby-red blouse, some underwear, tennis shoes, toothbrush and toothpaste, comb and brush, Tampax and deodorant, some apples and cold sausage. In the pocket of her jacket she carried a jackknife with a four-inch blade.

Everything had been thrown together in a hurry when she slipped past her mother's room and down the stairs. There'd been another party last night and someone lay passed out on the sofa and snored. For a moment she thought it might have been Sonny and her heart pumped in her throat, even though she knew he was somewhere down in Calgary that night. She nearly tripped on an empty can on her way to the kitchen and grabbed for it in terror as it rattled across the floor. She waited for someone to come and get her, waited for the lights to go on in the upstairs hallway. But the house remained dark and silent and she took the apples and sausage out of the refrigerator, too anxious to look for anything more, and went out the back door, making sure that she made no sound when she closed it.

They lived north of Calgary, near Crossfield, in a farmhouse on about one hundred and forty acres of land that was leased out for sugar beets to one of the big combines. They hadn't farmed for years, not since her father had left. The only thing they used the land for now was when Sonny or somebody got drunk enough and went out to shoot up some of the beets in the middle of the night. Except one night, she heard screaming from the basement that lasted a long time. Afterward, Sonny and some other men carried shovels and several heavy plastic garbage bags out to the field. They wouldn't let her in the basement, and when she finally went down there, the concrete had been washed clean and it smelled of disinfectant and blood. Nobody ever talked about that night.

The yard in front of the house was filled with half a dozen vehicles. She dug with her fingers to find the hood latch on the first car, the one parked closest to the house. She hooked it finally and lifted the hood over her head. I forgot my damn gloves, she thought, and almost laughed. It didn't matter because she wasn't going back in that house. She stepped around to the side near the battery and cut the eight distributor wires one by one, feeling the cold greasy wires between her fingers, sawing through them with the blade of the jackknife.

It took awhile, maybe twenty minutes, to cut through all the cars. She was strong but the weather was cold and whenever she heard something, a fox scuttling through the field, a truck far out on the highway driving into Calgary, she stopped and waited.

Jenny was eighteen, even though she felt old before her time. After what her father had done, she knew what she was doing was the only sin that really mattered to any of them at the farm. She was leaving.

She took only rides that she found in truckstops and the small towns along the way, even though they might be going just a few miles. The rest of the time she walked, and hid whenever she heard a car coming down the road from Calgary.

For a while, she followed the path of a hawk in the sky above her as it circled over the empty fields. Even though the day had warmed, there were still patches of snow on the ground and in the deep gullies on either side of the road. Some of the fields were lined with rows of soft green winter wheat, others were covered with brown stubble. When a rancher let her off at the entrance to his ranch, a long straight dirt road that disappeared in a clump of sugar maples, he invited her home to have something to eat. Through the barren trees, she could see a big white house, a pair of blue enamel feed silos, and several outbuildings.

The rancher was in his midtwenties and had light brown hair, almost the same color as her own. When he asked her to the house, he did so with such an earnest smile that she wanted to hug him. Instead, she turned him down and sat by the entrance after he'd gone and ate one of the apples and a piece of sausage. She was still hungry but wanted to save the rest. There were still a few diners along this stretch of the Suffield highway and later, after it got dark, she might risk a meal at one of them and maybe find another ride.

Jenny watched the goshawk as it sailed away from her. She

closed her eyes and felt herself rising with it. That was where she wanted to be. In her mind, the image was so vivid that she saw herself from high overhead, the western mountains, a bright glint of something rolling over the highway toward where she stood. She wanted to disappear. She imagined herself vanishing with the hawk until she became nothing more than a small speck in the haze of blue, and then gone. Jenny opened her eyes with a start.

She'd forgotten about the Trans-Am. It was still in the goddamn barn where Sonny had parked it the week before. Christ, how could she have forgotten it? How could she have been so goddamn stupid? She looked around wildly, thinking that he was already nearby but there was nothing on the road in either direction.

That didn't mean anything and she knew it. Sonny would come after her and it really didn't matter when or how long it took. He'd be there. Jenny tossed the apple core into the gully and started walking, glancing over her shoulder now and then to see if she could catch a glimpse of something she knew was gaining on her.

She felt it coming long before she saw the car. It was like an evil rumbling in the ground underneath her feet, something foreign that disturbed the natural order of things. The air seemed to close in around her and there was a strange taste in her mouth, a metallic sensation that was like fresh blood.

Jenny hurried along the road until she found a place where the runoff had carved out a section of the shoulder and left a small overhang. She swung the knapsack off her back into the gully and followed it, trying to step carefully down the side without leaving any traces. Patches of icy snow clung to the shaded sides. Against it, her breath seemed almost blue. She pressed herself into the hollow, hunching her shoulders into the ground's frozen contours, and held her knapsack to her chest.

Five minutes later she heard the crackle of the exhaust as the Trans-Am sped down the highway, the sound as clear and distinctive as a voice. It roared past where she hid and she waited until long after it was gone before she climbed out of the gully onto the road. He would only go so far before turning around, running back and forth down the highway until he found her. She had to find a place off the highway before he came back.

She could see the car in her mind: white on white, he called it, a white lacquer finish with mother-of-pearl swirled into the paint so that it glittered in the sun, and a white leather interior. The wheel wells were painted red and he had small lights mounted behind each wheel. At night, the underside of the car glowed a dull red and the mags glistened.

Then he had the words painted on both rear quarter panels with the same red paint in a long flowing script. He told her he read them in some magazine. He said that's what he wanted people to think when they saw him coming. He held on tight to her shoulders, so tight that it hurt, and made her read them out loud: "The Angel of Death."

Forty-five minutes later, Jenny locked the bathroom door of the diner and took off her jacket and tossed it over the top of the stall by the sink. She ran the water in the small white porcelain sink. There was a ring of rust stains around the drain and the surrounding porcelain had yellowed. She filled the sink and splashed water on her face.

The water was soft and tasted of chlorine, not like the hard, sweet well water on the farm. She pulled up her sleeves and washed her face and hands with the pink liquid soap from the dispenser above the sink. When she finished, she dried herself with a handful of paper towels and ran her fingers through her hair several times before pulling it tight in back. The rows made by her fingers stood out in thick cords over the top of her head.

Her hair was short, trimmed to just the edge of her turtleneck in back but left thick and uneven along the sides. She held her head one way and then the other, examining each side in the cloudy mirror in front of her. It was still a girl's face, she thought, but you had to look hard for it now. Once there may have been a thin veneer of innocence but that had vanished long ago, peeled away like dead skin.

She wasn't pretty, Jenny knew that, but she would always be attractive in a bruised kind of way. She was aware of it, and how it affected the men around her and sometimes she did little things to accentuate it: the way she crossed her legs,

languidly scratching the soft skin of her inner thigh; a smudge
of eyeshadow that made her dark eyes even darker and even
more secretive. She carried her sexuality on the surface. She
did it easily and effortlessly. There was no sexual guilt in her
at all. Sonny told her she looked like a tramp and she thought
that might be true as well.

But not now. Now her face appeared flat and pale, so white
it was like a mask, her mouth a misshapen pink smear. Only
her eyes remained vivid. Even in the dingy light of the
cramped bathroom they shimmered like pieces of ebony.

Before Jenny put on her jacket, she lifted her sweater and
turtleneck up past the middle of her back and turned around,
glancing over her shoulder to see. She stared at the marks on
her back for a few seconds with mute curiosity before she
pulled down her sweater again. Something rattled against the
bathroom window. Outside, raindrops danced across the
pebbled glass.

She slipped her jacket on and looked at herself in the
mirror once more. Her eyes shone harder than before, as if
someone had spilled hot liquid on their dark polished surface.

Dane saw her through the front window of the diner. At
first, from what he could see in the instant when the wipers
cut through the heavy rain, he thought it was a man, but then
she turned around to look briefly at the van. He couldn't get
over the fact that her hair was nearly as short as his. She sat
by herself at the far end of the counter and seemed to be the
only person in the place. Where was her car? Maybe she
belonged to the owner, he thought, or maybe she just worked
there. He turned off the engine and watched rainwater bleed
down the windshield.

Dane shut the door to the van and walked quickly through
the downpour into the diner. He stood in the doorway and
looked around. From the kitchen, he heard the sound of
music and the sharp rattle of silverware banging together.
The girl turned around—he could see how young she was
now—and stared at him over the row of worn wooden booths
that stood between them. The left side of the diner was closed
off with a rope looped between two dining chairs. Next to the
counter, near where the girl sat, was a large glass cake display

with a single chocolate cake inside. The room was brightly lit and smelled like grease.

The girl continued to stare and it bothered him. He shook the water off his hands and took a seat at the other end of the counter, away from her. She now stared out the window as if she expected someone else to come through the door after him.

The door to the kitchen swung open and a thin man with bushy black hair came through it and stopped to wipe his hands on the stained white apron around his waist. He smiled at Dane, a smile that seemed to stretch across his narrow face before it disappeared into a flat antiseptic line.

"Don't suppose you two want to move a little closer together?" he asked. The girl ignored him. "Didn't think so."

He looked down at Dane and his smile returned momentarily.

"Coffee?" he asked. Dane told him yes and pulled a small faded pink menu from between the napkin holder and a half-empty bottle of ketchup. "How about you down there? More coffee?" The girl shook her head. "I guess that means no." He whistled while he filled a cup for Dane. "I'll be back in a minute," he said when he finished, and vanished through the door into the kitchen.

Dane drank half a cup before the cook returned. This time he grinned at Dane and raised both eyebrows. "What can I get you?" Dane ordered scrambled eggs and bacon with cottage fries and toast. "Be about ten minutes," the cook said. When the food came, he set out two jars of jam for Dane, orange marmalade and strawberry. Dane spooned great gobs of both on the toast while he ate. It was his first meal in a restaurant since leaving the canyon. Until then, he'd bought packages of cold meat and bread and milk and made sandwiches and ate them in the van. This was the first time he felt safe enough to eat out. He wiped the plate clean with the last piece of toast and had another cup of coffee. It seemed like very little could go wrong. At the other end of the counter, the girl was still looking out the window.

A car pulled into the gravel parking lot of the diner, the headlights cutting a wide flashing arc across the rain-covered window. Dane saw a white Trans-Am park beside the van.

The driver left the car lights on after he stopped and they shimmered brightly through the steady rain. The driver sat in the car for several minutes, a distorted, almost unrecognizable silhouette in the front seat.

Dane thought there was something odd about the car. The ground looked red, as if the underside of the car were on fire. He wondered if the girl saw it, too, but when he turned toward her end of the counter, she wasn't there. His eyes moved past the counter and saw the door to the bathroom swing shut as the edge of a shadow slipped past it. He watched the driver get slowly out of the car and stand next to the van for a moment and peer through the window.

There was a whirl of noise behind him and Dane spun around to see the face of the cook framed in the small service window. The cook stopped the spinning metal order rack with a finger, then brought the same finger to his mouth and tapped it softly against his lips just as the front door opened.

Chapter 11

JENNY SLIPPED QUIETLY off her seat and was through the bathroom door before the car came to a stop. She didn't have to think about it. She knew it was Sonny, knew it when she saw the red lights of the car as it turned into the parking lot. The bathroom door eased shut, and her fingers found the window latch and she pushed hard on the handle and snapped it open, scraping one knuckle against the metal lip. Blood oozed into the tiny white crater and she stuck it in her mouth and sucked it clean before she hoisted herself up and butted open the window with her head. She tossed her knapsack out the window and pulled herself over the window ledge and hung with her head straight down for a few seconds. Rain battered the back of her head and ran into her nose and eyes. She pulled her legs through the window and landed on the rocky ground in back of the diner on both knees. The pain was sharp and instantaneous.

Jenny rolled on her side and rubbed her knees, trying to drive away the pain where the stones had dug into them. Through the rain, she saw something scurry across the ground just a few feet from where she lay. She stood up quickly and grabbed her knapsack. A large rat ran out from between a row of plastic garbage cans underneath one of the kitchen windows. She could see it in the light. It sniffed the air hesitantly and then hurried back between the cans.

The shock of it woke her up and she dashed down the back of the building, past the row of garbage cans, ignoring the pain in her knees, stepping as carefully as she could over the slippery stones, stumbling once and almost falling as she neared the end of the building and then stopping, body pressed up against the wall, amazed when she looked back and realized that she had run less than forty feet. She wanted it to be more, she wanted it to be to the ends of the earth, the universe, anywhere he couldn't get to her. The wind blew the rain into her back and she turned around to let it spray across her face. It felt like cold needles plunging into her skin. She shook her head and moved around the corner of the building without looking, wondering as she stepped into the darkness if she was going to walk straight into Sonny's terrible hands.

But there was nothing on the other side, just some broken-down cardboard boxes and a pile of railroad ties that smelled strongly of creosote and an old oil barrel that seemed to glisten even in the darkness. She moved around the objects to the corner of the building nearest to the parking lot. The van blocked most of it but she could still see the front end of the Trans-Am sticking out under the edge of the overhang. A line of rainwater poured down over the sleek white hood and splashed in a red muddy puddle beneath the grill.

She stopped herself from slamming the side of the building with her fist. There was no place left to go. It wouldn't take Sonny long to go through the diner and find the open window. Why didn't she remember to shut the goddamn window! It was too late to worry about it now. If she ran for the road, he'd find her right away, and she knew what would happen then. Sonny had a big hunting knife with a serrated edge and he'd use it on her. He'd start with her face. Once he was finished with that, it wouldn't much matter what else he did to her.

She could stay outside until he left but he'd just circle the diner like a shark and wait her out. Besides, where would she hide out here? Beyond the light of the diner there was nothing but an endless flat plain. If she did manage to lose him out here in this rain, she could be dead of pneumonia in less than a week. Already she was soaked through to the skin and shaking like crazy from the cold.

Jenny took one more look at the parking lot and the van. The driver's side door was only twenty feet from where she stood. She couldn't remember whether or not you could see it from inside the diner but she decided that she didn't really have any more choices left. She remembered the face of the driver looking down the counter at her. What struck her most was the color of his skin, a lifeless bone white.

It wasn't an unkind face. But the way he had looked at her seemed more curiosity than anything else. After that, he hadn't said anything to her, hadn't made a pass, had basically ignored her. She wondered if he'd been in prison. They were like that sometimes, the ones just getting out, quiet, afraid to say anything; they were outside and they still needed the feeling of walls around them to make them feel safe, especially at night. They didn't sleep much, not for a while at least. A few didn't want a woman to touch them, either. One of them had told her it just didn't feel right after so many years without it. But he wanted to look. She stood in front of him while he masturbated with rapid little jerks of his hand. When he finished wiping himself off, he thanked her and told her to leave him the fuck alone.

It was a strange thought but it carried her from the corner of the building to the door of the van and inside.

At first, he didn't talk to Dane and didn't bother to sit down. He was older than the girl, probably in his late twenties, and wore jeans and a kind of black vinyl jacket that Dane had never seen before. The name Sonny was stitched in red over one pocket.

Sonny's hair was slicked straight back and he wore a small gold hoop through his left earlobe. A single bead of water clung to the end of it, then dropped onto the sleeve of his jacket. His eyes flitted around the diner, a careful examination that was meant to look casual, but Dane saw it immediately. He also saw the way Sonny's hand kept opening and closing in a rhythmic grasp that seemed like the slow and labored breathing of some small savage animal.

Sonny spoke slowly and carefully as if he were afraid of using the wrong words. His voice carried with it the faint hint of an accent, a kind of suppressed guttural lilt.

"Either one of you see a girl in here?" Sonny asked, looking at the abandoned plate and coffee cup at the end of the counter.

"There was a girl," the cook said, following Sonny's gaze, "but it was awhile ago."

"How long?"

"Half an hour, maybe forty-five minutes," the cook said.

Sonny looked at Dane. "That right?"

"I didn't see her," Dane said.

Sonny tilted his head to one side.

"How long have you been sitting here?"

"Twenty minutes," Dane said.

Sonny leaned against the counter and pointed toward the front window. Behind him, the cook cleaned a thumbnail with a small paring knife and wiped the blade on his apron. It left a grimy half-moon on the white cloth.

"That your van out there?" Sonny asked. He asked casually but his fingers gripped the edge of the counter and the skin across the ridge of both knuckles was taut.

Dane sipped his coffee and nodded.

"You see anybody on the road tonight? Hitchhiker maybe?"

Dane shook his head and answered no.

"You want coffee or anything?" the cook asked Sonny, and held up the steaming glass pot. "Some eggs?"

Sonny managed a half grin. "I'm going to look around," he said, and headed straight for the bathrooms. The cook shrugged and poured a cup for himself.

Sonny pushed open the bathroom door. Dane hoped that the girl wasn't still hiding in there, that somehow she'd gotten away. He looked outside, wondering where she might have gone.

It was warm inside the van. The air was heavy and filled with a sharp musklike odor that reminded her of ammonia. All Jenny could think of was that it smelled like a kennel. Behind the seats was a heavy black curtain. She just hoped to Christ he didn't have some kind of dog in back. She slid over the driver's seat and crawled between the seat and the curtain, a narrow space, perhaps four feet wide, loaded with several cardboard boxes, a rolled-up sleeping bag, and two large duffels that lay angled on top of one another like sleeping children. Jenny crouched between the boxes and the sleeping bag and ran her hand across the back curtain and pulled it to one side.

In the darkness just beyond the curtain, something stirred, something that was much bigger than a dog.

Sonny emerged from the bathroom and made his way down the counter. He walked with a casual menace, still wearing that half grin, enjoying himself immensely. The cook wiped off a stainless-steel creamer with his apron and watched him. Sonny paused when he got to Dane, and then stepped through the opening in the counter by the kitchen door and the cash register. He leaned over the cook.

"Where's your back door?"

"On the other side of the walk-in," the cook said. He set the creamer on the counter.

"The window in the john's open," Sonny said. "Water's all over the goddamn floor."

"So?" the cook answered.

"So?" Sonny said. "If you lied to me about the girl, I'm going to come back and tear your fucking head off." He said it pleasantly, no connection between what he said and the tone of his voice. "You got a flashlight back there?"

The cook took his time answering. "Above the door," he said wearily.

Sonny went through the door to the kitchen. A few seconds later, Dane heard a loud metallic crash, then the sound of the back door banging open. The cook stared down at the counter and shook his head.

"It's nothing," the cook said after a while. "Some pans I had stacked up. The guy's tough, he kicks pans around." He picked up Dane's check and crumpled it. "The eggs are on me." He slipped his other hand beneath the apron and pulled out a black snub-nosed revolver. "You might want to think about leaving now," he said. He looked around the diner. "This is my place," he said. "If he comes back in here, I'm going to kill the cocksucker."

* * *

At first, Jenny felt a kind of numbing terror that left her frozen in place, fingers pressed against the rough fabric, her breathing barely audible against the chatter of rain on the roof of the van. She saw the dull yellow glimmer of the wolf's eyes, caught in a shaft of light that spilled between the curtains from the front windows of the van, clouded only by the small trails of vapor that escaped from both sides of the half-open jaws. The wolf flattened himself along the floor, moving into the deeper darkness of the corner of the van, nails scraping on the metal surface. A high-pitched growl, almost a whine, began in his throat.

Jenny heard the sound, a treble counterpoint to the thunder of the rain, but she chose to ignore the warning. For some unexplainable reason, her own fear began to fade. She could feel it. It seemed to break away from her in fragments, like pieces of a cliff tumbling into the sea.

She withdrew her hand from the curtain and sat very calmly in front of the wolf. In the dark closeness of the van, she could *feel* the wolf more than she could see him. Hidden in the corner, he was only an outline, an immense black shape that seemed to change constantly. Even in the darkness, she felt the heat rising off him and the still intensity of those eyes. She began to hum, almost unconsciously, a bit of a tune that she had nearly forgotten, an old lullaby. The growling wavered.

Jenny kept humming, staying very still. For a while she lost the melody and her humming became a soft indistinguishable drone before she found it again. The growling stopped. The wolf lowered his head slightly, enough that the thin shaft of light from the front of the van crossed his muzzle, just catching the corner of one eye and changing the yellow into what looked like a wedge of purest gold. The black wolf was the most beautiful creature she had ever seen.

Jenny laid her head back against one of the duffels. The wolf dropped his head and rested it on his front paws, still watching her carefully. She closed her eyes until everything around her grew faint and indistinct and all that was left in her mind was the darkly eloquent face of the wolf and her own humming as it drifted through the silent van.

The sound of Sonny's voice snapped her awake.

Sonny came up behind Dane from where he'd been standing at the far end of the building just as Dane opened the door to the van. The half grin on Sonny's face was gone and he held a big silver flashlight in one hand. He swung it in a short arc across his chest and caught it stiffly in the palm of his other hand. The light flashed across the empty field beyond the diner. Wisps of steam rolled off the glass face and drifted into the darkness.

"You in a hurry to leave?" Sonny asked.

Dane turned to face him, trying to decide what he was going to do if Sonny came at him with the flashlight. He might have to kill him and he didn't want to do it, not here, not now. Let the cook do it. Right now he only wanted to get away from these people before anything happened to the wolf.

Dane closed the door gently and stepped away from the van. "What do you want?" he asked.

"Something that belongs to me," Sonny said. He wiped the rain off his face with the sleeve of his coat. "What's in the van?"

Dane was tired of the game. He pointed to the front of the van. "Look for yourself."

"I can see what's in there," Sonny said. "Show me what you got around in back."

The decision was made for him.

Sonny followed him around to the back of the van and watched while he unlocked the rear doors. Dane pushed them open and clapped his hands twice.

"What the hell was that for?" Sonny said, and aimed the flashlight into the dark interior. The light caught the wolf as he stood upright in the back of the van, ears flat against his head, muzzle pulled back against sharp white teeth. It was like gazing into another world. In the glare of the flashlight, the wolf was like some half-mad prehistoric thing come back to life, ready to kill him.

Sonny swore once and scrambled backward toward his own

car. The flashlight fell from his hand and flipped end over end like a baton. The light flashed over Dane's face and then across the back of the van, the rain distorting it into a carnival gloss as the flashlight spun downward.

In those flashes of light, those moments when he first saw Dane's face and then the wolf, Sonny decided that whatever secrets Dane had locked in the van, he wanted no part of them.

What he thought he saw, what he *remembered,* was like two pictures cut from a time-lapse sequence, the first picture in the sequence in the process of becoming the other: Dane's sharp features, his dark, mad eyes made even darker by the heavy rain, transformed into the elongated black grimace of the wolf as it crouched. The moment was a frightening stab of revelation for him. What Sonny understood best was what he could beat down with his fists. He thought that if he moved, the thing that stood in front of him would tear him apart.

The flashlight struck the gravel and shattered. The light flickered twice like distress signals and went out. Dane picked it up. Sonny backed up against the trunk of the Trans-Am and stared at the open doors of the van, seeing only the black shape inside.

"What the fuck is that?" he asked incredulously. Dane laid his hand on the front of the van's rear door as if to bring the wolf out, and Sonny jumped.

Dane's muscles were rigid from the tension and he let his hand move down the surface of the door. The wolf crept forward in response, tracking Sonny's jerky shuffle, and Dane knew what would happen if he turned the wolf loose now. After being cooped up in the van, the wolf was at the far edge of his control. Once he let the wolf loose, Dane wouldn't even have to signal. The animal would kill whatever stood in the way.

"A wolf," Dane said finally. He clapped his hands twice and waited to make certain that the wolf settled down before he locked the doors again.

He felt like a man who had survived a terrible fall. It was only just beginning and it had nearly gotten out of control. What would happen when they got to New York? The question was like a knife at his back. He wanted to get the hell away from the diner and he wanted to do it fast.

Sonny stayed close to his car and watched as Dane climbed into the van. "A wolf," he said to himself. "I don't fucking believe it."

Dane started the van. Water poured off his clothes and formed a puddle at his feet, splashing over his legs when he shifted into reverse. With his arm, Sonny blocked the glare of the headlights as the van swung around, and called after it, his voice tired and faint: "What the fuck you keep a wolf in there for, anyway?"

A few miles down the road, when he was certain that no one was following him, Dane pulled the van off the road into a ragged turnaround cut out of the shoulder. Away from the diner, the rain seemed less intense. He kept the engine and headlights on and the heater running to dry out his wet clothes. The windows grew cloudy with moisture as though the rain itself had come inside.

Dane was suddenly exhausted and everything else was forgotten. The drumming of the rain on the highway filled the van like a meditation and he let it carry him along until his consciousness drifted almost out of reach.

The girl slid back the curtain covering the wolf, and the sound, as piercing as a scream, brought him back. He snapped open the curtain directly behind his seat and she gasped at the unexpected sound. Her startled face seemed so small and white against the dark fabric that she looked like a child caught in a game of hide-and-seek.

Dane stared at her; his shock and disbelief merged at a single hypnotic point. Her hand rested against the floor of the van, fingers buried in the wolf's black fur. His feeling of betrayal was sudden and overwhelming, like a sharp plunge into an icy pool, then over just as quickly. He was shocked at the speed of the change. Whatever his expectations had been, they were shattered now beyond redemption.

The black wolf lay next to the girl, calm and relaxed, allowing her to stroke his broad back gently with the tips of her fingers.

She took her hand away and cradled it in her lap, still playing the child. When she spoke, she didn't sound like a child at all. Her voice had depth. It was separate from the delicacy of her face, making it all the more striking.

"What are you going to do to me?" she asked.

Dane looked in the rearview mirror. Behind the van the road stretched out, black and empty. The thought entered his mind before he even realized it: he could do anything he wanted to her.

How could he possibly tell her now what he was thinking?

Chapter 12

$\sim\sim\sim\sim\sim\sim\sim\sim\sim\sim\sim\sim\sim\sim$

VAN OWEN TOLD them to turn the two pumas loose just after sundown at the northern end of the preserve, which would give the big cats a few hours to get used to the terrain before he staked out the goats near the shoot. There were two shoots altogether but they were using the main one, roughly near the center of the preserve, a rectangular wooden platform built in the wide crotch of an immense oak that overlooked a small clearing. The platform was fifteen feet above the ground, surrounded on four sides by a heavy wooden railing that came almost to shoulder height and was covered with heavy black canvas that could be left up or taken down depending on the weather.

It was warm tonight, no chance for an early spring rain, so they could leave the roof open.

It was nearly ten o'clock now. Van Owen walked through the preserve toward the shoot. He came in from the north side, following the trail of the cats as they made their way toward the shoot and the goats. They were big animals, close to seven feet long and almost one hundred and seventy-five pounds, skittish and easily spooked. A loud noise could send them off in six directions at once. But judging from the trails they left, the cats that were somewhere in the preserve right now were still groggy from the tranquilizers.

They were only a day and a half away from the Peruvian

rain forest where they'd been trapped, and already doped twice: once when they were captured and again so they could be smuggled out without any problems from customs or without tearing each other to shreds during the twelve-hour flight.

They wandered through the preserve like a pair of drunkards, Van Owen thought, and the idiots waiting for them at the shoots would be lucky if the cats even knew the goats were there. This time it was a bunch of insurance executives, another special group that the society had been forced to cater to lately because of what everyone referred to as a "shortfall in our current portfolio." Van thought about kicking them the hell off the platform. Let them go *find* the cats, see if they can sell them a little whole life.

Van Owen moved along the trail until it started to rise and he came to what appeared to be a large outcropping of rock, several gigantic boulders that surged out of the ground in a semicircle, leaving a small scooped-out basin in the middle. He climbed into the center and looked down over the southern half of the preserve. From the cluster of rocks, he could see the lodge building in the distance and, to his left, hidden behind a thick row of Austrian pines, the bluish lights of the command trailer.

This particular group of rocks, called OBSERVATION MODULE #5 in the architectural plans, was artificial as was about fifty percent of the preserve. That was the idea; it gave the illusion of reality without any of the danger. Insurance executives, or any other kind of executives for that matter, could kill whatever they wanted without worrying whether they might not make it to next week's board meeting because something had eaten their liver.

There were four other rock clusters, each of varying height and design, placed strategically throughout the preserve, as well as a thin stream that meandered through the center of it like a miniature jungle river, turning back on itself in picturesque tangles.

The preserve was roughly one square mile in size, a little over one-third of the total land that the society owned in Delaware County, about two and a half hours northwest of New York City. It was surrounded by an electronic web of lights, cameras, and fences. The cameras and lights were mounted in the trees on all four sides and at each of the five rock clusters.

The electric fence consisted of fourteen strands of high-density copper wire that made it impossible for anything to get out of the preserve once it was inside. The voltage could be raised so that whatever came in contact with it would be knocked cold. All of this was run from the command trailer.

With the nightscope, Van Owen spotted one of the pumas as it moved slowly along the edge of the stream. The cat wobbled over to the water, dropped down, and drank. He lowered the scope in disgust. They'd overdone the dope again. They expected them to be a little groggy; it made them easier to shoot. But the one by the stream was half dead and would probably be all the way dead by morning. The other one was probably just the same, maybe worse.

He raised the scope again and looked for the second cat. It took him a few minutes but he found it, resting comfortably on one of the other rock clusters, tail flopping back and forth. Van Owen wondered if the cat was as bored as he was with this latest piece of shit they were calling a hunt.

From the direction of the shoot, he heard one of the goats bleating, followed by the sound of nervous laughter. On the rocks, the puma stood up suddenly, the lionesslike head turned toward the sound, finally catching the scent of the goats. While Van Owen watched, the cat made its way down the rocks and jumped to the floor of the preserve.

He swung the scope toward the shoot. Two of the men were climbing down from the platform, spreading out on either side of the goat. They knew about the doping and had decided to be brave. The second cat was nowhere to be seen. Van Owen grabbed his rifle and climbed down the rocks.

He could have warned them, of course, could have used the small radio on his hip to let them know that the cat that was stalking them wasn't doped up at all; in fact, it was very much alive.

But why spoil a good thing?

A few minutes later, the first cat also picked up the scent of the goats and made its way slowly toward the shoot, ambling along the trail, head down, tongue out, rocking unsteadily.

Van Owen stayed several yards behind it on the trail, downwind, thinking that the other cat had probably already circled the clearing once and settled down to watch for a while. If one of the hunters got too close, the cat might decide to pull back or it might attack. It might do anything.

You just never knew with cats.

As soon as the goats started bleating again, Van Owen moved through the woods toward the shoot. The drugged cat was hypnotized by the scent of the goats and kept going until it reached the edge of the clearing. There it stopped and looked at the goats tethered twenty yards away. The cat raised its head as best as it could and sniffed the air.

The goats went into a frenzy, bleating and banging into one another, trying to break loose. Amid all the sound and commotion, the drugged cat simply walked into the center of the clearing and clubbed the nearest goat to the ground, raking the neck of the animal with its claws and sending a fan of blood into the air.

One of the salesmen stepped into the clearing and put a bullet into the cat, knocking the animal over backward as if it had been punched. The cat rolled twice and the salesman put another slug into it before the animal stopped moving. Another man dropped his gun where he stood and joined the shooter to look at the kill. Someone up on the platform began to clap. The two on the ground picked up the dead cat and held it between them.

From where he was watching, Van Owen saw something move on the other side of the clearing, almost directly behind the two men congratulating themselves on their bravery. He fell back into the shadows and moved quickly around the perimeter. Some of the others climbed down from the platform.

The other cat lay in a fresh bed of ferns, body flat against the ground, hidden by the delicate green fronds that curled around the animal's flanks like feathers. As the other men joined the two in the clearing, the cat began to back away, shuffling backward with its huge hind legs until it sensed something behind it.

Van Owen jumped up suddenly and hissed at the puma. The cat rolled on its shoulder and slashed at him, ripping through the air between them. Van Owen raised his hands like claws and hissed again. One of the men holding the dead cat heard the noise and looked at the woods but saw nothing. The goats began their frantic bleating again. The startled cat scrambled to its feet and took the easiest escape route it could find.

It ran into the clearing, directly toward the crowd of men who were busy patting one another on the back.

The one who had done the shooting and was now holding up his prize saw the reddish-brown blur burst out of the woods and screamed. The men around him scattered; some tried to reach the tree; others tried for the woods. The cat tore through the terrified goats and swiped at the legs of one of the men as he made a mad dash for the trees. Then it turned on the first man. He held the carcass in front of him like a shield and screamed for someone to shoot the other cat. A cloud of dust billowed around them.

The cat rose on its hind legs and clawed viciously at the man, catching his left forearm with her claws and tearing through the khaki jacket into flesh. He screamed again, louder this time. His arm turned bright scarlet.

One of the other men picked up his gun but was so frightened that he grabbed it by the barrel and ran toward the center of the clearing swinging it like a club. He struck the cat in the middle of the back, knocking it to the ground, but the momentum of his swing carried him too far and he fell on his side. The puma rolled and lunged for his face.

Van Owen shot the animal in the shoulder and then again in the neck. It dropped dead across the man's legs. The man screamed incoherently and tried to kick the cat away from him, scrambling to get away from it. He picked up the rifle and, on his hands and knees, began to beat the animal with it as if he expected the cat to rise from the dead and attack him again.

The wounded man still held the other puma in his arms. He stared at both animals and then at the blood pouring down his arm and told the other man in a voice so eerily calm that it sounded mechanical, that everything was going to be okay, he could stop hitting it now, that it was over and it was going to be okay.

Then he held out the dead cat in front of him and asked someone if they could please take it because he was feeling very light-headed all of a sudden and needed to lie down. He saw Van Owen coming toward him in a burst of light and couldn't understand, even while his knees gave way beneath him and Van Owen's face loomed overhead, why the hunter was smiling so much.

It took thirty-eight stitches to sew up the executive's arm. The doctor who did it said that the guy was lucky that whatever it was he ran into hadn't cut into muscle and bone or he probably wouldn't have an arm right now. He picked up the pile of bloodstained gauze with both hands, opening a waste container with his foot.

"What the hell was it, anyway?" he asked, but nobody answered him. They just left him standing there with a bunch of bloody rags in his hands.

Van Owen took the limo back to the city. There would be some complaints from the board about tonight's accident. He could hear them already. They might sue, they might cancel their membership, their insurance rates would go up. He didn't care. He sat alone in the backseat, feeling as tight as a coiled snake. The feeling had been growing for months. The one small spasm he'd felt after the hunt had been only a momentary flash and now the anger and the yearning were back, worse than before. It was like something that he couldn't control had invaded his bloodstream. He could feel it moving. He closed his eyes and dug his fingers into the velour seat and waited for the motion of the ride to calm him down.

It grew worse after the driver dropped him off at the apartment. He felt like a trapped animal there, pacing in front of the wide glass windows that looked out over the park and beyond, like the view of another country, the lights of the West Side. He fixed himself a drink and then another, but the liquor only fueled his restlessness.

A little after three in the morning, he called for a taxi to take him downtown.

It was three-thirty in the morning and the fare was for someplace on Varrick, an area of warehouses and grim storefronts that at night looked as if they had all been painted the same drab shade of gray. The cabdriver kept looking in the mirror at his fare. There's a club down here, the fare told him. What kind of club did they have down here, the cabdriver wanted to know, because this place looked as grim as a sewer to him.

"You sure this is right?" he asked again, and the fare nodded. "You tell me where, okay?" Another nod.

The cabdriver thought of something funny. "I guess it doesn't matter which side, does it? I could drop you in the middle of the street, who'd care?" The fare didn't laugh and the cabdriver figured that along with being screwy and strange, the prick had no sense of humor at all.

Van Owen saw it on the right, up ahead, a single blue spotlight over an unmarked door, perhaps the only spot of color for blocks around. The cabdriver slowed at the intersection and Van Owen tapped the plastic barrier and told him to pull over.

The cabdriver took the fare and wished Van Owen luck, common courtesy even if the guy was a prick, because he figured that anybody who wandered around in a place like this at nearly four in the morning was going to need more luck than there was on the whole goddamn planet.

When his eyes adjusted to the darkness inside the club, Van Owen could see, just ahead of him, not more than fifteen feet down a wide hallway, a high oval arch decorated with dark green ornamental tiles that made it look like the entrance to a Moorish courtyard. Instead, it led to a smallish dance floor lit from above with a star made of blinking white lights. A few people were dancing, one or two couples, while the rest sat at several small tables scattered around the edges of the dance floor. Two women, one dressed in what seemed to be a white sheet, the other in a simple skirt and blouse, danced with their hands on each other's shoulders to music that popped and crackled to the rhythm of the lights.

A black man in a white T-shirt and slacks and leather wrist bracelets stood behind a counter near the entrance to the dance floor and moved casually to the music. He took Van Owen's coat and wallet and placed them in a small locker. He spoke with a soft Jamaican accent.

"I know your face," he said. "Nice to see you again." The black man held up a mask. "You want one of these things?" Van Owen shook his head. "No, I didn't think so." He put the mask away and grinned. "Maybe you like to dance first, lively up yourself?" Van Owen headed for a set of narrow stairs next to the archway.

"I can tell you're in a big hurry tonight," the black man called after him. "Enjoy yourself, man," he said. "Happy hunting."

The hallway at the top of the stairs wound around in a gentle crescent toward a dim warren of rooms and alcoves. Some appeared empty, others were filled with people. A man and a woman on their knees bent over a woman, a fleshy triangle on the dark floor of one of the rooms, seen through the open door. They spoke to one another in voices that blended with the sounds coming from other rooms nearby. Van Owen heard a scream and felt the sweat rise on his skin.

Electric candles glowed every few feet in the hall, and he swam slowly through the flickering light, a growing tightness around his eyes as he squinted to see. People moved around him like shades, neither curious nor afraid. Midway along the curve, he saw a naked woman leaning out of a doorway, her skin as white as flour. A man in a mask gripped her breasts as he pounded into her from behind. She leaned her body into the hall in an odd cranelike gesture, head erect, and reached out to pull Van Owen to her. Her mouth was slack and she made little coughing noises each time the man slammed into her. He pushed her hand away. She shut her eyes, the rejection already forgotten, and clutched the hands across her chest, rocking them gently as if they had somehow become her own.

The hallway ended in a pair of doors. He listened momentarily at the one on the right before opening it. Inside the narrow room a woman with hair that hung like two black wings on either side of her face sat naked on an ornate metal-frame bed with her hands held together demurely between her knees.

She was small and delicate, almost Oriental in appearance, her skin so pale that the veins looked like ribbons of sea grass just beneath the surface. She kept her eyes to the floor until he stood in front of her and then she brought them up slowly, lingering over his hands and arms. Her eyes were wide, and so flat looking that they seemed to lack dimension, even color, empty of everything except a great inarticulate need that only she could feel. Her lips were outlined in bright red gloss, some of it dribbled across her cheek. She opened them slightly and brought her hands up in front of her small breasts.

Her hands were tied loosely together at the wrists with a piece of cord. Van Owen felt his mouth go dry. She stood up slowly, hair falling down to cover part of her face.

She slid to her knees in front of him and pressed her hands against his groin, letting the warmth of her fingers play over him. He struck her once, a glancing blow that snapped her head sideways. She looked up at him through the dark veil of hair, her red mouth hanging half open. Her breathing quickened.

The next blow was like a thunderclap in the tiny room.

Part III
SPRING/SUMMER

Chapter 13

LANGE LOVED HIS evening run in Central Park. It put just the right spin on the end of the day, he thought. In the mornings, before breakfast, he did a thirty-minute stretch workout in one of the spare bedrooms that had been converted into a private gym. At noon, three times a week, he played squash with a senior partner from another investment firm. He had been playing racquetball until he saw one of the younger account executives from his own firm, someone he had interviewed, playing in the court next to his one day and promptly switched to squash, something slightly less egalitarian. Before dinner, three evenings a week, he ran.

He usually took his dog with him, an eighteen-month-old Doberman named Victor, and walked up Fifth Avenue from their apartment house at Sixty-eighth Street to the Seventy-ninth Street traverse and into the park.

His run began there, just north of the boathouse. From that point, Lange ran around the lake, skirting the outer edges of the silently wooded ramble, and then headed for the bridlepath on the other side of Park West Drive.

When it was dry, he ran along the side of the bridlepath to the ballfields, then east again to the carousel where he would swing alongside the center drive toward the statues at the entrance to the mall. Since the park was always closed to traffic when he ran, Lange could have stayed on the road with the rest of the late-day joggers. Instead, he ran on the shaded paths that spread like so many capillaries off the main thoroughfares. At that time of day, he had them almost completely to himself.

Lately, while he ran, Lange tried very hard not to think about his third wife.

He was going to divorce her soon; he'd talked to his lawyer about it already. It was just a question of waiting for the right set of circumstances. Over a year ago, as soon as he'd returned from Canada, he'd hired the same detective agency he had used on his first two wives to find out what she'd been doing. That she was unfaithful to him was a given, but the scale of her infidelity staggered even him. His other wives had had affairs; this one was conducting a liaison with most of the Upper East Side. The turnover rate was astounding. Her appetite had been one of her prime selling points, but it had been getting out of hand. Still, he would miss it. He already did.

They didn't screw anymore, hadn't in months. The last time he'd tried, he'd been drunk and she looked contemptuously at his wilted cock as if it had been some sort of helpless and pathetic insect.

Lange thought about her as he rode down in the elevator of his building. The silvery interior of the car, the soft creamy light that flared up from the opaque white sconces on the walls, the gentle mechanized hum as he slowly descended the shaft, put him in an almost forgiving mood.

The mood took him through the apartment building's elegant salmon-colored lobby and into the street, Victor on his six-foot chain leash tugging him north along Fifth. The dog was nearly full-grown and, despite extensive training, still a little awkward. He didn't possess the alert spring-wired step of the others Lange had seen. The trainer had told him to have patience, that the dog was still young. Lange didn't believe a word the trainer said. Lange yanked Victor's chain and the dog's legs splayed comically before it straightened up. Lange's forgiving mood abruptly vanished.

If the dog didn't shape up soon, it was going out the goddamn door with his wife.

The weather was cool for the middle of May, not much

rain, the air crisp. The sky was beginning to cloud over, and that cut the early evening light, eliminating all shadows. The trees weren't in bloom except for the big sycamores that seemed to ring much of the park. The rest of the trees were swathed in a greenish haze, their edges tinged with blue in the approaching darkness.

Lange stopped just inside the park and warmed up for a few minutes, stretching his calves and leg muscles while the dog sat and stared silently at two young black men who emerged from a darkened stone archway carrying a large silver portable stereo that drowned out the rumble of traffic from Seventy-ninth Street. Lange wondered why it was that every time he heard one of those things, it was always playing the same song. They saw Lange and the dog and ambled away into the center of the park. He continued the warmup.

With his hands on his hips, Lange first stretched from side to side, pumping hard to the left and then to the right. He saw hints of movement through the trees, shadows of other runners along the drive at the top of the steep slope above him. Lange stretched out his calf muscles and stared into the green mist of the trees.

The dog jumped up suddenly and began to whine.

Lange wrapped the chain leash twice around his hand and jerked it hard, pulling the dog's neck down. Victor nearly fell over. Lange continued stretching. The dog whined again and twisted his head toward the arch. Lange stopped stretching. He thought for a moment that the two blacks might have come back but there was nothing there, only the half-moon mouth of the arch and the shaft of pale light from the other side as it opened into the treelined path beyond. Except for the steady noise of the traffic, the park was silent.

"Goddammit," Lange said, and jerked the dog's chain again. He was tired of warming up. With Victor at his heels, he ran up the path toward the arch. He ran slowly at first, then faster as the tunnel swallowed them up. They burst through the darkness to the other side as if passing through some invisible barrier. He was running in the opposite direction from his usual run, a strange thing for him to do. The change might be interesting, he thought as he skirted the boat pond and picked up speed, his arms pumping close to his sides. Victor ran next to him, big feet galloping smoothly. Lange had noticed that when the dog ran, it lost most of the awkwardness that seemed to overwhelm it standing still. Whatever had been bothering the dog before was forgotten. The dog might not be so bad after all, he thought.

Near the entrance to the mall, Lange broke into a sweat and unzipped the hooded sweatshirt, exposing a T-shirt with a small, dark green insignia over the right breast. Several runners passed him in the opposite direction by the ballfields, the only ones he'd seen so far, one or two even nodding their acknowledgment. Lange ignored them all and focused instead on the white sepulcher of the G&W building rising above Columbus Circle.

He passed Tavern on the Green, the surrounding trees aglow with hundreds of miniature white lights. A gold Mercedes sat idling next to the entrance while two women, one in a white leather pantsuit, embraced one another under the restaurant's canopy. Lange followed the fence around the edge of Sheep Meadow and then crossed to the bridlepath. Another arch, sunk in the darkness between walls of thick vegetation and rock, stood straight ahead.

Lange felt the beginnings of a stitch in his side and slowed his pace, one foot slapping in front of the other on the cindered path. Clusters of hoofprints covered the ground like tiny craters. Once he was inside, his breath sounded like the roar of a train as it echoed in the darkened archway. The other end seemed miles away.

As he neared it, the dog began to growl.

They broke out of the tunnel and Lange heard voices and the screech of music. The two blacks stood in the shadows of the stone wall and pointed at him as he ran past. They blurred with the landscape, a ripple of movement, crazy laughter that rose over the music, the red glow of a cigarette, the smell of marijuana, the booming sound of their voices that echoed behind him.

Lange ran on along the path, the shock of their sudden appearance settling over him near the playground by the lake. He slowed just enough to feel the tingle settle into his stomach and looked at the Doberman. He hadn't shied away from them, Lange thought, suddenly pleased. He reached down and patted Victor on the top of the head. The park was nearly deserted now and the tremors in his stomach vanished and he ran down the path beside the shelter of the wooded ramble without a worry. Lange crossed the drive and turned again toward the first arch. He decided to sprint the final yards through the arch. Outside it was almost dark. Inside the tunnel, it was as if they'd moved hours ahead into the night.

The ground was soft inside, muddy in parts, and his eyes caught shadowy impressions as he raced through it, the rocks on each side rugged and uneven like the walls of a canyon, the ceiling stones lined with the patchwork marks of the cutter's blade. He could hear the whine of the dog as it pulled against him with almost every step.

The Doberman stopped abruptly. The chain closed tightly around his hand. Lange felt a sharp pain as the pressure crushed the bones together. He tried desperately to unwrap the chain but the dog started to drag him backward. He grabbed the chain with his other hand and yanked hard, lifting the dog off his feet. Then and only then did he notice what stood at the end of the tunnel.

A shape waited for him. It appeared suddenly like an apparition. The shape parted, revealing a mirror image. A man and a large black dog blocked the tunnel exit. The man stood with his back to the light, the black dog lay in the dirt with his head erect and stared at him.

Victor whimpered at his feet and pulled the chain across his legs. Lange dropped his hand and the chain played out behind him. The man did an odd thing. He clapped his hands. The black dog stood up and Lange felt the first real rush of fear crawl over his skin. The creature in front of him was enormous. It seemed to rise right out of the ground.

Victor went berserk, barking and thrashing on the end of the chain. Lange let him go. The Doberman ran out of the tunnel, the chain trailing between his legs like some kind of long metal tail. It seemed almost comical.

He tried to say something to the man, anything, but his throat closed around the sound like a fist and he found he couldn't breathe. The man reached in his pocket and took out what looked like a small silver whistle. Lange had one last thought before the man brought the whistle to his mouth. The man had been waiting for him here and now he was going to die. The creature was going to kill him. He ran. As Victor had.

Dane watched him run and waited until he reached the end of the tunnel before he blew the whistle and released the wolf. The wolf covered the distance quickly and caught up with Lange in the middle of a small grove of trees just to the right of the tunnel entrance. The wolf grabbed Lange's arm and dragged him into the dirt. Lange tried to pull his arm loose. The wolf bit down harder, snapping the forearm, shredding the sleeve, and ripping apart the flesh underneath. Arterial blood spurted down his arm. He clutched frantically at the arm. Blood ran through his fingers. The wolf struck again, tearing apart the muscles along his neck and shoulders. Lange tried to roll over to protect himself but already he was too weak from shock. He lay on his side, helpless, his head thrown back, throat exposed, and watched as the wolf lunged forward. He had time to scream only once.

The wolf seized him by the throat and whipped him savagely back and forth. The force of the movement shattered his larynx and windpipe instantly. Tissue, bone, cartilage, everything collapsed under the pressure. Lange's body shook uncontrollably. His wounded arm swung free. Blood splattered over the hard ground.

The wolf let go and then bit down again, sharp teeth cutting through the carotid artery. Seconds later, Lange was dead, the vertebrae in his neck crushed, his spinal cord severed.

The wolf held him like that until Dane blew the whistle again. He released the dead man almost instantaneously.

The kill had been strangely silent and created a momentary stillness before the noise of the city rushed in on Dane. The noise seemed to bring the night with it; everything around him turned the color of charcoal. Dane looked but he already knew what he would find: exactly what he had found earlier. Nothing. The park was empty, abandoned. He clapped his hands and the black wolf trotted to his side. The wolf was panting slightly. Dane ran his hand down the side of the wolf's head. It came away covered with dirt and blood. He saw Lange's body, an unrecognizable lump in the center of the dark grove, no different from the rocks that lay strewn throughout the park. High above the trees, a row of lights came on in one of the apartments. They shone down like blind white eyes in the night sky.

An hour later, after it began to drizzle, the Doberman found its way back to the body. Shivering in the cold rain, the dog padded delicately toward it, lifting each leg carefully as if the ground had become electrified. At the slightest sound, a car horn, the heavy rumble of a truck, the dog stopped, frozen in place, and looked around frantically. Close to Lange's body, it began to whine and pushed at the runner's shoes, resting side by side, the toes turned straight down like a dancer on point. The dog explored the rest of the body, poking at it, licking one of the hands, a whimper in its throat. The head lay in a circle of blood-soaked ground the color of tar.

The Doberman stopped, confused by the smell of blood and the scent of the wolf that clung to the open wound. The dog backed away from the body, growling, its ears pressed back. The smell of the wolf was all around and the dog twisted and turned, biting at the air in a sudden frenzy to get away from it. But the smell seemed everywhere and the Doberman, angry and frightened, finally turned on the body to kill the scent.

When it was over, the dog lay down a few feet from the body and waited for its master to awaken from his terrible sleep.

Chapter 14

WHEN JENNY HAD spoken to Dane for the first time in the van, he hesitated before answering her. He was a little like Sonny, she thought, the way he would look at you as if he had something waiting for you in the back of his mind. But when she looked in his eyes, she saw something stricken in them, a flutter of revelation; there was a secret in those eyes. Sonny's eyes weren't like that. They were like mirrors, they showed you your own fear.

"Who was he?" he had asked her, a practical question, and Jenny had answered him in her own practical way. She had turned her back to him and pulled up her jacket and shirt and held them there, her chin resting on the top of her arms like a woman lost in thought. She felt him move closer to look at the bruises that ringed her shoulders and mottled the skin of her lower back. She saw the shadow as his hand moved to touch the small puckered mouths of the burns that ran down the ridge of her spine, but he pulled back without touching them at all, as if he could feel some residual heat from the wounds the way she sometimes did at night when her skin was taut and feverish and she was afraid that Sonny would come to her room again.

Most of the time, Sonny had slept with her mother except when he got drunk. If he'd been drinking, he'd wait until four or five or sometimes until dawn, then he'd come into her room and use her. Her mother didn't care. She'd stopped caring years ago, so far back that Jenny couldn't even remember when her mother had looked at her with anything other than envy and suspicion.

She'd fought Sonny once and not even the first time. The first time she had been so surprised that she was struck dumb when she woke up with his body on her. He pinned her down with one hand, stuck two fingers in his mouth, and rubbed them between her legs and shoved himself inside her.

The next time he came to her room, she hit him in the face with a hairbrush and broke his nose. Sonny wiped away the blood and punched her hard in the stomach, so hard that she couldn't eat for two days because of the pain and she was terrified that he'd broken something deep inside her. She lay doubled over against the headboard. He picked her up, blood dripping from his nose onto her neck and her cheek, and held her facedown on the bed and hurt her some more.

After that, she didn't fight him. She began to think of her body as a kind of glove, a thing without thought or feeling. When he was inside her, moving hard, even hurting her, she refused to feel it. She kept her mind blank; if she thought about anything at all, it was getting away.

Kneeling in the back of the van, she decided she had shown him enough of her secrets. She let her clothes fall and raised her head. The man said nothing, gave no sign of what he was thinking. He seemed to be making up his mind about her.

The wolf stared at her, his eyes cloaked in indifference. Her hand caressed the animal's back and the man followed each stroke. The look of hurt on his face was so deep that she almost gasped.

"My name is Jenny," she said. Her voice was loud inside the van.

He turned away from her when he spoke as if he was afraid to let her see him.

"Jenny," he said quietly, "why don't you ride up front?"

She climbed into the seat and he looked at her briefly before he dropped the van into gear and pulled out onto the highway again. "My name is Dane," he said, and the words died in the silence that followed. They rode for a while without speaking. She leaned forward to look into the side mirror every few minutes to make certain there was no car following them.

"He won't follow us," Dane said to her.

"You're sure about that?"

"Yes," Dane said. The way he said it put her at ease.

"Where are we going, Dane?"

It took him a moment to decide that he would tell her only part of the truth, enough to keep her with him. Once they got there, she might be useful. She could help look for a house, get them settled, deal with dozens of things he knew nothing about. The idea seemed dangerous at first but if he could just keep her out of the way, there might be no risk at all. It suddenly seemed like a mistake to leave her behind.

"New York," he said at last.

"I always wanted to see New York," Jenny said. She sat back in the seat and shut her eyes. Now, she thought, we each know a secret.

It took nearly two weeks to find the place he wanted, a small frame house just a few hours northwest of New York. He'd looked for the place only in that area. When she asked him why, he said it was near a hunting lodge that he'd read about one time. He'd seen pictures of it, he told her, and liked the way it looked. It seemed to make as much sense as anything else he did and she soon forgot about it.

Inside, there were two rooms and a cramped kitchen downstairs, two more rooms and a tiny bath at the top of the steep stairs on the second floor. Near the bath, a door in the ceiling led to an unlit attic. The walls were covered in the same dingy green wallpaper, some of it so faded now that they looked bleached, and there were waterstains everywhere. In the living room there was an old stone fireplace. A cracked and chipped mantel cut from a single oak beam ran through the middle of it, the top hidden beneath a layer of dust and cobwebs. Small black spiders covered it with hairline tracks. The front door was cut between the two front windows at the bottom of the stairs. One side of it had angled several inches below the other as the old house had settled into the rocky ground.

The dining room was directly behind the living room.

Directly behind that was the kitchen and the back door. A single window faced the garden; the glass was so old that some of the panes had turned milky white in places.

In one corner of the dining room, a doorway led down to a half basement with damp stone walls that flaked bits of dirty white paint onto the uneven dirt floor. The old furnace sat on an island of pitted concrete against the wall.

The backyard seemed almost as small and cramped as the rest of the house. It ended abruptly in a stubby rock-strewn hill and a piney woods that stretched around three sides of the property and as far back as she could see into the hills.

Each day she dug in the yard, pulling up bits of sod and rock to fashion a garden. It kept them separate at first and gave her time to watch him, to learn what he was like. The distance between them seemed to make him uneasy. He brought her packets of seed, fertilizer, some stakes, and a tight roll of chicken wire to make a fence, stacking them on the bare wooden picnic table by the back door like a kind of offering.

The house came furnished with odd pieces of furniture. No two pieces matched except for the set in the back bedroom, a dresser and bed and night table made out of maple and stained the color of mud. There was an old sofa and a low rocker with a pressed wood back in the living room and a square red enamel table in the dining room and four metal chairs with vinyl seats.

The house was covered with white asbestos shingling that sagged in places like an old suit of clothes, and the roof was green with moss. There was a graveled road that ran half a mile from the front of the house. A dirt driveway snaked off the road and petered out in the high saw grass that grew everywhere except around the front door where Jenny had cut it with a sickle.

Jenny slept in the bedroom near the back. Dane took the one in front. She'd gone with him to talk to the woman who rented out the house.

The woman had hardly paid any attention to Dane except to take his money for six months' rent in advance. He'd paid her in cash and she counted it in front of him, and nodded once when she finished and stuffed it into a man's worn leather wallet that she kept in her jacket. Her hands were large and the edges of her fingers were black with dirt.

She took hold of Jenny's arm, a surprisingly gentle touch for those hands, and walked her through the house and told her she was welcome to whatever she could find in the attic. There might be some extra furniture up there, she said with a smile. She even showed her the old phone they could use and not have to pay for. "The only thing you can do is call out, nobody can call you," she said. "But it's free. Can't complain about the price." In the backyard, Jenny asked her about a garden.

"I had one out here," the woman said. "We used to grow tomatoes and squash because that's what Pru liked." The woman rubbed her index finger with a large callused thumb and looked at her. "My second husband."

"Do you still have a garden?"

"Not anymore," the woman said, the words coming slow. "He died."

They'd moved into the house that night. The frequent rain turned the night air cold. Jenny would build a fire and sit on the sofa reading. Along with the furniture in the attic—an old three-legged table, a pitcher and washbowl tinted a light violet, a quilt rack, a set of dishes—she'd found a box of old novels and *Reader's Digest Condensed Books*. She had never been much of a reader but she started to read them, slowly and carefully, one by one. There was little else to do at night, especially without Dane.

He was gone most of the time now. The sound of the van starting up in the mornings before sunrise would wake her. She would look out the side window of her room and watch the headlights as they wavered across the yard and he would be gone. He would return to the house at night exhausted and withdrawn. She always left a plate of food for him. Sometimes, when she couldn't sleep, she'd come downstairs to find that he had taken only one or two bites and gone to his room. Sometimes the light would still be on and she would have to sneak past his door. They lived like brother and sister. It was a relief. For a while, at least, she forgot about her body.

She cleaned and cooked and took care of the house and went shopping with him. He was as self-conscious as a small boy, even in the small IGA where they bought groceries. He spoke to her in whispers as they walked through the aisles.

"It's the noise," he'd told her in the van.

"What are you going to do when you get to New York?" she had said. He looked at her without smiling as if she had betrayed him somehow.

During part of the day and at night, Dane kept the wolf in the basement. Dane fed him there, too, several pounds of raw meat that left a trail of blood across the dining-room floor as he carried it in his bare hands to the basement.

When Dane was home, he took her and the wolf out for walks in the surrounding hills in the late afternoons. The wolf came alive during those walks, running ahead of them and disappearing into the thick woods. She could have stayed in those woods forever. Dane and the wolf pulled her away from everything she'd known before; she remembered the farm where she felt like she'd begun to die a little each day. When she was with them, it was her past that died instead.

Her days were as hopeful as dreams. She began to live like she had always imagined she might, free and alive. The more her feelings grew, the more frightened she became of losing what she'd found. But she learned to forget her fears, the same way she learned to forget her past, and for a short time her dreams were real, and for the first time she let those dreams carry her away.

When Dane began to take the wolf with him during the day, and then at night, the dream disintegrated so gradually over the weeks that its slow disturbing motion seemed as languid and harmless as falling leaves. When it became real, all that was left to her was the emptiness of the small house.

That the wolf was gone was the hardest for her to take. Dane's absence didn't bother her as much; she was used to his silence, the way he locked himself in his room, and even his sudden disappearances. She never asked where he went or what he did or where he got the money. It wasn't any different from her life on the farm. All her life, she had been used to mystery.

She asked him once if she could take the wolf out alone. He sat her down and spoke to her in a stern voice.

"I don't want you to ever take him out by yourself," he

said. "I want your promise on that." She nodded her agreement. "You don't know how dangerous it is right now."

But she made mistakes. One morning she thought the van was gone, and she looked inside his room. There was a narrow single bed covered with a plain olive blanket and a small dresser. The sparseness of the room struck her as terribly sad somehow, almost like her own room at the farm, and she was suddenly sorry that she'd looked.

Then she saw a small notebook lying open on the floor next to the bed. She knelt on the floor and turned to a page at random and began to read. It was Dane's journal. As she skimmed the pages, she caught a glimpse of her name and somewhere next to it, like a stray bit of light caught in the orbit of the sun, the word *love*. She was so startled by the idea that he might be falling in love with her that she stopped to read the page. She held the book up and a piece of paper fell out, filled with names and addresses in New York. They seemed so strange in the context of the rest of the journal that she read through the names carefully, curious about why he'd written them down.

There was a sudden shadow above her head and Dane pulled her up roughly by her arms and spun her against the wall.

"What are you doing in here?" he shouted at her. She tried to get away but he pinned her against the wall and wouldn't let go. He yelled again, "What do you think you're doing?"

"I didn't know!" she yelled back, and then she closed her hands over her eyes and pressed her face against the wall and waited for him to hit her. Her one thought was how could she have been so wrong about him?

He gripped her arms hard until she cried out in pain, then let her go. He stepped back and looked around the room, everywhere except at her, his eyes coming to rest on the open notebook.

"I didn't know," she said again. Dane only shook his head and waited for her to leave.

But she'd already seen what he'd written about her.

That had been a week ago and he'd hardly spoken a word to her since. She kept to herself, enduring his silence without protest. Now she sat alone in front of the fire and waited for them to come home. It was late, the room cold despite the warmth of the fire. She read for a while and then closed her eyes.

The sound of water running in the kitchen sink woke her up. She stepped into the dining room. Dane stood in the kitchen doorway drying his hands, the wolf beside him. He turned toward her in surprise. She saw something on his face, a dirty brown smear on one cheek and more down the front of his shirt. It looked like blood.

Without warning, the wolf rushed through the doorway, his head low, and raced toward her along the wall. She knelt down to greet him and stopped almost immediately. The wolf left a chalky smudge of reddish-brown stain along the dining-room wall. There was no mistaking it now, it *was* blood. Jenny froze. Dane clapped his hands hard. The wolf stopped immediately and leaned heavily against the wall. His fur was wet and glistened from the rain. Jenny looked down at the floor. A pool of pink water had formed at her feet.

Dane gently pulled the wolf away and led him toward the basement. He opened the door. The wolf climbed down the stairs.

"What happened?" Jenny asked. He kept his back to her, doing something with the door.

"He got into a fight," Dane said. He closed the door and turned around.

He was lying and she knew it. "What about you?" she asked.

"I'm all right," he said.

She walked into the kitchen for a towel. "There's blood on your cheek," she said when she passed him. His hand moved slowly to his face.

Jenny wiped up the dining-room floor on her hands and knees. When she finished, she stood and looked at the basement door. There was a new lock on it now.

That night after the first killing, Dane wrote in his journal:
"I expected to feel something after the killing tonight of the man named Lange but I felt nothing. It must be done, the

139

others, too. But I don't know why I didn't feel anything. Just emptiness. It meant no more to me than killing a rabbit."

He looked at what he had written and stopped. Moments later, he began again.

"A few days ago, I found Jenny reading one of my journals. I'm almost certain that she saw the names. They won't mean anything to her unless she sees something in a newspaper but that seems unlikely. She is as uninterested in the outside world as I am. She spends most of her time in the garden, digging and weeding with great determination. The only thing that interests her more than the garden is the wolf. She is more confident around him every day. I don't know what makes her so fearless.

"The woods here are so much smaller than in Canada, even the land seems smaller. The wolf moves through it quickly, especially at night. He can adapt to anything. Most of this seems so new, even after several weeks here. One thing that is almost the same is the silence. It's like it must have been before people were ever created.

"The one other thing that seems familiar, for reasons I still don't understand, is Jenny. Even now I have trouble calling her by name. It's been so long since names meant anything to me. It's been so long since people meant anything to me. She has become so much a part of what I'm doing that it's hard for me to imagine when she wasn't here. My feelings toward her have changed and I have to fight to control them all the time.

"I don't know what to say to her. So far, the silence seems to be enough for both of us."

Dane had been awake for hours when he heard Jenny leave her room. He lay motionless on top of the bed, his body stiff with tension, and waited until he was sure she was all the way downstairs before he slipped out of his room after her. He stood at the top of the stairs and listened for the sound of a door opening but he heard only silence, the occasional drumbeat of rain from the trees being blown against the side of the house. He shut his eyes and listened again. The floorboards in the dining room creaked. Dane moved quickly down the stairs.

He stood at the bottom and listened, a little startled when

he heard her voice. She was singing. The words were unclear but the melody was familiar, an old lullaby that he remembered hearing as a child. He was halfway across the living room when he realized that she wasn't at the table. She was sitting beside the basement door singing to the wolf.

It startled him so much that he stopped in the middle of the room to look at her. She leaned her head toward where he stood and he stepped back into the dark shadows of the room.

It was such a simple thing, and so unexpected. For the first time since it had all begun, he was afraid of her.

Chapter 15

THE SQUIRREL WAS out early the next morning in the park. The two uniforms pulled past her on the park's East Drive and waved. The Squirrel gave them the finger. It was their morning ritual; they waved, the Squirrel wordlessly told them to fuck off.

The Squirrel continued up the East Drive to the mall and stopped among the statues where she seemed to be at home feeding the squirrels that gathered there each morning to wait for her. There were half a dozen other places around the park where she fed other squirrels at other times. The Squirrel made her rounds with the punctuality of a gamekeeper. She wouldn't feed pigeons or starlings. If a pigeon started hanging around while she was feeding the squirrels, she went after it with a stick. She only fed squirrels. That was how she got her name.

She carried a large plastic bag filled with bagel crisps, two-day-old jellied donuts that oozed over the bottom of the bag, peanuts so bad that their shells had started to turn green, leaky boxes of raisins, granola and sunflower seeds, anything she could pick up on her way to the park early each morning. Nobody knew where she lived or what her real name was or if she was crazy or not. She didn't dress rich and she didn't dress poor. Better yet, she didn't smell. They assumed she was crazy but since she never spoke to anyone except in sign language, they were never certain of it.

The Squirrel finished her first feeding by the statues and walked up the mall toward the terrace on the other side of Olmsted Way. It was closed for repairs, the whole of it surrounded by cyclone fence. No workmen yet, they'd be there later, rebuilding the chevron-patterned brick walk, cleaning and repointing the gray stone wall that ran around the edge of the terrace walk and the fountain below. Some of the decorative crowns on the wall were wrapped in plastic that had turned nearly the same color as the wall.

The Squirrel stopped to look at the fountain through the fence. No matter what the weather, the Angel of the Waters was still green. The fat little cherubs beneath still stood for Purity, Health, Peace, and Temperance. The Squirrel knew these things but no one ever asked her about them and she never bothered to tell anybody. On one side of the terrace was a huge gray rock, her second stop. The rock sloped upward, revealing the etched lines of glacier scars. The Squirrel sat down on the edge of the rock nearest the path and doled out some pieces of bran muffins that she'd found behind a D'Agostino's. After her second feeding, she walked east toward the boat pond and turned right on the path by the arch to her third stop, the small grove of trees just on the other side.

This morning, though, her squirrels weren't waiting for her. Instead, there was a dog in the middle of the grove. It appeared to be sitting on a log or something. She looked closer. The log had feet.

She was going to go after both of them with her stick but when she reached the grove, the dog growled menacingly at her and she reconsidered. She wondered if the man was injured, unable to speak. The dog's eyes followed the woman while she stepped carefully through the trees around the edge of the grove until she came to a spot where she could see the man's face.

Except he didn't have one.

The patrol car was parked in the lot near the boathouse at the east end of the lake. The two uniformed officers inside sipped coffee through holes torn in the plastic tops of their styrofoam cups. They had an hour and a half to go on their eight and so far nothing had happened. Earlier, somebody had reported a dog running loose but they hadn't seen anything. They hadn't looked too hard but it was nothing to work up a lather over. The driver, whose name was O'Donnell, had been on the force for twelve years and in the Central Park Precinct for four. His partner's name was Jackson. He'd been with O'Donnell for a little over two. O'Donnell liked Jackson. He thought Jackson was okay, especially for somebody who went to Columbia.

O'Donnell looked at his partner's pants. "New?"

"Got 'em cleaned."

"About time," O'Donnell said.

Jackson grinned. "Where are we going to eat?"

"Someplace where you won't spill anything on your nice clean pants."

"You mean where they got napkins, shit like that?" Jackson said.

"Forks too," O'Donnell said.

They both sipped their coffee in silence. Jackson looked out the window at the East Drive.

"Goddamn," he said.

"What is it?" O'Donnell said, and leaned forward in the seat so he could see.

"I don't believe it," O'Donnell said.

The Squirrel stood on the other side of the drive. She waved to them. Her tiny arm swung back and forth like a metronome. She crossed the drive and walked toward the car.

"She's coming over here," Jackson said. His voice was tinged with awe.

"Maybe she just wants to see who she's been flipping off all these years."

"Maybe she's making a mistake," Jackson said.

But it wasn't a mistake. The woman kept coming, her short legs working fast underneath her plain black raincoat. Jackson could see that she wore white orthopedic shoes.

"What do I call her?" Jackson said.

O'Donnell looked surprised. "Squirrel," he said. "That's her name, isn't it?"

She was out of breath when she reached Jackson's window and had to rest before she could speak. When she did, they were both astounded, as much by the way she said it as by what she said.

"Excuse me, officers," the Squirrel said in a voice that sounded as if it had rolled all the way there from the Back Bay. "There's a man and a dog over in the grove." She pointed in the general direction.

"By the archway?" Jackson asked carefully, afraid to upset her.

"That's right," she said. "I don't really know how to put this." She paused and patted each one of her cheeks. "His face," she said.

"What about it?" O'Donnell asked.

"Well, it's not there." The two policemen looked at one another. "If you ask me," the Squirrel said thoughtfully, "I think the dog ate most of it."

They parked the car on Cedar Hill and walked toward the trees, O'Donnell a few feet behind Jackson.

"It's a Doberman," Jackson said.

"I hate things that bite," O'Donnell replied.

"My girlfriend likes to bite," Jackson said.

"When she can find it," O'Donnell said. They were about forty feet from the grove and the dog growled at them.

"Let's move around a bit, confuse him," O'Donnell said. "You take one side, I'll take the other."

Jackson worked his way around slowly until he could see the man's face.

"Oh, Jesus," he said despondently.

"Dead, right?" O'Donnell asked casually.

"As dead as your dork," Jackson said. He bent down so he could get a better look at the dead man without getting his pants dirty and tilted his head to the side. One of the dead man's eyes remained open, a tiny white island in a pulpy red sea. The rest of the face was gone. Shreds of skin and tissue hung down like strings of cheese. Jackson couldn't tell what had happened to him. He moved a little closer, ignoring the growling dog. The dead man's throat hung open like a second mouth.

"I think he got sliced," Jackson said, and drew his index finger across his throat. The movement spooked the Doberman. The dog lunged at Jackson who fell over in a panic and scrambled backward across the muddy ground on his butt.

O'Donnell drew his revolver and shot the Doberman twice. The dog flipped over on its back and died, two fist-sized holes in its side.

Jackson stared at the dog and then at his partner. O'Donnell straightened up and held his revolver at his side. "Well?" he asked Jackson.

"Justifiable use of firepower," Jackson said.

O'Donnell nodded. "Your pants are shot," he said. The seat of Jackson's pants was smeared with mud. "I'm going to call this in," O'Donnell said. Jackson told him to bring back the camera and O'Donnell nodded. He climbed slowly up the hill to the car. A single jogger stood next to it, trying to get a better view. O'Donnell waved him on.

Jackson wagged a finger at the dead Doberman. "Bad doggie," he said. Then he stood up, took out a small black notebook, and began writing it all down.

Detective Charles Yates was always amazed at the disturbance a public death created. People seemed so anxious to get close to it, even the people whose job was to get right down in it; the detectives, the medical people, the press, the spectators, the goddamn birds in the trees, everybody wanted just a little taste, enough so maybe they could tell themselves they knew what death was all about. Yates knew. It was an unidentified male civilian in running shorts with his throat ripped open lying in the mud and a Doberman with two big holes punched in its guts.

There was no identification on the man and the dog wore a plain leather collar. It had rained during the night, threatened to rain again any minute, and the ground around the scene was muddy and pockmarked with footprints from everybody except possibly the dead man. When he'd first arrived, the area had been so clean that it looked like the bodies had fallen from the sky.

He wished they hadn't shot the Doberman. Not that it made any real difference to him but it made things messy.

There would be shooting reports for both officers to file and a hearing that he'd probably have to attend in case somebody wanted to know the impact of the shooting on this case in particular or the future of the NYPD in general, whichever they were worried about most that day.

The dog was only part of the problem, dead or alive. The Animal Affairs people could deal with that. But this one was going to attract attention, even if the dog *did* do it. One or two television crews had already been there and the rest would show up eventually. The sergeant was already talking to some reporters and that was as entertaining as bending over and chatting with your own asshole. But he had to do it this time because this was more than just one more dead civilian, this was a Dead Civilian in Central Park. For the press, that was a sure sign of the Decline and Fall of Our Fair City.

And they still didn't know what they had, even though they were handling it like a homicide right now. The medical examiner had already told them that the guy was dead and that he couldn't tell anything more than that until after the autopsy. The situation, even for the park, was worse than usual. The dog had generally just screwed everything up more.

Yates knew what else he didn't have. He didn't have a partner. Tito, his partner for four years, was in the hospital getting a new stainless-steel ball joint put in his hip socket. He wouldn't be back for another six weeks and they hadn't gotten around to assigning him a new one and nobody had come running up to Yates begging to be his sidekick. He didn't expect anybody to do that anymore.

He didn't have a girlfriend and for once in his life he wasn't looking. He didn't have a new car and he didn't have a lot of money in the bank.

What he had was a stiff in the park. If somebody had cut him up, it was going to get worse. There would be pressure, which meant that even though it was his case, there would be a task force. That would be like being caught in the middle of a stampede. The paperwork alone would kill him. Yates hated the very idea of a task force. Central Park could handle its own.

He agreed with the woman who found the body; he hoped the dog did it.

Yates heard his name and turned to see one of the crime scene detectives, a short unhappy-looking man with glasses and a bald head coming toward him around the edge of the grove. His name was Winn and he was never happy with anything.

"What'd you find?"

Winn pushed his glasses up onto the bridge of his nose.

"Close your eyes, what do you see?"

Jesus, Yates thought, is this a joke?

"We didn't find anything," Winn said when Yates didn't respond. "The rain got to the place first. Look at it."

It was a mess, Yates had to agree. The small crowd behind the blue wooden barriers watched the scene. What were they hoping for? he wondered. Fresh blood? Very little fresh blood here except for the dog. The guy managed to bleed himself clean hours ago. They took samples of the blood-soaked dirt around his neck. It seemed ridiculous but they did it. They worked on the You-Never-Know Theory. Something stupid always made the case, you just never knew what, so you took a sample of everything in sight.

"Tell me," Yates said.

"I don't have anything," Winn said.

Yates waited.

"We found a couple tracks under the arch," Winn said. "But they're in bad shape. I won't guarantee anything."

"What does that mean?"

"How should I know?" Winn said.

Yates noticed a Polaroid picture sticking up between the pages of the lab man's notebook. Winn always saved the best for last and he liked to be coaxed.

"What's the picture?" Yates asked.

"Not much," Winn said. "They got it when we rolled him over."

"Well," Yates said, "let's see it anyway. You never know."

Winn handed it to Yates. It was a picture of the dead man's chest. It showed a small green insignia, a ring of letters around a small circle, partially obscured by a large bloodstain

148

but he could still make out the words: THE NEW YORK SPORTSMAN'S SOCIETY. Yates looked a little closer. The small circle turned out to be the earth resting on the arched backs of two male lions.

"Are there more?" Yates asked.

"Of course." Winn handed Yates several different photos.

"I'll keep them," he said. "Is that it?" He looked at his watch. It was almost nine.

"That's it." Winn gave Yates a sour look and walked back toward the center of the grove where they were busy zipping the body into a greenish-black bag. Yates saw Jackson and O'Donnell talking to another detective and waved them over.

He watched them as they walked, the young one, so casual in his movement; the older, heavyset one who walked carefully, placing one foot in front of the other like a large lumbering machine. They walked around the trees. On the Fifth Avenue side, the area was blocked off by red plastic ribbon hung between the trees. It gave the scene something of a carnival background. By the time the two men stood in front of him, Yates had a broad smile on his face. He had already talked to them once that morning and heard Jackson's description of what they'd found. Jackson, he remembered, had taken very good notes.

"What can we do for you?" O'Donnell asked. He was getting restless. They had paperwork to do back at the precinct.

Yates handed the photo to Jackson, who looked at it carefully and handed it over to O'Donnell, who held it out in front of his stomach.

"You ever hear of the New York Sportsman's Society?" Yates asked.

Both men said no, almost simultaneously.

"Find out where it is," Yates said. "If it's in the city, drive over there and see if they know who he is."

He pointed toward the body. Behind them an ambulance backed down the hill and stopped. The rear doors opened. Four detectives hauled the body up the hill, struggling on the slippery ground. A television camera crew followed them, bright lights shining even in the daylight.

"If you find it," he said, "just give them what you've got. Don't forget the dog." He said it to Jackson. "I want a name for this guy soon. Okay?"

"We took some body shots," Jackson said.

"Take them along if you think they'll help."

O'Donnell spoke as if he hadn't heard a thing. "Before or after our paperwork?" he asked.

"Before," Yates said.

The two officers walked off and left Yates alone. He took out a cigarette, lit it, and stuck the burnt match in his jacket pocket where it joined at least a dozen others. He'd worn it to too many deaths, he decided. The ambulance pulled out. Yates strolled back into the center of things.

He stopped to watch one of the officers pull the bag with the Doberman inside closer to the trees, out of range of the television cameras.

"When are they getting here?" Yates asked him. He meant the Animal Affairs people. Usually, the ASPCA picked them up, but not today, not with this mess.

"In a few minutes," he said. "That was half an hour ago." The officer stood up. He looked about twenty and a little simple. Yates knew he was neither. But the fact that he looked like Andy Hardy wasn't going to help him at all. "They said they were going to send Atwood," he said, and smiled.

Shit, Yates thought, and it's not even noon.

"They said he was out," the officer went on, "but they're going to beep him."

Yates looked at the sergeant talking to one of the television reporters. At least O'Donnell wasn't around to talk about blowing the Doberman away. That was one less target. If Atwood had found him, they could have all gone home. Atwood would have had the whole show to himself.

All they had to do now was get the dog out of there before he showed up and started mouthing off to the press. Of course, Atwood would mouth off to the press whether the dog was there or not. Yates thought about it for a moment and shrugged.

Either way you looked at it, he was fucked.

* * *

"I want three dozen," Michael Atwood said. He waited while the woman dipped into the big fish tank with the white mesh strainer and lifted out a fist-sized scoop of goldfish. The tiny orange fish slithered around in the strainer as she poured them into a plastic bag half filled with water.

She dumped another full strainer into the bag. "Is that enough?"

"Almost," Atwood said cheerfully.

The woman filled the strainer again and poured the flopping goldfish into the bag.

"That'll be fine," Atwood said. A smile rose to the surface of his face. The woman didn't see it. She was on her way back to the counter, spinning the bag in her hand, wrapping the blue tie around the twisted plastic, ignoring her customer.

The bill came to $13.50. Atwood paid with a credit card. He hefted the bag. Enough for a week, he thought. The beeper in his pocket went off suddenly, like a warning against whatever he had been thinking. He jammed his fist into his pocket and shut it off. The woman behind the counter didn't even bother to look up from her seat.

"Can I use your phone?" Atwood said. "I work for the city." He reached for his clip, the one that held the gold shield with the blue enamel center that identified him as Chief Veterinarian for the Bureau of Animal Affairs for the City of New York. He held it out for the woman to see. She looked at it closely and set the phone on top of the counter.

"Cute badge, Doc," she said.

Chapter 16

THE BUREAU OF Animal Affairs worked out of a handful of cramped offices on the seventh floor of an old court building on lower Broadway. There were four veterinarians assigned to handle an average of two thousand animal complaints a year for the entire city of New York. The only thing they didn't have to worry about was the circus and barking dogs. Barking dog complaints went to the Environmental Protection Agency because technically they were noise pollution. Nobody bothered the circus no matter what they did because it was pointless.

If you attacked the circus because the cages were too small or the animal feed was rotten or the animals were injured, you ended up looking like a seriously disturbed person. Everybody loved the circus, even the mayor. Atwood knew this because Atwood had tried it. The mayor called him up to tell him that if Atwood ever decided to shut the circus down again, the mayor was personally going to bury him up to his ears in elephant shit.

Animal Affairs was understaffed and underbudgeted. Atwood's office was a ten-by-fifteen beige rectangle with a metal desk and a wall of metal shelves and file cabinets. There were two aquariums on top of the cabinets. One held an African side-head turtle in about an inch of dirty water that Atwood had impounded because of the risk of salmonella.

It was called a side-head because it pulled its head in its body sideways. The other was empty, the sides stained with an inky residue, the dry bottom layered with gravel and the creamy white skeletons of hundreds of tiny fish.

He used his own car and had long ago given up on central supply to provide him with anything except the forms he needed to write a brief history when a dog bit somebody. You could get forms from supply in a matter of hours. Anything else took six months. So he bought everything himself and filed for expenses because it was easier. Vets got comp time instead of overtime. Atwood never took it. He kept working because he liked it.

The backseat and trunk of Atwood's car were filled with boxes of hypodermics, distemper serum, several nylon nets for trapping bats, blankets, a portable weather gauge for temperature readings in the park—when it hit ninety degrees, they shut the horse-drawn hacks down—heavy leather gloves, posters, pamphlets, trash from hundreds of takeout Chinese dinners, an illegal dart gun, and a dozen vials of Ace-Promazine tranquilizer and a plastic cat cage that he had stolen from the ASPCA offices on Ninety-second Street.

He had been at Animal Affairs for eleven years, made $31,673 a year, and had been bitten only once in all that time. He got his picture in the paper every so often, usually for things like wrestling a fifteen-foot boa constrictor out a pet shop door or saving a lion from the mess of someone's Manhattan apartment.

In eleven years, he had ordered only one animal destroyed, a German shepherd that had been left alone with a seven-month-old child. The mother was out for the day and had forgotten to chain it up. Some animal rights lawyer fought the order, claiming it was inhumane. The dog was not vicious, he said. Atwood told him that if he thought the dog was such a goddamn prize, why didn't he take it home so it could play fetch with the wife and kids.

Mostly it was the animals that suffered. Atwood considered it his job to keep their suffering to an absolute minimum. The most amazing thing about the job was that no matter where he went, everybody, the police who waited around while he figured out what to do about an apartment filled with cats, the pet store owners who wanted their pictures taken with him, the secretaries in his office who sat together in one corner going over the reports and license applications, the guy at the ASPCA who hosed down the cages, everybody called him Doc.

Atwood flashed his shield at the officer who waved him through the blockade on the park's East Drive. He could see part of the roped-off area from the road, most of it obscured by trees and the orange and white ambulance that was making its way slowly up the hill. A television camera crew stood in the wake of the ambulance and panned across the scene. Small clusters of the police, a handful of spectators, one or two reporters, all seemed frozen into a modern urban still life as they watched the ambulance lurch onto the road.

Atwood searched for the dog. Maybe Emergency Services had gotten there first and tranquilized it. Then he saw the body bag almost hidden behind the trees. He started down the hill.

The dumb bastards did it again, he thought, a small bubble of anger rising in his guts.

Yates saw Atwood coming and stepped out of the way. There was bound to be trouble and there was nothing he could do about it anyway. Yates put out his cigarette on the nearest tree and deposited the butt in his pocket.

Atwood unzipped the bag and stuck his hand inside to remove the dog. He found the gunshot wounds right away, put his fingers in the middle of the first hole, pulled it out and stared at his bloody hand. He dragged the dog out of the bag and looked at the two gaping holes in the side. Other than the wounds, the dog appeared normal. The detective leaned against the tree with his hands behind him and watched the veterinarian.

"Who shot the dog?" he asked Yates.

"Not me, Doc," Yates said.

"Well, who the hell did?" Atwood looked around for something to wipe his hand off with and settled for the ground.

"The officers who found the body."

"Did they see the dog attack anybody?"

"The man was already dead when they got here," Yates said.

"Where was the dog?"

"Sitting on the body."

Atwood shoved the Doberman into the bag and zipped it up.

"So they just shot it?" he asked. "Why didn't they wait for Emergency Services?" Whenever cops had to deal with anything out of the ordinary, they usually called Emergency Services first. Emergency Services had everything except surface-to-air missiles.

"The dog went after one of them," Yates said. "His partner shot it." He lit another cigarette. The smoke hung like moss between the shafts of morning sunlight that shone through the branches.

"On the assumption that the dog just killed somebody."

"No," Yates said calmly. "I think he shot it on the assumption that it was about to bite a big chunk out of his partner's ass."

Atwood gripped the end of the bag tight and lifted. The dog wasn't as heavy as it looked lying on the ground with its guts shot out.

"Does anybody *know* if the dog killed somebody?" Atwood asked.

Yates shrugged and looked at his watch. "The medical examiner is going to make that determination just as soon as he gets a chance."

Yates's voice sounded natural and unperturbed. Things happened, it said, people did the best they could, it was too early to go scalp hunting, give it a rest.

Atwood's bubble of anger burst.

"Was it the owner?" he asked. If it was, it might explain a lot, why the Doberman had turned on the man and why it stayed to protect the body. An unresolved conflict between instinct and training. It was pathetically human.

"Probably," Yates said. "We don't know who the victim was yet."

"I'll have it tested for rabies," Atwood said. "I don't think they'll find anything but I'll let you know."

Yates fished around inside his coat and took out the

photographs Winn had given him and handed them to Atwood, one by one.

"Does that look like a dog attack to you?"

Atwood dropped the bag and looked through the photographs. He shuffled through them quickly at first, too shocked to say anything. Then he went over them again, sucking in his breath slowly each time. It was as bad as the evening he had walked into the second-floor tenement and saw what was left of the seven-month-old. The child was wrapped in a clear plastic bag on the small table. A loopy trail of blood ran across the kitchen floor and the faded green carpet in the hallway toward one of the bedrooms. The shepherd had been tranquilized and he told them to take it to the ASPCA. Its legs were wired together. The two cops had hung it on a broom handle and carried it out on their shoulders. Someone threw a towel over the child's remains and apologized to him for not having a regular body bag that small. Atwood noticed the child's arm just before the towel covered it. The skin was so smooth and white that it looked like a piece of china.

The pictures in his hand were just as bad. He tried to connect the viciousness of the attack with the thing in the bag at his feet. He closed his eyes and tried to imagine what it must have been like but stopped; the pictures were too vivid. Atwood opened his eyes and found Yates looking at him almost sympathetically. He pressed the photos together and handed them back to the detective.

"It could've been an attack," he said. To say it seemed to diminish it. He wondered if Yates felt that, too. "It probably was," he added. Atwood thought of something else. "I'll tell them to save the head for the autopsy."

"Good," Yates said, and put the photos back in his jacket. "Ever see anything like that before?"

"Only once," Atwood said, and was ready to tell him the story but Yates didn't seem interested. The detective took a deep drag on his cigarette.

"What would make an animal do that?" Yates asked. Smoke seemed to chase the words out of his mouth.

Atwood shook his head. He could've made something up but the truth was he just didn't know. Nobody knew.

Another cop had asked him the same question in the tenement kitchen. He didn't know then, either.

Van Owen knew it was Lange the moment the young cop showed him the photograph but waited until the cop gave him one more, a picture of the dog. A pair of hands held the Doberman's head up by both ears. The narrow muscular jaw hung open, the tongue lay like a large pink flatworm over one side. Van Owen studied the picture. Even dead, the dog managed to look ridiculous. He asked to see the picture of Lange again. Maybe they had one of someone holding *him* up by the ears. That would have been perfect.

It was George Lange all right. He could tell by the hair and the ears and the shape of his head. Van Owen tried to imagine what had happened to him. It looked like somebody went after his face with a pair of pinking shears. His right eye was still open, what was left of it. Van Owen wondered if he had seen the end coming.

He took both pictures and laid them side by side on his desk, snapshots from an odd menagerie. Lange's body had the bloated look of something that had been left out in the rain for a while. That's what happened to you when you thought you were prince of the city, Van Owen thought.

The two cops had been waiting for him when he arrived that morning. He noticed that the older cop sat down in the leather chair nearest the front door to his office and was examining the room, going over the bookcase and the pictures on the wall, probably trying to figure out how much it all cost. He didn't seem to care whether Van Owen liked it or not. The young cop stood, more concerned with Van Owen's reaction to the photographs.

Van Owen stacked the photographs together and handed them back to him. "I know him," Van Owen said. "His name is George Lange." The young cop took out a small notebook. "With an *E*," Van Owen told him.

He took the membership book from the desk and opened it. "He lives at 872 Fifth Avenue." He spun the book around. "You can read it yourself." Now it was Van Owen's turn to wait. The young cop wrote everything down quickly.

"His business," the cop said, reading the book. "Law firm?"

"Investments," Van Owen said.

"Stocks, bonds, that sort of thing?"

Van Owen nodded.

"How well did you know him?" the black cop asked.

"I knew him as a member," Van Owen said. "Not much more than that."

"Do you know if he ran in the park every day?"

Van Owen shook his head.

"Anyone who might have something against him?"

Most of the people who worked for him—his partners, whom he cheated regularly, his friends, his wife; Van Owen thought there might be a few hundred more.

"No," he said.

"Any problems with the marriage?"

His wife fucked everything that walked, crawled, or had been dead for less than three days. Lange had let her. Van Owen didn't see that as a serious problem.

"Not that I know," he answered.

The young cop wrote something on a page of the notebook, tore it out, and handed it to Van Owen. It was a phone number.

"Thanks for the information," he said. "If you think of something else, give me a call."

Van Owen folded the piece of paper in half and slid it into one corner of his desk pad. The older cop rose slowly out of his chair.

"Any idea what happened to him?" Van Owen asked. He was professionally curious.

The young cop shrugged. "They won't know until after the autopsy." Behind him, his partner snorted.

"They're not sure," the older cop said in a voice that sounded like wet cement running down a drainpipe. "I think he got his face chewed off."

Chapter 17

AN ASSOCIATE MEDICAL examiner at the M.E.'s office named Tieneman got to Lange's body a little after noon. The body had been in a tray for half an hour, gone to X-ray and was now on one of the eight steel surgical tables in the main autopsy room down the hall from the vault area. Plastic tubes buried in each wrist drained what little fluid there was left from the body. Tieneman removed the tubes and small flecks of coagulated blood as thick as glue splattered across the sheets that hung down the sides of the table and onto the white tile floor.

The facial wounds looked bad but they were only superficial. The skin had been torn—shredded was more like it—but the major muscles remained basically intact. Tieneman turned to the neck and let out a long sigh. The neck was a real mess. For the next hour, Tieneman cut through the damaged tissue, examining, measuring, comparing the various pieces of bone and ruptured muscle. He did the same with the wounds to the right arm and shoulder. When Tieneman finished, he put down his scalpel. There wasn't anything else he could do at the moment. He was waiting on a set of teeth.

Yates arrived with the Doberman's head in a brown paper bag that one of the lab techs had given him, the brain removed and tested, the teeth scraped clean of their residue of human tissue, smeared on a slide and examined, the eye

159

sockets empty but still moist. He could have had it sent over from the lab but things got misplaced over there and he didn't want to argue with anybody about it, and besides, it was still his case. The detective stood behind Tieneman and watched his back while the pathologist bent over the body. Tieneman spoke so low that Yates could only make out a few words. Yates hated the smell of the place, the stench of chemicals and decay. It got in your hair and clothes.

Finally, Tieneman straightened up. "I don't think you've got a homicide here," he said. "But that doesn't mean you don't have a big problem."

Yates stepped to the head of the table and stared down at what was left of George Lange and waited for Tieneman to explain. Without a homicide, he was out of a job. The pathologist held up the dog's head with both hands and opened the jaws.

"About seventeen centimeters," Tieneman said. "Give or take one or two. Enough to do the kind of damage that was done here." He pointed to the face. "Maybe even here," he said and circled his finger over the arm and shoulder. "But not here." He pointed to the throat. "And this is what killed him," he said.

Tieneman set the dog's head on the table. "I think the arm wound was made first," he said. "That's how he was dragged down." He grabbed Yates's arm with his bare hand and shook it. "The muscles in his forearm were all torn in the same direction. After that, there were several strong bites to the neck. One or more of them crushed his neck and cut his spinal cord in half."

Yates said nothing. He rocked back and forth on the balls of his feet.

"The main reason I think those two wounds came first is because there was a lot of hemorrhaging in the arm and neck areas but very little in the face," Tieneman said. "That would indicate that the face wounds came later—*after* he'd bled for a while. I want the lab to look at some more tissue samples and to make a comparison with those teeth. But I know what they're going to find." He tapped the dead man's shoulder as if to get his attention. "There was more than one animal involved in this." Tieneman pointed to the dog's head. "This one didn't kill him." The look in the pathologist's eyes was clear.

We shot the wrong goddamn dog, Yates thought.

By the time he arrived at the precinct later that night, the sergeant had already been on the phone to his captain in Manhattan North. The captain in turn called the lieutenant and ordered half of the thirty-five new officers that they'd just assigned to discourage the park's numerous drug dealers reassigned to dog patrol. The lieutenant didn't think that his cops were going to be too enthusiastic about chasing after some crazed killer dog and he figured that the union would have something to say about it. The union rep told him he thought the captain was clearly out of his mind. Four extra units were added and coordinated with the foot patrols so that nobody was more than a hundred feet or so from the safety of one of the cars and everybody felt better.

The patrols went on through the four-to-twelve shift and the twelve-to-eight and nobody found a thing except two mangy strays hiding underneath some bushes near the bandshell. The men swept their flashlights across the bushes and the dogs' eyes lit up like marbles. They drew their revolvers and called for backup. The dogs, scared and hungry, waddled out with their heads dragging the ground. The units pulled up, doors flew open, shotguns were leveled across car roofs. The dogs rolled over on their backs, wagged their tails, and pissed happily all over themselves.

Michael Atwood lived on West Fifty-first. It was once called Hell's Kitchen but now everybody called it Clinton for reasons Atwood never bothered to understand. It was an area of empty factories, taxi garages, and tenements. During the winter, the wind came hard off the river and blew the wet snow through the tenements as if trying to hurry it on to someplace else. In the summer, the streets were as dry and dusty as a desert town. There weren't any artists there yet and kids still played in the street below his window. He'd lived there for six years and felt like he had the place all to himself. He loved it.

He lived on the second floor of a red brick tenement. The

apartment was old but clean; the living-room floor angled down slightly toward the street and the bathroom was small but the bedroom was large with a nice pair of windows in back and a fire escape. It was everything Atwood needed.

Atwood took himself, a worn leather satchel full of reports, a bag of groceries, and the plastic bag of goldfish up the two flights of stairs and opened the door. The living room was dark, the curtains drawn tight against the dim red glow of early evening.

Before Atwood could turn on the light, something crawled over his foot and nibbled at the hem of his pants. He flicked the switch and looked down.

A bright green parrot with a red beak and weak dumb eyes squawked and continued to peck at his pants. Atwood dropped the satchel. The bird jumped and fluttered away from the noise, bobbing its head in a loony motion as it waddled across the floor.

The carpet was strewn with shredded pieces of the *Times,* the edges of the faded newsprint curled up like strips of leftover ribbon. In the corner furthest from windows, there was a large metal cage with an open door. Newspaper covered the floor below the cage, empty sunflower seed husks covered the newspaper. The parrot shrieked twice.

"Please," Atwood said. The parrot had no name. Atwood had never been able to think of one. Finally he had decided that the bird was better off without a name. Lately he was beginning to think that the bird didn't deserve one. The parrot bobbed its head several times and hopped up on the arm of a nearby chair. From the chair it attached itself to the bottom of the cage and walked around the side until it perched on top and clawed at the side of its head.

Atwood hefted the bag of goldfish and walked across the room toward a large galvanized tub that sat beneath one of the windows. He sat down on the floor and tapped the side with his knuckles. Water splashed and something slithered over the bed of stones in the bottom of the tub. Atwood looked inside.

A greenish-white crocodile, nearly a foot long, peered at him with buggy yellow eyes. The animal's thin jaw opened and closed. Atwood opened the bag of fish and poured a quarter of it into the tub. The crocodile caught two fish in its mouth and bit down. Slivers of orange flesh fell from the sides of its mouth into the water and sank. The surface shimmered with fish scales.

Atwood watched the animal eat, amazed as always by its voraciousness. After each feeding, it rested in the shallow water, surrounded by the writhing bodies of the fish still left alive, and pulled the thin white membrane up over its eyes. It remained still for several minutes as if in a trance. Then its eyes would open again and the tiny reptile would tilt its head in the direction of the moving fish and strike. It reminded Atwood of what he'd seen that afternoon, the photographs still clear. He sat down next to the tub and rested his head against the window sill. He opened the window and let the cool breeze blow against the back of his neck.

Atwood had no words for what he was feeling, just like he had no words to answer Yates's questions that afternoon. Sometime in the last twenty-four hours a man had been killed by his dog and the dog had been killed in turn by the police. The fact that he hadn't been there to prevent it irritated him.

In the far corner, the parrot squawked and shifted lazily from one foot to the other on top of the cage. A door opened somewhere in the building and he heard the sound of strange voices. Down in the street, a child laughed.

The symmetry of life and death was complete; it worked without Atwood's presence. That irritated him, too.

He got up to make dinner, the one activity of the day that he enjoyed almost as much as his job. Each morning before work, he would open one of his cookbooks and pick out several recipes at random. He felt that this chance selection added a bit of drama to his evening meal. For instance, tonight he was having oysters florentine with sweet and sour pork on Spanish rice. He dumped the bag of groceries on the counter and went to work.

While driving into work the next morning, Yates remembered what the medical examiner had told him when he asked what kind of dog they were looking for this time. "Big and real upset," the pathologist said, a description Yates considered colorful and reasonably complete. But they had found nothing so far, just a handful of wet mangy strays. It had not been a good night for anybody. Now he'd have to call Atwood when he got to the station, allow one more intruder into it.

He turned into the precinct parking lot off the Seventy-ninth Street traverse and parked as close as he could to the maintenance department lot next door. Yates drove a seven-year-old Oldsmobile Cutlass. The car was now a sour-looking blue with freckles of rust along both rear quarter panels. A long strip of molding hung loose on the passenger side door. Yates didn't care. It was paid for and it worked.

It was like the rest of his life. He had gotten married when he first joined the force and divorced three years later. The divorce was no big deal, he thought now, just two people who were too young to know that it wasn't ever going to work with them. There were no children and he never thought about getting married again, at least not seriously. He lived with a woman for several months once but that didn't work out either. It was pleasant and convenient and even that seemed to grate on his nerves.

He lived in the same two-bedroom apartment on the Island that he'd lived in for nearly ten years. Every year he told himself he was going to do something with the second bedroom, turn it into a study or something, but he never did. It stayed the same, an abandoned place filled with broken furniture and cardboard boxes, thick with dust.

A television van was parked in the center of the lot. Yates was walking up the sidewalk when another one pulled into the driveway. At least he didn't have to talk to them. He ambled down the steps into the precinct lobby. A camera crew milled around near the front desk getting in everyone's way while a constant stream of police worked their way around them. The walls of the lobby were covered with two-tone paint, sea green and a bright glossy blue. The scene reminded Yates of something he had seen at an aquarium: a swarm of captive fish swimming through a reef. A reporter from the *News* saw him and pushed toward him. Yates ducked into his office.

The office for all six detectives assigned to Central Park consisted of three small rooms. The one at the end was the sergeant's office; the other two were first come, first served.

The whole place was a dump. The city said they were going to redo the building. Yates wasn't sure it was worth it. He spent as little time there as possible.

Someone had taped the front page of the *New York Post* to the wall near the door. One of the other detectives pointed silently toward it as Yates walked past. The details of the killing had already leaked out. It didn't come as a complete surprise; he just hadn't expected it so soon. He wondered if Tieneman had talked and decided it wasn't important. Everybody talked, nobody kept anything to themselves anymore. He stopped and read the headline and shook his head. It was going to be just about as bad as he'd figured.

Atwood woke up late the next morning but instead of driving straight to work, he walked to the Eighth Avenue newsstand to get the paper. There was a fruit stand not too far away and he decided to pick up some apples, maybe even some pears, for his lunch.

The morning was warm. The high clouds over the city were moving out to sea, leaving behind a clear spring sky. Atwood reached for the *Times* but it was the front page of the *Post* that caught his eye. He grabbed the tabloid in both hands and pulled it toward him. The headline came into focus, sharp black letters inside a red border.

DOG PACK SLAYS PARK RUNNER, Atwood read. Below the headline was another line, words so concise that they possessed the same grim clarity as the epitaph on a gravestone: "A Horrifying Death, see Page 3."

Chapter 18

~~~~~~~~~~~~~~~~~~~~~~~~~~~~~~~~~~~

DANE CAME AWAKE immediately. He brought his head up and turned slowly toward the open window. Nothing but the faint flutter of the wind. With his eyes closed, he listened for the sound that had woken him, the shuffle of footsteps through the long grass in front of the house. When he heard it again, the sound had shifted, coming from the side of the house now. There was more, a noise like ragged breathing, almost a cough.

Dane slid out of bed and crossed the narrow room, picking up pieces of clothing as he went, slipping into pants and shirt quickly, carrying his boots and knife with him into the hall. He put on the boots and tied the laces twice around each ankle. The knife he kept unsheathed in his hand. At Jenny's door, he stopped and tried the handle, surprised to find that it twisted open at his touch. Through the narrow crack he saw her form beneath the sheet, one arm clutched around a blanket that lay tangled across her neck.

He left her door open and crept down the stairs, pausing in the middle of the living room to listen, then went straight toward the rear of the house and the kitchen. Whatever was out there was moving away from the house toward the woods. At the back door, he undid the lock and slipped out, squeezing himself through the narrow opening into the yard.

He kept close to the back of the house, the blade of the knife pressed against his leg to keep it from flashing in the moonlight. At the corner, he brought the knife up next to his head, ready to slash downward at whatever was waiting on the other side.

Dane stepped out suddenly, the knife slicing through the air. To his right, near the edge of the woods, something scurried away into the trees, leaving a trail of disturbance through the tall grass. Dane glanced at his feet, then along the side of the house. There was nothing there. He moved halfheartedly toward the woods and heard the last remnant of the creature's escape, the sigh of the grass as it settled back into place. It was a ghostly sound and it stopped him from going any further. What was he chasing? Was he so out of control that he chased after strays in the middle of the night?

The moon escaped one of the clouds and its light drained the earth at his feet of all color. He turned around to face the house and felt an unexpected danger from it.

The house that moments before had seemed dark and peaceful had somehow been turned into an enemy. He knew what it was. Even now, it pulled him in, turning his fear into something that he thought he had buried deep in long-forgotten ground.

The house that had become a home each day seemed to change a little more. Each day grew longer, the sun warmer. Leaves covered the trees in the surrounding hills. Dane dug up the rocky soil in the backyard and Jenny planted the garden, arranging the narrow patch in neat rows of seedlings, beets, carrots, onions, string beans, lettuce, and tomatoes. He put up a two-foot-high chicken-wire fence around it, pounding down the heavy wooden stakes with a rubber mallet he found in the basement. The wolf dozed in the sun of the morning, as serene as the landscape.

He had brought her along as a buffer, someone who could smooth the way for him as she had done with the landlady. Two people living together were easier to understand. They drew less attention. People might start to wonder about a man living by himself in the hills, a hermit. Curious children might come to spy on him. But they'd leave a young couple alone, especially if the woman who owned the house spread the word in town that they were all right.

Now nothing was right. Dane crossed the yard, angling toward the garden to avoid going back inside. A light upstairs caught his eye. Jenny stood naked in her bedroom window, hands braced against the casing, and looked down at him. The light that shone behind her in the room seemed to warm the edges of her flesh like heat from a hidden sun. He couldn't see her face, only the dark golden outlines of her skin and the glow of the light as it played through her hair.

One arm fell from the side of the window and she hooked her hand on her hip. Her fingers moved and disappeared into the darkness of her thigh. Dane felt himself growing hard and he turned away, embarrassed.

Then a deep vein of anger opened up inside of him. His hands were wet with sweat and the knife slippery, the sharp metal warm and close. It was all vaguely familiar, like feeling the touch of blood for the first time.

He looked up to see her vanish from the window, her shadow like the edge of a curtain waving in the wind. For a moment the room was hot and bright, the next moment it was completely dark. Dane crossed the yard to the back door and stepped quickly through the kitchen. He felt himself being pulled toward the stairs but turned to the basement instead, unlocked the door, and standing before the dark abyss, clapped his hands twice. The black wolf, a shape solidifying out of the air, ran up the stairs to him. Dane's fingers felt for the silver whistle in his pocket.

Jenny was awake when she heard Dane open the door to her bedroom. She didn't move but kept one eye half open. He stood in the doorway and watched her and she felt frightened and excited all at once. The exhilaration drained the energy from her legs and sent it hurtling like a fist into the pit of her stomach. Her breath seemed to leave her by osmosis, passing through the pores of her skin. Then he was gone, leaving the door open behind him like an unanswered invitation.

It was like the other times recently when she caught him

looking at her. He would stare until she met his eyes, then he'd turn away. A brief glimpse was all she had ever had of him. When he let the wolf out, she stayed near the animal and felt him watching her constantly, the way Sonny used to watch her when they were in a crowd, carefully making certain that he was close enough to reach her if she tried to get away. Dane's stare unnerved her until she discovered the fear behind it, the glimmer of uncertainty that she saw in his eyes just before he dropped them. She knew why he had brought her this far; she guessed that when the woman who owned the house began to question them and Dane held back and let her talk. His fear was new. She knew the precise moment that it had started, when he brought the wolf home that night, when she told him he had blood on his face.

Jenny waited until she heard the back door open and climbed out of bed. She looked down from the window and saw him creeping along the side of the house. He held something against his leg. When he got to the corner, he lifted it and she saw the knife blade as he swung back against the wall. He's hunting something, she thought. The rest of her thoughts followed so quickly that it seemed like a revelation. Of course, she thought, that's what he does when he goes away. That was why he needed the wolf.

The wolf was his only weapon, even against her.

Jenny remembered turning on the light only after she'd seen Dane walk across the yard toward the garden. She stood in the window and watched him, knowing that he was unaware of her. The night air chilled her bare skin and pulled it taut. Finally he looked up at the window. In the light, his face looked as white as the moon. One hand caressed her hip, trying to bring some life back to her frozen skin.

Jenny looked down again and saw Dane start for the house. She left the window in one quick motion and shut her door, pushing the small end table under the knob. She was certain that he had somehow read her thoughts and that he was coming after her. Her back was against the table when she realized the light was still on. Her hand brushed the switch.

Below her, the basement door opened and she heard him call the wolf up the stairs.

That was all until she heard the back door swing open and bang against the side of the house. She rushed to the window and knelt down in front of the sill. Dane ran straight across the yard with the wolf beside him and climbed up the bluff at the treeline. The two figures disappeared instantly, like stones sinking into a black spring.

Chapter 19

~~~~~~

FOR WALKER, the funeral had been an enormous amusement. To be dragged out to Connecticut, to some ridiculous upper-class cemetery off the Merritt Parkway, to listen while a round-faced little minister—Lange turned out to be Methodist, of all things—droned on about the Kingdom of God or some such nonsense, broke up the monotony of another working day. The minister, Walker noticed, kept licking his lips all during the ceremony as if he were addressing a banquet table covered with food and not the pewter-gray bronze casket that contained the last remains of George Harold Lange.

For reasons that Walker never quite understood, the service wasn't held until nearly a full week after he read about the killing in the newspapers. He understood that there had been some problems with releasing the body, what with the bizarre circumstances surrounding his death. Being murdered by your own pet in Central Park wasn't an everyday occurrence, not even in New York.

Lange's entire firm showed up. Walker stood with most of them outside the white canvas tent reserved for the immediate family, friends, and a small handful of executives who all seemed rather pleased with Lange's early departure. His widow, on the other hand, looked bored and irritated. She sat with her long legs crossed, the hem of her black dress pulled up past her knee while her foot carved tight angry circles in the cool morning air.

She also seemed very interested in Van Owen. The hunter sat almost directly across from her on the other side of the coffin and stared impassively at the crowd on either side. For the widow, he had a small sympathetic smile. His eyes seemed to glitter when he bestowed it on her.

Walker was surprised to see Blackburn and Carroll at the funeral. They stood together just a few yards away. The lawyer had gained a little weight; the doctor looked as trim as ever. Carroll nodded his acknowledgment through the heads of the crowd. Blackburn rolled his eyes upward and waved. Walker had forgotten that the lawyer was a funny man. It was too bad they hadn't gotten together more over the past year. Just once, he thought, drinks at the society. The previous August, wasn't it? Walker couldn't remember the last time he'd been there. He'd let his membership lapse and now he was getting computer-written letters every week reminding him of it.

The minister turned to say a few words to the family. The widow looked up at him through her veil and sucked hard on one cheek. He moved down the row. A woman Walker took to be one of Lange's younger sisters—his parents were both dead—began to sob loudly. The widow stood up immediately and stepped around the minister.

She patted one corner of the coffin as if to wish its passenger good luck and walked over to where Van Owen stood. He bent his head to hear what she was saying over the sobbing and her words carried. Walker heard them quite clearly. So did everyone else.

"I could use a fucking drink," she said.

The service broke up rather quickly after that.

Blackburn approached him, with the doctor reluctantly in tow a few minutes later. Blackburn laughed and shook his hand, while Carroll smiled politely and watched the crowd. All three turned to watch Van Owen walk past with the widow on his arm. He stopped and gave them a curt snap of his head. "Gentlemen," he said quietly, and continued on his way. The widow did nothing to control her laughter.

"I hope his dick falls off," Blackburn said after the couple got into Van Owen's car, a dark brown Jaguar coupe. Walker burst out laughing. Carroll seemed distracted and stared in the direction of the far end of the cemetery, toward a series of low grassy hills. He was looking at a pair of figures who stood on the crest of one of the hills and seemed to be watching them. He'd noticed them when he first arrived and glanced at them occasionally during the service. They hadn't moved. It didn't mean anything. It just seemed odd.

Blackburn moved beside Carroll. "What are you looking at?" the lawyer asked.

"Nothing," Carroll said. But Blackburn wasn't in the mood to get brushed off twice in the same morning.

"Those two, right?" he said, and pointed. "I saw them when I came in. Big deal."

"Who?" Walker asked.

"Up there," Blackburn said, and pointed again.

It strained his eyes but he finally saw what the lawyer was pointing at.

"Oh, isn't that sweet," Walker said. "A boy and his dog."

Now it was almost a month later, the third week of June already, and Walker's memory of the funeral had faded. The summer preview issue was finished, which meant he could begin to relax; the rest of June was slow, so was July; August was a tomb. The weather had turned unexpectedly hot during midweek and Walker felt as if he were suffocating when inside. The walls of his office seemed to press ominously inward. His mind drifted during editorial meetings, snagging on odd hooks. Lange's funeral was one. It came back to him at Monday's meeting. He couldn't get over how glad he was to see Blackburn, how much fun it had been, and he wondered if there might be an article in there, something on funerals being the cocktail parties of the 1980s. The idea had definite possibilities.

After the funeral, the two of them had gone to the Oak Bar for drinks. Carroll had even joined them for awhile before he said he had to leave. It had happened when Blackburn brought up the wolf hunt. He saw the muscles along Carroll's jaw tighten, and the doctor stood up almost immediately and said that he had to get home. It was like Blackburn had whispered a magic word and the doctor was gone. Until then, Walker hadn't realized that Carroll felt that guilty about it. The odd part of it was that he and Carroll were practically neighbors. The doctor and his wife had just bought a co-op on Eighty-seventh Street, not more than four blocks from where Walker lived.

After Carroll left, Walker and Blackburn ate dinner at a steak house off Sixth and had ended up back at the Plaza for more drinks. Blackburn's personal life was in a state of flux and he was more than a bit lonely. His wife had filed for divorce and ordered him out of the house in Connecticut, and it would be at least two more weeks and probably longer before his new apartment would be finished. Until then, he was staying in a hotel. When the evening broke up, they promised to have dinner again. He'd just dropped Blackburn a note about it, in fact.

Walker was sorry now that he'd let his society membership lapse. On his desk was another computerized letter, reminding him that if he renewed his membership before the first of August, he could do it at the old rate. After August, the letter said, there would be an increase. Walker folded the letter in thirds and stuck it in his jacket pocket. He'd write the check this week.

Now that everything was in order, Walker began to think about visiting the Ramble again. The last time, nearly three weeks ago, had been a great disappointment. The place was absolutely disgusting, filled with derelicts and some malignant teenagers who seemed to have dropped in from another planet where intelligence was apparently a criminal act. Walker knew that everyone considered that part of the park dangerous but that was precisely its allure. That business with the stray dogs was cleared up after they captured a few of them. He didn't take stupid chances, and besides, it made him feel young again.

The graphic designer was long gone, along with his chairs. Walker was actually relieved when he left. He saw him occasionally but the moments were few and fleeting, a rushed hello on the street, a glance and a wave across a bar. It didn't come as a total surprise to him that the designer had taken up with a young woman this time. Anyone with money, he thought, and the gossip was that she had lots of that.

She was small and thin with a passive quality that Walker found annoying the instant he met her. He noticed a bruise the size of a quarter on her cheekbone and wondered if the designer's temper tantrums had escalated somewhat since they'd been together.

But that had been over six months ago and now the designer and his little waif were history. Summer was here. Warm weather had broken through the chill of spring. The city was alive again. He couldn't bear to go back to his apartment tonight.

It was Wednesday. Walker grabbed the cricket bat from beside his desk and stood up. Why not tonight? He gazed out his window at the evening sky, the sun a crest of muddy orange somewhere over New Jersey, and swung the bat to and fro across the toes of his shoes. Why *not* tonight?

He'd take himself out for dinner, maybe some pizza with fresh basil at that little place on Fiftieth, that would set the mood, and after that, a stroll down Forty-second and then to the park. The decision put him in a bright mood. He called the restaurant for reservations himself, and when he finally got through, his voice sounded so cheerful it was almost a chirp.

Chapter 20

IN THE CENTER of the Ramble, the city disappeared.
Dane could never quite get used to the sudden transformation
even when he returned to it the second and third time after
following the editor through it. At night the city was a distant
hum, like a faint vibration trapped underwater, the surrounding forest filled with dark crannies and treacherous pathways
that wove through the rocky hills, twisted, and fell off into
hidden crevices and muddy pools filled with debris. A stream
ran through the middle of it, full and swollen, and emptied
into ponds edged by deep crimson azaleas and then down a
long cascade into the lake.

In another spot, the path descended through a deep and
narrow gorge and underneath a high stone arch that led to a
small bridge spanning the cloudy green water of the lake.
Stepping through the arch for the first time, Dane felt a sense
of release, a feeling of absolute freedom. But it ended as he
crossed the bridge and the cars drifted past along the park's
West Drive again. He had to stop for a moment and shut his
eyes tight, squeezing out the sensations that pelted him like
sparks.

That was what it had been like trailing Walker for weeks:
days and nights of watching, discovering the man's patterns,
the streets he walked home, where he ordered his groceries,

what time he slept, learning the repetition of his life—and waiting, always waiting.

He'd taken the wolf to the man's funeral, hoping to share some of the shock of seeing all of them together for the first time. He had stayed far back in the hills where he could still see them but be too far away for them to identify the wolf and him. But there'd been no shock, only an undercurrent of recognition. He knew what they were, and standing there, he began to wonder if that was going to be enough to carry him through it. Beside him, the wolf sniffed the air, picking up the myriad smells of the crowd. Dane wondered if the wolf could smell the four men they were hunting. Of course. In the mountains, the wolves remembered dozens of smells, scents that had taken them back to game trails a year old.

One of the men, the lawyer, pointed toward him and he felt his stomach tighten and his legs tense, ready to run. But they were only curious about him and soon lost interest, filing away with the rest of the crowd toward the line of cars parked along the black asphalt road.

The wolf had not stirred, had not grown alarmed when the men pointed up at the hill. That was the difference between them. He had lost something coming here; he thought too much and it brought him nothing.

He felt himself reaching a dead end until he followed the editor into the Ramble that first time. All that first day, there had been a sudden unexplainable break in the man's routine, as though he were aiming toward some point that Dane hadn't anticipated. That night, when Dane watched him stalking through the Ramble, everything became clear, the weeks of frustration over. The man had even looked at him and smiled; Dane, not thinking at all, had smiled back.

For Walker, time ended just inside the Ramble. The editor waited until his eyes adjusted to the absence of light and, like a man entering the sanctuary of a vacuum, stepped into the black woods.

The Ramble was alive with men. They strolled about like boulevardiers. They paired off, whispered to each other, and slipped away without another sound. Walker was excited almost immediately. He watched the furtive glances, the secret gestures that bound them all together. A young boy, probably not more than fifteen, smiled shyly at him but Walker turned away and moved deeper into the Ramble, unaware of precisely what he was looking for but wanting it desperately just the same.

The wolf seemed confused and agitated by the men in the Ramble. The men thought they were moving quietly but the wolf heard each sound distinctly, the scrape of a heel on the rocks, a cry escaping between clenched fists, even the hiss of shallow breathing. The wolf's head twisted back and forth as he tried to follow each sound, his eyes wide and alert.

Dane watched as Walker followed the path across the small bridge and down toward the lake, turning off at the last moment and moving even closer to the water. Dane stayed just inside the trees, near where the small river fed into a long finger-shaped pond, and waited.

Walker stopped by the water's edge and Dane saw the silhouette of another man move next to him. Dane clapped his hands quietly and the wolf swung his head around toward the lake.

The black man was tall and narrowly built with a face like an elongated slab of black marble and eyes that caught the light from across the lake. He was sitting on the grass by himself when Walker came by, and when Walker stopped and spoke to him, the black man stood. He moved his body so carefully that it reminded Walker of someone slowly unraveling a piece of ribbon from around a package.

Beyond a few meaningless words of greeting, banalities that Walker hated even as he spoke them, they had little to say. The black man pulled the sweater he had tied over his shoulders closer to his neck and Walker asked him if he was cold.

"A little," the man said. Walker rubbed a hand up and down his back. "That's nice," the man said, and touched Walker's hair. Without another word, they walked off together in the direction of the trees at the edge of the Ramble.

Dane lost sight of the wolf and the two men. They disappeared in the trees up ahead of him, like shadows melting into shadows. He ignored his first feelings of panic and moved forward, knowing that they had to be somewhere just beyond the range of his vision.

The ground was fairly level until just past the treeline, where an outcropping of rock blocked his way. He climbed around it, until he could finally see where the two men had gone. His hands caressed the rough surface of the rocks.

He could leave now, he thought. The idea was so compelling that he stopped completely, his hands frozen in place on the rocks. If he left the wolf now, this instant, he could be safe with Jenny. He seemed to choke on her name. He already knew the answer. The wolf had become his only connection to her. Without the wolf, there would be no link between them, nothing to hold her to him. In his mind, he saw himself falling without hope of ever coming to rest. Was that what he wanted?

His hands released the rocks and he moved forward through the trees. From where he stood, he could see the two men. They were directly ahead of him, no more than thirty feet away. One stood with his back braced against a tree while the other knelt in front of him, head moving slowly, hands holding on to his waist.

Dane looked to the left and saw the wolf approach slowly along the treeline. He clapped his hands as a warning. The two men turned toward the noise as the wolf broke into a run. They had time enough to see the animal hurtle through the air. The black man screamed, a high-pitched shriek, and shoved Walker away from him. Walker tried to stand but his foot twisted and he stumbled backward. The wolf struck him hard in the chest and they rolled toward the lake.

They broke apart. Dane could see them outlined against the shimmering water of the lake, and he trembled as he watched, fascinated by what he could no longer control.

The wolf moved back, shoulder muscles rippling, jaws distended, and then struck at the man, again and again. Walker tried to escape but each time his hands slipped on the blood-slicked ground beneath him. He made one final attempt to stand. He got as far as his knees before the wolf pulled him down for the last time.

The black man ran without looking back. At first he ran

directly toward the lake but then turned south at the edge of the water toward the bow bridge. He ran with an almost comic intensity, his long legs pumping higher and higher. He screamed as he ran, the sounds escaping in little squeals, like air leaking from a balloon.

When Dane finally emerged from the trees, the wolf was waiting for him, just as he somehow knew the animal would be, sitting beside the body, guarding the kill against all intruders except Dane. Up close, the smell of the blood was very strong. The wolf bent down and licked at the wet grass next to the body.

Dane clapped his hands. The wolf looked up, confused by the new sound, and edged closer to the dead man. Dane clapped once more, slamming his hands together hard. This time the wolf obeyed. But there was a second of hesitation, as if the wolf had been waiting for someone else.

He could hardly look at the body. The sight of it only seemed to mystify him. He stood back, wondering how he had lost so much control in so short a time.

It was Jenny, he thought. Her power over the wolf had extended this far. She was taking away what was his and leaving him with nothing.

The thought seemed to burn across his vision, twisting what he saw into mad unrecognizable shapes. He felt betrayed by everything, even his own eyes.

Chapter 21

ATWOOD NEVER REMEMBERED his dreams and that suited him just fine. His waking life was interesting enough. In the mornings, his mind was empty. He thought it was a perfect way to start the day. Whatever was missing, he never could quite imagine. When the phone woke him at eleven-thirty, it had the effect of yanking him fully awake out of a complete void. He was sprawled in one of the living-room chairs, legs splayed awkwardly in front of him, arms dangling loose over the sides. He'd forgotten to go to bed again.

He lurched out of the chair and into the kitchen and pulled the phone from its cradle. The unfamiliar voice was very matter-of-fact. The message sounded well rehearsed.

There was a new body in Central Park.

Could he come down and take a look?

Yates felt his control over the case slipping away from him and thought there wasn't much he could do about it. It was the very nature of things. There was a word for it but he couldn't remember what it was.

"And it's all your fault," he said to the dead man. The body was zipped into a body bag with only the face left exposed. The dead man's features had settled into a look of confusion and surprise, as if he didn't quite understand the detective's accusation.

Yates unzipped the bag and examined the rest of the body. The worst wounds were on neck and chest, and the front of the body was covered with fresh blood. They were lucky to get his wallet out before it was soaked through completely. He looked at the end of the man's right arm. The wrist was nearly severed. The hand hung on by a thin piece of tendon. One of the attendants had stuck the hand in a clear plastic bag and taped it to the rest of the arm. Yates made him do it so the hand wouldn't fall off and get lost.

The attendant didn't seem to care one way or the other about the hand. He found a plastic bag in the ambulance and wrapped it up. It reminded Yates of a piece of vouchered evidence. He examined it closely. Tucked inside the plastic, the hand looked just like a woman's white linen glove.

He shut the bag, covering up Benjamin Walker's face. It would have to be a well-known magazine editor, one more sign that things were out of his control. He would have been happy with anyone else, with the possible exception of the mayor or a nun.

"How big?" the black man asked Atwood. "It was *real* big. I've never been so scared in my entire life."

Atwood sat next to the man in the backseat of one of the unmarked police cars and tried to take notes.

"I know," Atwood said. "Can you remember anything else?"

"Isn't that enough?"

"What color was it?"

"Black," the man said. He took out a cigarette and lit it. Even though both doors were open, smoke filled the car. "It was big and black and it killed that man." He was very serious when he said it.

Atwood didn't respond but it sounded like the punch line to a joke to him. He looked the other way and saw Yates watching them.

"I need a better description than that," Atwood said.

"I don't know what else to tell you," the man said, and stared off into space. He sounded tired. "I just want to go home."

Atwood scribbled some wavy lines across the top of the page.

"All right, all right," the man said, and pointed at the open notebook. "It looked like a dog, a great big dog." Atwood held the pen still on the page. "Aren't you going to write that down?"

"What kind of dog?"

"How should I know? You're supposed to be the expert."

"Like a German shepherd?" Atwood said. "Something like that?"

The black man closed his eyes.

"It looked like a shepherd," he said, and opened his eyes wide. They were badly bloodshot, the whites riddled with tiny red veins. "But it was bigger than that," the black man said. "A lot bigger."

It took Yates about ten minutes once he got to the scene to realize that he was just going through the motions. After he was finished with his master sheet, he'd turn it over to the sergeant. The sergeant would give it to the captain and the captain would give it to the deputy commissioner and the deputy commissioner would call in the head of the Manhattan North task force and tell him not to buy that retirement condo in Pensacola just yet.

A killer dog running loose in the park was strange enough to warrant dumping the whole thing in their laps. That was their job. And they wouldn't do any better than the rest of us, Yates thought. They'd end up nailing some matron's poodle to the deck and that would turn every reporter in town sideways. The press was going to go completely batshit over this one. They were practically out of control already, an angry mob strung out behind the barricade, yelling questions, shooting pictures of anything that moved. Yates had seen them like this before. They were getting ready to lynch somebody.

All because some goddamn magazine editor wanted to get his jollies in the park. Everybody was looking to get into trouble these days. Yates just wished they wouldn't waste his time unless they were really serious about finding it.

Entropy, Yates thought, that was the word. He was fighting entropy all the way. He would keep his head down and move ahead, that was the best he could do.

Atwood was finished with the witness. The man looked a mess but that wasn't any of his business. No comment required. No additional statements, thank you very much. Cooperation, he had been told, was the key to a successful investigation. Two uniformed officers came to pick up the body and Yates told them to leave it for a few minutes.

"What'd you find out, Doc?" Yates asked when Atwood approached him.

Atwood stared at the body bag and shrugged. "He said it was bigger than a German shepherd."

"What else?"

"That's about it," Atwood said, and stepped around the end of the bag.

"Any ideas about how we're going to catch it?"

"I'm not sure we are," Atwood answered vaguely. He kept staring at the body; he wanted it to sit up and tell him where to look.

"What the hell's wrong with you?" Yates asked. His voice was low but it got Atwood's attention.

"Nothing's wrong with me," Atwood said. "I'm wildly enthusiastic about what I'm doing. I'm licensed by the city." There was a genuine gleam in his eyes.

Yates motioned for the officers to take the body away.

"Wait a minute," Atwood said, but it was too late. They picked up the bag and carried it toward the ambulance. There was an explosion of television lights from behind the barricades. The mob of reporters followed them, falling over themselves to get to the ambulance.

Yates looked at his hands. In the harsh light they were white and bloodless, just like the dead man's. "I want to ride with them," he heard Atwood say. The screaming from behind the barricades made it hard to hear. The veterinarian pointed to the ambulance.

"What for?"

"I want to look at the body," Atwood said. He was serious now, trying to make a good impression on Yates.

They were closing the ambulance doors, trying to clear a path so they could get through the mob.

"You already saw it," Yates said.

Atwood shook his head. It was a nervous little gesture. "I want to *examine* it," he said.

He knows something, Yates suddenly realized. The whole idea seemed implausible.

The ambulance started to pull out but the crowd stopped it before it could move more than a few feet.

"Go on," Yates told him, and Atwood sprinted toward the ambulance, yelling for them to wait. The driver looked at Atwood and then at Yates. The detective waved his approval, an act of generosity that cost him nothing.

To his surprise, Atwood waved back. He looked very happy, climbing into the back of the ambulance, like a schoolboy setting out on some new adventure. What sort of secrets could a schoolboy have?

It was cold and noisy in back. The air conditioner roared and the reporters banged on the door demanding to be let inside for a look at the dead man. Atwood braced himself in one corner while they rocked slowly through the crowd. The driver kept his window up and yelled at them through the glass. The reporters yelled right back.

The nurse sat stiff and silent in the passenger seat. She stared straight ahead, even when a photographer angrily slammed his hand against the window and left a huge greasy palm print in the middle of the glass. They made it through the crowd and bounced around the edge of the lake in the direction of the boathouse. The driver smiled at the nurse. He was small, muscular and inordinately cheerful.

"You all right?"

"I'm fine," she said. Her voice was almost a whisper.

"You sure?"

"Yes," she said. Then, quietly amazed, she said, "I've never seen people act like that before."

"They're creeps and assholes," the driver said. "If they were real people, they'd be cabdrivers or something like that." He swung his head around. "So who are you?" he asked Atwood.

Atwood took out his wallet and showed the driver his shield.

The driver shrugged and twisted the wheel hard to the left to avoid hitting something.

"Could you turn the air conditioning down?" Atwood asked.

"Sure," the driver said, and turned off the fan. "My passengers are usually in no condition to complain."

"I'm going to take a look at him."

"Be my guest," the driver said. "You're the only one in here with a badge."

"Do you need any help?" the nurse asked politely.

"Maybe," Atwood said. "How are you at zippers?" The nurse smiled. He loosened the straps that held the body on the cart. When the straps were off, he unzipped the bag and pulled it open.

He was startled by Walker's face. Except for the ashen color of his skin, he looked like a man who had just dozed off. His shirt and jacket were stiff with blood, and Atwood had to press them back to make them stay in place so he could examine the wounds. He peeled away one side of Walker's shirt. Pieces of the material stuck to his fingers. He stared at the gaping bites in the man's chest, at the half-dozen places where pieces of flesh the size of his fist had been torn out, and immediately closed the man's shirt. He didn't have to see any more. The answers were there in front of him.

He straightened up the man's shirt, feeling a little odd suddenly to be dressing a corpse. He closed the jacket quickly and pulled it tight. When he did, he felt something hard and small right near the hem. He opened the coat and searched through the bloody lining. A piece of paper, folded several times and soaked completely through with blood, was stuck in one of the smaller pockets. Atwood slid two fingers into the pocket and pulled the paper out. Some of it stuck to the lining and peeled away from his fingers like layers of skin.

He unfolded what was left of it carefully. There were white confetti patterns across the top of the page where the blood hadn't soaked through. He laid it open on the body bag. It was an ordinary form letter except for a partially obscured insignia on the bottom of the page. With his finger, he wiped away some of the blood and smeared it on his pants, leaving a rust-colored stain. The insignia now appeared to be a drawing of the earth resting on the arched backs of two lions. Beneath the insignia, in lettering so clear even the blood couldn't obscure them, were the words THE NEW YORK SPORTSMAN'S SOCIETY.

"You looked at this on the way over?" the pathologist asked Atwood. It was sometime after three o'clock in the morning. Atwood didn't know the time exactly because when he'd looked at his watch, it was stopped. It must have broken during the day and he hadn't noticed it.

He sat on a metal folding chair behind and to the left of the pathologist, which gave him an eye-level view of the corpse, making it a ridiculous kind of landscape; the knees became foothills, the head and face a mountain crest, the pubic hair underbrush on a snow-white plain.

"Felt compelled," Atwood said to Tieneman. The pathologist continued weighing the dead man's organs. They had gotten him out of bed for the autopsy but he didn't mind. He didn't mind Atwood being there ahead of him, either; he just didn't know quite what to do with him.

"What do you mean, compelled?" Tieneman asked when he finished with the weighing. He stopped for a minute to exercise his fingers, flexing them over the open chest cavity, glancing at the wounds along the man's neck and all the way down his right side. The wounds were worse than the last one. He didn't think it was possible but there it was, right in front of him.

"Because of the way it was described to me," Atwood said.

Tieneman released the retractors and closed the flaps of skin.

"Oh?" Tieneman said. "And how was that?"

Atwood stood and looked down at the man. An aerial view, he thought. Under the lights, the man seemed shriveled, all except for his face, which retained its unexpected calm. Atwood marveled at it. The pathologist seemed to read his mind.

"They look that way sometimes," he said. "Like they're asleep. It's the adrenaline. It stimulates the blood vessels near the skin, smooths it right out." Tieneman ran his hand over the surface of the man's arm. "How *did* they describe this?" he asked.

"Not *this*," Atwood said. "The animal that did it. There was a witness this time."

Tieneman raised his eyebrows but said nothing and began his examination of the neck wounds. Even though they were the only ones in the room, all of the overhead lights were on as if they expected visitors at any moment. The empty metal tables with their burnished steel tops looked almost inviting, like hotel beds waiting to be filled.

"Do you *know* what did this?" he asked.

"I don't know for sure," Atwood said.

"What do you *think* did it?"

"A wolf," Atwood said. "The way the man described it to me, that's the only thing it could be."

Tieneman returned to the body. His hands peeled back the torn flesh and slipped inside one of the wounds.

"You figured it out just on the description?" he asked.

"Not entirely," Atwood said. "There were the wounds. I've never seen dog bites like that."

"You've seen enough bites to be sure?" Tieneman asked. He felt around the interior of it with his fingers, trying to measure the destruction underneath. It felt enormous.

"Yup," Atwood said. "Millions."

Tieneman removed his hand. "A wolf," he said, and looked down at the body. "I guess that would do it."

Atwood felt relieved.

Now what the hell was he going to do?

Atwood's family were working poor. His mother worked behind the lunch counter at Woolworth's while his father picked up odd jobs in the neighborhood. He was the man the neighbors called when the washer needed fixing for the fifth time or a bathroom needed quick painting. It was an honorable and necessary trade.

When he was nine, his father brought home a dog from the pound, a mongrel he named Dollar because that's how much it cost his father to get him released. A few months later, when the dog became sick, they took him to a local veterinarian. The doctor examined Dollar and told them the dog had distemper and would have to be quarantined for what was then very expensive treatment. His father agreed to pay for it a little bit each week until Dollar was cured.

There was an old black janitor who swept out the kennel. Atwood would see him every time they went to pay on the bill. He would stand outside the wire fence by the kennel, hoping to hear Dollar's bark. The black man would nod a friendly greeting at Atwood each time, as if to say that even though he couldn't see inside, everything was okay.

One day they came to pay but instead of going inside with his father, Atwood went straight out back. The black man was down on his knees, pulling up weeds alongside the fence.

"You got a dog in here?" he asked, and the question took Atwood by surprise. He thought the man knew.

"Yes, sir," Atwood said, and described the dog. "His name is Dollar," he said.

"Your daddy's been payin' on his bill, hasn't he?"

Atwood nodded and for no other reason except the look in the man's eyes began to feel afraid.

"That dog is dead," the black man said. "I buried him myself not more'n a week after you brought him in."

Atwood backed away from the fence and walked home alone. His father must have found out because by the time he got home, he was sitting on the front steps, waiting to tell Atwood he was sorry that he couldn't save his dog.

Atwood made up his mind then what he wanted to do with his life. He wanted to save things.

It was still dark when he got home from the autopsy. He sat in his apartment and fingered the piece of paper he'd taken from Walker's coat and kept without telling anyone. The parrot perched on his shoulder and cooed in his ear. Atwood knew exactly what he was going to do.

He was going to start with the wolves.

Chapter 22

THE WOLVES RAN toward him in the bright moonlight across the snow. Behind them, beyond the frozen lake and high above the thick line of trees, the aurora rippled across the sky in vibrant streaks of yellow and green. The wolves were chasing something, he could see the tracks in the snow. The light made it hard to see but it was probably a deer, weak from hunger and exhaustion and sluggish in the heavy crusted snow. It could have been a man, Atwood thought. The same rules applied.

"Are you Michael Atwood?" a voice behind him asked. It was a woman's voice but coarse, one that had been scratched and scarred over the years from too many cigarettes, too much talk.

When Atwood turned around to greet her, he saw how short she was and automatically dropped his gaze. She smiled at him, a pretty feminine smile at odds with her rough masculine voice. The smile was gone as quickly as it appeared, a throwaway gesture. She held out her hand to him.

"Dr. Hendricks?" Atwood asked, and reached down to grasp her small hand.

She nodded toward the exhibit directly behind him. "Is this what you came for?" she asked. "The wolves?"

Dr. Hendricks stepped around him and stood closer to the glass. They were in the middle of a long hallway lined with other exhibits, part of the North American Mammals section of the Museum of Natural History, one of the smaller first-floor displays in the museum. She was fifty-one years old, a trained field biologist who no longer felt at home there and spent all of her energy watching over the museum's massive collection of exhibits. She knew the mammal exhibits best. They were the ones she felt most affectionate about and she found herself returning to them again and again.

"They look so intelligent," she said. "Even with glass eyes." She pointed down into the exhibit at the tracks behind the two wolves.

"Wolves gallop," she said. "I don't suppose you took the time to read the descriptions?"

Atwood shook his head. It was like the beginning of a lecture.

"I didn't think so." She cleared her throat. "When they run, they place both hind legs between their front legs, so the first prints you see are always the rear feet." She pushed her hands forward against the glass. "There is a moment when they are completely free of the ground. They actually fly, you see."

While she spoke, a small crowd gathered behind her to listen. They caught her by surprise and she gave them a sharp smile and an even sharper nod of the head, gestures that to Atwood seemed to be careful impersonations of human behavior, skilled reproductions, like everything else around them.

She led him back toward the main display area. As they passed silently through the exhibits, he saw that almost all of the animals were staged in some kind of predatory activity and he wondered why he hadn't noticed it before. They sat down on a bench in front of the grizzly exhibit. The female grizzly was tearing apart a rotten log looking for ants and grubs. There was the obligatory cub up a tree.

"It's always been much too cute for my taste," Dr. Hendricks said. "Everyone else seems to love it."

"I had a teddy bear that looked just like that one," Atwood said, and pointed at the female grizzly.

"You must have had a very bizarre upbringing," she said.

"Reasonably so," Atwood said.

She looked at him closely. His skin was pale white, his eyes bright and impish. He looked a little feverish to her.

"Are you all right?" she asked.

"Everybody asks me that," he said. "I should pin a happy face to my forehead, save them all the trouble." He smiled at her. "Trust me," he said. "I'm at the very top of my form. I need to know about wolves."

"So you can find the one they say is loose in the park?"

"So I can save it," he said.

She was going to ask from what but the look on his face was so beatific that she stopped herself.

"Why don't we go down to the restaurant," she said, feeling as if she had to protect him suddenly; the feeling unnerved her. "You can buy me some coffee and I'll try and tell you what you want to know about wolves."

They sat at one of the small tables in the center of the museum restaurant. Above them hung a life-size model of a blue whale. The room was dominated more by the whale's rich hues than by its enormous size. The air seemed contaminated with it.

At first their talk was general and she spoke to him in the familiar tones of a tutor repeating a well-rehearsed, if slightly dull, lecture. When she finished, he realized nothing she said would help him. He could have learned as much from a book, he thought. Maybe if he tried leading her in the right direction, she might come up with something that could help him.

Everything he believed was built on a handful of facts; he was like an anthropologist, reconstructing an entire human skeleton out of some tiny fragments of jawbone. First, after several weeks of searching, the police had found no trace of a wolf—or even a large dog, if he wanted to hedge his theory a bit, which he did not; no dog could have inflicted those wounds, the autopsy convinced him of that—in the park. To Atwood, that meant only one thing. The wolf wasn't in the park *except* when he was brought there to kill. Second, the fact that two members of the same club were killed within weeks of each other was too glaring a coincidence to ignore. He decided that it wasn't a coincidence at all. It was deliberate. That meant that someone was controlling the wolf.

There was no way around it. Someone had used the wolf to kill two people.

He told her nearly all of this, keeping only the relationship between Walker and Lange to himself, and waited for her judgment. There was nothing else to present to her, only the certainty of his feeling. He felt like a student waiting for his semester grade.

"I think you're looking for something that isn't there," she said but with a quick smile. "I could be wrong, of course." She smiled again. "You obviously believe it, don't you?"

"Is it possible?" Atwood asked.

"Anything is possible," she said. "But I can't verify whether what you've said is true or not. You understand that?" She paused as if uncertain of what to say next. "It's possible but that's not quite the same thing, is it? I don't have the same kind of feeling for it that you do, obviously. I couldn't. I wasn't there."

"You think I'm crazy?"

"Is that what you really want to know?"

"Probably," Atwood said. He was running in a circle and about to bang into himself.

"I don't think you're crazy," she said. Perhaps a little mystical, she thought, but quickly changed the subject, suddenly afraid of taking it any further. "Let's assume for a moment that you're right, that someone has trained this wolf to kill for him. Do you have a motive?"

"No," he said.

"Do you think there are going to be more killings?"

"Yes," Atwood said, facing the possibility for the first time. "I don't *know* how I know that." For the first time, he sounded angry when he spoke. It surprised and frightened her.

"It doesn't matter," she said, almost to herself. "You believe it." Once again she had the urge to lead him to safety. It lasted only a few seconds, and when it was over, she was astonished by how close she had come to accepting his story.

How utterly fantastic it all was, she thought, the sheer force of his fantasy. He had tried to engulf her in his own delusions and nearly succeeded. She moved back in her chair as if the extra distance would protect her from him somehow.

She had never thought of saving anyone in her life and, she realized now, it was the one thing Atwood wanted. Why hadn't she seen that in him, the crusader waiting in the wings? She felt the museum, its cold and weary hallways, its dry dusty exhibits, its appearance of life, pull her back into its careful symmetry. He had nearly taken it from her, just as others had tried. A new crispness crept into her voice. At first Atwood didn't seem to notice.

"Have you told the police your ideas?" she asked. "I think you ought to, you know. You work for the city. They'd have to consider your theory seriously, wouldn't they?"

Atwood shook his head, the change in her voice registering at last.

"Well," she said. "I really have to be going. I hope I've been able to help you." Dr. Hendricks straightened herself up, ready to leave. She wiped her hands lightly on the napkin and replaced it, neatly folded, beside her empty glass. As he helped her from her chair, she smiled quickly. Her smile wasn't directed at him, he realized, but at one of the exhibits on the other side of the room.

Class dismissed, he thought.

Atwood returned to his office and sat around feeling useless for nearly half an hour before calling the Sportman's Society. The woman who spoke to him was cheerful and polite and wouldn't tell him anything when he asked about Lange and Walker. Any questions regarding their membership would have to go through the president, a man named Van Owen.

"Is he around?" Atwood asked.

"I'm sorry," she said cheerfully. "But he'll be out of the office for the next few days. I can have him call you when he gets back."

After several minutes of wrangling, he finally got her to reveal the man's location. He was staying at the society's private lodge, about two hours out of the city. Atwood tried calling the phone number she'd given him. No one answered.

He gave up and went next door to talk to Peterson, one of

the other veterinarians. Peterson was overweight and cynical, a department veteran who had been there longer than anyone else, even the director. He drank diet soda and smoked herbed cigarettes and his whole office smelled like rotten cabbage. When Atwood asked him about the society, Peterson responded with surprising vigor.

"Stay away from them," Peterson said. "They know too many people."

"Name six," Atwood said.

"I don't *know* six people," Peterson said. "All I do know is when I point a finger in their direction, I get it chopped off."

Atwood was surprised. Peterson seemed genuinely upset.

"What was the complaint?" he asked.

Peterson frowned. "They were having one of those game dinners," he said. "Zebra steaks, that sort of thing. Someone said that they were also serving a few endangered species on their menu. I was told to leave it alone."

"Who told you that?"

"The powers that be," Peterson said. "Who else?" He threw his hands in the air dramatically, then laid them nervously on the desktop. He's avoiding something, Atwood thought. All that motion for such a minor insult. That wasn't like Peterson.

"That doesn't seem like much," Atwood said blandly.

Peterson lit a cigarette and blew the smoke in Atwood's direction. "I was also threatened," he snapped.

"You were what?"

Peterson glared at him. "You heard me," he said.

"I heard you," Atwood said. "I just find it a little bizarre. Who would threaten you?"

"Have you met their president?" Peterson asked.

"Van Owen?" Atwood said. "Not yet. I've been trying to reach him."

"Forget it," Peterson said, and blew more smoke at him. He seemed to be pushing Atwood out of the room. "Stay away from him."

"Did *he* threaten you?"

"He said he was going to cut my head off," Peterson said. There was real fear in his voice.

"He did what?" Atwood asked. He definitely wanted to hear more about this one.

Peterson only stared at him. "Read my lips," he said, and refused to say any more about it. Atwood left. He loved being warned off something. It gave him the perfect excuse to charge ahead.

That same day, Van Owen left the city early to spend a few days at the lodge, to get away from the business and the stack of messages on his desk. At the lodge, there'd be time to get himself ready for what he knew was coming. Blackburn knew it, too. In the last few days, the calls from the lawyer had become frantic. Nothing, of course, from the good doctor, not a twinge of fear or curiosity. He wondered if Carroll even realized that he was standing in a very short line.

They were being hunted. Van Owen knew it. From the moment he'd seen Walker's face on television, he knew it. He should have been aware of it before this, that was his only mistake. The announcement by the medical examiner that a wolf, or "wolflike animal," was responsible for Walker's death and that there was evidence linking the animal to the death of George Lange, seemed familiar, like a vague memory pulled suddenly into focus. He began to laugh, loud, violent laughter that he could feel twisting out of his control. Without much of a struggle, he let it go.

He expected the police to ask him about the Walker killing, but to his surprise, no one did. He thought it was odd until he checked the records and found that the editor's membership had lapsed several months before and he hadn't renewed it.

But what surprised him the most that day was the appearance of Michael Atwood.

Van Owen crossed the Tappan Zee Bridge. It was a cool morning, a little chilly for late June. The bridge was still shrouded in a fog that hung high over the water and drifted across the roadway in front of him. He continued north on the thruway until it crossed the expressway at Bear Mountain and drove west into the Shawangunk Mountains. There were few cars on the road and he drove undisturbed through a landscape littered with billboards for the Catskill resorts. An hour later he turned off onto a two-lane county road and drove another twenty minutes or so to the entrance of a long dirt road, marked by a small wooden sign, that led to the society's lodge and private hunting preserve.

He kept a room for himself in the back of the lodge, a small windowless box with a bed and an old knotty-pine dresser and small oval mirror hung on the wall above it. When he pulled into the stone-covered parking lot beside the lodge, a huge log mansion built to Adirondack proportions, his mind was focused on that solitary cell; it was the only place that could hold him now.

No one was there to greet him. The main building was deserted. With no new group expected for at least a week, it would remain that way for several more days. Karl, the lodge's burly manager, had his own four-room apartment over the garage and kept pretty much to himself. With the club's growing prosperity, they had added a more elaborate security system around the lodge and the new hunting preserve. It kept out trespassers and lowered their insurance premiums by nearly sixteen percent. The security guards and the rest of the staff lived off the property, commuting to the lodge from the small mountain towns scattered throughout the area.

He carried two pieces of luggage, a khaki duffel that he slung over one shoulder as he stepped from the car and a large black metal case. The air was clean and filled with a dry sweetness, like an autumn field rich with hay. His boots crackled on the white stones. The colors of the surrounding forest, from bright green to solemn gray, glistened in the midmorning warmth. A stream of sparrows soared overhead and dove into the safety of a hedgerow of chokecherry trees that formed a border across one side of the lot.

Van Owen walked toward the front of the building and the wide porch with the heavy wooden railing that stretched the length of the entire building. The high overhanging roof blocked out the sun during most of the day and left the entrance in deep shade except for very late in the afternoon, just when it touched the tops of the distant trees and made the front windows shimmer with streaks of red and orange. At that hour of the morning, the entrance looked closed and dark as though the building itself were still asleep.

He climbed the front steps, broad descending curves of dark red oak, each step supported by squat columns of pointed stone on either side. The sky above the building was clear and blue, but the chill of early morning clung to him like smoke. He shook it off and continued up the steps into the lodge.

He crossed the enormous main room, striding over the heavy rugs that covered the wooden floor with their medieval tapestry illustrations, lords and ladies in formal dress, stag hunting behind a brace of hounds. On the walls were other hunting scenes: men on horseback in red and green waistcoats; elephants on the African veldt, tusks thrust skyward while they stumbled and died; seas of buffalo, antelope, and elk, huge canvases that dominated the room with their dark violent colors and separated it from the real world with their somber antiquity.

Van Owen detested the room and felt the urge to destroy it, to rip through its ornamental veneer. Even this morning, when his mind was far away, he could feel it like a vague twinge in a muscle that had never been used. He opened the door to the first-floor rooms. The hallway was dim and the air smelled stale. He turned left into a shorter hall, darker than the first. At the end of it, like the last stop on a seldom-used railway spur, he unlocked the door to his room. Van Owen set his bags down inside and let the silent darkness surround him.

He moved around the unlit room by memory, feeling his way toward the open space at the end of the bed where he stood and waited for it to come again, like it had come that last day in Bangkok.

Van Owen could see the girl again as she knelt at his feet. He stood by the bed and remembered. The smell of smoke, as soft as a breath, whispered past his cheek.

She was telling him a story, how her family had been killed by the Ar'rang, a spirit of great evil that lived in the jungles close to her village. The Ar'rang was a grotesque dwarf with an enormous misshapen head and arms like huge black wings that beckoned to the villagers at night. The dwarf would call to them in a delightful feminine voice, promising whatever they wished for most: riches, sexual favors, power. The Ar'rang's breath was scented like incense, a deep smoky musk that filled the jungle with its seductive odor. If they responded to the dwarf's call, those huge black arms would pull them to their death, for that misshapen head contained a huge ravenous mouth full of sharp white teeth.

As Diap told him the story, she trembled in fear. She believed in the Ar'rang, just as she believed in the other ghosts and spirits. They were as real to her as the river, as real as Van Owen, who felt a bit of warm-scented air pass his lips, the smoky flavor that lingered on his tongue, just as it had that night in the jungle when he had massacred her family.

From the first moment Van Owen had seen her in Bangkok, he had become obsessed with having her. Her father, the head of one of the seven opium families in the country, dismissed him with a curt wave of his hand; he was just another round eye, a bit of white-skinned malignancy, not to be taken seriously. His obsession grew like a dark embryo inside of him. When the family moved to their summer home in the mountains, he followed them.

For two months, he lived and hunted in the jungle near the village. He grew more and more reckless, slipping easily past the guard dogs into the family compound at night, as invisible as any spirit. Inside the house, he would stand over Diap's bed and watch her sleep. She was like a magnet, drawing him farther and farther away from himself. He would wake up at night in the jungle, erect, his body covered with sweat, and dream of her face next to his, her eyes locked into his own. He killed several of the dogs and dragged their bodies back into the jungle for food.

When he seemed dangerously close to losing himself completely, he killed two local farmers and mutilated their bodies. Stories of the Ar'rang began to spread through the village. It was expected that Diap's father would offer payment to rid the village of the evil spirit. To show his lack of fear, he took his family to a private shrine in the jungle several hundred yards from the village, near the fields where the red poppies grew.

It was a night of rain, all sound washed away in the

downpour. As they marched back along the path, he slipped out of the jungle and struck Diap across the head and carried her to the shrine. When he finished with the rest, he left a trail of hacked and dismembered bodies all the way to the edge of the village. Even now he could hardly remember what had happened except that when he finally went back for her, he found the heads of the family on the stones in front of the shrine, eyes open, staring blankly into his. He couldn't remember putting them there. When Diap awoke, he spoke one word to her, Ar'rang, and she cried out in fear. She went with him obediently, his property now, to do with as he chose.

Months later, they were in Bangkok. He sat in the large wicker chair with a high back and arms that cradled his own in their deep curves. The folds of his black silk robe fell open at his chest and knees. He saw that he had grown erect.

Diap stood up and presented herself to him. She was naked, her brown skin like satin, tiny adolescent breasts, nipples the color of dark wine. He reached out and cupped one hand over her public bone. His fingers slipped between her legs and he watched her move slightly higher on her toes to spread herself open to him. Her eyes fluttered and rolled back. He kept his secret until the last.

"I killed them," he whispered to her, and her eyes flew open.

With his other hand, Van Owen brought the small bone knife out of his sleeve and slit her throat, holding her body upright against his with his silken arms, which must have looked to her like huge black wings as the blade, so white, so sharp, cut deeper and deeper. The light faded from her eyes. His orgasm was swift and sudden, a point of pleasure as sharp and perfect as the blade. He looked at himself and saw the colors, red, black and more, a slippery white swirl that hung between them like tiny strings of pearl.

In the back room of the lodge, Van Owen awoke from the memory cleansed and alert, a man at the start of a long journey. He switched on the lamp by the dresser, opened the black case, and began to assemble what was inside.

* * *

By early afternoon, the day had become swelteringly hot, an almost tropical heat that seeped through even the shaded areas of the preserve grounds surrounding the lodge. The change was unexpected and Van Owen emerged from the preserve drenched with sweat. He'd spent the better part of the morning and early afternoon walking through the grounds of the preserve, covering it carefully, talking to the guards who were on day duty, finding the hidden places he had forgotten, and memorizing their contours and locations.

The path from the lodge to the preserve entrance was broad and straight and carefully maintained. The edges were trimmed with wildflowers and white birch logs that had to be replaced each season and gave it something of the look of a formal garden path.

A narrow porch with steps at each end ran across the back of the lodge and was used mainly by the staff after late summer dinners when the members had finished eating and were all busy in the main room drinking and telling lies to one another.

Van Owen came up the path and saw a tall thin man standing by the porch. In the sunlight he seemed pale and indistinct, a kind of human mirage, as if the light had eaten away all his sharp edges. But closer up he saw that the man's eyes were bright with expectation, and even before he introduced himself, Van Owen knew it was Michael Atwood. He had been insistent over the phone and Van Owen had put him off. Now he had shown up here and Van Owen suddenly understood the reason for his insistence. Michael Atwood looked like a man who had finally discovered his great purpose in life.

Whatever it was, he seemed reluctant at first to share it with Van Owen. After he introduced himself, all he could seem to manage was a curious stare.

"They said you might be here," Atwood said eventually. "I took a chance."

"You do that a lot?" Van Owen asked.

"What?"

"Take chances," Van Owen said. He peeled off his shirt and hung it over the porch railing. Atwood stared at his bare flesh, at the scar tissue that covered his shoulders and arms. He had the feeling he was staring at a relief map, a topographical representation of the man's life.

"Not as much as I'd like to," Atwood said.

"Then this must be a real special occasion for you," Van Owen said. He gazed across the property toward a small path that led to the other side of the woods. Atwood might prove to be useful, he thought, if only for comic relief.

"I have some information about the two men who were killed in Central Park," Atwood said. "I know they were both members here." He waited for Van Owen's reply but the man seemed to be ignoring him. "Are you listening to me?"

"Oh, I'm listening," he said. "I'm just curious why anyone would drive two hours out of his way to tell me something I already know." Van Owen did not look around. "You must think I'm dull." He sounded greatly disappointed.

Atwood shook his head. "Someone had those men killed," he said. "He used a wolf to do it."

"Is that what the police think? Or is this your own peculiar theory?"

"They don't know that Walker was a member here," Atwood said. "I haven't told them yet."

"You *are* taking chances," Van Owen said. "And the part about the wolf?"

"I thought you might know something about that," Atwood said. He tried to make the words sound casual but they came out like an accusation.

Van Owen turned around. He spoke in a low voice and Atwood had to bend down to hear. "Is this some sort of personal crusade you're on today?"

"It's not a crusade," Atwood said.

"But it is, isn't it?" Van Owen said. "It's like a sickness. I can smell it on you." He sniffed the air contemptuously. "Or is that just the stink of fear?"

"Maybe it's my cologne," Atwood said.

He was suddenly aware that Van Owen was standing no more than a few inches in front of him and it surprised him that he hadn't seen him move, only that the hunter was there and he was staring straight into his eyes. They were as glassy and impenetrable as the surface of a northern sea and they forced Atwood back against the porch. He felt the wood bite into his spine.

"You're a bigger fool then I thought," Van Owen said.

Atwood wanted to push him away but he was trapped against the porch and couldn't move. Van Owen studied him closely. The hunter's eyes seemed to open up, and when Atwood looked into them, he could see the emptiness there. For just a moment, he believed he was looking into the eyes of a corpse. Then the feeling passed and Van Owen stepped back and grinned.

"I'll bet you're a slow learner, too," he said.

Atwood didn't answer. Van Owen turned and walked toward the small path into the woods. The only thing Atwood could do was follow.

He lost him on the path and then found him again, standing behind a row of small wooden tables, lined up across an open field. At the other end of the field were several large hay bales. All had circle targets on them except one which had the black silhouette of a man on it. Van Owen stood with one hand on what looked like a small bow that lay at an angle to him on top of the table. Atwood could see that it was a small black crossbow about a foot and a half long with a hand grip built like a pistol.

The hunter held it up for his inspection, elbow braced against his hip, turning the bow slowly in the air in an oddly familiar stance. The arms of the crossbow curved back toward the ground like two powerful wings trying to pull away from his grip. The bow's flat black finish made it look blunt and unforgiving.

"Like to try it?" he asked. When Atwood shook his head he clucked like a schoolmaster.

"It's called a triforce," he said. "The shaft and the grip are made from die-cast aluminum. The bow is reinforced laminated fiberglass. The whole thing weighs less than two pounds." He reached down and picked up a short stubby arrow with a head of bright copper from the table. "The bow is strung with seventy-five pounds of tension. It can fire one of these—they're called bolts, not arrows—at nearly sixty miles per hour." He slipped the bolt into the bow with one hand and pulled the slide ratchet back, locking the bolt in place.

"At that speed, you could put one through a tree. It's accurate up to one hundred feet. For instance."

He swung the crossbow around directly in front of Atwood and fired it at the human target, pausing for only a few seconds to aim. The bolt tore a gaping hole in the target's head and disappeared into the hay bale. He walked to the target, motioning for Atwood to join him. He switched the crossbow to his left hand and swung it between them with the steady rhythm of a warning beacon. Dust clung to his arms and chest in cross patterns like the skin of a snake.

They found the bolt buried halfway into the ground several yards beyond the hay bale. Van Owen pulled it out and wiped the dirt off on the still-wet grass.

"Any more questions?" he asked.

"Yeah," Atwood said. "Did you actually threaten to cut somebody's head off over a dinner menu?"

Van Owen racked the bolt into the crossbow. "You *are* a slow learner," he said, and walked to the front of the range. Atwood moved away in the direction of the path, far out of the line of fire, and watched Van Owen step up to the line, turn quickly and shoot. The bolt whistled through the air and hit in the same place, tearing away what was left of the target's head.

Van Owen loaded the bow again and fired, the bolt striking the center of the chest. He loaded it once more, his hands moving rapidly, loading, aiming, firing, an action so fluid and strong that Atwood thought it must be an optical illusion, some kind of deadly magic.

Van Owen turned toward him, his elbow braced on his hip, the crossbow tilted toward the sky. Atwood realized now why it looked so familiar. He'd seen his father standing like that, in a picture taken in front of a burned-out German tank during the war, a triumphant smile on his face. The bodies of several dead enemy soldiers were stacked on top of the tank, charred arms and legs dangling behind him.

It was a warrior's stance, he thought, probably the only time that his father had ever felt victorious in his whole life.

Atwood moved down the path, out of the bow's range. He understood what Van Owen was doing. The man was getting himself ready to hunt for the wolf. Atwood moved quickly, pushed along by a growing feeling of urgency. Whatever Van Owen knew about the wolf, Atwood was going to find out. He had to find out. Right now, he was the only one who could.

He was going to save the wolf. It was his war; he wanted his own victory.

Chapter 23

FOR DAYS AFTER the Walker killing, Dane slept late and woke up tired and empty. He moved cautiously around the house until he could get outside in the sun, which made him feel alive again. On the steps behind the house, leaning against the door, he watched Jenny working in the garden. Sometimes very early, while he drifted half asleep in his bed, Dane thought he could hear her get up, the sound of her footsteps down the hall to the bathroom. And always, when he came outside, she was there, crouched in the dirt, tearing weeds from around the young plants and tossing them very deliberately behind her.

During those days, he would watch her closely, study her the way he did the wolves, noticing the small physical details that made up the whole of her life. Her skin had begun to change color, to darken in the sunlight, especially her face and neck. Small delicate freckles, like a spray of tiny flowers, appeared on the backs on her hands. Her hair grew longer and curled against the collar of her shirt. When she caught him staring at her, he would look away quickly. But occasionally, he would meet her eyes and be surprised to see his own sense of curiosity reflected there.

But if he stared too long, the curiosity gave way to a hardness that came from someplace deep inside her that left him bewildered and frightened again. She had grown into something that he could no longer control.

She moved according to her own rhythm, behaved according to her own natural law. That morning, when he came outside, Jenny wasn't in the garden. At first he thought that she'd taken the wolf, but when he checked the basement it was still locked. He circled the house, thinking she might have been working in the front yard, but she wasn't there either. He looked through the woods, moving slowly and deliberately. If she were lost or hurt, she might cry out. The woods were silent as if she had simply gotten up and walked away. The thought left him with an empty desolate feeling. He hurried back to the house to see if there was anything in her room that might tell him where she'd gone.

When he came out of the woods, Jenny was in the backyard cutting the stems off a handful of wild daisies and putting them one by one in an old vase.

She held the vase toward him. "What do you think?"

"They're very pretty," he said.

"I found them in a field down the road. They're all over." She set the vase down on the back step and nodded toward the woods. "You were out early this morning."

Dane shrugged, afraid that she might see how glad he was to find her. But she didn't seem to notice.

"Can we let the wolf out?" she asked, and picked up the vase, holding it close to her, as if she were saving it for a special present.

He unlocked the basement door and clapped his hands. The wolf bounded up the stairs and brushed hard against his leg, nuzzling his head on Dane's hip. Jenny was in the kitchen, cutting up some short ribs, mixing them with some ground beef for the wolf. It was something she did each morning now when he was there—did without being asked. Dane watched her cut through chunks of rib. Flecks of the white fat clung to her fingers. She sucked the bits of raw meat from her fingers, licking the soft skin between them with her tongue. Jenny saw him in the doorway with the wolf and held the bowl in her hands and waited. The wolf trotted to her side immediately. She put the bowl on the floor and watched the animal feed. Dane couldn't take his eyes off her.

"When you look at me," she asked him, "what do you think you're going to find?"

"I'm not trying to find anything," he said.

"You're just looking," she said, making it sound like an agreed-upon fact.

"I like to look at you," he said and she surprised him with a smile so warm that he wanted to hold her face in his hands so he wouldn't lose it.

"Let's go outside," she said when the wolf finished the bowl of meat. She worked in the garden and he took one of the chairs from the dining room and sat a few feet away. The wolf lay in the grass along the edge of the garden, his head thrown back in heavy rest after eating. They said very little, comfortable in what seemed like old habits. To Dane, it was as silent and perfect as a painting he had once seen, families resting together on a riverbank looking forever at ease.

He saw her reach behind her and run her hand down the wolf's flank. Dane watched her hand move and suddenly remembered the way she appeared in the window, the ruby-gold color of her skin against the light, the way she had gazed down at him. He closed his eyes and saw her again, like an old familiar dream. He watched the wolves mating and moved closer to see. Except this time when he looked down to see the gray wolf, it was Jenny who smiled seductively back.

If he touched her now, he thought, he could hold her scent on his fingertips, the same way he held his image of her in his memory. He opened his eyes and found her staring at the wolf instead.

"I miss him when you take him away," she said, not bothering to look at him when she spoke. "Where do you take him, anyway?"

His feelings died with her question. In their place came not fear or rage, but something much darker, a feeling of overwhelming dread.

One part of his mind had died but another sprang to life. For a few hours he'd almost forgotten that it was time to hunt again.

* * *

There were times that Jenny did not see Dane at all. Even when they were together in the house or outside in the garden, he would seem to fade from her vision. At other times he would vanish for hours and she would be left alone in the house with the wolf locked behind the basement door. She wanted to put her fist through the thin wood as though she thought she could free the wolf and herself with a single blow.

They were both trapped in this house, held down by whatever power Dane had over the wolf. At times, like gravity, that power extended to her. She could feel it when he stared at her. He'd been doing a lot of that lately, watched her like he wanted to pry open the back of her skull and peer inside. When he got too close, she would pull herself in close, burrow down to the hard place deep inside her.

She'd felt Dane drawing nearer to her for the past several days. They were in the garden and she knew he was going to touch her. She could see the warmth there when he opened his eyes. At first, she deliberately jarred him with her indifference. But before she could change it, before she could take it back, he'd vanished, taking his secrets with him. Now, once again, he was gone before she woke and didn't return until late at night. He would eat by himself and then sit on the steps, sometimes until well past midnight. The night before last, he'd taken the wolf with him and they were gone nearly all night. She lay awake and waited for them, wishing that she could escape with them.

What was he hunting out there? What was his secret? Every man she had ever known had secrets. A few were like Sonny; they wore them on their face. His was simple; he liked to hurt people. You had to be blind to miss that. The funny thing was, so many people wanted to miss it that it turned half the human race into a sick joke. Little girls wandered into the farm like dull-eyed sheep, looking for whatever pain he could give to them. They seemed to need it like air.

Other men kept their secrets inside, hid them in their private rooms and dark chambers. She knew them, too. They were like little boys when they came to her, hardly able to say the words for what they wanted. She liked to make them tell her what they wanted her to do, and when they did, she felt herself growing excited despite their fumbling advances.

The wolf had no secrets to conceal from her. Discovering the wolf was like discovering a brand-new piece of herself that she'd never expected to find, something powerful and pure that would change her forever if only she would let it. When she was with the wolf, she felt alive and complete, like a woman being courted for the first time by some beautiful creature out of myth. When she touched the wolf, she felt his power run through her body.

That was why Dane was afraid of her, afraid of what she knew, of what she might do. She could escape from him today, tomorrow, anytime that she chose. The idea had occurred to her again a few days before when she'd gone to pick flowers. A ragged pickup truck that she had seen once or twice on the road slowed down on its way past the field. As it went by, she saw a hand wave through the open side window and disappear behind a veil of dust. She could have waved back, even forced the driver to stop and take her with him. It would have been easy, so much so that it might as well have been a dream. But without the wolf, the dream would have remained empty. And Dane?

When she cut him off that morning, she was startled to see the warmth die so quickly in his eyes. She wanted to say something to bring it back but it was too late; she hated him a little for making her feel that way, just before she began to hate herself for hurting him without thinking, the way Sonny might have struck her, a casual sort of violence that seemed normal, everyday.

What she longed for now was something clear, a life without confusion and turmoil, without secrets. If she was careful, she could make his secrets her own. If she was careful, she could have everything she wanted.

She wanted the wolf. With the wolf beside her, she thought, no one would ever hurt her again.

The van woke her early. She listened to the noise of the engine fade and waited for the silence to settle over the house. It came on abruptly, like a door slamming shut on the world. Even the house itself seemed to exist without sound. It drove her from her bed and downstairs, anything to escape the void that threatened to swallow her up.

She spent most of the early morning drinking tea on the back steps until she couldn't stand it any longer and she set off down the driveway to the road to wait for the ragged pickup truck she knew would come along almost any minute.

The truck was late but when it came, she easily waved it down. The driver was in his early fifties with gray stubble on his face and smelled of fresh-cut wood and creosote and said he worked in a lumberyard out on the highway.

He had a picture of his family taped to the dashboard and told Jenny each of their names and what they were doing with their lives, which, for some reason, left her feeling sad. He said very little else except that, yes, he'd give her a ride into town if that's where she wanted to go.

He dropped her off at the main corner. The town seemed smaller than the last time she'd been there with Dane; the colors of the buildings looked dull and faded. She could feel the grit under her feet as she walked down the narrow pitted sidewalk to the small coffee shop at the end of the block with its back leaning out over a debris-strewn ravine.

The restaurant was crowded with men, the air sharp with the smell of cigarettes and coffee and the sound of harsh laughter, and eggs frying on the open grill behind the counter. The men watched her as she crossed the room, looking for a place to sit, then went back to eating when she found a seat at the counter, next to a man with a black T-shirt and jeans. A worn leather jacket hung over the stool. He scooped it off the stool with a bandaged left hand so she could sit down.

His hand looked stiff and he hoisted the jacket carefully and dropped it on the floor next to him. The bandage was gray with dirt and there was a spider web of brownish bloodstains across the back of it. He took a big bite out of a fried egg sandwich and smiled.

"That looks good," she said.

He swallowed hard. "Which one?" he said.

"The sandwich."

"You bet." He looked at his bandaged hand. "I can't do shit with this." He grinned at her. "Haven't even tried." He dropped the sandwich on his plate and turned to the newspaper at his elbow, flipped through a few pages and shoved it away from him. "I don't know why I read that trash," he said. "It just makes me feel foolish."

The waitress took Jenny's order with the sullen aggression of a woman used to waiting on men and having them to herself. Jenny held her hands around the cup. They had stayed cold all morning and only now could she feel the warmth finally seeping through her skin.

"Cigarette?" the man asked her, and she shook her head. He lit one and blew the smoke straight up in the air. "You live around here?"

"No," she said.

"Just passing through? I get that urge myself occasionally."

She took a sip of coffee and wondered if that was really all she was doing. Sometimes she thought that she'd learned to lie so well that she could no longer tell the difference.

The man finished his coffee and picked up his jacket. "Here," he said, and pushed the folded paper over to her with his bandaged hand. "See what a sorry mess the world's in these days." He stood up and was gone before she could thank him. The waitress brought her food and she ate first, savoring everything, relaxed, even ordered another cup of coffee before she opened the paper and read the front page.

Afterward, she took the paper outside, held it close to her, and found a place along the banks of the ravine where she sat in the morning sun and read the story again. The headlines screamed: KILLER WOLF STILL LOOSE, and below that, "Citywide Hunt for Creature."

On the inside, a pair of grainy black-and-white pictures gave her faces to go along with the names she'd seen on the paper in Dane's room. She read the accounts of both killings and tried to connect the pictures, so gray and still, like the faces of statues, with the horror they described.

Then she remembered that there were three more names on Dane's list, three more deaths, three more gray and lifeless faces. She closed the paper and lay back in the grassy stubble of the ravine and watched the sunlight move through the trees on the other side like refiner's fire, turning them a bright clear gold.

It took until midafternoon for her to walk home. She accepted no rides, and even when they slowed down and waited for her, she waved them away, watching as they drove off shaking their heads. She wanted to send them running, throw something to hurry them on their way. When she saw a familiar sign, she got off the highway and walked through open fields to the house, glad to be free of the road.

In the silence that surrounded her, the anger built until she felt that it must have somehow equaled his. How else could a man drive himself across a continent just to kill? The thought consumed her as she walked across the fields, the wet grass silently lapping at her feet and legs like delicate green waves. In that silence, she felt a kinship growing, enveloping the hard place next to her heart with its purity.

She waited for Dane until nightfall. When he did not return, she took a hammer from the kitchen and tried to smash open the lock on the basement door but only managed to splinter some pieces of the wooden frame. The lock remained in place. In the aftermath of the pounding, she could hear the wolf pacing nervously up and down the stairs.

She dropped the hammer and ran upstairs to Dane's room, throwing open drawers in a frenzy to find the key. The notebooks could wait. She pulled out one of the smaller drawers and dumped it in the center of the bed, spilling papers everywhere. She pushed the papers aside and saw the key next to a small silver whistle, both on a brass key ring. She scooped them up and hurried downstairs.

As she unlocked the basement and clapped her hands, the wolf bounded up the stairs to greet her and rubbed hard against her legs. She pressed her back against the door and closed her eyes, thinking that this was either the beginning or the end of everything.

Two weeks after the Walker killing, Dane began watching Blackburn's building. After a few days, he realized the lawyer wasn't going to come out. Three days before, Blackburn had made one quick trip at night to Van Owen's apartment. Carroll had been there as well. They had stayed less than an hour and then both had gone home. After that meeting, Blackburn remained inside his apartment. A large delivery of groceries was made the very next day.

He spent part of the next afternoon near Carroll's office and his apartment. The doctor had taken his family away. The receptionist told him that Carroll was on vacation and was not expected back for at least two weeks.

Van Owen's routine was the same. Dane knew the hunter had gone to the lodge for a few days, but he was back now and working as if nothing had changed at all. If anything, he seemed more visible, more open, giving Dane a free hand, challenging him to reach for him. At first he was afraid that Van Owen was setting him up somehow. But as he watched the hunter for another few days, he realized he was wrong.

He's enjoying this, Dane thought. He knows I'm hunting the others first and he's waiting his turn. Dane left Van Owen alone and went back to his vigil at Blackburn's apartment.

It was in a new building on Fifty-fourth Street between Lexington and Third, a gilt shell, pristine and expensive, lost in the shadow of Citicorp Center. It was twenty-three stories high with a staggered tier-shaped pedestal roof illuminated by rows of multicolored spotlights that made it look like a stack of children's wooden blocks.

The lobby was painted antique gold and silver with splashes of black lacquer on the walls that resembled gigantic potted ferns. The top five floors including the penthouse were still being finished, and there was a continuous stream of workmen in and out of the ground-floor garage. The architect had added a narrow covered alleyway next to the garage for deliveries, but since that was blocked with construction material and trucks, all deliveries had to come in through the garage.

Blackburn's apartment was on the seventh floor. Dane picked up that information and a floor plan of the building from the real estate agency handling the sale. On the fifth day, he arrived early and double-parked the van near the garage entrance and settled down in the front seat to watch.

The van looked like so many others on the street that no one took any notice of it, not even the police, who drove by occasionally and stopped to talk to the Con Ed crew working on the main circuit line underneath the street. Dane felt invisible.

Finally he got out of the van and walked into the building. He walked past the trucks, the workmen and movers, watching the confusion and the noise of the traffic as it passed through the lower overhanging entrance to the garage. No one stopped him or questioned him as he got on the elevator and rode up to Blackburn's floor.

He spent over three hours inside the building, learning about the place. He knew what floors were occupied and what apartments were vacant; he found out where the workmen took their breaks and how much security was left after the workmen went home. The building was filled with movers. There were so many crates and boxes stacked in the halls that in some places you couldn't get through. He talked to some of them and found out what he needed to know, and by the time he left, he had figured it out.

It was simple and dangerous but it'd been right in front of him all the time.

The woods were cold and damp, the chill night air held low to the ground by the canopy of leaves. Thin wisps of ground mist clung to her legs before they drifted apart like frail spirits and disappeared. Jenny carried a flashlight and, with its narrow bright beam, followed the wolf's trail. The sweater that she wore seemed to keep the cold close to her skin. She shivered every few steps and the beam stuttered into the underbrush before she could bring it back.

The wolf sensed where to go. He would roam through the woods ahead of her, often vanishing in the darkness beyond the light, then suddenly reappear at her side. If the wolf was out of her sight for too long, she clapped her hands and he would come running back to her immediately, sometimes emerging from the woods directly behind her as if he had been stalking her. The feeling unnerved her, especially when he was out of her sight, because she couldn't hear him.

Whatever noise the wolf made blended into the other sounds of the night, as if he'd been transformed into the darkness itself.

They had left the house and yard and climbed up the small ridge and gone straight into the woods. For a while she could still see the light from her bedroom window through the trees. When that was gone, she tried to keep her bearings, tried to remember the position of the house but soon that was gone as well and she gave up caring about it completely. There was a trail of sorts. She could see it in the light, a path littered with broken ferns, appleweed, and the stripped limbs of saplings, a path that the wolf knew instinctively.

Occasionally she would stop for a few minutes and cover the flashlight with the palm of her hand and let the night close in over her. Once, she turned off the light, clapped her hands, and felt the wolf slide against her and curl his huge body around her legs. She knelt down and wrapped her arms around his neck and held him close and listened to his heart beating through his thick fur.

The house was somewhere far behind them now. Jenny couldn't tell where they'd come from or where they were going. She'd lost all sense of direction. Noises shifted and moved through the trees. She heard a harsh rustling noise behind her, like the sound of something traveling at great speed along the ground, and turned around, only to find that it had already passed her and was moving out of range. When she swung the light, she saw nothing.

The wolf ranged farther ahead of her on the trail, and when she clapped her hands, it took longer and longer for him to come back, until finally he didn't come back at all. She stood in the middle of the path, the outer edges of the light forming an oblong circle around her feet, a misshapen cell of pale white and deep black shadows, and listened.

In the distance, or what she thought was the distance because she was too disoriented to tell where anything came from anymore, she heard the sound of an animal running hard through the underbrush, tearing across the woods, branches and twigs snapping in syncopated rhythm like the chattering of frightened birds. She thought that it must be the wolf and she clapped her hands hard. The sharp noise pierced the darkness. What she heard next was something different and terrifying, the sound of running multiplied over and over again. Jenny lifted the light and saw a blur of movement through the trees and felt herself stumble forward as if she'd been pushed.

She moved toward a tree directly in front of her, thinking that she was walking directly into whatever was out there but she had to have something at her back. She reached the tree and braced against it, balancing with one hand while the other pointed the flashlight at the ground.

The running stopped, replaced by the deep sound of panting, the way dogs panted on hot afternoons at the farm. Something moved on her left and she slid down the face of the tree, reaching out with her free hand for a rock or stick to throw at it. She felt only dirt and grass and the velvet crush of damp moss before she found the rough edge of something hard. The rock wouldn't move, it was buried too deep in the ground. It seemed so pathetic that she almost laughed. All she had left to defend herself was her hands, a flashlight, and one small silver whistle.

She raised the flashlight toward the path. On the other side, just beyond the edge of the light, she saw a pair of hungry yellow eyes staring back at her. At first she thought it was the wolf and felt a moment of relief. She raised the flashlight higher. It was a large black German shepherd, ears flat against the sides of its head, jaws open, a shimmer of saliva sparkling in the light. Behind it, other eyes flickered and winked as the pack moved back and forth in the light and waited. The lead animal growled. Jenny held the flashlight steady and saw the rest of the pack move closer into the light.

She backed up hard against the tree. The flashlight slipped from her hand and rolled along the ground out of reach. Without knowing what would happen, she dug in her pocket for the whistle, tugged hard as the key caught on the edge of her pocket, heard the fabric tear as it gave way, pulled too quickly and felt it slip out of her fingers onto the ground somewhere near her leg.

She searched for it frantically with both hands, her breath

coming faster and faster. The key stuck between her fingers. She grabbed the whistle tight in her fist and brought it to her mouth as the pack moved toward her in shadowy formation.

There was something wrong in the house. Dane sensed it the moment he opened the back door. He stopped immediately and stared into the kitchen. All the lights were on but the house was perfectly still. It felt haunted and empty. Dane wondered if somehow Van Owen had found the house and had taken Jenny and the wolf with him.

Dane walked through the kitchen and into the dining room, taking everything in at once: the newspaper on the counter, the block-letter headline, and then the open basement door. He ran upstairs and burst through the door to his room, knowing that it wasn't Van Owen but Jenny who had ransacked his room, Jenny who had taken the wolf away from him, Jenny who had betrayed him.

The full impact of what she had done hit him and left him feeling more alone than he ever imagined it would. He was going to have to find her now and stop her.

Then another possibility occurred to him. What if something had happened, what if the wolf had stopped her already?

The woods felt as desolate as the house. No sound, no sense of life, only darkness and an awareness of his own fear. If she had lost control of him, if the wolf had been threatened or confused, he would have turned on her first. Dane was almost certain of that. And afterward? He had no idea what would happen. If she fought him or tried to run, it would only have made it worse. The animal's own confusion might slow him down but it wouldn't stop him.

He hurried along, moving through the dead silence on instinct. He stayed with the trail, stopping every few yards to pick up the sound of anything that might be moving with him. Perhaps, he thought, the wolf was even hunting for him.

The deeper he moved into the woods, the more uncertain he became of what might have happened. The place seemed alien to him suddenly and he half expected the landscape itself to attack him. Instead of hurrying, he slowed down. Fear made him awkward and blind. He stumbled over a small rock and nearly fell. A branch sliced against his cheek like a sharp claw. He thought he heard something moving through the trees but it was his own echo returning to haunt him. What if they were both alive? What if she had learned to control the wolf? His thoughts drove him forward along the twisted narrow trail, thinking that he might find some escape only if he could outrun them.

The sharp odor of fresh blood stopped him. He moved off the path and crouched in the protection of the underbrush. The scent was strong, something killed within the last twenty minutes. It had probably happened while he was tearing through the house. That explained the silence. A fresh kill would clear out the woods, send deer bounding frantically away from the smell, drive the other animals into hiding. He crept forward until he could see the path ahead more clearly. Something was half sprawled across it. The rest of the body lay hidden in the weeds. On the nearby ground, partially obscured by a large tree, he saw a small ball of light with a white-hot center.

It was a flashlight. Jenny must have lost it in the attack, had it knocked from her hand before she died. She might have even tried to reach for it as she fell across the path, might have even crawled the last few feet to get it, thinking that it would protect her somehow. All sense broke down; his fear of her, of the wolf, of what might have happened, all was lost when he thought of her dying. Dane rose out of the weeds and stepped forward, keeping the tree between him and what lay on the other side. He reached down blindly and picked the flashlight out of the weeds, wiping off the moisture from the glass. He pointed the light at the body.

It wasn't Jenny. It wasn't even human. It was a dog with the throat torn open, its dirty white fur matted with blood.

Dane saw her only seconds before he heard her voice.

She stood in the path with the wolf by her side, holding the silver whistle in her hand so he could see it. Her face looked extraordinarily pale, the bones hard against her skin, and the faint smile on her face showed him nothing. He lowered the flashlight. He felt more comfortable in the dark, unable to see her or the wolf. In the dark they were only distant shadows, like the mountains at night, things he thought he understood.

"We've been waiting for you," she said.

He reached behind his back and felt the knife handle slide into his palm. Jenny and the wolf moved toward him along the path, her hand still outstretched. The wolf was exhausted. He walked slowly on stiff legs. Blood dripped down his jaw from a torn right ear. Dane raised the flashlight.

"There's another one over there," Jenny said, and pointed to her left, just on the other side of the tree. "I killed it with a rock." Dane saw the outline of the dead animal in the weeds, a dark mongrel. "The rest of them ran."

She held the whistle out for him to take. "I don't need this anymore," she said. For the first time, Dane saw that her hands were stained with blood. He closed her fingers gently over the whistle and pulled her closer. Jenny put her arms around his waist and pinned the knife against the small of his back as though she had already known what he was thinking.

Unexpectedly, the wolf leaned hard against his leg and Dane felt Jenny take hold of him, as if they both suddenly needed him for support. He let the knife fall and slipped his arm around her shoulders to keep her from collapsing. She reached down and dug her hand into the wolf's fur and held on tight.

"Take us home now," she whispered to him.

The wolf sat between them, dozing by fits, his great body stretched out to its full length in front of the couch. Every now and again, his front legs shook in the throes of a hunting dream. When Dane stopped talking, he turned to watch him sleep, seeking shelter in the silence.

He told her everything. She listened without interruption and never took her eyes off him while he told her about the wolf pack, the hunters, Walker and Lange and Blackburn and Carroll and, finally, Van Owen.

"Will you take me to the lodge?" she said. "I want to see it."

"Yes," he said. "I promise."

She opened his hand and held hers against it. To his surprise they were almost the same size. She dropped her hand and stared at the wolf who seemed to tremble under her gaze. "Aren't you afraid of losing him?" she asked.

Dane lied again and told her no, not knowing which would have been worse, the truth or the lie, only that the lie was easier to believe.

Jenny entered his room. She felt safe and serene, no longer the victim, no need to escape, no need to run. Tonight had been a baptism. She put her fingers against the door and pushed it open gently, stood in the doorway, and smelled the dry stale air of his room, the scent of his body, the sweet wet smell of her own, the scent of the wolf as faint as moonlight in the air.

She thought he might wake up when she opened the door but he slept on. This, she thought, was all that was left. His head rocked slowly back and forth, then stopped. Maybe he was dreaming about her right now, she thought. She closed her eyes and arched her neck back until her head grazed the wall and remembered what it had been like, scrambling on her hands and knees over the wet ground, the dog pack circling her. The high scream of the whistle startled the dogs and they shied from her. Then she saw the wolf burst out of the darkness into the center of the pack. The dogs attacked and the wolf fought them all, whirling around to meet each one, keeping the pack at bay, keeping them away from her.

A rock broke loose in her hands, and when one of the dogs came close to her, she brought it down hard, again and again, until the animal stopped moving. The wolf seized another one by the neck and flung it back and forth and then pinned it to the ground, biting deep into its flesh. The animal squealed and died. The rest of the pack, even the German shepherd, scattered into the trees. The wolf flung the animal aside and turned to face her. She tried to call him but her voice seemed harsh and distorted, no longer her own. Her voice shocked. The wolf cocked his head and listened. He moved toward her cautiously, each step slow and deliberate, as if he were uncertain of what she wanted.

She felt so weary that she could barely raise her head to watch him as he approached. She struggled to bring her hands together, to make some kind of signal that he would understand. Instead, she could only hold them in front of her, like a child beginning her prayers. Perhaps that's what I'm doing, she thought. After that, she gave up. She leaned against the tree and waited for him to come to her.

As he got closer to her, the muscles along the wolf's shoulders gradually relaxed. Finally he hung his head and stood next to her. She put her arms around his neck and pulled him close, burying her face deep in his fur. When her strength finally gave out and she couldn't hold on any longer, he lay on the ground next to her and licked the blood on her hands.

Jenny opened her eyes and knelt at Dane's bedside, saw his face and his half-open mouth clearly, remembered other mouths in other rooms, saw them as things that were no longer hers, and pressed her fingers against his lips and watched him awaken. His eyes opened suddenly and he started to sit up but she pushed him back with only her fingers. He seemed to fall against the bed as though he were weightless, a feather drifting in the wind.

She bent over and kissed one of his nipples, gently sucking the dark flesh into her mouth until she felt it grow hard. Dane arched his back, his hands circling her back, the heavy calluses on his palms scratching her shoulders. Without a word, he lifted her onto the bed and moved over to make room. She lay next to him and listened to his heart pound and then sat up, throwing one leg over him so she could see his eyes when he slid into her. But when she looked, his eyes were closed, shut tight against whatever power she had.

"Open your eyes," she said, and felt him swelling inside of her. She took his face in her hands and said again, "Open your eyes. I want to see you." He came suddenly, and when he did, his eyes opened wide in a kind of fearful release.

He slipped away from her gradually, shrinking a little at a time. She laid her head on his chest, shivered gently, and felt his wetness flow out with him. She touched herself and brought her hand to her mouth.

She could taste him on her fingers, as warm and bitter as her own tears.

Chapter 24

IT WAS THE second week in July but Blackburn hardly noticed the change. He had other things on his mind. A week ago he and Carroll had gone to see Van Owen and he could still see the jackallike grin on the hunter's face when Van Owen opened the apartment door to let them inside. Blackburn hurried past him. The first thing Van Owen said was, "You look like a man who needs a drink."

He'd been right. Blackburn had needed a drink that night. He also needed a drink and a gun and that freak with the wolf right *there* in front of him so he could shoot the son of a bitch dead.

Carroll had come in after him looking like a funeral director, his face serious and dour, worse than the lawyer remembered from the hunting trip. Blackburn thought of Walker and the trip and almost started to laugh until he remembered what had happened to him. Christ Almighty, Blackburn thought, the man had gotten his goddamn joint chewed off by some crazed *wolf*, that's what it was, some goddamn *monster* animal, and that was no joke. He couldn't open the bottle of scotch fast enough. His stubby fingers twisted the cap so hard that it fell into the round metal sink below the open cabinet and whirled around and around like an ivory ball on a roulette wheel.

Carroll passed on the liquor. Well, fuck you, Blackburn

thought. He drank a quick one and poured another, adding a few ice cubes this time to water it down. He had to be sober enough to phone his lawyer later so his soon-to-be-ex-wife wouldn't eat *his* dork for dinner.

Blackburn carried his drink over to the windows and looked over the city and the park. Van Owen could probably point out the spots where Lange and Walker got killed, he thought. The prick probably wished he could have been there to help. The park was dark, a rectangle of black cloth laid over the bright busy lights in the center of the city. Blackburn had never felt so unbalanced in all his life. He half expected the windows to explode and hurl him to the street far below. He turned to face Van Owen and Carroll. They were looking at him as if they expected *him* to explode.

"What are we going to do?" he said to both of them. He used his courtroom voice. It boomed across the room. Carroll looked shocked by it.

"Yelling won't help," Carroll said.

"The fuck it won't," Blackburn said, and looked at Van Owen. "What are you going to do about it?"

"There's nothing I can do right now," Van Owen said blandly.

"You could kill the son of a bitch!"

"Who's that?"

"The motherfucker with the wolf!" he screamed.

Blackburn wanted to throw his drink at him. Instead, he finished it in one large gulp and shook the empty glass at him. The ice cubes rattled like stones.

"I think we should go to the police and tell them what we know," Carroll said quietly. "At least they'll know what's behind it."

Van Owen looked at Carroll and thought, You stupid bastard, you really think it's going to be that easy? Blackburn didn't argue with the doctor. That was a bad sign. It meant they were both going dead simple on him.

"That's a real good idea," Van Owen said to Carroll. "Who's going to believe it?"

"If we all tell them the same story," Carroll said.

"That there's a mountain man running around New York killing people with a wolf," Van Owen said. He glanced at

Blackburn. "That should be an easy one." The lawyer was listening to him now. "Are you going to tell them *why* he's doing it?" Carroll nodded. "What would your patients think about a thing like that?"

Carroll tried to muster a certain dignity and failed. "I'd explain it to them somehow," he said.

"Shit," Van Owen said. "You can't even explain to yourself." The hunter crossed the room to the liquor cabinet and poured himself a short bourbon and drank it. He wiped his mouth off with the back of his hand.

"Let me explain a few things," Van Owen said. "If you go to the police, the Canadians are going to be involved. I can guarantee that. At the very least, they'll bring charges against the three of us. With all the publicity, they might even want extradition."

"For shooting a bunch of wolves?" Blackburn said derisively, but Van Owen cut him off.

"It's illegal to hunt wolves in Canada without a special permit," he said, raising his voice for the first time. "I didn't tell you that, did I? And they don't like Americans who go up there and slaughter them from helicopters. It's not enough to get you disbarred, I know. But it'll be ugly enough. Your business will take a beating. Your wife'll cut your nuts off." Blackburn winced. Both were quiet, they seemed too frightened of him to speak. "Have you two got the picture now?" he asked. "Are we clear on this?" Neither one answered.

Carroll finally broke the silence. "Then what are we going to do?"

"Stay out of the park," Van Owen said very seriously, and laughed out loud. Blackburn looked ill. Carroll managed to look shocked and ill at the same time.

"Christ," Van Owen said. "You people have no sense of humor."

"This isn't very funny," Carroll said. He acted like he was ready to leave.

"Don't you find the irony fascinating?" Van Owen asked.

"What's so ironic about getting your dick chewed off?" Blackburn wanted to know.

"In Walker's case," Van Owen said, "it was his dick that got him in trouble in the first place."

226

"What the fuck's the difference!" Blackburn yelled. "He's dead, isn't he? He got killed by a wolf in the middle of New York City and he's dead!" He pounded the back of one of the chairs. "If I had that motherfucker right now, I'd rip his fucking head off." He shoved the chair away from him and looked at Van Owen. "You want to tell me some more about how ironic everything is?"

"I want to tell you to shut up," Van Owen said flatly.

"There's no need for that," Carroll said.

"You too," Van Owen said, and pointed a finger at him. Carroll stepped closer to Blackburn. Van Owen's finger tracked his movement like the barrel of a gun. Right then, Carroll decided he was going to run. He had never run from anything in his life but he was going to run from this, take his family and get away from the insanity he could feel everywhere he turned. The man with the wolf was insane. For good reason, perhaps, but insane. Van Owen was obviously a madman. He could go to the house in New Hampshire. Take a few weeks off. By then, the police would find the wolf and it would all be over. Carroll felt a sense of relief now that the decision had been made. He was surprised at how easy it was to accept his cowardice.

"Excuse me," he said. His voice was calm and controlled, the way it was in surgery. This was the same thing, like cutting away a bad sickness. The lawyer was nervous and ill-at-ease, hoping for someone to save him from his own hideous past. Van Owen, so cool and self-contained, waiting for another victim. Carroll couldn't believe that he had actually put himself in the man's power. Not anymore. "Excuse me," he said again, and started for the hallway and the door.

Carroll stopped directly in front of the lawyer and patted him on the arm. "Take care of yourself," he said.

"Where are you going?" Blackburn asked, more bewildered than before.

Carroll said good-bye to Van Owen, who was so silent he might not have been there at all. He reached the end of the hall and heard Blackburn yell at him just before he shut the door.

"What the fuck do you think you're doing? Get the hell back here!"

Carroll hurried toward the elevator. It opened before him as if it had been waiting to carry him away, and when the doors closed and the walls enveloped him, he began to feel safe for the first time in weeks.

"He's decided to run," Van Owen said. He put a hand on Blackburn's shoulder and drew him back into the living room.

"What do you mean run?"

"I mean *run,*" he said, and wiggled his fingers like a pair of fast-moving legs. "Away."

"That son of a bitch," Blackburn said. "He can't do that."

"I'm not going to chase him."

"Then what the hell are we going to do?" Blackburn asked again. This time his voice was desperate.

"Let him go."

"What?" the lawyer said. He was lost in his own fear and seemed not to have heard.

"I said, we let him go."

"So what am I supposed to do? Wait in my apartment for the wolfman to make up his mind?"

"No," Van Owen said. He was smiling again.

"You got something planned," Blackburn said. "What is it?"

"Just stay in your apartment for the next week or so. I don't care who comes in, just don't go outside. Can you handle that?"

"Sure," Blackburn said. "Where will you be?"

"Don't worry about me," Van Owen said. "Just do what I tell you and maybe you won't get turned into lunch meat like your queer buddy."

That had been a week ago and the groceries he'd had delivered when the siege began—that was how Blackburn thought of his apartment now, a medieval fortress surrounded by barbarians—were getting a little low and he didn't want to deal with another delivery boy. The first time they'd sent this Puerto Rican gangster who stood about four feet high, with slick black hair, a greasy mustache, a gold star in one earlobe, tight pants, an orange sleeveless T-shirt, and a cigarette hanging from the corner of his mouth. He waltzed into Blackburn's apartment with the groceries and immediately started to case the place. He could see the little beaner making notes in his mind, like where the stereo was and the potential take from antique ivory statues over the fireplace. He gave him a buck. The beaner looked at it contemptuously and dropped it on the carpet before he strutted out, muttering in Spanish. Blackburn almost laughed. He should introduce the beaner to his wife. They could come back and clean him out together.

Blackburn didn't like delivery boys. They were looking for places to rip off, and if you were stuck in your apartment, you were at their mercy. He'd seen *Deathwish,* he knew what went on, and it didn't matter where you lived. East Side, West Side, Trump fucking Tower, security didn't mean shit anymore.

At the moment, he was waiting for a television set to be delivered and it proved his point. His new neighbor had called that morning and asked if Blackburn could take delivery of a new television that was arriving at three that afternoon. The neighbor said he was going to be out all day, maybe even overnight, and that if they had to reschedule the delivery it would take another two weeks. Blackburn was a little perturbed and asked about the desk holding it or something, but the neighbor told him that the desk man had said that they could only hold it at the delivery entrance in the garage, but with all the people going in and out down there, they couldn't guarantee it would be there when he came to claim it, and if it was, he'd have to move it himself because most of the crew were too busy with the people moving entire apartments full of furniture into the building and they weren't going to make time for just one television set. See? Security didn't mean shit anymore. Blackburn agreed to take delivery just because of that, and because the neighbor agreed to bring Blackburn the groceries that he needed. The guys who delivered major appliances were different than the greasers humping their three-wheelers through the streets. Guys who delivered televisions were professionals. They had uniforms and everything.

Blackburn was almost glad to be staying inside. Ever since his wife had filed for divorce, his life had been turned into a garbage dump. His work slipped, and for the first time he let some of the associates pick up the slack. That had worked out all right, at least, the single bright spot in the oversized pile of shit that had become his existence. His whole life tasted sour. The fact that some maniac with a wolf was out to kill him seemed appropriate. He couldn't even use the goddamn balcony that came with the place. Now if he could only figure out what the hell Van Owen was doing about the wolfman. There was nothing new in the papers, but who believed that crap anyway? Besides, if Van Owen did kill the guy, he wasn't going to hold a press conference to tell everybody about it.

The delivery service called later that morning and said they were going to be a little late with the set, closer to five than three. Blackburn didn't care. He wasn't going anywhere. He was in for the duration, that's what his old man used to say.

Chapter 25

ATWOOD WAS AWAKE and dreaming, staring through the trees and shrubbery and the intricate pattern of the wrought-iron grating surrounding the small private park at the entrance to the New York Sportsman's Society in Gramercy Park. He'd been parked in nearly the same spot every day for so many days he could barely remember. The monotony of watching affected him like a sedative. He might have been asleep because what he saw seemed like a dream. The park itself was a fantasy and Atwood expected the laughter of women and the clatter of carriage wheels behind horses' hoofs to startle him at any moment.

Instead, there was only the stern statue of actor Edwin Booth in the center of the small private park. His brother had murdered a president and Edwin had dragged that cross of history with him from place to place for another thirty years. Edwin had lived in Gramercy Park, Atwood remembered, and wondered whether the aging actor had stood at the window overlooking the tiny park and wept for his renegade brother.

Now it was the middle of July and nothing had happened. Van Owen arrived by taxi at ten o'clock each morning and left a few minutes after six in the evening. His schedule never changed. Atwood wasn't discouraged. Something was going to happen. Van Owen knew something about the wolf and Atwood was going to stay with him until he found out.

Van Owen didn't go out for lunch, and if he did, Atwood didn't see him leave. There could have been a back entrance but Atwood didn't know that, either. He didn't even know whether Van Owen was actually *in* the building during the day or if his precise schedule was just for appearances, a charade to keep Atwood occupied. Sometimes he fell asleep and woke up feeling guilty and embarrassed. On the third day, it had rained in the afternoon. He'd let the water blow across his face through the open car window to keep him awake. After a while, he began to wonder if telling Yates what he knew wasn't such a bad idea after all. He weighed the notion and dismissed it.

He hadn't told the detective anything yet because he didn't trust him. Yates would shoot the wolf first and worry about the ecological ramifications later, if at all; the detective might even shoot *him*. Another idea occurred to him. Maybe he wouldn't have to tell Yates everything, just enough to get the detective on his side. That might work. It was certainly better than speculating whether a dead actor ever got depressed. He could always try something new and go to work. He'd been in the office only once in nearly a week, and then only to grab some reports and papers. By now, even the secretaries would be complaining about him.

He looked at the pile of reports on the seat next to him, almost all of them from people who were certain they had seen the wolf prowling through their neighborhood. One woman had called from Queens to say that the wolf had eaten her schnauzer. He began to wonder exactly what *had* happened to the schnauzer. The reports piled up, one after another, an entire city hysterical with fear and suspicion. The hysteria was infectious. He wasn't immune, either. Why else was he sitting here? The lady with the missing schnauzer would have to wait; he already had his hands full.

It was almost one o'clock. Atwood ate his lunch, a bagel and cream cheese and a cup of coffee. The coffee was cold, the cream a shattered white crust floating on the surface. Five more hours of this to go, he thought, but he was wrong. At three o'clock, for the first time in over a week, the pattern broke.

Van Owen came out of the entrance alone and walked briskly toward Lexington. At first Atwood was too startled by his unexpected appearance to do anything but stare as he walked away. Van Owen stopped at the corner of Twenty-second Street to look around and then continued north on Lexington, slowing down to glance at something in the street. Atwood waited until he was one more block away and followed him on foot, crossing to the dark side of the street. He narrowed the gap between them to a single block and hung back close to the buildings.

They stayed that way well into the Fifties. Van Owen moved quickly through the crowd of slightly stoned office workers out for a stroll in the sun, pausing only when the lights were against him. He never seemed to stop completely. He was like a runner, in constant motion, hands shaking at his sides, head turning this way and that, watching the people around him. He acted like a man with someplace important to go.

By the time he crossed to Park and then Madison and finally Fifth, Atwood knew exactly where. In his excitement, he had to slow down consciously to keep from climbing all over Van Owen's back.

Van Owen walked up Fifth Avenue on the Central Park side to the entrance by the children's zoo. Atwood lost him momentarily in a crowd of children but found him again almost immediately, walking north rapidly along the park's East Drive. Van Owen seemed to be in a great hurry now and Atwood had to struggle to keep up with him. The muscles in his legs hurt. His right calf began to cramp and he bent to rub it, hobbling beside the traffic like a crab.

Just past the fountain, Van Owen changed directions and started walking toward Atwood as he came charging up the path after him. Atwood jumped off the path and scrambled down the hill toward the lake. When he looked up, he expected to see Van Owen heading in his direction but the hunter was gone. He'd lost him. Atwood debated what to do and then ran back up the hill.

He reached the top in time to see him cross the bow bridge into the Ramble. Atwood hesitated, afraid of a trap. The hunter disappeared into the green maze of the Ramble. Atwood decided the hell with it and plunged in after him.

It was like chasing a ghost. He would catch glimpses of Van Owen only now and then, always in unexpected places, as he disappeared behind an outcropping of rock or down one of the twisting dirt trails that meandered through the trees. The Ramble was filled with deep ravines choked with bushes, cul-de-sacs and sudden drops, winding paths that sometimes stopped in the middle of nowhere—a wilderness in miniature.

After a few minutes, Atwood was completely lost, switching back and forth on trails and hills that seemed at once familiar and new. His only way out was by following Van Owen, something that had become increasingly difficult. He would be climbing down a ravine after him and glance up to see Van Owen fading into the trees high on the other side, directly opposite where he'd been only seconds before. Atwood began to believe that Van Owen was the reincarnation of something unnatural.

He stayed just behind him for what seemed like hours, losing him, finding him; they played a strange game of tag through the Ramble. It seemed Van Owen was leading him somewhere but he had no idea where. When he passed through the narrow stone arch, he expected to find Van Owen perched on the high rock walls like a harpy, waiting to swoop down on him, but the sloping walls were bare, the only sign of life a pair of faded initials scratched on the rock with white chalk.

Atwood moved past the cave, now sealed like a tomb, and down to the lake. To his left, he saw Van Owen stop at the water's edge and then climb back into the Ramble just north of where they'd first entered at the bow bridge.

Atwood ran as fast as he could to catch him but slowed when he realized where Van Owen had finally led him. A few wooden police barriers were still up; the rest were in a pile off to one side. Long strings of red plastic tape lay scattered over the ground around the site. The rest, sagging and stretched out of shape, hung limp between the trees, protecting a scene that no one cared about anymore. He remembered what it had been like—the crowds, the lights, the police wrestling the mutilated body into the back of the ambulance.

Van Owen had led him to the place where Walker had died. This is it, he thought, there's a joke here somewhere and it's on me. No point in trying to find Van Owen now. He sat down and looked out over the water, the bright green algae floating like a ribbon around the shoreline. A slug curled up on the toe of one of his tennis shoes and he flicked it on the grass.

Van Owen had left him stranded in the park. In a matter of minutes, his alternatives had shriveled up and died. No merit badge today, Atwood thought. He could sit there forever or he could do what he should have done in the first place. He stood up and brushed off his pants.

Good joke, he thought. Let's see if Yates gets it.

Van Owen left Atwood staring at the lake. If he stayed by the Ramble long enough, maybe someone would do him the great and good favor of beating him to death. It was a distinct possibility, one of the reasons he'd led Atwood into the Ramble in the first place. He thought it might teach him a valuable lesson. The other reason was to have a little fun. Now the fun was over. If he gets in my way again, Van Owen thought, I'm going to take care of his problem for him.

He'd seen the veterinarian parked outside the society the day after he got back from the lodge and every day after that. It didn't matter that he left by the back entrance an hour after he arrived and returned the same way. When he left by the front door at the end of each day, Atwood was where he'd been eight hours before. Van Owen wondered what the veterinarian would have done if he'd put one or two rifle slugs through his windshield right next to his head. Might have brightened his day for him.

He cut back through the Ramble toward the Seventy-ninth Street traverse and out of the park. At a garage near Fifty-ninth and First, under the bridge, he picked up the rental car he'd been using for the past few days and drove to Blackburn's apartment.

Van Owen had spotted the battered blue van about the fourth day of his surveillance of the lawyer's apartment. He hadn't noticed it before because it blended so well with the different vans and trucks parked everywhere around the building. It was there every day, parked in almost the same spot, sometimes until well after dark.

He only saw the silhouette of the driver. It seemed to shift slightly with the angle of his vision, an outline as mutable as the light itself. For a while he allowed himself a certain amount of fascination with the driver but that quickly faded, replaced by the urge to get on with it. He willed the driver to move, to take some action, but day after day the driver only watched and waited and never took his eyes off the building.

Now, after leaving Atwood in the park, he saw that the van was no longer there. The change in the pattern made him uneasy at first, but then, as he searched for some sign of the van and its missing driver, his uneasiness melted away. It was today, he thought. He could feel the anticipation growing in him, swelling through the pit of his stomach and into his chest. It was coming toward him, he could sense it. His feelings were as strong as the first shifts of wind just before a storm.

Late in the afternoon, the van appeared. It descended slowly and carefully into the garage. He climbed out of his car and walked to the entrance and watched the driver get out. It was the first time Van Owen had really looked at him.

The driver was young and tall, and seemed uncomfortable in the delivery outfit. A cap covered his head and he walked deliberately across the concrete dock as if he was afraid of stumbling. Against the stale white concrete he looked slight, almost transparent. From a distance, his face seemed the same chalky color as the garage walls. Van Owen could only guess at the rest. The eyes would be clear, gray or blue, the mouth a soft gash in the middle of those ascetic features. He could only imagine his voice. Like the eyes, it too would reek of clarity and purpose.

A young woman got out of the passenger side and opened the van's rear doors. Van Owen moved closer, stepping into the shadow of the overhang. A group of construction workers, laughter booming, strode past him. She looked his way but saw only the men. As he watched her from the shadows, she dismissed them with a glance.

The driver came out and together they loaded a large crate onto one of the carts. They spoke briefly and she climbed back into the van and backed it out. The driver pushed the cart toward one of the three freight elevators and waited. Another couple came out of the office and got on with him.

Van Owen focused his attention on the woman, saw her face as she drove past him, and memorized her pale childlike features. She was achingly familiar, like a ghost come back to haunt him alone, and he felt the first clear rush of excitement just watching her. He followed the van as she drove around slowly, circling the surrounding blocks searching for a parking space until she double-parked near a group of pay phones just off Second.

At first he didn't understand what they were doing, then realized the answer. The driver couldn't risk bringing the wolf out during the day, not after a killing and not with so many people around. They were going to wait until after dark when there was little or no chance of being seen. It was a simple, workable plan. She would call and he would bring the wolf out at a set time. It wouldn't take more than a few minutes to bring the van around to the garage to pick them up. The chances of getting caught were negligible.

He had expected the driver to be alone. But now the girl was here and suddenly other possibilities opened up before him. As he walked back to the building, he kept her face alive in his mind.

The wolf had been the target, the man the means to that end; now they were only stepping-stones. All he had to do was take them one by one until he reached her.

Chapter 26

DANE PARKED THE van in the garage and spoke briefly to the man in the office who was busy with a moving-van driver and a young couple who wanted to know if he could help them move two grand pianos into their apartment. He told Dane not to bother him with rinky-dink shit like a television set and told the driver to hold on for a minute, then turned to the couple with the pianos and asked them if they were out of their goddamn fucking minds.

Jenny closed the television carton and helped him load it onto one of the carts on the loading dock. He hadn't argued with her when she'd climbed into the van that morning. It seemed a little late for that. She had coaxed the wolf into the empty television carton without any trouble and sat down with him for a few minutes to make the animal feel at ease. "It's not much worse than the basement," she said. The wolf had remained quiet and subdued all the way into the city.

They didn't speak to one another during the long ride. Words were unnecessary and pointless. Like they had been last night. It was his first time with any woman and he tried to find a safe place in his mind to hide what had happened between them but couldn't. He needed her and resented her and could not bring his feelings under control.

He pushed the cart into the center of the freight elevator and pressed the button for the seventh floor. At the last moment the young couple got into the freight elevator with him. He was afraid they might notice something about the carton but they barely acknowledged him. They were too busy arguing with one another over what to do with the two pianos. They got off on four.

On seven, Dane pushed the cart down the deserted hall to the apartment. There were no workmen on Blackburn's floor; they'd finished up several days before. He pressed the doorbell and waited for the lawyer to let him inside.

The doorbell chimed. Blackburn peered through the peep-hole and saw a young man in a blue uniform with a clipboard standing next to an enormous cardboard television carton. The man smiled at him, a warm ingratiating smile. He opened the door and looked at the carton.

"What the hell am I supposed to do with that?" he asked.

Dane shrugged and started to push the cart inside.

"Wait a minute, wait a minute," Blackburn said, and stopped it with both hands. "Where are you going with that thing? Can't you just leave it out in the hall?"

"They told me to deliver it to this apartment," Dane said. "They didn't tell me to leave it in the hall."

"You always do what you're told?"

Dane nodded.

"Shit," Blackburn said, and stepped back so he could get the cart in the apartment. "Take it in the living room." The lawyer stepped into the kitchen to get out of the way. Dane parked the cart in the middle of the room while Blackburn stood in the kitchen doorway and stared at it malevolently.

"When's he going to pick this thing up?"

"I don't know," Dane said. "You have to sign this." He handed Blackburn the clipboard.

The lawyer looked over the sheet. "There's nothing on here," he said.

"I know," Dane said. "It's easier to fill them in later."

Blackburn handed it back to him. "I don't sign anything that's blank," he said. "I don't care if it's easier for you or not." He glanced again at the carton. "You mind if I take a look at it?"

"Not if you sign this," Dane said. Blackburn rolled his eyes and scrawled his signature across the bottom of the sheet. He made it so illegible that no handwriting analyst in the world could read it anyway.

Blackburn leaned over one end of the carton. "Hey," he said. "Did you know this end is already open?" He poked his head up. The delivery man had a small silver whistle in his hand.

"What's that?" Blackburn asked.

"It's a whistle," Dane said.

"What the fuck you need a whistle for a TV?" he asked, and looked down at the box.

The front of the box opened explosively, knocking him on his back. The wolf attacked immediately. Blackburn got to his knees and threw his arms around the animal. Together they rolled across the carpeting. The wolf tore at the lawyer's face and chest, lunging and pulling back. Blackburn managed to sit up, his face covered with blood. He grabbed the wolf by the front legs and tried to hold him down. The wolf slid forward. The lawyer swung at him with his fists, pummeling the animal on the shoulders and neck. The wolf began to collapse under the terrible pounding.

Dane slipped the knife out of his belt and stepped into the living room, afraid he might have miscalculated, that the wolf might lose. Blackburn yelled triumphantly and pounded harder on the wolf's back. The animal's hind legs gave way and the animal fell sideways on the carpet. Dane moved in with the knife.

Blackburn raised both hands together like a club but the wolf rolled out of the way and his fists slammed against the floor. The wolf shook himself hard and lunged for Blackburn's neck. His jaws raked the side of Blackburn's head, tearing his scalp and cheek wide open.

Blackburn pressed a hand over his torn face and kicked the wolf away from him. Blood poured out between his fingers. He aimed his other hand at the wolf but the animal stayed back. His fist swung wildly through the air.

The wolf attacked again, ripping the lawyer's arm from the elbow to the shoulder. Blackburn looked up at Dane, half blinded by blood and fear, and cried for help. Dane backed away from the dying man and closed his eyes. He didn't want to look at the lawyer again. Blackburn tried to get away. He crawled into the hall on his hands and knees, stumbling every few feet as the wolf struck him again and again. His body shook with each new attack. A spray of blood danced up the white walls. He collapsed a few feet from the door, arms and legs splayed out on the carpet.

He blew the whistle but the wolf refused to stop, even after Blackburn was dead, and Dane had no strength to intervene. He stayed in the kitchen and waited for the wolf to finish. When the sounds of the killing stopped, he clapped his hands once and held them together in front of his face and breathed deeply.

He felt the wolf approach. The animal leaned against the wall beside him, panting heavily. The wolf was so exhausted that he was unable to raise his head. A strand of dark pink saliva dripped from the point of his open jaw, twisting like a piece of string onto the floor.

The wolf shook himself off, a gentle wobble, and padded into the living room and lay down by the shattered carton. He put his head between his paws and went to sleep.

Dane looked at the kitchen clock. It was ten minutes to five. The killing had taken only twenty minutes; it felt like an eternity to him. It would be several hours at least before he could leave, before he knew that it would be safe to use the freight elevator.

He sat down on the couch and watched the wolf sleep. Then he dragged Blackburn's body out of the hall and propped it against the front of the couch. After that, he wandered about the apartment, looking through Blackburn's things. In a small hand-painted box on top of the desk, he found a dozen or more new credit cards; the shelf below the liquor cabinet held a stack of pornographic magazines and video cassettes. Dane went into the bedroom. In the drawer of the nightstand, he found a pistol, a small-caliber automatic. He put it in his pocket without thinking.

When he was finished, he felt himself growing tired. To stay awake, he turned on the television set in the living room and watched a young woman announcer read the news. The lead story was about the wolf killings.

While the police hadn't completely given up their search for the wolf believed to be responsible for the deaths of two people in Central Park, she said, there was still no progress in the case and no indication that there would be any in the near future. A police spokesman came on to explain how difficult it was to patrol an area the size of Central Park with the manpower they had available but that they were doing all they could to keep the park safe. The latest theory they were following was that the wolf was someone's escaped pet.

Dane glanced at the dead man and was startled to see that his eyes were wide open. He tried to shut them but no matter what he did, they remained half open. He looked like he was squinting at the television set. The announcer smiled at both of them and moved on to the rest of the day's news.

Chapter 27

$\mathbf{Y}$ATES FELT LETHARGIC. He sat in the tiny side room away from the other detectives and waited. The waiting was the hardest part because it got into your blood and slowed you down. He sat in his shirtsleeves with his feet up on the desk and leaned backward in the chair. The back of the chair dipped dangerously toward the floor.

One of the detectives stuck his head in the room.

"You got a visitor," he said. "Atwood."

Yates let the chair come forward slowly. At least it's a break in the monotony, he thought. Since the death of the editor in June, little had happened, something that the newspapers still screamed about nearly every single day. Yates didn't know what else to do. Nobody did. The task force had canceled all comp time, they had extra patrols out, emergency services stayed on alert; they even had a new patrol plan approved by the commissioner's office. The newspapers got agitated, the public grew restless, everybody wanted something to happen. Everybody waited.

Yates peered into the lobby. Atwood was sitting at the prisoners' bench just down from the door to his office. The veterinarian stared at the big chain that hung from the wall and stretched across the wall behind the bench. There were no holding cells in Central Park. They handcuffed the prisoners to the chain. What are we going to do if we get the wolf in here? Yates thought.

Yates watched him for a minute. He looks nervous or something, the detective thought, the same way he looked the night he and Tieneman figured out it was a wolf. So maybe he knows something else. Yates shrugged. He'd talk to him.

The veterinarian stood up as Yates approached. "Thanks for seeing me," he said.

"How could I miss you?" Yates said, and led him back to his office.

Yates resumed his position in the chair. Atwood sat on the edge of the desk. Yates moved his feet to make room for him. He lit a cigarette and stuffed the burnt match in his shirt pocket.

"So what's new and exciting?" he asked.

"I was trailing somebody into the park," Atwood answered. The veterinarian seemed abnormally pleased with himself. Somebody else with a bright idea, Yates thought.

"You were doing what?" he asked.

"I followed a guy named Van Owen into the park this afternoon," Atwood said. "You know who he is?"

"Your date?" Yates said just to keep the conversation going. He knew who Van Owen was but it didn't matter. Atwood was going to tell him anyway.

"He runs the New York Sportsman's Society," Atwood said. "He's hunting for the wolf." The idea seemed to engage Yates. He swung his feet off the desk.

"How do you know that?"

"I called him," Atwood said, making it up as he went along. "He's a hunter. I figured since it was one of his people who got killed, he might try something. He said he was thinking about it." Atwood paused. "I think he might be after the publicity."

"Where's he now?"

"I lost him."

"Where was that?"

"In the park somewhere."

Yates smiled. It sounded like so much horseshit to

him but maybe it would keep Atwood out of trouble. Maybe not. Right now the veterinarian looked like he was trying to make up his mind whether or not to tell Yates everything he knew. He had the feeling that for the time being, the veterinarian had decided it was easier to lie.

"What are you doing here?" he asked him.

"I thought we might ride around the park for a while," Atwood said. "See what we can find." He played with the edge of the desk.

Yates ignored his suggestion and attempted a smoke ring. It flowed from his mouth and broke into several pieces.

"I don't want the wolf killed," Atwood said. "That's the truth."

"I believe you," Yates said. He did. The detective stood up. He'd ride around with Atwood for a few hours, help him chase Van Owen around. If he waited long enough, maybe the veterinarian would tell him the rest of the story. It beats sitting around all night working up a shine on my ass, he thought.

"Mind if we eat first?" Yates asked.

"No," Atwood said. "I don't mind. I'll get my stuff."

Chapter 28

DANE HAD FALLEN asleep with the television on and was dreaming of the woods. He stood alone inside the entrance to an immense cathedral of trees, the long open nave canopied with broad green limbs. He raised his arms and watched while the particles of light that drifted above him seemed to settle in his outstretched hands. All around him the air was alive with light; it cascaded from the sky, falling in graceful movements, dancing across the heavens. The air was clean and fresh, the smell of pine and resin, new grass and spring, rushed toward him from the far end of the cathedral. Dane reached down to touch the wolf but the animal was gone. He looked all around but he was alone, lost in this immense empty forest. When he looked up again, the sky was on fire and the burning limbs reached down for him like blackened skeletal hands. Something howled in the distance, a roar like a train through a tunnel that turned into a scream.

The shrill ring of the phone jarred him awake and broke him free of the dream. It screamed at him from the other side of the couch. Next to it, the dead man's head had slumped rigidly to one side, his heavy chin thrust forward, lips frozen in a deformed smile. There was a movie playing on the television.

He got up from the couch and nearly fell over the carton in the center of the room. He turned off the television with a slap of his hand, wishing he could smash the screen with his fist, reduce it all to wreckage, and stumbled for the phone. The dead man's face seemed to stare at him through the half-closed lids. Why couldn't he force them shut? He picked up the phone and listened.

"Dane?" Jenny's voice was a whisper in the room. She spoke his name again, stronger this time, the first tremors of fear becoming apparent. The line crackled between them. She spoke his name once more and he could feel her drawing away. In another second she would hang up the phone.

"I'm here," he said. "Don't hang up."

"Is everything all right?"

The dead man smiled at him. Dane looked away. His foot slipped on part of the carpet next to where the dead man was sitting. Blood came off the sole of his shoe like a piece of dark red taffy.

"Yes," he told her. He felt his own voice getting weaker. Behind her, he heard the sound of traffic, a horn and the squeal of tires. "Where are you?"

"I can't hear you," Jenny said. "You're going to have to talk louder."

"Where are you?" he asked again, louder this time. It was an effort for him. His hand shook holding the phone.

"A few blocks away. Don't ask me anything else because I don't know." Something must have distracted her because there was a short pause. Maybe she was trying to figure out where she was standing. Maybe she was thinking of running away. "How soon should I be there?" she asked.

He wanted her there right now but instead told her to be at the loading dock in twenty minutes. It would take him that long to get himself and the wolf ready to move again.

"How is he?" Her voice was full of concern.

At first he was confused by the question. Did she mean Blackburn? Dane looked down the hall and saw the bloodstains on the carpet, the door, the walls. There was blood everywhere he looked. The answer to her question was easy: he was dead. The wolf stood up and stretched, watching him constantly. Dane realized that Jenny was asking about the wolf. The animal walked over and sniffed at the body.

"There's no problem," Dane told her. He thought he heard her laugh.

"And what about you?"

"I'm okay."

Jenny laughed. This time he heard her clearly. Her laugh was sharp and loud, like the sound of breaking glass.

"Then both my men are safe," she said, and laughed again. He couldn't tell what the laughter meant or what she was thinking. Her laughter stopped abruptly as if it had come up against something hard and unyielding. "I'll be there in twenty minutes," she said.

The wolf lay down next to the body, taking possession of his kill, one paw hooked over the badly torn right leg. He clapped his hands and the wolf responded by slowly raising his head. Dane was suddenly afraid to move, thinking that this was the time the wolf was going to turn on him. He stepped back and clapped again. This time the wolf came to him.

The front of the carton was torn and it took him several minutes to work it into shape to take out of the building. He had to coax the animal back in the carton and once, but only once, the wolf growled and snapped at him. Dane pulled his hand away quickly. There were several long red streaks across the back of it where the wolf's teeth had raked his skin. It was a clear warning. He had to get the wolf out of the apartment soon.

Dane wheeled the cart down the hall and into the freight elevator. When he looked back, he had to catch the cry that rattled in his throat, forcing it down with the last remnants of his will. His hand knotted into a fist.

Running the length of the hall from the apartment door, the parallel tracks of the cart were clearly etched on the carpet. Without realizing it, without even seeing it, he'd left a trail of blood behind him.

Jenny saw Dane on television. He was pushing the cart down a long hall that seemed so dark and cramped on the small screen that it looked like a tunnel. He stopped at the elevator and pressed the button. When it didn't come immediately, he pressed it again and again, slamming the button hard with the heel of his hand. He glanced up in the direction of the camera and looked away, dropping his face toward the floor. The elevator opened and he was gone. A few seconds later, the picture on the screen changed and a new hallway appeared. She was the only one who saw it. The guard was asleep at the desk, his head on his arms.

She stepped out of the office and quietly shut the door behind her. She stood next to the elevator with her back to the wall and waited for him.

The elevator doors opened but instead of Dane, out stepped someone who looked sick and frightened and who grabbed her arm and said in a ragged voice, "We've got to get out of here now."

She pushed the cart toward the van but he took hold of the handle and spun it around. "Leave the carton," he said. "Get the wolf in the van."

"They'll know where it came from," she argued. "We can't just leave it behind."

"Then do it now," he said angrily.

She shoved the carton inside, then coaxed the wolf through the back doors and pushed the cart away. It bumped against the wall and rolled to a slow stop next to the office. She helped Dane down the concrete steps and into the passenger side. He kept looking around to see if anybody was going to stop them.

"He's asleep," she said. "I checked." Dane seemed so confused that she wasn't sure he understood what she'd told him. She started the van. "I saw you," she said, but Dane wasn't listening. He had his eyes closed while his hands shuddered and twitched. She backed the van around and gunned it out of the garage.

She followed his directions and drove straight toward the

river but there was a Con Ed truck blocking the street. He told her to get on the River Drive but that seemed wrong to her. Instead, she turned back into midtown. She drove the van as best she could, half remembering a map of the city, half listening to Dane's confused directions, and tried to find her way north, the only way she knew that seemed safe to her.

Dane drifted in and out of consciousness, telling her first to get to the bridge and then yelling for her to take a completely different route. She was lost in the glut of traffic and one-way streets, turning in what seemed like an endless circle that carried her back to where they'd started. Finally she stopped listening to him and tried to find her own way out of the city.

She pushed the van harder, dropping it into second and running fast through yellow lights that glared red when she passed beneath them. The city became a blur—buildings, cars, horns, people, everything joined together in a stream of light that flashed by her window. The only thing she saw was directly in front of her, the red eyes of taillights, bright, then dim, as endless as the empty hallways she had seen on the television monitors in the dead man's apartment building.

In the back of the van, behind the curtain, she heard the wolf pacing anxiously, bumping against the sides when she took a corner too fast or slid by a taxi on her way to another corner, another street. A sign pointed toward Central Park, and for whatever reason, she took it. He woke up suddenly and yelled at her to stop. She kept going. At the last moment, Dane tried to reach her hands to keep her from turning but it was too late. She twisted the wheel away from him and drove into the park.

Dane was fully awake now and the vividness of the sensations that surrounded him astonished him: the glare of headlights, the sound of the wolf pacing back and forth, the clatter of his claws on the metal floor of the van, the smell of the damp earth and trees mixed with the stench of carbon monoxide, Jenny's labored breathing, loud and repetitious, each gasp escaping through the ragged opening of her half-open mouth; everything had an edge, cut sharp as a razor.

He rolled down his window and felt the heat of the night air pour into the van. Behind the curtain, the wolf snarled at something unseen.

Dane reached for Jenny's arm, to pull her away from the wheel, but she smashed at his arm with her fist and kept the other hand locked on the wheel.

"Keep your hands off of me!" she screamed. The strength of her voice pushed him back against the door.

"Get us out of here!" he yelled.

"Then tell me how," she screamed back, "because I don't know!"

Up ahead, a traffic light went from green to yellow. At first she sped up to reach it but slowed instead and then let the van slide to a stop. She felt like she was suffocating inside the van. The one thing she wanted to do was run, break through the barrier of dark impenetrable air that circled her face and seemed to close off her throat.

"Why are you stopping?" he asked.

She couldn't speak, she could barely even move. He took her arm. This time she had no strength to fight him.

"We have to get out of here now," Dane said. His voice was thick with urgency and fear. "Don't you see what it's doing to him?"

Jenny pulled back the curtain and looked at the wolf. The animal crouched in the far corner of the van, his ears thrown back, the fur on his neck and shoulders bristling, watching both of them.

The wolf remembers, she thought, this place, the other killings. She couldn't control him now, any more than Dane could. Her control was as much a mirage as his.

The light changed to green. She inched the van ahead, touching the brakes gently before shifting into first. The van stalled. Something rammed into the van from behind and she was thrown against the wheel. Dane bounced headfirst into the windshield, holding out his hands at the last moment to break the impact. The wolf tumbled forward along the floor, fighting to keep himself upright. He slipped and rolled against the back edge of the seat.

In the side mirror, Jenny saw what had hit the van. A taxi driver backed his cab away from the van, leaned out the window and shook his fist at her. Without thinking, she opened the door and stepped to the pavement.

Dane screamed at her to stop but it was too late. Jenny turned just as the wolf scrambled up and over her seat. She held out her arms as if to stop him and for a moment the wolf hesitated.

As she swung the door shut the wolf leaped clear of it and out of the van, passing so close to her that his fur brushed the side of her face. She fell back, clinging to the door, and watched the wolf bolt across the open road and into the park.

Dane climbed across the seat to the driver's side, trying desperately to reach her. Jenny looked up at him once, saw the fear and anger in his eyes, and raced after the wolf before he could stop her. The wolf vanished into the darkness, then Jenny. Dane felt as though he were tumbling backward into a deep and troubled sleep, as though the world around him had slowed and died.

The taxi driver stepped out of his cab and kicked the side of the van.

"What the fuck are you two doing here?" he yelled. "Playing hide-and-seek? Get this piece of shit moving!"

The noise jarred Dane alive. He started the van and pulled away, still lost, still uncertain of what there was left for him to do. He wanted to run. The memory of flight was so strong that it was like being sucked into the current of a river. It pulled him along, dragging all his other feelings to the bottom. He decided not to fight but to give in, to surrender to the emptiness of it all. The park seemed noisy and frantic, a place filled with disturbance. He couldn't stand the noise any longer.

He shut his eyes for one brief second and turned the van away from the park into what he imagined was the silence of the city beyond.

Van Owen was two cars in back when the taxi struck the rear of the van. From where he sat, it looked like a kind of startled nudge, something a frightened animal might do to shove its way out of danger. Then he saw the girl get out. He rolled down his window so he could hear her, hear the sound of her voice. He wanted to draw her to him now, pull her in close. She turned and opened her arms to someone inside the van.

He saw the wolf leap out and almost knock her down. The wolf was a blur of motion, his paws barely touching the pavement before he scrambled across the road and into the park. Van Owen reached for the door handle and snapped it open, thinking he might catch the girl before she got back into the van. But instead of climbing into the van, she ran after the wolf.

The cabdriver got out and approached the back of the van. He kicked the side of it and yelled something, shaking his fist at the open door. The scene had all the qualities of a badly dubbed film. Everything was vague and disjointed and he suddenly felt trapped in the line of cars behind the van, exposed, unable to move quickly.

He eased the door shut and waited, watching both sides of the van. He felt the urge to do something, to push everything along, but he forced the feeling away, hammered it down with his will. Wait, wait, he whispered to himself, in a kind of mantra, something will happen soon, wait, wait. He expected the girl and the wolf to emerge from the park at any moment. His blood sang with the idea of it.

Unless the man had changed his mind. He spun the thought around in his mind, testing each facet of it. Maybe by setting the wolf and the girl free, that was exactly what he had done. He held it tightly for a few seconds and then discarded it. It wasn't what the man wanted.

Then the most extraordinary thing happened. An arm reached from inside the van to shut the door and the van drove off.

Van Owen spun the wheel hard and pulled around the taxi, sliding in behind the van. He saw a reflection of the man's face in the side mirror of the van, a face that was white with terror. The face floated in the glass, then dissolved into a serpentine shape and then into nothing, a reflection of black sky.

He stayed with the van. There'd been no change of plans, he thought, only a stupid mistake that had turned to his advantage. The girl and the wolf were loose in the park. The man was going after them; he was going to save them. It was so pathetically easy. Van Owen had seen it all in the man's tormented face.

The man drove the van erratically, first going as far east as Park Avenue, then turning around and cutting back through the park on the Eighty-sixth Street traverse. On the left the Museum of Art glimmered through the trees like an enormous mausoleum. The van sped through the green light on the traverse road and through the dark tunnel to the West Side. At Columbus Avenue, it turned south and raced between lights.

The van turned onto Seventy-ninth and stopped in the middle of the block between Amsterdam and Broadway, a wide stretch of the street with several restaurants and small shops on either side. A car was pulling out. The van pulled up behind it and waited and then slipped into the empty space.

Van Owen stopped near Broadway and kept the vehicle in his rearview mirror. He backed up a few feet and double-parked. The man was already out, running up the street toward the park.

He got out of the car and hurried after him, staying close to the buildings that changed from storefronts to apartments and townhouses the closer they got to the park itself.

The man never looked back, he was so intent on reaching the park. Van Owen loped along, following the outlines of his elongated shadow on the sidewalk, watching it fade in and out of the light, while the sounds of the city washed over him. It was like the beginning of a great hunt and he felt himself rising to it, thinking of the wolf and the girl and how strangely everything had turned out. He had been here before. He could see the end coming and felt something hot and wet flowing through his fingers. The sensation was so real that he had to look down to see that his hands were clean, that he had imagined it all. Not much longer, he thought. The one thing that stood in his way was only a few yards ahead of him.

The man dashed across Central Park West into the park without bothering to look. Van Owen stopped at the edge of the darkness to listen. The man's footsteps were sharp and clear, the sound of his breathing an echo that followed their frantic gait. He plunged in after him.

Van Owen had no weapon with him but that didn't matter. He had his hands. He could do more damage with those than with any weapon imaginable.

Chapter 29

"THIS IS WHERE he brought you?" Yates asked. He stood on the Ramble side of the bow bridge and smoked a cigarette. His car was parked several yards away by the Cherry Hill fountain. Atwood shrugged.

"Maybe it was a joke," Yates said. "Maybe this guy got tired of you playing Bulldog Drummond on his time." Atwood refused to rise to the bait and stepped over one of the red plastic lines that was still up.

"Where's your sense of humor?" Yates asked. They had been driving around now for a couple of hours and Atwood's story had only gotten more vague. Yates didn't mind at first. He was happy to be out of the station. Now he was tired of the veterinarian's virgin act; the guy was either going to put out or he was going home. Yates walked back to the car. Let him poke around in the dark.

When he got in the front seat, he saw Atwood's bag and opened it up. Right on top he found the dart gun and the plastic case full of tranquilizer darts. He put them back inside. Atwood was serious about saving the wolf. Jesus, Yates thought, I got a goddamn hero on my hands.

Atwood opened the door and slid inside.

Yates pulled out of the park and turned downtown.

"Where are we going?" Atwood asked.

"I'm taking you home," Yates said. "I've wasted enough time tonight. You want to tell me where you live?"

"I don't know about that," Atwood said. "Can I trust you?"

"You could take a hike," Yates said. The detective seemed to be losing his sense of humor, so Atwood gave him his address. They drove along in silence. Atwood rolled down his window and looked at the people on the street.

"Hey, Atwood," Yates said out of the blue. "You got a permit for that dart gun you're lugging around?"

"You looked through my bag?"

"No," Yates said. "I located it with my X-ray vision."

Atwood pulled his bag toward him. "I don't believe it," he said angrily. He zipped it up and then shoved it on the floor. "Who the hell said you could search my things?"

Yates slammed the car to a stop by the curb. Brakes squealed behind them. Horns screamed. Yates ignored them. He whirled around in the seat and stuck a finger in Atwood's startled face.

"I'm going to use numbers," Yates said. "That'll make this easy for you to remember. One, I don't need permission to search your crummy bag. I'm a cop. I got a license from the city. Two, I'm tired of dicking around with you. If you've got some information, fine, you tell me. If you don't, stay out of my way." He withdrew his finger. Atwood thought he could see a hole in the air where it had been.

"Now," Yates asked again. "Have you got a permit for that thing?"

"More or less," Atwood said. "I never sent in the form."

"More or less, it's a felony," Yates observed. "So's withholding evidence." He pulled the car away from the curb.

I'm not withholding evidence, Atwood thought, I'm only editing it. The detective's outburst had shaken him up but it hadn't changed his mind. He still didn't trust Yates.

"Let me have a cigarette," Atwood asked.

Yates pulled one out of his pack. Atwood took one and held it to his nose. "There're some matches on the seat," Yates said.

"I just like to smell them," Atwood said.

Yates grabbed the cigarette from under Atwood's nose and stuck it in his mouth. He picked the matches up off the seat, bent the cover back, folded a match over, and pushed it across the strike pad with his thumb. The match popped and flared.

"You get tired of sniffing around," he said, "you be sure and give me a call."

Scout's honor, Atwood thought.

The patrol unit was parked in the back of the parking lot behind the public rest rooms near the Seventy-ninth Street traverse. From there, it had a fairly clear view of the bottom third of Belvedere Lake, the museum, and the expanse of the Great Lawn. The two policemen inside the unit were young and had been pulled into what Task Force Command called the Park Patrol Enhancement Squad (PPES). Anyone could sign up but it had to be on a regular rotation basis and it meant a lot of overtime. The men referred to it as the Piss Patrol.

The driver had a round black face and kept his hat on the seat next to him. His partner was white and wore his pushed back on the top of his head like a cowboy.

The black cop leaned his head out of the window.

"Did you hear anything?" he asked.

"I heard something. What did you hear?"

"I don't know. I thought I heard something, too."

His partner laughed. "I think it's your brain dying of syphilis."

"Fuck you," the driver said, laughing as well. His laughter stopped as though it had hit a brick wall. "Listen."

His partner took off his hat and leaned his head out the window. Yes, it was definitely something, he thought, a rustling like bits of paper being scraped together.

"Whatever it is, it's moving," he said.

"Quiet," the driver said.

Both men listened again. The rustling stopped.

The driver got out and walked a few feet to the back of the car and stared into the Ramble.

"You see anything?" his partner whispered.

"Not a damn thing," the driver said.

He's pissed, the white cop thought. His voice had that *tone* to it again. The driver had been a Marine. His partner figured that was where he'd picked it up. People always picked up something like that in the Marines, something that they didn't need at all.

The driver stood beside the door but said nothing.

"You want to call somebody?"

"Like who?" the driver asked.

"The detectives," his partner said. "Who else?"

"Not yet," the black cop said, and pulled the flashlight from under the seat. "I'm going to see just what's out there."

"It's supposed to be a wolf," his partner said, but not loud enough for the driver to hear. He was wrong. The driver stuck his head through the open door.

"You believe that wolf shit?" he said.

The white cop shrugged. "Shouldn't I go with you?" he asked.

"Wait in the car."

The white cop persisted. "I think I ought to come with you."

"I know what you think. You got a lot to learn. I'll be back in five."

He watched the black cop disappear into the ramble. I'll give you five minutes, he thought, and if your black ass isn't back in this vehicle on time, I'm going to get the whole goddamn task force down here. *That's* what I think.

Dane worked his way into the Ramble, the one place he knew the wolf might go. It was closest in the animal's memory. He wanted both of them with him, safe and alive. The thought of it gnawed at the pit of his stomach as he moved through the thick woods.

He forced himself to slow down, to slow everything down, to kill the fear before it had a chance to grow. A huge slab of rock bulged out of the bare dirt beneath his feet. He stopped beside it.

That was when he heard it, a sharp intake of breath from the darkness to his right, the direction he'd come from only seconds before. As he listened, the sound moved toward him. Then it faded. Dane turned so that his back was against the rock. He heard another sound, the minute scrape of a heel against stone that was almost immediately swallowed up by the surrounding trees. The sound was closer now.

Someone was stalking him.

Dane dropped silently and crawled along the ground to a point where the trees opened into a worn dirt gully that snaked up a narrow peaked hill just above the rock. He crept through the gully, feeling the bits of exposed stone and the jagged edges of broken roots dig into his belly while he climbed with agonizing slowness. A few feet from the peak he stopped and listened again.

He heard other sounds, the murmur of voices, fractured and broken by their passage through the trees, the trill of water cascading over the narrow rocks, the distant clatter of automobiles, and the squeal of brakes; each sound, even the beating of his heart, was as clear and distinct as if it were a single note played to an empty room.

He saw it this time, at the bottom of a steep incline near the small stream that meandered through the ramble. To the right was an algae-covered pond surrounded by soft marshy ground. To the left, another pond, smaller, a shallow stagnant backwater. Between them, the briefest glimmer of white skin. In no more than the flutter of an eye, it was there and gone.

Dane slipped over the top of the hill, certain that sooner or later, whoever was below would follow him. All he could do now was to put a little more distance between them.

The black cop knew just where he wanted to be because he'd been there during the day. He'd done a little reconaissance, nothing major, just a walk through the Ramble to see what was there. Nothing much, he'd decided, except rocks and dirt and a lot of ugly white men. No wonder the guy lost his lunch in here. A place like this didn't belong in the city. The city was all sharp angles and noise. This place was quiet and soft; the edges blurred together after a while. He damn near broke his neck climbing around it and that's when he'd discovered a primitive lookout, a crumbling stone platform in the middle of everything. He'd decided it was a good spot to be and he'd memorized the path to it in case he had to find it again in the dark.

Which was what he was doing right now. He kept his flashlight off so he walked through the woods exactly the way he remembered it, never missing a step. It had a nice spooky feel to it, like there was something out there waiting for you, you just didn't know what it might be. He was ready for it, whatever it was. He felt real good about it, loose, ready.

He worked out every day in the decrepit weight room behind the main precinct building and was amazed how few cops actually kept in shape. Why bother, his partner had said. So you don't end up a fat ignorant motherfucker when you hit forty, the black cop thought, and so you'd be ready when a good opportunity came along. Like it was right now. He was going to blow this wolf or whatever it was away and get the fuck out of the Piss Patrol for the rest of his tour of duty.

He reached the lookout and scanned the area. On his third sweep, he saw something slip through the trees below him near the little stream and another quick blur of motion that came from a steep hill back to his left.

He waited a few more seconds and saw the first shadow climb out of the ravine and move up the hill. The black cop slid off the lookout and crept through the underbrush after it. Whatever it was, it didn't look like a wolf to him. He stuck the flashlight through his belt and took out his revolver.

He was going to have a good time tonight, he thought. Playing hide-and-seek in the dark with live rounds.

The wolf led Jenny deeper into the Ramble. The animal moved surefootedly along the dirt paths, staying just a few feet ahead of her so she could follow his movements, compensating for her lack of knowledge of the terrain. She stayed with him, running low over the rocky ground, breathing in rhythm with each step to muffle the sound of her passage.

If there was a time to escape, she thought, it was now, even though she had no idea how she would get out of the city with the wolf. Where he was leading her, she didn't know, except that he seemed to be circling toward the lake. She could see the reflection of the lights on the water through the trees.

She followed the wolf off the high ground and climbed onto a path that wound down past high rock walls. What little light there was vanished completely. She slowed, afraid to move any faster. In the near distance, she heard the sound of the stream.

A hand struck like a snake from the high stone wall and wrapped around her mouth, dragging her into darkness with such strength that she was lifted completely off the ground. She kicked her legs wildly but hit only air. The hand closed tighter while the other groped around her waist. Jenny bit down hard on the fleshy part of the palm and let up only when she heard Dane whisper her name.

He pulled her with him and backed around the edge of the wall. Behind him, the rocks fell away into a wide ravine and the stream. She wrapped her arms around his neck and felt the wolf slide between them and push his nose against her breast.

From the bottom of the ravine, there was a flash of bright light and another voice.

"Don't you move, motherfucker," the voice said. "Not a goddamn inch."

Van Owen didn't stop running, not when he realized that he'd lost track of the man, not even when the light exploded out of the darkness and he saw the man and the girl crouched in the illuminated darkness above, not even when he realized that the man standing on the edge of the stream with the flashlight and gun in his hand was a cop. If he stopped now, the cop would probably turn and shoot him.

He saw her eyes move toward him, a momentary flicker. She seemed so real that he wanted her right then, wanted to feel her moving beneath him. The desire was so strong that he almost lost his footing. He saw the rock directly in front of him, brought both feet together, and pushed off.

At the noise, the cop swung around and Van Owen hit him with the point of his elbow in the side of the throat. The cop dropped the light and crumpled. Van Owen grabbed the light and brought the large heavy end up into the man's face. The cop snapped open like a jackknife and tumbled backward against the side of the ravine. Blood sprayed across Van Owen's face; he could taste it on his tongue. All he could think about was getting to the girl just a few yards away.

In the darkness, he struck out again with the flashlight and felt it break against stone. He shifted his aim, using the broken end like a spear. It caught the black man in the chest and the man cried out. Van Owen leaned hard on it, trying to push the flashlight deeper into the man's flesh.

The cop raised his gun and pulled the trigger. The concussion exploded in Van Owen's ear and he rolled away from it. The cop, blind with blood and pain, fired the gun until it was empty.

His partner in the patrol unit heard the first shot and sat up. The other shots came in quick succession, each one seeming to get louder as it echoed through the trees.

His fingers were suddenly filmy with sweat. He grabbed the radio mike, dropped it, picked it up again and screamed into it.

"Unit twelve. Shots fired, officer down. Request immediate backup. Ramble Station parking lot."

He remembered to release the mike. The response crackled out of the speaker.

"Unit twelve, we need a clarification of your situation."

"Just send the goddam backup," he screamed.

"Backup is on its way," the speaker said. "Can you see the officer?"

"No, I can't see him," he yelled. "He's in the middle of the Ramble."

A wave of static washed over the car as he waited for a reply.

"Shit," the speaker said.

It was only a matter of minutes before the first backup units converged on the small parking lot. Now there were five other cops with him, moving close together through the ramble. He moved away from them and tried to follow his memory of the gunshots. It didn't matter that he was going to get his ass reamed for letting his partner go off alone in the first place; that was history. It only mattered that he find him first.

He heard his partner's voice through the trees. Except that it didn't sound like his partner. It didn't sound like anything *human* anymore. It sounded like a wounded animal, a moan so dark and painful that he had to brace himself to keep from screaming out loud in response. He'd never heard anything like it before. The light from his flashlight played over the mud and rocks and picked up bits of shimmering green from the surface of the stream.

He heard the moaning again, the same sound over and over again, like the cop was trying to say something. Christ, he thought, what the hell had happened out here?

He moved down into the gully, stiff-legged and awkward, half stumbling over the rocks, afraid of what he might see in the flashlight's beam.

He held his breath and raised the light slowly.

His partner's face was smashed. His jaw moved slowly up and down, broken teeth clicking together. He still had the gun in his hand, stretched out beside him on the bloody ground.

The injured cop opened his eyes and stared at his partner. He started to say something, his jaws working hard to get it out. It was like watching a corpse come back to life. He coughed hard and spit up a mouthful of blood. The white cop knelt beside him. He heard the sound of a helicopter. A searchlight weaved toward them through the trees.

The white cop held his partner in his arms. "Take it easy," he said to him, "just take it easy."

The noise of the helicopter was louder now, a deep rhythmic boom settling over the trees. The blades sucked the air from around them and sent dust and bits of leaves swirling around their heads. The searchlight found them.

A voice called over a loudspeaker. "Do you need assistance down there?"

The white cop waved his hands and yelled that he needed a doctor. He didn't know if they could hear him or not, so he yelled it several more times.

The helicopter backed off a little but kept the light on them. The white cop turned around to see his partner holding up three fingers of his right hand and grinning with his bloody broken mouth. The white cop began to cry and covered his eyes with one hand to hide the tears.

"Were three of them?" he asked. He got down close. "Is that what you mean?"

The black cop pressed three bloody fingers hard against his partner's cheek and fainted.

Van Owen slid into the water at the mouth of the stream and his feet sank into the muck at the bottom up to his ankles. He stopped moving, leaned forward, almost floating, and carefully lifted each foot out. The sound of a helicopter fluttered over the lake. He raised his head out of the water to see the searchlights and then the helicopter itself maneuvering over the trees, coming to a stop above the place where he'd attacked the cop.

He swept through the water toward the black outlines of a small bridge. Green scum clung to his cheeks and his hair. He swam on his back, with only his head showing. The helicopter twisted and turned over the trees. He kept swimming.

They'd gotten away, the girl, the man, and the wolf, all three of them. When he found the path, they were gone and he heard the sirens and the distant thump of the helicopter and the sound of the cops as they worked their way toward him. There wasn't much time. He could see them, flashlights shining through the trees. He climbed down the slope and made his way to the edge of the lake. The cold water took his breath away.

One opportunity missed but so much gained. He understood the man now and that put them on equal ground. The man was no longer a mystery, he had a face, a form. Van Owen already knew his weakest point.

The man wouldn't risk the wolf getting loose again, not like tonight. Next time the animal might not be so easy to recapture. That would change whatever plans the man had made.

And that would make it easier for Van Owen to kill him.

He stayed under the bridge for over an hour while the police searched the park. Another helicopter was brought in and they swept the whole area unsuccessfully. Footsteps and voices pounded over his head while the sky was lit with shafts of light from the helicopter searchlights. He lay in the cool water and thought about the girl, the way her face had looked when the light first hit her, full of fear and surprise, the way it might look in his hands.

Jenny waited in the small park on the north side of the Museum of Natural History for Dane to bring the van. She sat huddled in the dark beside a broken bench with her arms wrapped tight around the wolf's neck and hung on like a dead weight. Police cars cruised by slowly on Columbus Avenue. One of them turned a spotlight on the park but it swept high over their heads and missed them completely. The ground was wet, the air thick and humid. Jenny shivered, cold despite the wolf's warmth. The animal was alert and kept his eyes on the street.

She had no idea who'd hit the cop but somehow she thought it was important to find out. There hadn't been any time to think about it in the park. After the first shot, Dane had pulled her to her feet and they were off, running along the narrow path, the wolf out in front. She seemed to skim over the ground like a stone over a lake. They were already across the small bridge when she heard the helicopter and looked back to see it swoop down on the ramble. Dane jerked her arm hard and they ran faster. They crossed the park's West Drive and kept running until they reached a wide gravel path. From there they raced through a tunnel and climbed the last few feet out of the park. They stopped just before the sidewalk and hid behind the high wisteria bushes that grew along the top of the wall and obscured their view of the street.

They were across from the museum. He told her to take the wolf and wait in the small park on the other side of the building. She did it without a word, stepping away from the safety of the bushes onto the sidewalk. When she clapped her hands, the wolf followed her instinctively. They crossed the street. Just a girl and her large dog. Cars and pedestrians passed without a glance, strangers in a hurry to be someplace else. The small park was deserted except for one or two drunks who were stretched out on the benches along Columbus.

They'd waited less than five minutes when Jenny saw the van pull to a stop around the corner from the museum and flash its lights once. A few minutes later, they were driving up Broadway and then Riverside Drive and north on the thruway, finally free of the city.

The wolf curled up against the back of her seat and slept, oblivious to everything. Jenny wrapped herself in the rhythm of the highway, closed her eyes. She laid her head against the window and listened to the purr of the wheels, feeling each vibration. She was never going back, she thought, no matter what happened. Dane could do whatever he wanted to, finish the killings if that's what he thought was important, but if he tried to take the wolf away from her again, she was going to stop him. The wolf belonged to her now. She reached behind her seat and laid a hand on the wolf's flank. The animal stirred and moved closer. Jenny held onto his fur, lacing it through her fingers.

The van slowed and she opened her eyes. Dane let it drift to a stop on the shoulder. In both directions, the highway was deserted, just like the night he'd picked her up in Canada, the night she'd asked him what he was going to do to her and he had stared at her for a long time, not saying anything until at last he turned away and said, "Nothing," and pulled back on the highway as though nothing at all had happened. But even she could feel the change. She could see it in the way he looked at her for the rest of the trip.

She turned in her seat, ready to use everything she had if he tried to hurt her. Like before, it took him a long time to say it.

"We can't take any more chances like tonight," he said. "We have to end this thing soon."

It wasn't what he said that struck her as odd or different but the way he said it. He looked nearly the same as he had that first night. The skin around his eyes seemed bruised and puffy and his hair was longer and pushed back off his forehead, exposing the deep furrows in his flesh. It was his voice that had changed.

When he spoke this time, there was nothing behind it. His words were an artifice to protect him from a loss that had already occurred, one that had finally caught up with him, as he must have known it would.

She stared at him until he turned away.

"The other man in the park tonight," she said. "Who was he?"

"I didn't see him," he said, but she swept it aside. It was almost too easy.

"Yes, you did," she said.

"Van Owen," he said.

Before, he was only a name; now the name had a face.

"He's the one you're really after, isn't he?" she asked.

"Yes," he said finally, and started the van.

There was something else that Dane hadn't told her but it didn't matter. She'd seen it for herself; Van Owen had been in the park tonight hunting for *them*. She watched Dane's grim, tired face as he drove. They'd been lucky tonight. She doubted it would happen again.

The first three had been easy. Killing Van Owen would be a battle, one that they might lose.

Jenny lay in her bed and listened to Dane's footsteps as he stepped quietly down the stairs. She waited for the sound of the back door opening but it never came. She climbed out of bed and slipped on a shirt. The house was still, like a sleeper undisturbed. He moved so silently, she thought, he could be anywhere. She felt a brief fear, and looked behind her. The hall was empty.

The stairs seemed to bend with each step, as if the wood were some rough and heavy fabric, pliable to her touch. A few steps from the bottom, she stopped, hoping she might hear him, wondering where he might be. But there was only silence and she reached the last step and stood in the doorway.

"I couldn't sleep," Dane said. He sat on the floor near the far corner of the darkened room. Without asking, she crossed the floor and sat down. The silence was like a wedge between them. She had the feeling that she was interrupting some kind of ritual, a ceremony she wouldn't understand.

He felt different, distant and cold, as though he had made up his mind, come to some understanding of himself that had nothing to do with her or the wolf, while she still had so far to go.

She got to her knees, ready to leave.

"No," he said. "Stay here."

He reached for her, let his hand rest softly on her arm. Her fingers worked their way to his and she held on, trying to squeeze warmth into his flesh.

"It was quiet like this at night," he said suddenly. "In the canyons. The wind stayed high above the trees. The skies were so clear."

He said it as if he were still there, as if he could open the door and walk into the canyon, away from everything. She wondered if he was aware of what had happened to all of them, if he had any real understanding of what he'd done.

She fought her feelings toward him, fought until she reached a balance between need and fear. Her fear had kept her alive; she'd survived because of it. No matter what happened, she would not let go of that. A cautious truce was the best she could manage.

"Is that what you write about in your journals?" she asked. "Your memories?"

"No," Dane said. "There's more."

"What?" she asked.

"My life," he said. He spoke as if it had already ended.

She pulled him toward her without thinking. To her great surprise he offered no resistance. He laid his head against her neck, his breath warm on her skin. His hands pushed underneath her shirt with an urgency that surprised her.

She moved back and lifted the shirt over her head. Then she pulled him on top of her, feeling his weight settle on her hips. The cold pinch of his shirt buttons cut down through the hollow of her chest. She wrapped her legs around his waist, pushing down with her hands on the small of his back, forcing him hard against her. She slid one hand between them so she could feel him. The motion made him gasp.

He slid off her. She caught one of his hands and moved it between her legs, forcing her thighs together to hold him there. He gripped her tightly, his hand stiff and unyielding. She could feel the cool tips of his fingers buried in her flesh. She opened the front of his pants and ran her hand up and down to make him hard. She released him and closed her mouth over his. The stubble on his cheeks scratched against her face.

Dane took off his pants and kicked them into a pile at his feet. He started to unbutton his shirt but she stopped him. She did it herself, kissing his chest all the way down, while her hand stroked him.

She lay back and pulled him on her, holding him with one hand while she guided him, then pushed hard on his back to force him inside of her with a sudden thrust. She pushed against him at the same time with her hips and curled her legs over his.

He threw his head back and cried out. She held his face against hers and rocked slowly.

There was time enough for this, she thought, that was all. This was what she would take with her when she left.

It was nearly two o'clock in the morning and Yates was finally finished with the mess in Central Park. After the crime scene unit had found some animal hairs stuck to the rocks near the scene, the head of the task force had taken over as a matter of course. That left Yates with the lunatic fringe. They had been crossing his desk at the rate of about one every hour. So far he had six UFO sightings and one voodoo sacrifice involving a goat. The fact that a member of the Piss Patrol had gotten his head kicked in while stalking through the ramble in the dark didn't surprise Yates at all. The cop was a cowboy. He was surprised it had taken as long as it had for him to catch his lunch.

The park had been closed off almost immediately but so far nothing had turned up. The search continued. It would probably taper off in another hour or so with much the same results.

Still, the night wasn't a complete bust, Yates thought. Atwood had slunk off in the middle of everything like a man with a guilty conscience and Yates had to grin. The boy was going to come in handy one of these days and he didn't even know it yet.

Then there was Van Owen. He pulled his master sheet from one of the file cabinets and read the part that referred to him. It was short, not more than a paragraph. He had paraphrased most of the report except for one line: *Subject appeared undisturbed by the entire incident including photographs of the deceased.*

The fact that Van Owen hadn't reacted to anything wasn't necessarily unusual—people were unpredictable when it came to death—but Yates had singled out the description just the same. Something had struck him about it, a pure gut reaction. Now, as he reread it, the feeling was even stronger. Atwood had known about him, had known enough to follow him into the park, and that only added to it. He wanted to know a little more about Van Owen, where he lived, what he did during the day, where he went at night. For that matter, he wanted to know more about Atwood. He just didn't want to tell anybody about it, not yet. He put the file away and stepped into the lobby, looking for a couple of cops he knew who owed him favors.

Chapter 30

BLACKBURN'S NEIGHBOR NOTICED the tracks on the carpet the next morning. When he returned home later that night, the stains were still there and it looked as though they'd gotten worse. He took out a small black leather notebook and wrote down the time and nature of the offense. He was going to let the front desk know that this sort of thing was not acceptable.

The following day, the young woman at the front desk said that it was the first she'd heard of it but that it would be taken care of as soon as possible. But when he returned that afternoon, the stains were still there and now there was a smell in the hallway as well, a faint putrid odor that seemed to be coming from the apartment next door. He called the desk. The young woman apologized and said that someone would take care of it first thing in the morning.

There was someone in the hall the next morning, scrubbing the carpet with a large machine. The young woman from the front desk was there as well.

The smell was worse than before. Even the carpet cleaner was aware of it. He switched off the machine and leaned against the wall, smoking a cigarette. The smoke helped to mask the smell.

"What is it?" she asked him.

"It smells like something died in there," the carpet man said.

The woman knocked on Blackburn's door but got no answer. She knocked again. The carpet man reached over her head and pounded on the door. It sounded like somebody banging on a steel drum in the middle of an empty auditorium. She made him stop.

"Just trying to help," he said, and returned to his vigil against the wall.

Finally, even though it broke several building rules, she took out her master key and unlocked the apartment door. At the last moment, something made her step back, a sharp stab of apprehension that she felt deep in the pit of her stomach.

"You got cold feet?" the carpet man asked. He gently moved her out of the way and grabbed the handle. The door stuck on the blood-soaked carpet. "No problem," he said. He put his shoulder against it and shoved the door open.

The smell was definitely stronger with the door open. Still, it wasn't that bad. He straightened up and pushed the door open a little more and stepped further into the apartment.

"Holy shit," he said when he got to the living room.

What had once been human was now a bloated heap next to the couch. One hand, as gray as stone, stuck out from the body at an angle, two of the fingers twisted around each other like pieces of wire. The rest of the fingers were missing. It looked like something had chewed them off.

Yates isolated himself from the activity in the apartment. He sat in a leather chair in the far corner of the living room and stared at a piece of paper while everyone worked around him. They did their jobs and he ignored them, ignored the flash from the strobe lights of the photographers, the detectives sifting through the contents of the dead man's garbage on the kitchen table, the groans of laughter when somebody found the guy's missing fingers beneath the body and held them up in a plastic baggie so everybody could see.

The air conditioning and disinfectant had softened the smell in the apartment by the time Yates got there. Now the place smelled a little like moldy flowers. Detectives from the Nineteenth Precinct had taken the call. They took one look at the body and called Yates.

The detectives from the Nineteenth already had several working theories when he arrived: maybe this was the guy with the pet wolf who was eating people in the park and maybe it wasn't; maybe this was a *friend* of the guy with the pet wolf and maybe it wasn't; maybe this guy had a very strange sex life.

Yates examined the body and the apartment, pacing from the living room to the kitchen to the blood-splattered hallway. One of the detectives from the task force asked him to look at the kitchen. The cupboards and the refrigerator were overstocked and there was a list on one of the counters for more.

"You couldn't get any more food in this place if you used a truck," the detective said. "It's like the guy was stocking up for a siege."

That's what it seemed like. Even though no one was absolutely certain, the people at the front desk couldn't remember the lawyer leaving the building in the last few weeks. The visitors' log showed that no one had come to see him during that time as well. Yates wanted to talk to the dead man's neighbor, but after they found the body, the man had eaten a handful of tranquilizers and gone to bed.

The day man on the delivery dock was a little more helpful. He remembered a tall thin guy delivering a television set two days before but that was about it. He couldn't remember the guy's truck or where he was from or what he looked like beyond the fact that he was tall and on the thin side. Nobody saw him leave, either.

The lawyer's wallet and whatever the detectives could find in the apartment that looked interesting had been dusted for prints. Yates expected nothing in the way of usable prints and was rarely disappointed. As evidence, they were highly overrated. The evidence, including the wallet, had been vouchered and put aside for Yates to look at, everything except the collection of pornography in the liquor cabinet.

Yates took the material into the living room and stood by one of the chairs that faced the sliding glass doors and the balcony. Before he sat down, he checked the doors. They were locked and braced with a metal rod. The curtains were drawn as well.

He pulled them back. Nice view. Why does a guy close off a view like this? Because he's afraid somebody might be looking in, that's why. He was scared, even on the seventh floor. The lawyer *was* under siege but who was out there?

Yates left the questions alone and pulled a coffee table over in front of him and laid the material out on it. The detectives put the apartment material in a plastic bag to keep it separate from what had been found on the body and Yates went through it carefully, piece by piece. It was like sorting through somebody's life, trying to figure them out, a job he always liked. It didn't matter whose life it was, either; it was *somebody's* and that's all that mattered.

The letter slipped past him at first. He read it without seeing it and was ready to move on to the next one before realizing what he'd found. There was no sudden flash of recognition, only a sense of quiet surprise. He leaned back in the chair and read the letter, a short note from Benjamin Walker to Blackburn, saying how terrific it was seeing him again and how wonderful the evening turned out to be despite the funeral and Van Owen.

He looked again at the date of the letter. It was too close to be a coincidence. Yates had no way of knowing but he was willing to bet that the funeral was George Lange's. The detective pushed the thought aside and concentrated on the rest of the material. He had a connection between the three dead men now. The only problem was he didn't know what it was. There was nothing in the rest of the apartment stuff but he went through it twice to make certain.

Finally he went through the wallet, a scratched and worn burgundy alligator number, thick with money—nearly five hundred in small bills—and a handful of credit cards, some of which Yates didn't even know existed. He didn't understand why the lawyer needed to carry so much cash around with him. The guy had more credit cards than he'd ever seen and he wasn't even counting the dozen in the box on the desk. He figured Blackburn could have gone from New York to Fiji without breaking the sweat on a five-dollar bill.

There was more. Blackburn was a member of the New York and New Jersey bar associations, the Vertical Club, although judging from the lawyer's heft, he didn't make it there too often, the Princeton Club, and the Stanford Alumni Association. There were a few more bits and pieces, some phone numbers and addresses that would need to be checked out, but nothing of any real significance until the very end when he found another card, a membership to the New York Sportsman's Society, and everything seemed to fall into place.

Chapter 31

YATES HAD NEVER been to Gramercy Park, not in all his years on the force. It was an oversight, he decided. He pulled up in front of the New York Sportsman's Society that afternoon but before going inside, he took a brief stroll around the park, staring curiously over the wrought-iron railing at the statue in the middle of it. Sometimes there seemed to be as many statues in New York as there were people, he thought; the statues just had better manners.

Van Owen's secretary was cool to him at first but cordial after he flashed his shield for her. She didn't know if he was still in but she would certainly check.

"Take a seat," she said. "I'll be right back."

Yates sat down in a high-backed green leather chair, the kind that he always associated with British movies, and waited. On the table next to the chair was a glossy fishing magazine, *The Compleat Angler*. He'd been fishing once in his life, the summer he and his ex-wife had gone to Maine for two weeks. He had made two important decisions that summer; he didn't like fishing very much and he didn't like his wife at all. The magazine was pretty good, though. He started to read an article about fly fishing in Scotland because he liked the clothes one of the fishermen was wearing.

The secretary returned with a warm smile on her face and showed him into Van Owen's office. Yates wondered if the man was sleeping with her. She was young, she was attractive, she looked like she could talk without cue cards. He couldn't decide.

Van Owen looked young, too, that was his immediate impression. After he shook hands and sat down in one of the leather office chairs—the place had more leather than most of the weird bars he'd been in—he decided that his first impression was way off. It didn't upset him but it did make him more curious. Who the hell was this guy?

He was a couple inches shorter than Yates, firm handshake, polite smile, good muscle tone. The guy stayed in shape but he didn't look like a fanatic. Short hair, maybe ex-military, he appeared to be casual about everything when in all probability he wasn't casual about a thing. Van Owen kept his eyes on him all the time, a man used to being in control. So let him be in control, Yates thought. After they sat down, the detective noticed a reddish bruise on the right side of his face. It started just below the rim of his cheekbone and stopped at his hairline. Yates looked away quickly. Van Owen didn't seem to care.

"Nice place," Yates said. The windowless office was on the small side, fifteen, maybe sixteen feet square, and that was probably by choice, Yates thought. Three walls were an off-white. The wall behind Van Owen's desk was paneled with dark brown wood. A pair of wooden filing cabinets stood behind the desk. Next to the filing cabinets was another door.

A large glass-front bookcase took up most of the wall to his left, an ornately carved wooden clock dominated the other. Yates noticed that the clock wasn't working, and looked all around.

Some old-fashioned prints, hunting scenes it looked like, were clustered behind him on both sides of the front door. An empty wooden coat rack stood in the right corner, partially obscuring some of the prints.

Van Owen nodded his appreciation. His face was lost in shadows that even the large brass desk lamp couldn't penetrate. Yates realized that the light in the office had been dimmed on purpose. It made him feel a little claustrophobic, the first time he could remember feeling like that. It was like sitting in a cave. He expected to hear echoes and the sound of water dripping in subterranean pools. Caught in the edge of the light, Van Owen's eyes shimmered.

It's like watching an animal, Yates thought. I'm not going to get a goddamn thing out of this guy. I'll be lucky if he confirms his own name. He smiled at Van Owen.

"I understand you identified George Lange for a couple of our patrol officers," Yates said.

Van Owen didn't say anything. Yates took out a small notebook and pretended to skim through it looking for the date.

"It was back in May," Yates said. "Let me see if I can pin that date down for you."

"I know when it was," Van Owen said. His voice sounded funny, like he was speaking from the bottom of a well. Yates wondered what other tricks the guy was going to try on him.

"Then you remember it?"

"Yes."

"Good," Yates said, and consulted the notebook again. "He was a member. Am I right?"

Van Owen nodded. His eyes went opaque and lost their shine. He forgot that the detective was in the room with him. He began to feel light-headed, a delirious sensation, delicate as gossamer. In his mind, he saw the face of the girl again, felt her skin beneath his fingers, watched her twist and turn in pain. It brought him back to the room and the man sitting on the other side of his desk.

Yates took an envelope from the breast pocket of his sport coat. "Here," he said, "let me show you something."

He laid pictures of the three dead men across the front of the desk so he could see their faces. "It's the damnedest thing," Yates said. "All three were members here and all three of them are dead." Van Owen kept his eyes on Yates. "They died the same way."

"What a tragic coincidence," Van Owen said.

"They were all killed by a wolf."

Van Owen said nothing.

"It's a real mystery," Yates said. "I thought you might help me out with it."

Van Owen picked up the photos. He glanced casually at each one. They were black-and-white, taken with a flash, full of bloody details. Insubstantial images, Van Owen thought. He could remember the real thing. He fanned them out in his hand like playing cards.

"Why would I want to do that?" he asked.

"So I don't have to come down on you like a fucking hammer," Yates said, mostly to see what would happen. Not much, he decided.

Van Owen laid the photos down on the desk. The bruise on his face began to throb in time to his heart. He could feel each cell, each molecule fill with blood; each one whispered his name. Compared with what he knew, the detective's threat seemed as insubstantial as the pictures in front of him. The man was as transparent as ice. He wanted to be rid of him.

"It's better if there are two of you," Van Owen said. "With one, you never know who you're talking to, the good cop or the bad cop." He paused. "Which one is it this time?"

Yates ignored the question and pointed at the wooden cabinets. "If I could have a look at your files, it would save me some trouble."

Van Owen pushed the photos across the desk. "You don't need a hammer," he said. "You need a warrant."

Yates shrugged. "I thought I'd give it a shot anyway." He looked closely at the bruise on Van Owen's cheek. "What happened to your face?" he asked. "Powder burn?" He touched the skin near his own eye. "Awfully close."

"It's not as bad as it looks," Van Owen said.

"You're a lucky man," Yates said. "Those things can go off when you least expect it."

"I don't believe in luck," Van Owen said. "Everyone I ever met who thought he was lucky ended up dead." He nodded toward the photos.

"I'll bet you're right about that," Yates said, and collected them. "Do you know a city vet named Atwood?"

"I know the name," Van Owen said.

"Ever meet him?"

"Once," Van Owen said. "It was a while ago. June, I think."

June? That would have been after the Walker killing. Yates realized that the veterinarian had been way ahead of him on this thing and it suddenly made him angry. He was tired of being a day late and a dollar short. When he got back to the office, he was going to jerk the little fuck's chain.

"What would someone like you have to say to a fruitcake like Atwood?" he asked.

"He wanted to know about wolves," Van Owen said. His eyes began to gloss over again.

"What'd you tell him?"

"I told him they were dangerous. I also told him to stay away from them." Van Owen's eyes opened briefly, a flare of light in the dim room. "I don't think he took my advice."

Yates got to his feet. The conversation had just about run out of steam. He thought about asking Van Owen about what he was doing in the park the other night but decided to hold back. It wouldn't do him any good. He was talking to a man who was no longer there.

Instead, he spoke to the secretary on his way out.

"Do you have anything on this place?"

"Of course," she said, and handed him a rather large brochure. "Take it," she said. "They're free. Anyone can have one."

"I guess that means me," Yates said.

It opened up like a map, with color pictures and a rhapsodic description of the society's facilities in the city and at a hunting lodge in Delaware County in lower New York State, just a few hours away. He pretended to read it carefully.

"They really have all this stuff there?" he asked.

"Like what?"

"Oh," he said, "I don't know." He turned over the brochure and started to read. "An environmentally designed hunting preserve protected by electronic fences and twenty-four-hour supervision. I'll bet that means they've got guards, right?"

"It's a terrific place," she said, and smiled at him without showing her teeth.

"You've been there?"

"Only once."

"Shoot anything?"

She laughed. "No. I just watched."

He decided right then that she wasn't sleeping with Van

Owen. She probably had a boyfriend who was a psychologist or something. She liked to watch.

"Are you thinking about joining?" she asked.

"Maybe," Yates said. "Who knows? I might get lucky."

"I hope you do," she said pleasantly.

"Are you out here all by yourself?"

"Just me," she said. "That's my job."

"I'll bet he never tells you if he's going to be in or not," he said. "That's not fair."

"How'd you guess that?" she said.

Yates smiled sympathetically.

"There's nothing I can do about it," she said. "He's got his own private entrance. He comes and goes anytime he pleases."

"Is that so?" Yates said.

Chapter 32

YATES SHUFFLED DOWN the steps into the precinct lobby and made a quick left turn into the office. He swung the door back hard and heard it bang against the wall behind him. A clerk named Hilde who had been assigned to the precinct for the investigation looked up from one of the desks. Hilde was a large black woman with a silver front tooth. Yates had liked her immediately when she told him she didn't call nobody sir except her daddy and he was twenty-five years dead, the worthless son of a bitch.

Hilde was alone. Yates looked in both the other offices but the sergeant and the rest of the detectives were gone. This was all he needed.

"What the hell is this?"

She took one look at his face and held up her hands.

"Don't yell at me," she said. "I didn't scare 'em off."

"Where are they?"

"In the lounge watching TV," she said merrily. "I believe they expecting you."

The lounge was a twenty-by-twenty-foot room directly behind the task force office. The lounge was where everybody hung out between shifts or when they didn't want to go home right away. It had soft-drink machines, a big color television set, and furniture that would have looked good in a dump.

The floor was warped plywood. There were rust stains from a leaky roof on the walls. The plastic on the front of the soda machine had a fist-sized hole in it. Somebody had tried their hand at interior decoration and taped an old Clyde Beatty Circus poster on one of the boarded-up windows. The poster was covered with dozens of little tiny holes. Somebody else had used it as a target in a knife-throwing contest. It hardly mattered. Yates thought that most cops were slobs. The lounge was a clubhouse for slobs.

The sergeant and the missing detectives were indeed watching television. Half of the task force was with them, eyes glued to the screen. One or two of them acknowledged his entrance with a nod as he moved toward the sergeant who stood by himself in the back of the crowd, his hands pushed down deep in his pockets. He looked like a man who clearly expected to wake the next morning with a brand-new asshole.

"You're not going to like this," the sergeant said to him.

Yates looked at the television. Chuck Scarborough was talking about a breakthrough in the wolf killings. Earlier today, he said, sources close to the investigation had told NewsCenter 4 that a third man had been killed, this time *inside* an as-yet-unidentified high-rise apartment building in midtown. Because of the bizarre circumstances surrounding that killing, police were now leaning strongly toward the theory that all three had been murdered and were not the victims of random animal attacks as first thought.

"This is great," Yates said, loud enough for everyone to hear. "This is all we fucking need." A few heads turned, most decided against it. The sergeant looked at the ceiling.

There was another new and unexpected development in this story, the newscaster said. In just a few seconds they were switching to a live news conference at the Department of Health where the chief veterinarian from Animal Affairs was expected to offer his own confirmation of this astonishing new theory.

Yates was almost certain the sergeant was right. "I haven't liked anything else today," he said to him. "Why should this shit be any different?"

The sound went out for a few seconds. Chuck looked intently into the camera and the picture switched to a man standing on the sidewalk before a crowd of reporters. Directly behind him Yates could see the edge of a large stone column and the metal frames of some scaffolding. Further in back, he could see people watching the crowd from behind a row of dirty glass doors.

The camera closed in on the speaker and Yates saw Atwood.

"I have a statement to read," Atwood said. Yates didn't wait to hear it. He told two task force cops in front of him to pick the veterinarian up for questioning.

"Can't we hear what he has to say first?" one asked.

"Do it now," Yates said. "We'll take notes. You won't miss a thing."

Atwood felt a little weird. He stood in front of the reporters and couldn't hear the words that were coming out of his mouth. They faded in and out like bad reception, lost in the noise of the reporters and the cameras and the crowd of onlookers who had gathered around him, spilling over the sidewalk and into the street. Traffic stopped, horns blared, drivers yelled obscenities at him, reality moved further and further away. He was nearly done with his statement and he wanted to go home.

"There is at least one person behind these killings," he said. One of the reporters yelled for him to speak up.

"How's this?" Atwood yelled back, and the reporters laughed and told him that was fine. Atwood shook his head. "All right, all right," he continued. "At least one person is behind these killings, someone who is directly responsible." He stopped there and added, "Including what I understand was another one this morning. This is the person I want to reach now."

"Who is it?"

"I don't know," Atwood answered.

"Is this person a man or a woman?"

Atwood lowered his statement. "I don't know that either," he said. "There may be more than one person involved. I just don't know."

Someone asked if he thought a gang was behind the killings.

"Could be," he said, and the crowd exploded, hurling questions at him all at once. The reporters surged forward and drove him toward the glass doors of the building, now packed with spectators. Atwood looked and saw one of the secretaries from Animal Affairs, her face pressed against the glass. She waved at him and smiled.

Atwood felt a hand on his shoulder and someone yelled a question in his ear.

"How'd you get the information? Did the killer give it to you?"

Atwood shoved him out of the way. "Hey," he yelled at the crowd of reporters. "Let me finish my statement. I'll answer your questions when I've finished my statement."

No one listened to him. He looked at a sea of lights and cameras and faces and no one heard him at all. The crowd was completely out of hand. A piece of the scaffolding shifted, bits of dirt and wood fell on the heads of the reporters. Somebody screamed and part of the crowd moved into the street.

"Just let me finish," he said. He was talking directly into one of the cameras now. The cameraman bore down on him, the camera only a few feet from his face. Atwood decided he had only a few seconds before it would be time to bail out of the mess he'd created. He stuck his face into the lens.

"I can save the wolf," he said. "I can help you. You have to trust me. I'm the only one who can help you. He'll kill the wolf if he gets the chance. You know that." He looked directly into the camera and yelled out his phone number over the noise, hoping that whoever was out there would remember it.

Someone pushed the cameraman out of the way and stuck a microphone in his face. Atwood shoved him away and tried to open one of the glass doors but it wouldn't budge. They'd locked him out of the building. He worked his way down the front of the building, yanking each door handle, trying desperately to get away from the hands and the noise that were tearing him apart.

At last one of the doors opened. Atwood twisted his body around the edge of the door, felt himself being pulled to safety inside. From the other side of the glass, the faces of the reporters looked distorted and grotesque. Atwood let himself be carried away, down the high-ceilinged corridor, his heels almost skimming the marble floors, catching only brief glimpses of everything while they whisked him along, the peeling white paint on the walls, a brushstroke of red graffiti, the startled faces of everyone as he rushed past. They hurried down the broad steps toward the back of the building. Atwood let them pull him through the bare oval lobby and the revolving doors and into a waiting car.

One of them opened the back door and helped him inside, holding his head down so he wouldn't hit it on the edge of the doorframe. He slumped against the seat and felt the car accelerate from the curb. He heard a scream, a high-pitched wail that surrounded the car, following it down the street. He realized he was in a cop car and started to laugh.

The cop on the passenger side turned around in the seat. He took out his shield and slapped Atwood's arm with it. The veterinarian looked up.

"Out of the frying pan," the cop said. "Into the fucking fire."

It was late and except for the woman behind the counter they were alone in the small grocery store. Dane waited at the counter while Jenny took her time walking up and down the narrow aisles, picking out cans of food and placing them in the blue plastic basket. There was a small portable television on the counter next to the cash register and the woman watched it intently. She had thick fleshy arms that stuck out of the sleeves of her T-shirt and a heavy jowled face that quivered whenever she shifted her weight from one arm to the other.

"That's something, isn't it?" she said to Dane. He turned around.

"What?"

"The TV," the woman said, and moved the television set around so he could see. She turned up the volume and Atwood's voice blared over the wooden shelves of the tiny store.

Jenny hurried along the aisle and stood behind Dane to watch the tiny black-and-white image on the screen and listened while Atwood pleaded for their trust.

Dane hadn't heard her come up. When he looked back, her eyes were riveted to the screen. She hardly noticed he was there at all.

Chapter 33

AT LEAST ATWOOD was having a good time, Yates thought. Taken by itself, his theory about the wolf had the quality of a vision, a kind of heretical religious experience. But if Yates added the story to what else he knew, it made slightly more sense. If Yates looked hard, he could see the faint edges of a pattern begin to emerge. The cop who'd nearly gotten his head and chest kicked in, and who would probably end up with a partial disability once they let him out of Albert Einstein, said there were three—a man, a young woman, and the one who crippled him. Atwood said that was Van Owen and Yates was inclined to believe him.

But so what? Yates thought. It left him nowhere. He still had no connection other than circumstantial between any of them, not between the three dead men and Van Owen, not between Van Owen and the wolf. None of it was worth anything because there was no motive for the killings, only the fact of their death and their membership in the Sportsman's Society. Van Owen was the key, but to which door? Was he only after the wolf or was there something else? Did he know the killer? Did he know why?

He could legitimately request a warrant for the society's membership files and he asked the sergeant to put a routine order through Police Plaza instead of through the task force—which would have hurried things up and half an hour later he would have been listening to it on news-radio. He wanted this one low priority. If Van Owen knew what was coming, his lawyer would be all over the place with one writ after another. Yates could hear the lawyer already.

What about the fact that all three were society members? Purely coincidental—they all carried Blue Cross/Blue Shield, too. Why weren't the police requesting those records, why only his clients' files? Where was Van Owen the night of Blackburn's murder? At home, and there would be fifteen witnesses lined up to prove it. Even the secretary would probably lie about it. What about the bruise on his face? The lawyer would laugh that one to death. The list would go on and on. It was human nature. Yates kept his own council and called in his favors and put the routine warrant request through Police Plaza. So far, his clandestine surveillance of the hunter had turned up nothing.

The sergeant looked at him skeptically when he made the routine request.

"Is there something going on here that I should know about?" he asked Yates.

"You want to know about it?" Yates asked back.

The sergeant thought about that for a few seconds and left him alone.

For a man who'd just been given a thirty-day suspension without pay, Atwood was in a good mood. He sat on the desk and munched a granola bar. Yates had seen the suspension coming. The mayor didn't like his bureaucrats to get their mugs all over network television.

"Van Owen wants to kill the wolf, you know that," Atwood said.

"I know," Yates said. "You told the whole world, remember."

"It's the only thing he wants," Atwood said.

That was the extent of their conversation after he'd had the veterinarian picked up. He listened to it for a few more minutes and shut the office door. Atwood looked apprehensive. Maybe he expects a good beating, Yates thought.

"Let me tell you what I want," Yates said. "You're going to

work for me from now on. You do nothing unless you clear it with me first." Atwood swallowed hard but nodded his agreement. Yates took the granola bar away from him. "And there's no eating on the job," he said.

That was a day and a half ago, a week since they'd found Blackburn's body, and nothing had happened since then. The papers were in an uproar over what Atwood had said but the veterinarian refused to come out of his apartment. Van Owen went about his business. Yates told the surveillance cops it didn't matter how close they got to him, the hunter would make them within the first twenty-four hours anyway. Yates didn't give a damn. All he wanted to do was squeeze the guy as much as he could.

It was close to midnight. Yates sat with his feet up on the desk and stared at the green chalkboard propped up against the window. The air conditioning was off and the tiny room was warm, the air heavy with the smell of cigarettes and sweat. The pictures on the bulletin board were beginning to curl up in the heat.

He crushed his cigarette out in the tiny aluminum pie plate he'd been using as an ashtray for the past two days. The thin metal buckled and snapped. Gray soot and stale cigarette butts spilled onto the top of the desk. He blew them away and sent a cloud of ash into the air. The fallout drifted down on his shirt and pants.

On the chalkboard he had drawn a large triangle. At the top of the triangle he had written the word *wolf*. An arrow off it pointed to the words *woman??* and *man??* Near the left-hand corner of the triangle he wrote the names of the three dead men, *Lange, Walker, Blackburn*. Beside the right-hand corner, he wrote *Van Owen* and *Sportsman's Society??*

Below the triangle, he underlined the question: *Why a wolf???*

This was what he had. He stared at it for a few minutes, then he wrote the date of each murder next to the victim's name. He sat down and looked at it again. Of course. There were several weeks between the killings because the killer needed time to learn each man's routine. Or he needed that much time to pick *out* a target. Maybe he hated hunters in general and these guys were just random choices.

He rubbed his eyes with the heels of his hands. It was late, he was alone and feeling foolish. To conclude at this late date that the killer needed time to stalk his victims was not exactly the pinnacle of intelligent police work. I'd do better if I had 3-D glasses and a secret decoder ring, he thought. He opened his eyes and looked at the chalkboard again.

Who was next? Atwood thought it would be Van Owen. Maybe Van Owen and the wolf would kill each other off. That wouldn't be so bad, Yates thought. I'd buy tickets to that.

"Detective Yates?"

He swung his feet off the desk. A tall, gaunt man stood in the doorway, one hand braced against the wall while he leaned on it for support. He looked exhausted, Yates thought, a man who'd come a long way with a lot on his mind. The flesh around his eyes was red and swollen; his clothes were wrinkled and there was a large coffee stain down the front of his shirt. Despite his appearance, he acted calm.

But that doesn't mean he isn't crazy, Yates thought.

The man in the doorway nodded toward the chalkboard.

"My name is Carroll," he said. His voice was ragged and unsteady. "I can answer that question for you," he said.

Yates looked at him like he'd just descended on a beam of angelic light.

"I can tell you everything you need to know," Carroll said. Yates was on the verge of throwing him out when the man's eyes moved to the pictures on the bulletin board. He didn't cry out or scream or look away as Yates expected him to do.

"I was in New Hampshire," Carroll said calmly. "I saw it on the news. I didn't realize."

He stared at the pictures quietly, drained of all emotions except one. The effect was overwhelming.

Yates thought he had never seen such sadness before.

Atwood drank from the tap in the kitchen and splashed cold water in his face and ran his wet fingers through his hair to keep himself awake.

The parrot waddled into the kitchen and pecked at his bare feet. Atwood tried to pick the bird up with his toe but the parrot moved away. Atwood reached down and the parrot climbed on his hand.

"So," he said, "you think this is going to work?"

The parrot gave a strangled squawk that sounded like a rat throwing up. Atwood took that to mean the parrot didn't give a fuck. A realist, he thought.

Yates had made him an offer, one he felt inclined to accept. If he didn't, Yates was going to persecute him for the rest of his life. That's what he said, at least. The deal was simple: if Atwood stayed by the phone and waited for them to call, Yates would give him a chance to save the wolf.

"As far as I'm concerned," Yates had said, "the wolf is innocent. I want whoever's behind it."

"What if they don't call?" Atwood had asked.

"Then we're both in the shithouse," Yates had said.

Now there was a guard at his front door and he was waiting anxiously for the operations van to show up so they could set up a trace. Yates screamed and yelled to get one and it was due anytime. So far, they were okay without it. He'd had only a few crank calls, people who sounded like they were drooling into the receiver, so he still had hope that nothing major would happen before Yates got there with the van. He wasted time staring at the linoleum and talking to his parrot. He was going batshit and he knew it.

The phone rang. He dropped the bird in the sink and raced down the hall to the bedroom.

The phone rang again.

It seemed to be coming from the other side of the bed. Atwood dove across the mattress and reached far underneath the bed. He felt the cord in his hand and pulled the phone out. It rang once more. The receiver tumbled across the floor. Atwood grabbed it.

He heard a girl whisper, "I saw you on television the other day."

He pulled the phone into bed with him and cradled it against his chest like a baby. He wondered if she could hear his heart beating.

"Are you the girl from the park?" he asked.

"Yes," she said.

"How do I know you're the girl?"

"I don't want to play these games," she said. "If you don't believe me, hang up."

He couldn't bring himself to do that. "Wait a minute," he said, and thought of a question only she could answer. "Who else was in the park that night?"

"Who else?" she asked.

Please answer me, he thought. He felt like a child pleading for a Christmas toy.

"You mean Van Owen," she said. Her voice was edgy. "There, did I pass your little test?"

"Yes," he said, and didn't know what to ask next. Where the hell was Yates? He thought he heard her cry. "Are you all right?"

"I'm scared, I'm scared to death. I don't know what he's going to do."

"You mean Van Owen?"

"No," she said. "Dane."

"Is that his name?"

"Yes," she said. "I don't know much more about him than that. Except he's getting worse all the time."

"Can you get away from him?"

"You don't know what it's like here," she whispered. "He's been crazy since the park. Sometimes I think he wants to kill us both."

"Us?" Atwood wasn't sure what she meant.

"The wolf."

"Is the wolf all right?"

"The wolf's fine," she said. "Dane's losing control over him. That's what's making him crazy. That and the killings. He hasn't stopped talking about the last one, the one in the apartment. It sounded like a real bloodbath."

"Why is he doing this?"

"I can't tell you," she said. She raised her voice and then caught herself. "They killed his family, that's all I can say. Stop asking so many questions."

"I can't help you if I don't ask questions," Atwood said. He found himself whispering, too. The girl was silent. "Why'd you call me?"

"You think I'm wasting my time?"

"No," he said. "What's your name?"

"Why?" she said. The tension in her voice was strong.

"You already know mine. If I know yours, it'll make it easier to talk to you, that's all."

"It's Jenny," she said. "I never liked it very much."

"I like it," Atwood said.

She laughed. "You can have it," she said.

"Where are you?"

"Why?"

"I could come and get you," Atwood said, and paused. "And the wolf," he said.

"Is that what you really want? The wolf?"

"No," Atwood said quickly. He was afraid of losing her. "That wasn't what I meant."

"Right," she said. "You're the one who wants to save him. Isn't that what you said?"

"Please," he said. The girl was quiet. Atwood thought she'd hung up. "Jenny?"

"The wolf can take care of himself," she said. "I'm worried about me."

"I can save both of you."

"Dane would kill you if you tried," she said. "Don't you understand that?"

His anxiety grew. He wanted desperately to keep her talking. "I could talk to him," he said. "Over the phone. Ask him to give himself up."

"You think so? Maybe he'd just add you to his list. He's got one, you know. I've seen it." She drew a sharp breath. "Oh, Christ."

"What?" Atwood sat up straight. The phone tumbled onto the bed.

"I think he heard me."

"Don't hang up!"

"He'll kill me if he finds out now."

He held the receiver away from him and screamed into it. "Don't hang up!"

The line went dead.

The room was silent and dark as if all the life had been squeezed out of it in those last few seconds. The dial tone, loud and persistent, the mechanized hum of another world, broke into the void. He dropped the receiver.

The van showed up about two hours later. Yates arrived early the next morning. He looked clean and alert, like he'd just stepped out of the dry cleaner's, right along with his suit.

"You're a tad late," Atwood told him.

"If she called once, she'll probably call again," Yates said, and looked around the apartment. "Why don't you get a rug in here or something?"

Chapter 34

VAN OWEN SPOTTED the cop the first day. It was hard to miss a man who ate all his meals in the front seat of a 1976 maroon Duster and dumped his trash out the window. Atwood didn't even do that. He made a quick check of the back entrance to the building. Maybe Yates had only sent the one as a warning; the cop had suddenly appeared the morning after the attack in the park. But nothing else, no search warrants, no interrogations. The detective was working on his own. The knowledge did not make him feel better.

He felt hemmed in by his small office. The room seemed abnormally silent and dark and the walls seemed to have a life of their own, expanding and contracting with every breath he took. He wanted to tear the place apart, rip out the walls, smash the furniture, anything to stop what he was feeling.

He went next door to the gym and worked out for an hour, sliding twenty extra pounds on the bench press, forcing extra repetitions on himself until the muscles of his arms burned and ached with each heavy thrust. But the workout only made him edgy; each step felt more like a spasm. In the shower, the sound of a locker door slamming shut him into a combat stance. The hot water poured off his back and swirled around his feet. For a split second, he looked down and thought he saw blood.

He could have gone to the club downtown, that might have

helped, but he needed something else now. If he could only find the girl.

He dressed and left by the back entrance. The kitchen was deserted. Van Owen stepped into a narrow alley behind the building that led to Twenty-first Street. Everything was quiet. The streetlights were pale yellow dots against the early evening sky. He'd gone only a few feet when he spotted the second cop.

"We got him," the cop said. He leaned down in the seat and talked on the walkie-talkie. His car was parked on the street to the right of the alley. Van Owen turned left. "He's going to Third," the cop said.

"You want me to swing around?" It was the cop in the Duster in front of the building.

"I want to see what he does first," the first cop said. He followed Van Owen to the corner, where he stopped and hailed a cab. Shit, the cop thought, and ran back to his car. He grabbed the walkie-talkie. "Move it," he said. "He just got into a cab."

Van Owen saw the second cop nose his car out into the avenue. As they went through the intersection at Twenty-third, the Duster ran the red light and pulled into traffic a block behind the first car. Van Owen tapped the plexiglass divider to get the driver's attention.

"Take me to Penn Station," he said.

"Where's he going?" the cop in the Duster asked.

"How the hell should I know?"

"You're right behind him is why." The Duster was stuck behind a blue Cadillac from New Jersey.

"What can I tell you?" the first cop said. "He's still going north." There was a pause, then a whistle. "Okay, here we go. He just made a left on Thirtieth."

"Stay with him. I'm going to cut over."

The first cop stayed behind him all the way to Broadway. The cab turned north.

"Where the fuck is he going now?" the cop in the Duster asked.

At Thirty-fourth Street the cab made another left and got

stuck in the block between Broadway and Seventh Avenue. The cab stayed to the left side of the street and inched forward. At Seventh Avenue, the cab swung through the yellow light and pulled in front of Penn Station. Van Owen got out and ran for the front stairs.

"He's going into the station," the first cop yelled. He played a hunch. "Get over to Eighth, watch the other side. I'm going after him."

The cop pulled around the building and turned into the cab lanes. He parked his car behind the line of cabs. One of the drivers told him he couldn't park there. He flashed his shield and barreled through the doors down the escalator toward the long wall of ticket counters. Van Owen wasn't there.

The cop ran past the ticket counter and pushed his way through the crowd of commuters into the waiting area. He wasn't there either. The cop stood beside one of the large square pillars and spoke into the walkie-talkie.

"I don't see him," he said. "How about you?"

"Nothing," the second cop said. "Nothing at all."

"Shit," he said. "I'm going to look out front again. He's got to be around here somewhere."

Van Owen approached the off-duty cab parked at the corner of Thirty-second Street and Seventh, just down from a cheap Chinese takeout place and a McDonald's. The cabdriver was eating a hamburger and shook his head. He spoke with a Russian accent.

"Not working," he said. "Dinner."

Van Owen laid a twenty-dollar bill on top of his hamburger and got in the cab.

"You're working for yourself now," Van Owen told him.

The driver tossed the hamburger on the seat next to him. He left the off-duty sign on.

"Free enterprise," the driver said, and pulled out. "Where you go?"

It was just dark. The cabdriver doubled-parked near the Port Authority close to Forty-second Street and finished the rest of his meal. He asked Van Owen how long he was going to be. Van Owen tossed another twenty into the front seat.

"Take a break," he told the driver. The Russian lit a

cigarette. Van Owen continued to watch the building and the people that came through its doors.

A young girl stepped out of the Port Authority and strutted casually down the sidewalk. She wore white slacks that closed tightly around her calfs and a long-sleeved green tube top that left her stomach exposed. A small yellow purse hung over her shoulder. Van Owen got out of the cab and stood in her way. She stopped and looked him up and down. Her eyes were heavy with mascara, her cheeks and lips bright with dark red rouge. Beneath all the makeup, she had the face of a teenager.

"You the sidewalk inspector?" she asked.

He shook his head. Her eyes looked a little glassy.

"Then you must have a problem," she said.

He moved close to her. He could smell her, a mingling of sweat and a sharp musky smell that she tried to hide with a sweet flowery perfume. She folded her arms as if to wrap herself in the scent. He took her elbow and pressed her up against the cab.

"What's your problem, honey?" she asked.

Van Owen rubbed his thumb across her cheek and smiled. The girl laughed nervously. He took a twenty from his pocket and closed one of her hands around it. She looked at him carefully.

"I guess your problem's pretty serious," she said.

He whispered something in her ear. She smiled to herself.

"That is serious," she said. "And it's going to cost you a hundred and fifty bucks."

Van Owen opened the door and she got into the cab. When they were on their way, she asked him for the rest of her money.

"When we get there," he said.

"*Right* when we get there," she said. She put her hand on his leg but he took it off. Fine with me, she thought. They rode along in silence. It was an easy half a yard, all he wanted to do was tie her up and beat off. She'd been tied up before, it wasn't a big deal. At least he didn't want to fuck her in the ass or something like that. That kind of pain she definitely did not need.

* * *

Beneath the robe, Van Owen was covered with sweat. It ran down his chest and his arms and flowed out over his hands to the ends of his fingers where it hung suspended until he flicked it away with a snap of his hands.

The girl was on her back in the bed, her hands cuffed in front of her. She pouted and spread her legs apart slowly. He watched her. She arched her back and pushed her crotch toward him.

She had small flaccid breasts and a thumb-size scar on her right hip. She shaved her crotch just above her pubis and he could see the dark black stubble. Below the shaved area, her hair was thick and wet and it fanned out across the inside of her thighs. She put her hands between her legs and tugged gently at it. Slowly she worked one finger inside of her and then brought it to her mouth. The finger disappeared between her lips. She pulled it out and offered it to him.

"Want some?" she said.

Van Owen said nothing.

"Suit yourself," she said, and stuck her hands between her legs again. She pushed one finger inside her, then two, keeping her eyes on him all the while. Her hand moved in and out, slowly at first, then faster. She pulled her knees back so he could get a better look.

"I could do this a lot better without these cuffs," she said. "I could really show you something then."

She turned over on her hands and knees and buried her face in the pillow. He knelt on the bed and put his hand between her legs. The girl moaned into the pillow. He pushed her open with his fingers and probed her, taking hold of the cuffs with his other hand and pressing them down on the bed.

She moaned again and moved back against his fingers, pushing them deep inside of her. She rocked her hips, gliding back and forth on his fingers. He took his hand away suddenly and she gasped out loud.

He parted the robe. Nothing, no feeling. He grabbed himself with one hand and stroked slowly. His fingers were oily and slick and they moved smoothly over his skin. Nothing. He couldn't get hard. There seemed to be no other way.

He flipped her over and straddled her. He sat on her hips and held her cuffed hands in the air over her head.

"What are you doing?" she gasped.

He grabbed her by the throat and jerked her toward him. One of her knees banged into his back. He barely felt the pain. It was distant and dull, something unconnected to the rage he felt. He squeezed her throat hard and felt her body begin to shake beneath his. He let go and she fell back on the bed.

"Get off me, motherfucker!" the girl screamed, and he took her by the throat again and squeezed, harder this time. Her eyes bulged. Black tears, thick and filmy with mascara, ran across her cheeks. The colors, black and red, struck some distant memory. He released her slowly and before she could react, he struck her, a backhanded blow that snapped her head to one side. She let out a sharp scream and he hit her again.

It's not working, he thought.

He struck again and again. Her head bounced back and forth in painful rhythm. With each blow her screams grew shorter until they stopped altogether. When he stopped hitting her, all she could offer him was a weak groan. He held her face in his hands and listened to it fade.

He reached into the pocket of his robe.

"You're the wrong one," he whispered to her.

He opened the tiny surgical razor. It clicked stiffly into place. He slid forward on her body until he was almost sitting on her chest. Her eyes fluttered open, narrow slits through her bruised and battered skin. She began to choke. He ran a hand through her hair and jerked her head back.

"You're not her," he said, and passed the razor gently across her throat. A thin red line appeared and grew wider as the first blood ran down her neck and collected in the hollow of her throat. Her eyes rolled up white. He said it again, louder this time, more a shriek than any recognizable language, and cut much deeper.

Chapter 35

THE WIRE FROM the bedroom stretched down the hall to the living room like plastic tubing strung from a vein. The man from the phone company opened the bedroom jack, attached the new wire, and rolled it off a small spool down the hall, stopping every few feet to staple it to the baseboard. In the living room, he clipped on the red test phone and called the operations van, a sixteen-foot motor trailer that was parked in the street and hooked into the main terminal block in the basement.

Yates tried to explain it to him. Atwood didn't need an explanation. He would wait for Dane or for Jenny to call again and try to keep them on the line while the police traced the call. Once they were found, Jenny and the wolf would be protected; Dane would not. Dane belonged to Yates.

The phone man wired two phones in the living room, one for Atwood and one for Yates. The detective had a hand radio for talking to the operations van. The phone man called the local test board to check out the connection and then left the two men alone in the apartment. There was a uniformed officer just outside the door, another two stationed at the front entrance. By now it all seemed excessive to Atwood. He wasn't expecting anyone. His expectations were on a much smaller scale now. He wanted Jenny to call him back.

Yates looked through the cupboards and sent one of the

uniformed officers to the nearest grocery store for supplies. Atwood had forgotten to shop and the only thing left worth eating was a box of graham crackers and half a jar of peanut butter.

"We don't have to eat like refugees," Yates said, and ordered enough food to last them through the weekend. Atwood hoped it wouldn't take that long.

Around two in the afternoon, they ate lunch together. Yates heated two cans of chicken soup and made grilled cheese sandwiches for them. The detective drank coffee; Atwood had a glass of milk.

Atwood enjoyed the meal, even enjoyed cleaning up afterward, warming to the simplicity of the routine. When he finished the few dishes, he returned to his seat by the window. Yates sat in the opposite corner near the parrot's empty perch.

The bird and the crocodile had been exiled to the bedroom. Yates wanted no distractions, nothing that might interfere with what they were doing. He drank another cup of coffee and waited, as patient as a rock. Atwood skimmed a magazine and watched the time slip away.

"Were you always a cop?" Atwood asked.

"No," Yates said. "I used to be a nun." He lit a cigarette, shifted one leg over the other, and rubbed smoke out of one eye. Each gesture came slowly, like sand shifting down a hundred-year-old slope, one grain at a time.

Atwood looked through the front window at the forest of antennas that covered the roof of the operations van. At both ends of the block, a squad car sat behind a line of wooden barricades. Only residents were allowed to pass the line. Directly across the street from the apartment, a gang of kids sat on their bikes. They leaned over their handlebars and stared at the operations van. One of them pointed at Atwood's apartment. Atwood waved. The kid gave him the finger and took off on his bike. The rest chased after him. He watched them go. Down the street, a television van stopped at the barricade. That's where they were headed. They wanted to see what they looked like on television. Wasn't reality good enough for them anymore?

"Who are you waving at?" Yates asked.

"My fans," Atwood said. He looked down again at the operations van. "What are they doing down there?"

"Your fans?"

"In that truck."

"Waiting," Yates said.

Atwood turned around. "I meant what's inside it?"

Yates got out of his chair. "Surveillance equipment," he said. "Tape recorders, video cameras, sweep mikes. They give us a clear patch to the phone company."

"You do a lot of surveillance work?"

"In my other life," the detective said. "Not anymore."

Atwood seemed suddenly uninterested in Yates's answers. "You know what I don't understand?" he said finally.

"What?"

"How they could kill his entire family. How could they do something like that?"

"Who knows?" Yates said. He turned on the television. "Let's watch a little TV," he said. "See if we made the news again today."

They watched the local and then the national news. There were pictures of the van in front of Atwood's apartment. A police spokesman said that it was routine surveillance, standard operating procedure in such cases. "We don't know what to expect, so we cover all the bases," the spokesman said. "We don't take any chances."

Yates laughed out loud. "But we sure do fuck up an awful lot," he said.

There were a few crank calls that evening, but not many. The best one suggested that the wolf had been sucked back into the fourth dimension by a device only the caller possessed; he was willing to sell, of course. Atwood was a little disappointed. It was a slow day even for whackos, he decided.

Nothing else happened until the phone rang again at four o'clock the next morning. Atwood had fallen asleep in the chair by the window with the phone on his lap. Yates had his head back and his eyes closed. He dozed, half awake, half asleep, drifting through the sounds in the apartment.

Atwood grabbed the phone with both hands to keep it from tumbling off his lap. It rang again.

"Hold it," Yates told him.

Atwood waited. It rang once more.

"Pick it up now," Yates ordered.

Atwood lifted the receiver. Yates lifted his at the same time. The line was dead.

Atwood was angry. It showed in his face, the way his hand trembled when he laid the phone back in its cradle. The veterinarian bit his lip and stared at the phone.

Yates radioed the van. "Yeah," he said. "False alarm." He nodded. "Yeah, I know."

"What'd they say?" It was Atwood.

"They said if this keeps up much longer, we can all go home." He went into the kitchen to make some coffee.

Atwood followed him. He stood in the doorway and watched Yates fill a saucepan with water. The detective spooned some instant coffee into a cup. "You want some?"

Atwood shook his head. "This sucks," he said.

"Relax," Yates said.

"You don't have to—"

"I know," Yates answered, raising his voice. He looked at his watch. "We got another thirty-six hours of this crap. You answer the phone, I'll keep my mouth shut and we'll both end up heroes. Okay?"

A smile flickered across the detective's face but to Atwood it seemed more like a mistake than anything else. He hesitated, realizing that it was the best he was going to get, and nodded.

The call came the second day, Saturday, a little after three o'clock in the afternoon. They lifted the receivers in unison, Atwood waiting just a few seconds longer to bring the phone to his ear, afraid that it would be another dead call. He heard nothing and looked at Yates. The detective stood, head down, one hand cupped over his other ear, listening hard.

"The girl said you wanted to talk to me," Dane said. His voice was mild, a quiet monotone. Atwood was surprised.

"Yes," Atwood said. "Dane?"

"I'm here."

"I was a little worried," Atwood said. "I didn't think you'd call."

"Just tell me what you want," Dane said.

"I want to help you," he blurted.

Atwood thought he heard him laugh. He wasn't certain. It might have been static on the line. How long did Yates say he had to keep him on? Three minutes? Five minutes? Atwood couldn't remember anymore.

"I don't think that's possible now," Dane said. "Not after what's happened."

"But if what Jenny said was true, if those men killed your family, then—"

"She told you that?" Dane asked. He sounded alarmed. "What else did she tell you?"

Atwood panicked. "That's all," he said. "She wanted me to understand why you're doing this."

"She had no right," he said. His voice sounded dreamy and far away. He said something else but Atwood couldn't hear him. I'm losing him, Atwood thought. Yates waved his fist, urging him to keep talking, to do anything to keep Dane on the line.

"Wait," Atwood said. "It isn't important. What's important is that we find a way to stop this."

Dane's voice lost its mildness. "You can't stop it," he said, and hung up.

Yates called the van. "Did you get it?" He listened and then threw the phone on the chair. "Dammit!" he said.

Atwood hung up quietly. "He'll call back," he said.

Atwood sounded so certain that Yates thought he'd misunderstood him.

"What?"

"I said he'll call back."

Atwood looked out the window. Down the street a woman in a heavy overcoat bent over a grocery cart to inspect something. She walked on, pushing her life in front of her.

"You sound pretty sure about it," Yates said.

"I just know it, that's all," he said. Yates shrugged and went to the kitchen. Atwood closed his eyes and leaned his head against the window. He pressed his lips against the glass. It was cold in spite of the heat.

Yates stepped out of the kitchen holding a glass of milk. He drank half of it and wiped the sides of his mouth with the back of one hand.

"There's some things I haven't told you," he said. "This guy's family, it isn't what you're thinking."

Atwood listened politely, even looked a little amused when Yates began. By the time Yates finished explaining what Carroll had told him about the wolf hunt, Atwood was silent, almost pensive. The detective asked him if he wanted anything to eat. Atwood said no and returned to his seat by the window.

He was still there when Dane called him an hour and a half later.

Atwood picked it up smoothly on the second ring.

"Dane?" he said. The voice came back to him, empty and haunted.

"I know what you want," Dane said.

"I want to help you," Atwood said. "That's all."

"The girl says you want the wolf."

"I can save it," Atwood said. "I can save all three of you if you let me."

"Then what?"

"I don't understand."

"What will you do with the wolf?" Dane asked. "Chain him up? Kill him?"

"No," Atwood said. "I won't let that happen."

"I know what you've done," Dane said. "I've seen the traps. They're all over the woods."

Atwood looked across the room at Yates. The detective pointed at the phone. They were playing for time now.

"What traps?" Atwood said.

"What kind of traps do you think?" Dane said. "Wolf traps. Black steel. Buried just below ground. You put them on the trails. I saw the pup drown." His voice had grown weak. Atwood had to listen carefully to hear every word.

"I didn't do it," Atwood said. "If you tell me where they are, I'll help you get rid of them."

"No, no," Dane said. "It's too late for that. They're everywhere now. I've seen them."

"If you just tell me where they are, I'll get rid of them."

"No, you won't," Dane said. "You're lying."

"I'm not lying," Atwood said. "I can help you."

"I have to go now."

"No, listen to me," Atwood said frantically, "I know what happened to your family."

"No, you don't," Dane said. "The girl doesn't even know." He sounded shaken by what Atwood had said, uncertain of what to do next.

"They shot the wolves," Atwood said. "The men in the helicopter came and shot them. You had to kill the men because of what they did."

His words spilled out and died in the silence on the other end of the line. Moments later the silence was shattered by Dane's whisper.

"Who told you?" he said. His words twisted and broke and ended in a mad cry.

"It doesn't matter," Atwood said quickly. "I know what happened. It's all right. Nothing bad has to happen again."

"No, no, no," Dane cried, over and over.

The phone dropped. Atwood heard it bang on the floor. He cupped his hand over the receiver and spoke to Yates.

"Something happened," he said. "He dropped it."

"Keep with it," Yates said. "They've almost got it."

"I'm going to ask for the girl," Atwood said.

Yates wasn't listening. He switched to the radio and spoke rapidly to the operations van.

Atwood counted off two minutes to himself, rocking in the chair, praying that Dane would come back on the line.

When he did, he spoke calmly.

"I let him go," Dane said.

"What?"

"I let him go. You won't be able to kill him now."

"You let the wolf go?" Atwood asked.

"Yes," Dane said.

Atwood was incredulous. This wasn't supposed to happen. The situation was spinning out of control.

"Where?"

Atwood heard something he thought might have been laughter.

"Guess," Dane said, and hung up.

He'd lost him. Atwood couldn't believe it.

"I think they've got him," Yates said. He gripped the radio with both hands and waited for confirmation from the operations van. "Come on," he said. "Come on." He stood stock still and closed his eyes. It was as close to prayer as he got.

"Yes," Yates said, and opened his eyes. He looked like he was hunched over the tiny receiver that he held against his ear.

Maybe they'd made it, Atwood thought. Maybe we can still save him.

"Fuck," Yates said, sounding more tired than angry. He pressed the radio against his forehead.

He brought it to his ear again. "I don't want an explanation," he said. "Just tell me what you need." He shook his head. "This is the kind of shit you should have planned for in the first place."

He threw the radio down and turned to Atwood.

"The guy's using a bootleg phone somewhere out in the boonies. The genius downstairs says he's got it pinned down to one county. *One fucking county!*" Yates slapped the back of the chair. "Now he says they need more time for the computer to work on it. Son of a bitch!" He strode across the room and opened one of the windows. *"One fucking county!"* he yelled. "You assholes better get it right next time."

Atwood was stunned.

"Don't you go simple on me, too," Yates said.

The phone rang.

"Get it," Yates said.

Atwood stared at the ringing phone like it had become radioactive.

"Get the phone," Yates yelled.

"What should I say to him?"

"I don't give a fuck what you say," Yates yelled. "Just pick up the phone!"

Atwood picked it up.

"Yes?" he said.

"I have to make her go," Dane said. His voice sounded small and weak. Atwood heard it and felt something begin to crumble inside. He touched a hand to his face. His skin was hot and covered in sweat. There was a roaring in his ears that threatened to drown out everything around him.

Yates waved at him. "Ask for the girl," the detective whispered. "Ask to talk to the girl."

Atwood swallowed hard and spoke. "Is Jenny there?" he asked. "Please, let me talk to her."

"I have to make her go," Dane said. "I have to make them both go."

"Please," Atwood begged. "Let me talk to her."

"I can't," Dane said.

"No," Atwood said. The word vanished like vapor.

He heard the phone drop and then something snapped, the scrape of metal on metal.

"What's going on?" Yates whispered.

The sound of the gunshot exploded from the phone. Atwood jerked the phone away.

The second gunshot snapped his head back like a blow. He stared at the instrument in his hand, trying to force himself to let go but he couldn't. He heard the sound of something heavy falling. He gripped the phone tighter and tighter until his muscles began to ache and he saw tiny white flashes of light in front of his eyes. He released it gradually, the tension ebbing through his open hand.

Yates sat down quietly in the chair and stared silently at the phone in his lap. He lit a cigarette and called the operations van.

"Yeah," he said. "Right. That's what it sounded like to me." He was tired and burned out and needed a good eight hours sleep and knew he wasn't going to get anything close to it anytime soon. He took a long drag, a kind of deep cleansing breath. The smoke felt harsh in his throat. It brought him back to life.

"How long's this going to take?" he asked. "That long? Okay. Let me know when you get it."

They told him it would take half an hour, maybe forty-five minutes. At least they had the time now, the guy in the van said. That was true, Yates thought. There wasn't going to be a big problem with time anymore.

Chapter 36

THE CAR TOOK the road hard. Atwood felt each bump in his bones. It was like riding a tremor; each one felt so strong that he thought his skin was going to explode from the shock waves. Behind him, the lights of the city faded into the rich black night. Other lights carried them along, the greenish-white haze of the sodium floodlights as they sped north on the parkway, the hidden glow of gas stations and all-night stores, the candlelight warmth of windows in the distant houses.

Yates drove fast, slowing only at the toll booths to flash his shield for the attendant and then they were gone again, picking up speed quickly. He and Yates rode alone. Somewhere behind them were three more detectives in another car. They made up a silent procession racing to sift through the remains. After the shooting, everything moved fast. Atwood kept up. He told Yates he deserved to be there. A bargain was a bargain.

Yates agreed. Nobody expected the guy to shoot the girl and then blow his brains out over the phone, although maybe he should have seen it coming a little sooner. Maybe. He could live with it.

The wolf wasn't going to be a big problem now, not where they were going. There they'd be lucky if they found the animal by next October. Yates smiled. That was something the New York State Police could handle. They loved the boonies. That's why they were never embarrassed driving around in their cars, those ugly yellow bastards, or dressed in those dink brown uniforms. You had to be color blind to be a state trooper.

But you had to give them their due or they would dance all over your face. They could make your life miserable in minutes.

When the trace went through and Yates saw where it was, he knew he was going to have to let the state have a piece of it. There was no way they weren't going to be involved. All he could do was try to limit their involvement. He told the sergeant as much and the sergeant agreed. They got Police Plaza to agree and had the rest of the liaison operation straightened out after tying up the lines between Albany and the city for an hour and a half.

The deal was simple. It would be a joint operation, divided equally by time and space and spheres of influence. The state police would arrive first, hold the place, and wait. Once Yates arrived with his troops, they would enter the house together. Until everything was secure, there would be an unofficial news blackout. No one at the scene was to make any comment whatsoever on the case. Any and all statements would be issued from Police Plaza.

Except for the wolf. The wolf had become the province of the state. The governor wanted the pleasure of announcing that particular capture from the capitol rotunda. It didn't matter to Yates anymore. They crossed the Tappan Zee and drove north on the thruway. Another hour at the most, Yates thought. He felt like he'd been cheated out of this one. He wanted to get there and see what was left. As for Atwood, the veterinarian looked like he was sinking through the front seat.

When they crossed the bridge, Atwood realized he'd driven this road on his way to see Van Owen at the lodge. Everything looked familiar, the curve of the road, the stillness of the trees. It cheered him up. Maybe he'd find the wolf after all.

He reached in the pocket of his coat and felt for the tranquilizer gun. His fingers closed around the grip, held it tight. Yates didn't even know he had it with him. Atwood closed his eyes and concentrated. This was his last chance and it was coming soon. One shot, that was all he needed.

The house was small and set back from the road. The field lay empty in front of it, washed in red and blue from the flashing lights of the police cars blocking the road, two pairs parked nose to nose a hundred yards down on both ends of the road. There were four more cars and a squat little ambulance parked in a straight line across the entrance to the dirt driveway, two mustard-yellow cruisers and the two unmarked NYPD cars. Occasionally one of the state cars trained a spotlight on the house. The light would sweep down across the white clapboards, then stop to focus on one of the windows for a few seconds. The intensity of the light made the house seem smaller and more vulnerable.

Yates was mildly annoyed by the flashing lights and the crowd of locals who watched them from behind the cars.

"I'm glad to see you people played it low-key," he said to the trooper in charge, a large man with a heavy chin named Bingham who took off his hat, ran his fingers through his thin curly hair, and put it back on, tugging it down on his forehead. They don't talk much, Yates thought. We must be having what they call a conversation up here.

"We can handle the back of the house," Bingham said. "You can have the front. You got any problems with that?"

Yates shook his head. "Just you and one more—max," he said, and signaled for two of the detectives to join him. "I don't want a crowd in there."

"Me neither," Bingham said, and raised a finger. "I hate crowds." A young state trooper climbed out of one of the cars and marched toward them.

The detectives followed the trooper at a more leisurely pace, hands in their pockets. They look like shit, Yates thought. One of them handed him a flashlight. He tested it. It didn't work. Yates banged the light against his leg. It still didn't work.

"Is this about the best we can do?" he asked the detective. The man mumbled something and shrugged.

"I can let you have one of ours," Bingham offered.

"No, thanks," Yates said. "We got another one. That ought to do it."

"It should," Bingham said, making it sound like it definitely would not.

Yates noticed that the one in Bingham's hand was big and yellow, the same color as his car. The lens was about the size of his head. It was probably nuclear-powered, Yates thought. They used it to bring down airplanes.

Shit, Yates thought, let's get this circus over with so I can go home.

"Come on," he said, and started down the driveway toward the house. Bingham shouted something. Yates looked back. The two state police cars turned on their spotlights and trained them on the house. The light blinded him and he covered his eyes.

When his eyes recovered, he dropped his hand and saw Atwood standing at the edge of the road. The veterinarian was staring intently at the woods on the other side of the house like he thought something was out there waiting for him. But what? The woods were deserted. There was nobody left alive inside the house, he thought. What the hell was he hoping to find?

The idea struck him all at once. Suppose the wolf was still in the house? Suppose the bastard had left it there, a little going-away present for everybody?

Christ on a stick, he thought, and told everyone to hold up a minute.

"Let's take it easy going in," he said. "We don't know what's in there. Okay?"

"Meaning?" one of the detectives asked.

"Meaning we don't know what we're walking into," Yates said. "So nobody charges in like the goddamn cavalry, okay?"

Bingham understood right away. "You think he might have left the wolf in there?"

"The idea crossed my mind," Yates said.

"Wouldn't we have heard something by now?" the other trooper asked.

"Maybe," Yates said. "You want to waltz in there by yourself and find out?"

315

"No, sir," the trooper said with a grin.

They continued down the drive. The fact that he'd missed something like that gnawed at Yates, and the more he tried to put it aside, the more it gnawed at him. He took out his gun and watched the others do the same. From force of habit he checked the cylinder, spun it once, and snapped it back.

The question still remained. Had he forgotten something else? If he had, it was a little late now.

They stopped at the corner of the house. Bingham and the trooper went around to the back, Yates and the two detectives approached the front door. The detectives waited on either side while Yates tried the handle.

The door was unlocked. Yates opened it half an inch, stepped back, and kicked it gently. The door slid open all the way. A narrow shaft of light, as slim and sharp as a nail, pierced the dark interior. The house smelled like gunpowder.

Yates saw a small couch and a doorway into what looked like the dining room. Beyond that was a door that probably led to the kitchen. He heard the sound of breaking glass and froze. The back door opened. A beam of light fanned out underneath the door and across the dining-room floor.

He stepped into the house. To his right was a stairway to the second floor. One of the detectives slipped in behind him and was already climbing the stairs. Yates told the other one to stay by the front door.

"Wait a minute," he whispered up the stairs. He took two steps at a time until he stood beside the detective. "Let me tell you what we're going to do here." The detective blinked at Yates. He looked nervous as hell. "Give me the light," Yates said, and pointed it down the hallway. There were three doors, one on the left, two on the right. He handed the flashlight back.

"I'm going to open the first door," Yates whispered. "You hold the light over my shoulder. If anything moves, shoot it. I don't care what it is. Shoot it. Okay?" The detective nodded.

Yates stood by the first door. The detective raised the light over his head, ready to bring it down quickly.

Yates grabbed the doorknob and shoved the door open in one motion, crouched at the same time, and swung his gun in front of him. The other detective brought the flashlight down and Yates followed the arc of light as it swept across the room to where it joined another arc from the front window.

He saw an unmade bed, the sheet spilling onto the floor, a small table with a lamp, a straight-backed wooden chair. Nothing else. The room was empty.

The door to the next room was half open and Yates heard water dripping just before he pushed it open the rest of the way with his foot. A bathroom. Yates pointed his gun at the bathtub and looked inside. Empty.

Downstairs, a door creaked open. Bingham and the other trooper were moving into the dining room.

The last room was another bedroom, slightly larger than the first. The bed was made. An empty water glass stood on a wooden nightstand. A towel lay carefully folded at the foot of the bed. The window shades were closed.

The detective leaned against the door. "I'm going to take a look at that first room again," he said, still whispering. He handed the flashlight to Yates. "I don't need this."

Yates swept the back room with the light. It looked innocent and empty, like a hotel room, as if someone had set it up that way. He couldn't imagine why they'd cleaned this one and left the other one in such a mess. He heard voices below him. They rose between the floorboards and floated through the silent room like the whispering of ghosts. Why did somebody go to the trouble of cleaning up the back room? Where were the bodies?

It struck him that he was asking the wrong questions. The right question was obvious. Why did they leave the front room like that? What was so important about it? Yates turned to say something to the detective.

The scream was sudden and loud. Yates swung the flashlight around in confusion. The scream grew louder and louder until it turned into one long continuous shriek of pain that came from downstairs and seemed to shake the floor beneath his feet.

He lunged into the hallway, thinking he still had time. From the front room, there was a snap, loud and sharp, like the cracking of a dead branch, a gasp of pain, and then a scream that drowned out the one downstairs.

Yates rushed into the front room. The detective writhed on

the floor near the side of the bed, entangled in the sheet, clawing frantically at his leg. He tore at the sheet with his hands, trying to pull it off. It was wound tight around his ankle. Yates could see the white fabric turning bright red with blood.

Yates pushed the detective's hands aside and tore at the sheet, ripping it away piece by piece until he exposed the ankle and the teeth of the black metal trap that were sunk deep into the flesh. Blood poured down his foot onto the floor.

Yates pinned the detective's leg with his knee, holding it steady while he tried to open the trap. It was almost impossible to get a grip on it. The man screamed and banged his leg against the floor as if he thought he could shake the trap loose. Yates pushed his hands away and shoved him against the bed. The man screamed louder and pounded on Yates's shoulder and back.

Yates couldn't get a hold on the trap. His hands kept slipping off the metal. He wrapped the sheet around the top of the trap and tried again. It worked.

Yates bore down as hard as he could and forced the jaws open. It was a struggle to keep it open. If he couldn't get the leg free soon, he was going to have to let go. The trap was too strong. Yates eased his knee off the man's leg and tried to pull the trap away from the ankle but the teeth were still tangled in the sheet and wouldn't let go. Yates felt the trap begin to close. The jaws moved an inch. Yates bent down with all his strength and held them.

"Get it out of there," Yates screamed. The detective started to move his leg back. Yates felt his arms start to give out. The trap closed another inch. One of the teeth bit deep into the man's ankle and he screamed again. Yates's hands slipped some more. The trap began to slide shut.

Yates heard someone running up the stairs.

"In here!" he yelled. Bingham rushed into the room. The trooper reached down and pushed the trap all the way open. The detective pulled his leg out slowly. The sheet caught in the teeth. Yates used one hand to tear the material away. The trap began to close again. Yates used his free hand to work the man's ankle out of the trap.

"Did you get it out?" Bingham asked. Yates nodded.

"Okay," the trooper said. "On three." He began to count. "One, two, three, now!"

They yanked their hands away at the same time and the trap snapped shut.

Yates tore off a large piece of the sheet and wrapped it around the detective's ankle and tied it off just above the open wound. The screaming stopped at last; the detective had passed out. Yates sat back against the bed and pulled the rest of the tangled sheet away from the man's neck and chest. He bunched it up and tucked it underneath his head. His hand brushed the man's face. The skin on his cheek felt cold and unnaturally soft, as though the bones underneath had vanished.

Yates heard shouting from outside. He raised himself and saw the ambulance as it bounced across the yard toward the house. Bingham held up the trap so he could get a good look at it. The policeman's hands were slashed and bleeding badly.

"You all right?" Yates asked.

Bingham smiled and set the trap down on the floor between them. Yates shoved it out of the way.

"How is it down there?" Yates asked.

"Okay, I guess," Bingham said. He spoke quietly and didn't take his eyes off the trap. "I wish I knew what the hell just happened."

There was more shouting. Somebody banged a stretcher through the front door.

Bingham pulled the trap toward him and held it in his lap.

"There was a pile of old clothes in one corner," Bingham said to Yates. "They seemed harmless enough. About two feet above them, in the wall, was something that looked like a bullet hole. I saw it. I guess my trooper saw it, too. I was going to tell him to be careful, not to mess it up."

Yates heard his name called. "In here," he said. Somebody started up the stairs. He looked at Bingham. The trooper was shaking his head.

"The next thing I heard was this son of a bitch snapping on his leg." He lifted the trap. "Your man came running in from the front. We got him free. Then I heard you two up here. I figured you were having the same problem."

"You find anything?" Yates asked.

"Like bodies?" Bingham said. "Nothing. Maybe they're in the basement but I doubt it." He shook his head. "We got sandbagged."

"I want the woods around the house checked out," Yates said. "I'm starting to feel like sniper bait."

"Good idea," Bingham said.

A face Yates had never seen before appeared in the doorway. "A stretcher's on the way. How's this one doing?"

Yates looked at the unconscious detective and thought that the answer to that question was pretty obvious.

"He's not going to dance much," he said.

Chapter 37

JENNY SAW ATWOOD from where she hid at the edge of the woods. He stood in the road by one of the police cars and stared right at her. She stepped back into the trees, afraid of what he might do. He continued to stare at her and then looked away as if pretending he hadn't seen her at all. It was an illusion, like her fear. He couldn't see her; she was invisible to him. She was invisible to everyone, from the police who rushed into the old house when the screaming began, to the crowd of spectators who stood behind the police cars, their faces stern and suspicious in the flashing lights.

She blocked out the noise, the screams, the cries for help, the whine of the ambulance as it swerved back and forth across the yard. It slammed to a stop at the front door. Men clambered out of it and rushed into the house with the first stretcher. They emerged carrying a man, one of his legs wrapped in bloody bandages. More police rushed across the yard after the ambulance and ran into the house. It no longer belonged to her, she thought. It had been taken over by strangers.

Jenny looked for Atwood again and found him. He had moved closer to the house and stood a few yards inside the yard. She could see his face clearly. Grief hung from his shoulders and weighed them down.

She touched the side of her face and felt the hot swollen flesh along her neck and jaw where Dane had struck her with the gun.

They had planned it together, worked out their escape so carefully. Once the fake murder and suicide were over, he said, they could take the wolf and go anywhere. He sounded so certain that she believed him. She watched while he dropped the receiver and fired the gun into the wall above a pile of old clothes in one corner of the room. But when he turned to face her, the gun held high, his face an empty mask, she thought that he had suddenly changed his mind, that he actually meant to kill them both, and she reached instinctively for the gun. He spun her away from him and struck her hard. She felt the side of her head explode and buckled at the knees. He caught her at the last moment as she stumbled headfirst into the wall.

She remembered feeling his arms around her and being carried into the basement. He cradled her head in the crook of his arm and laid her gently on the dirt floor. The smell of it made her sick. He held her shoulders while she threw up and wiped her mouth clean. He's going to wait until I'm finished, she thought, and then he's going to kill me.

Instead, he laid her on her side and tied her hands and feet behind her. Then he strung them together with another rope that he looped once around one of the big overhead beams. He left enough slack so she could move a few feet to either side if she wanted.

He isn't going to kill me, she thought. He's only going to leave me here.

Jenny was suddenly afraid that he wasn't ever going to come back. She struggled to speak. If she could just tell him what she felt, she could make him take her with him. But her mouth felt thick and swollen and her tongue seemed to hold back the words.

"Where are you going?" she whispered, but he gave no answer. His eyes were empty. She asked him again, pleading this time. Her head felt heavy and she put it in the dirt and closed her eyes and went to sleep. Before he left, he bent over and kissed her chastely on the forehead, his lips as cold and lifeless as marble.

When she woke, the low sun broke through the small basement windows and struck her face. She opened her eyes and saw the shadowy lines that ran across the wide dirt floor. The shadows looked like bars, and at first she thought that she was still in the basement of the farm and that Sonny was coming to kill her.

She twisted back and forth, trying to free herself, and banged the side of her head hard against the stone wall. The pain was enormous. It felt like her head was on fire. The sensation made her gag.

She pressed her face into the cool dirt and sang to herself, an old lullaby that was no more than a whisper at first but grew stronger as the burning feeling began to fade and the pain felt small and no longer part of her. Jenny pushed herself back against the stone wall and worked her way to a sitting position. She rested for a few minutes and looked around.

Because her hands and feet were tied together, she had to tuck her legs up underneath her body to keep from being bent backward. The rope ran under her right arm, up the wall, and then looped loosely around the beam. She slid slowly along the wall, dragging the rope with her. Bits of stone and loose cement broke off and dug into her back. Her shoulder caught on a sharp rock and her blouse tore open. Dirt and cement ran down the skin of her back. She rested a few minutes and moved further down the wall. The rope dangled free. A few more feet and it fell. The end struck her arm as it landed on the floor by her knees. Jenny closed her eyes and began to work on getting her hands and legs apart. It was easier than she'd thought. He had only wrapped the rope around the cords binding her hands and feet, and it was soon off. Now, if she could untie her feet, she could stand and move around the basement.

As long as she was careful and didn't fall over. If she fell now, she didn't think she would ever get up again.

Jenny let herself down carefully. She rolled over so that her arms and legs moved freely. Her face struck a rock and the pain shot across the side of her head and down her back. She cried out suddenly and closed her eyes. A shower of bright ocher burst across her eyelids. She waited until it passed, took a deep breath, and began to work the rope around her ankles loose. It took ten minutes. Her fingers ached and the skin on her legs was raw but she was almost free.

She got to her knees and then stood up slowly. Her head hurt so much that she had to stop every few inches and wait for the pain to subside before moving up the next few inches. She searched the floor and the nearby walls for a stone sharp enough to cut through the rope around her wrists, something that she could slip her hands over and pull down on with her weight. She found one. It was close to the stairs, away from the light, a triangular rock with a jagged edge across the top that stuck out several inches from the wall.

She stood on her tiptoes and caught the stone between her hands. She slid the rope over the top and began to move back and forth. The rope slipped off several times and the rock cut into her hands and wrists. She kept her balance and rubbed even harder. The rope began to fray.

She pulled at the partially severed strands, twisting her wrists. Her head throbbed from the strain. The rope split and broke apart. She pulled both hands free and held them up so she could look at them. They were covered with dirt and blood and the skin on her palms was scraped raw from the rock. There were red rope burns around each wrist.

She started up the basement stairs, slowly, pausing at each step to listen, marking each one like a passage through some enormous gulf of time. She had no idea what was on the other side of the door. It was only one more obstacle to get by, one more object to remove from her life. She reached the top of the stairs.

The door wasn't locked. She turned the knob and pushed it open. The smell of gunpowder was strong and the rags were still piled in the corner where he'd put them. He had left her knapsack on the table directly in front of the door. The knapsack wasn't the only thing he had left her.

Next to it were five small notebooks, each one numbered in the identical spot on the spine. He'd also left her a large manila envelope that had been folded over several times and taped together. She passed over it, uninterested, drawn more to the five small notebooks.

She touched the top notebook, ran her fingers across the face of it. The cover seemed warm to her touch, the texture as smooth as skin. She wanted to leave the notebooks there, undisturbed. She couldn't stop herself. She opened the top notebook and read the first line: "I followed the black wolf into the canyon at sundown."

She closed the book and put it back with the others. The knapsack was filled with her clothes, all the things she had brought with her. Everything was carefully packed, neat and clean as if a servant had done it. The only thing left unexamined was the envelope.

Jenny opened it and found the money. There must have been nearly five thousand dollars in the envelope, maybe more. She left the money on the table and picked up the notebooks. Underneath was a piece of paper.

"Get away as soon as you can," he had written to her in his small deliberate hand. "Don't touch anything in the house." Below that, he had written the words *I love you* but they were erased, their lines only faint impressions on the page, as if he were afraid to leave her with anything but a warning.

After he'd taken from her the one thing that mattered, the thing she wanted most of all.

She put everything in her knapsack and slipped out the back door. It came to her as she crossed the yard that she knew exactly where he was going.

He'd promised to take her there once.

The police cars arrived sometime after dark. She had no watch and no way to judge the time except that it was after sundown and she'd been sitting on the ridge behind the house when she first saw the yellow police car cruise down the road, turn slowly around at the other end, and come to a stop. The car was soon joined by several more. She lay flat on the ridge top and watched them for a long time before slipping off into the woods.

Now as she watched Atwood drift away from the wreckage of the house toward the crowd of spectators, she realized he was her last chance to reach Dane. She knew where he was but no idea how to find it, and even if she knew, she had no car, no way to get there quickly.

She hurried through the woods and circled around, finally coming out on the road several hundred yards behind the crowd of spectators. With her knapsack and her clothes, she looked like one more local, another sullen face in the crowd.

Atwood watched the ambulance roar past him across the yard. He couldn't stay there any longer and walked toward the crowd of spectators. The tranquilizer gun in his pocket felt useless to him now. They'd tricked everyone, he thought, and now they were gone. He just hoped they'd gotten far enough away. He nodded to the state trooper who stood guard over the crowd. He let Atwood by.

He turned to look at the crowd. Now he was like them; he could sit back and enjoy the show. The crowd didn't seem to be having too much fun. They stared at the unfolding drama without expression, thin faces and flat vacant eyes.

All except one.

She stood at the back and watched him instead, a young woman with a knapsack slung over one shoulder. Her eyes were alive; they glittered and danced, tried to draw him closer to her. Atwood stiffened, unable to move. She passed along the edge of the crowd, her unwavering gaze focused on him.

It's her, Atwood thought, it's Jenny. The realization forced him into motion and he started toward her. As he did, an older woman dressed in jeans and a sweater, so similar to Jenny that they might have been mother and daughter, took her by the arm and led her away. Jenny looked scared and Atwood was suddenly afraid that the woman was going to give her to the police and hurried to stop her.

"Who are you?" she asked him when he was a few feet away. She stood in front of the girl as if she were protecting her somehow.

"I'm a friend," Atwood said.

"Is that true?" the woman asked Jenny.

Jenny nodded. "I was trying to reach him when you stopped me."

"You could use a friend," the woman said to her. She turned to Atwood again. "You any good at it?"

"You bet," Atwood said.

The woman examined the bruise on Jenny's face. It was a long purplish smear that ran down her jawline and feathered across her neck. The bruise added a corrosive tinge to her face, Atwood thought.

"My first husband hit me," she said. "I let him get away with it once. Thought it was something he had to get out of his system." She searched in her back pocket. "Second time he did it I went after him with a kitchen knife. We didn't last long after that." She glanced at Atwood and looked Jenny straight in the eye. "You want to be careful who you pick from now on."

She pressed something into her hands. It was a set of car keys.

"You take my car," she said, and pointed down the road. Atwood saw a large gold car parked on the side a hundred feet away.

"It's just an old Ford. I got a couple more at home," the woman said. "When you get a chance, call and tell me where you left it." She stepped back, her eyes still on Jenny's face. "You better get out of here now," she said, and stepped into the crowd.

They walked quickly to the car. Atwood climbed in the driver's side of the Ford and waited for Jenny to tell him what to do.

"He's at the lodge," she said. "Do you know where it is?"

"I do," Atwood said. His fingers tightened around the steering wheel.

"How fast can you get there?"

"Do you care about the car?"

Jenny shook her head.

"No problem then," Atwood said.

He backed the car around and fishtailed down the road, his foot steady on the accelerator, gaining speed as they got farther and farther from the house. A police car with flashing lights passed him going the other way. Atwood hardly noticed it. The road was straight and wide. The Ford seemed to drive itself.

Chapter 38

THE VIEW FROM Carroll's bedroom closet was a narrow band of orange light from the bathroom reflected in the oval mirror that hung behind his small dressing table. Dane had been there for an hour, standing in the dark, barely moving, waiting for Carroll to return from his clinic, a suite of specialist offices behind a plain gray limestone facade on the corner of Eighty-first and West End Avenue.

He had been to the clinic earlier and had seen the police car parked in front. The officer had been talking to a young woman in shorts and a white halter top. It might have been a coincidence but when he returned an hour later, the same police car was still there. He used a pay phone a few blocks away on Broadway. Carroll's receptionist was very helpful when he asked to speak to him. The doctor was with a patient, she said, and wouldn't be free until eight. Dane thanked her and said he'd call him the next day.

Carroll's apartment was part of a cluster of buildings between West End and Riverside Drive on West Eighty-seventh that were joined by a courtyard in the rear. A high wrought-iron fence surrounded by shrubbery broke up the courtyard into separate spaces for each building.

He waited until dark and climbed the fence at the end of the narrow walkway crowded with piles of plastic garbage bags and newspapers bundled together with twine that ran between two of the buildings. He slipped over the top and catwalked down the inside of the fence. Lights flickered from the courtyard opposite Carroll's building and he heard loud voices and laughter and the sound of music. Someone was having a party. He crept along the wall. The courtyard behind the building was empty. Too much noise. On the other side of the fence, a glass smashed and someone yelled an obscenity.

The roof of one of the ground-floor apartments jutted out directly underneath Carroll's. Dane used the decorative brickwork on the corner of the building, a series of inverted pyramids that stuck out every few feet from the edge of the building like the prow of a boat, and climbed to the roof. He flung himself over the top and rolled across the tar and gravel. Below him, just visible above the wall, he could see the heads of the people in the other courtyard. They seemed too engrossed in what they were doing to worry about a solitary figure crawling around a neighbor's roof in the dark.

Dane crept forward, checking each window. The second to the last was unlocked. Scattered beneath it were several cigarette butts and an empty pack of matches. None of them looked fresh but it was hard to tell in the dark. There was no one home, he was certain of that. So where had the cigarettes come from? He pushed the window with his fingers and rolled out of the way.

Nothing happened. He pushed it open a little more and looked inside. From what he could see, the room was empty. He slipped over the sill and landed on a bed. When his eyes became adjusted to the dark, he knew where the cigarettes had come from. The room belonged to one of Carroll's children. Judging from the furniture and the decorations, it was the girl's room. She must have smoked on the roof so her parents wouldn't catch her.

He searched the rest of the apartment but there were no signs that anyone but Carroll had been there in the last few days. There were breakfast dishes in the kitchen but only for one. Three separate piles of unopened mail were stacked on the hall table. Dane flipped through each pile and put them back. He shut himself in Carroll's closet and left the door open just enough to see. A narrow field of vision was all he needed now.

He heard what he thought must have been Carroll's voice first. The door opened and a deep voice said quietly, "I don't think it's necessary."

"It'll just take a minute," someone with a heavy New York accent said. "I gotta do it." It was probably the policeman from the clinic.

Carroll said, "Would you like a glass of something? Iced tea? Coffee?"

"No, thanks," the policeman said. "I don't drink too much when I'm on a watch. Where am I going to put it, you know what I mean? Gets a little cagey in the unit."

Dane moved back into the recesses of the closet. He heard the policeman moving through the apartment, opening doors and looking into each room.

"Your windows are all secure," the policeman told Carroll.

"That's good to hear."

"You don't have too much to worry about now. I heard the guy got himself waxed."

"So you said," Carroll answered.

"I'm just going to check your bedroom and the bath and I'll be gone."

"I don't think anyone's in the bathroom," Carroll said. The voices came closer. The cop opened the bathroom door.

"You think so?" the cop said. "We had one creep used to like to hide in women's apartments—in the shower. He'd wait until a woman got on the can, then he'd jump out, shake his weenie in her face, and scoot down the hall like Br'er Rabbit. Woman couldn't do a goddamn thing, she's sitting on the toilet."

The policeman closed the bathroom door. "You're okay in here," he said.

"Good," Carroll said.

"Well," the policeman said. "I'll be going. You need anything, I'm downstairs."

"I'm sure I'll be fine," Carroll said. "Thank you for your help. And the ride."

"No problem," the policeman said. "It's part of the job."

Dane heard the door shut. Carroll sat on the edge of the bed nearest the bathroom. Dane could see him now, taking off his shoes first, tucking his socks into each one and setting them at the foot of the bed. He stretched and walked to the closet and slid back the door.

Dane's hand shot out and took him by the throat. Carroll had no time to scream, barely enough time to fill his lungs before Dane's hand closed around his throat and pushed him backward onto the bed. Dane put one knee on Carroll's chest and the other on his right arm. He squeezed the doctor's throat harder. Carroll's face turned dark red and his eyes bulged. He grabbed Dane's shoulder but his grip was so weak that it was almost like a caress. Carroll's hand dropped off. Dane eased his hold on his throat. Carroll gasped for air.

He waited until Carroll caught his breath and then tightened his grip again. The doctor shook his head, trying to make him stop.

"There's something I want you to do," Dane whispered to him. "If you do anything other than what I tell you, I'll kill you. If you try and warn the police after I'm gone, I'll come back and kill you and the rest of your family. Just the way you killed mine."

Carroll blinked and nodded. Dane let go of his throat and moved his knee off his chest and arm. Carroll sat up slowly. He held his throat and coughed. Dane stood over him.

"Listen to me," Dane said. "This is what I want you to do."

Carroll listened and nodded, too afraid to do anything else. When Dane finished, he asked Carroll to repeat what he had just said. The doctor repeated it, aware as he spoke that he was going to survive. He had been living under what he thought was a death sentence all this time but now that sentence had been commuted. He felt no flood of relief, only a numbing sense of guilt that he should be the only one left. The fact that the man was going to let him live was a condemnation of everything he had done to wash himself clean, to prepare himself for death. Now the opportunity was gone and the loss drained him of what little faith in himself he had left.

"Ten o'clock," Dane said. "Wait until then. I don't care if you call after that but not before."

The doctor nodded but still seemed confused by one thing.

"Why do you want him to meet you at the lodge?" he asked. "Why not the park?"

"Because I can't get him any other way," Dane said. It would be the completion of a circle. Van Owen would die on his own killing ground, not New York, but the place that he had helped create; Dane would turn that place against him. When it was finished, the wolf would go free. There was no hope of taking him back to Canada now. Tonight would be the end of it.

Dane turned to leave but Carroll took hold of his arm and held him back.

"Before you go," Carroll said, "I want to tell you what happened. I want to try to explain it to you."

Dane tore Carroll's hand loose and gripped it tight at the wrist. Carroll's face filled with pain.

"How are you going to do that?" he asked.

"Please," Carroll whispered, and bowed his head. Dane let go of his hand. The doctor began to speak. Dane listened to his voice, stripped of all cadence and tone, a flat whisper. Dane heard only the sound, and let the words die.

When he finished, Dane backed away from him. The doctor kept his head down, like a man awaiting sentence. When he looked up, Dane was gone. It didn't matter, he would do what had been asked.

He showered and cooked dinner but couldn't eat. After putting on clean clothes, he decided to leave early. If only he could convince Van Owen, Carroll thought, he might be able to end it without another killing.

Downstairs, he surprised the policeman by asking for a ride to the clinic. At the clinic, he entered through the Eighty-first Street side and then exited on West End Avenue and quickly flagged down a taxi.

He would do what he had promised, he thought as he directed the cabdriver to Van Owen's apartment.

He would do all that and more.

Van Owen thought Carroll looked like a man who'd just found salvation and was in a big hurry to spread the good news. His face had that feverish glow, his eyes shone, and he seemed barely able to control himself. Van Owen let him into the apartment, curious about the unexpected visit. At the same time he wondered if it might be a police setup. Had Yates wired the doctor up and sent him over?

No. Yates didn't seem that stupid.

"I have a message for you," Carroll said, and walked past him into the living room as if the hallway weren't big enough to accommodate the words. Van Owen followed him down the hall.

"I talked to him tonight," Carroll said. He stood with his back to the windows and wrung his hands together like some kind of mad prophet. "The man with the wolf," he said so there was no mistake.

"You did?" Van Owen asked. Here it comes, he thought. He felt his heart quicken. The tips of his fingers tingled like they'd been brought near the edge of a fire.

"He wants to meet you," Carroll said.

"When?" Van Owen forced himself to sit down. He turned his chair away from Carroll. He didn't want to look at him now, did not wish to see the doctor's overanxious face.

"Tonight," Carroll said.

"When?" Van Owen asked again, more sharply this time.

"Midnight," Carroll said.

"In the park?" Van Owen asked.

"No," Carroll said, and smiled.

Van Owen fought the urge to stand. If he stood up now, he wouldn't be able to stop himself. He'd beat the answer out of Carroll, and when he had it, he'd kill him with his bare hands. He breathed evenly through his mouth and felt the cool air whistle past his lips. The doctor was too ready to give up his secrets for that right now.

"There are conditions," Carroll said.

"There always are," Van Owen said.

"My conditions," Carroll said. "Not his."

Van Owen waited.

"I want you to let him live," Carroll said. "There's been enough killing. Let him go."

"And if I do?" Van Owen asked.

"I don't know," Carroll said. He was so serious now that Van Owen wanted to laugh. His voice slowed and grew faint. Carroll was a man unaccustomed to bargaining with death. "You have to have something, don't you?" he said.

"Of course," Van Owen said.

"Take the wolf," Carroll said, disgusted by what he was offering. "It's what you want, isn't it? Take the wolf and let the man go."

Van Owen stood up, completely in control. "I don't want him or the wolf," he said.

"What?" Carroll said. He was thrown off balance.

"I'm interested in something else."

"I'm not sure I understand. You're not going to kill him?"

"I'm not interested in him. I won't say it again." Van Owen smiled. "My own conditions." He'd run out of patience. "Where?"

"The lodge," Carroll said. "He said he'll meet you at the lodge at midnight." The words came out fast.

"Excuse me," Van Owen said abruptly, and left the room.

Carroll felt lost and abandoned. He'd just saved a man's life. There had to be more to it than this. He glanced down the hall to see where Van Owen had gone but there was no real way to tell; his bedroom door was closed, so were several others. Carroll returned to the living room and waited. He watched the lights of the cars as they swirled through the park. For the first time in weeks, he could look at the park without an overwhelming feeling of dread. The wolf was gone, the killings were over; once again it was just Central Park. Carroll managed a smile.

After ten minutes he began to get impatient. What was Van Owen doing in there?

"Hello," he said tentatively, and stepped into the hallway. The bedroom door opened.

"Hello," he said again.

Van Owen came out of the bedroom. He was dressed

completely in black. Even his face was black. Greasy smears ran down each cheek and across his forehead. In his left hand he held a small aluminum suitcase. In his right he held something that looked like a small black bow. Carroll started to say something, to ask the hunter what he was doing, but Van Owen wasn't listening. He raised the crossbow, pointed it at the doctor, and pulled the trigger.

The bolt struck Carroll in the chest and propelled him backward into the wall. The heavy shaft cracked the thick plate of the bone of his sternum and then tore through his aorta and heart muscle. He slammed against the wall. The bolt rammed through his rib cage and drove a full four inches into the plaster. Carroll's body slid forward down the shaft and stopped. He hung there alive for a few seconds more and died.

Van Owen secured the crossbow inside the suitcase. On his way out he stopped in front of Carroll's body. His head hung into his chest and Van Owen had to bend over to look at his face. The doctor's eyes were wide open, as if he were staring at his blood-spattered shoes.

Van Owen rubbed his fingers in Carroll's blood and wiped them across his face, mixing the blood with the black greasepaint. He took his time and proceeded carefully. He rubbed it along his hairline and under each eye. With the palm of his hand, he smeared the dark mixture under his chin and around the back of his neck.

When he finished, he lifted Carroll's face and ran his fingers down each of his cheeks. Not satisfied with the results, he drew his fingers straight across the doctor's forehead, three black and bloody lines, to mark a fool's death.

The two detectives Yates had assigned to watch Van Owen were not going to let him get away again. They were awake and alert and kept careful track of everyone entering or leaving the building. One of them recognized Carroll from a description. He made a quick note of the time and tried to figure out what it might mean.

A few minutes after ten, Van Owen left the building and walked past their car.

"Jesus Christ," one of them said. "Did you see that?"

"Yeah," the one on the driver's side said. How could he miss him? Van Owen was carrying a small black suitcase and his face was covered with greasepaint.

"What do you want to do?" Van Owen was a block down the street already. He was walking casually but he was definitely getting away.

"Where's the other one?"

"He didn't come down." He glanced anxiously in the side mirror. "What are we going to do?"

"Shit," the driver said. He opened the door and got out. "You take Van Owen. I'm going to check on the apartment." His partner slid over. "Stay close but don't spook him. If things start to break, call for a backup."

The driver watched his partner make a U-turn and drive slowly down the street. He took out his shield, held it up for the startled desk clerk, and pulled him into an elevator.

"You got a key on you?" he asked when the elevator doors closed. The desk clerk nodded.

"Good," the detective said. "Show me 1148."

They got out on the eleventh floor. The desk clerk turned right and stopped in front of a door in the middle of the hall.

"Open it and get out of the way," the detective told him.

He gave the detective the key and moved back. The detective opened the door and stepped to one side. Nothing, not a sound.

"Police," he yelled. He took out his gun. "Listen," he said, "if you're in there, I don't want any problems. I just want to talk." No reply. The detective took a quick look inside and saw Carroll's body. He slipped around the edge of the doorway and flattened out against the wall, his gun trained on the figure at the end of the hall. He was about to tell him to freeze when the guy fell straight down from the wall. Then he saw the pool of blood on the floor and the arrow sticking out of his back and thought, Shit, this guy doesn't have to freeze, he's stiff already. With Van Owen gone, the next big question was whether anybody else was hanging around.

He waved the desk clerk away from the door and moved cautiously down the hall. The apartment seemed to be empty but he went through it room by room. Van Owen's bedroom was the last.

The smell inside the bedroom was pretty bad. The bloodstains on the bed didn't look so good, either. The pillows and sheets were covered with them. He searched both closets but they were empty. That left the bathroom. He slid the door open with his foot. The door seemed unusually heavy.

The girl's body swung into view. She was hooked on the back of the door by her wrists. Her head was missing. He started to feel sick and closed the door.

Only one spot I forgot, he thought. He went back to the bed and lifted one of the pillows. Then the other.

Surprise, surprise.

Afterward, he sat down in the living room and called the sergeant. With Yates in New Jersey and this surveillance on shaky grounds to begin with, the sergeant would know how to handle it. All he wanted to do was get with his partner, so they could nail the creep in the makeup.

"Listen," he said to the sergeant when the operator put him through. "We got ourselves a couple extremely dead people here." He explained the situation and then asked about his partner. The sergeant told him to hold on, they'd try to raise him on the radio. He glanced at the body in the hall. "Hurry up," he said to the sergeant.

Van Owen stopped a few blocks north of his apartment building and looked back down the street. The detective tailing him in the car slowed down. He couldn't figure out why Van Owen had suddenly stopped. He looked in the rearview mirror, thinking that his partner might have followed him, but couldn't see anything. The street was empty. He pulled the car over, lit a cigarette, and waited. Van Owen stepped off the curb and walked toward him.

Shit, the detective thought. He took a deep drag on his cigarette and tried to act casual. Fat chance of that, he thought.

Van Owen approached the car.

"Excuse me," he said, and smiled.

The detective rolled down his window. "Yeah?"

Van Owen brought his hand up and shot him in the left eye with a small .22 caliber revolver. The gun made a sharp pop. The detective fell forward. His cigarette smashed on the steering wheel and sparks flew across the dash. Van Owen opened the door and shoved him over in the seat. The detective started to moan. Van Owen pressed the gun against the back of his head and fired twice. The detective stopped moaning. Van Owen closed the car door, dropped it into drive, and pulled away.

Five minutes later the radio crackled and someone asked for his location. He hesitated for a moment, then picked up the microphone and spoke rapidly, responding the way the cop might have, telling them that his suspect was heading north toward the far end of the park.

That was it, he thought when he finished. They either believed him or they didn't. And if they didn't, they still wouldn't be able to catch him in time. He laughed and ripped the microphone out of the dash and tossed it into the street.

The car was full of the smell of blood and death. The smell made him dizzy. When he looked at the dead detective, he saw only the girl. She was with him now and wouldn't get away again.

"Your partner's okay," the sergeant said. "He says your suspect's heading north on Central Park West. He's got a hunch he's heading toward the 106th Street entrance. He said he'll meet you there. Wait a second." The detective heard muffled voices. "Okay," the sergeant said. "You wait there. I'll get a couple units over to you right away. Then you're free to join your partner."

"I want some backup when I get up there," the detective said.

"You're going to have more backup than you've ever seen in your life," the sergeant told him.

Jesus, the detective thought, 106th Street. What a zoo that was going to be. At least the creep was dressed for it.

One of the state troopers told Yates he had a call. It had come into the police barracks at Scofield, a few miles away, and they patched it into the car radio. He could take it in the trooper's unit if he wanted. It was back from the crowds and not as noisy. Yates looked at his watch. It was almost a quarter to eleven. He glanced around him. The woods were filled with police, some with dogs, but no one was having any luck. He couldn't believe he'd been there for nearly three hours. The trooper escorted him across the road. Yates slid into the front seat. The trooper stood at attention by the hood of the car.

"This is Yates," he said. "What's the problem?"

"Carroll's dead," the sergeant said.

Yates sat the microphone on his knee and counted off several deep breaths before bringing it up again.

"What happened?" he asked.

"A detective found him at Van Owen's apartment with an arrow through his chest and his face covered with war paint," the sergeant said. "They also found a young girl with her head chopped off."

"What? Where'd the girl come from?"

"How the hell should I know? The detective said you ordered a surveillance on the guy. Is that true?"

"Where is he now?" Yates said. It was a shout. The state trooper turned around to see what had happened.

"I want to know if it's true about the surveillance."

"Forget the surveillance," Yates shouted. "Where the hell is Van Owen?"

"We don't know. The guy's partner said he was tailing him up Central Park West, heading toward 106th. That was forty-five minutes ago. Nobody's seen him or heard from either one of them since. His partner said that Van Owen was made up with blackface."

"You mean camouflage paint?"

"Yeah, that's what I mean."

"What else?"

"He was carrying a small metal case. The detective says he didn't think about it, but now he thinks it was probably for some kind of weapon."

"And nobody's seen either one of them?" Yates asked. "Find them, for Chrissakes!"

"We're looking."

"Shit!" Yates said. "Who's at the park?"

"Everybody," the sergeant said. "They've got the whole thing blocked off, every road, every entrance. Somebody said the mayor wants to call out the National Guard." The sergeant had to laugh. "I hope the guy's out there."

"Is that it?" What else could there possibly be? Yates thought. How much more damage could his case sustain in one evening?

"They want you back here, too," the sergeant said.

"It's going to take me awhile."

"They want you downtown. They already asked for your master sheet and the PD Five dupes."

"You give them what they wanted?"

"I didn't give them anything yet," the sergeant said defensively. "But if this thing falls apart any more, I won't be able to put them off much longer. They need somebody to blame. You look good. That's why I asked you about the surveillance." He waited for Yates to answer. When he didn't, the sergeant asked him again. "Is it true?"

"Yeah," Yates said. "It's true. Don't worry about it. You didn't want to hear about it and I didn't tell you."

"That's not why I asked," the sergeant said. "I know why you did it. I'll see what I can do for you. No promises, though."

Yates smiled. "You like getting your nuts whacked with a stick?"

"Hasn't happened in a while. Forgot what it's like."

"If it gets bad, don't do it," Yates said.

"If it gets bad, don't worry," the sergeant said. "How long will it take you to get back?"

"Hour or so. If I take my time, maybe two."

"I'd bust my hump on this one," the sergeant said. "Save us all an extra reaming."

Yates released the microphone. The state trooper had his back to the windshield. Yates shut the door behind him.

"Everything all right?" the trooper asked.

"No," Yates said. "Everything's pretty much fucked up."

The trooper tried not to smile but gave up.

"Tell Bingham we got a few problems in the city and I had to get back," Yates said. "Ask him to let the other detectives know I left. Thank him for me. Tell him I'll be in touch."

Yates walked to his car, started it, and then turned it off. Where was Atwood? He'd forgotten all about him. Yates called one of the troopers over and asked if he'd seen the veterinarian, but the trooper didn't know who he was talking about.

Yates looked from one end of the road to the other but couldn't find him. He started the car again. Atwood was probably searching through the woods somewhere. He had a habit of wandering off at the most inconvenient times, but that was not his particular problem now. He had problems of his own. Yates waited while the trooper moved one of the cars to let him out.

There were so many unanswered questions—starting with why Carroll had gone to see Van Owen and ending with the missing veterinarian—that it was like a fucking buffet. That meant he had a choice over which one he could tell them he didn't have the answer for first. So what? He knew the whole routine by heart. That's why he was on his way back to New York to get his dick whipped by a bunch of bureaucrats.

Tough shit, he thought, tough shit all the way around.

But he couldn't stop thinking. That was his real problem.

He drove for almost half an hour, running the questions over and over in his mind before they began to make any sense. When they were lined up a certain way, they connected with other bits and pieces of information to form what he began to see as an obvious pattern. The reason no one else could see it was because he hadn't told anybody else what he knew.

That was another one of his problems.

He saw a sign for a Gulf station in the distance and speeded up to get there.

The station was deserted except for one attendant who sat in a chair that was leaned up against a beat-up soda machine next to one of the open bays. He was young, maybe nineteen, and looked unhappy with his current lot in life.

"I need a good map of the area and I need to use your phone," Yates said.

"We don't have a pay phone," the kid said. "Maps are a buck fifty. Machine's right inside the door."

Yates yanked him off his seat. "I'm in a real big hurry," he said, and dragged the kid into the office. "Let's see how fast you can get them for me."

Chapter 39

~~~~~~~~~~~~~~~~~~~~~~~~~~~~~~~~~~~~~

THE TREES LOOKED like they were on fire. From where Dane sat on the crest of a hill a third of a mile north of the lodge, the large rectangular patch of forest directly below him appeared to be engulfed in silver-white flame.

His senses played tricks on him. He smelled smoke and ash and felt a wave of hot wind sweep up the hill and across his face. But it was only a trick, a bit of forgotten memory come back to surprise him. There was no fire, just the low spark of light that surrounded the edge of the preserve. The lights stayed on until midnight, which was less than an hour away. He knew the routine well; he'd been there enough times to know.

There were two guards in the trailer on the left side of the preserve and another who stayed in an apartment over one of the garages and came down only if there was a problem. Every hour until midnight one of the guards patrolled the gravel path cut next to the electric fence just inside the perimeter. He used a battery-powered three-wheel Overland. The inspection usually took just under twenty minutes.

After midnight the lights were activated only if something crossed the fence. The guards stayed in the trailer until six-thirty the next morning when the next shift arrived.

When a hunt wasn't scheduled, the patrol system at the preserve wasn't particularly efficient. The guards sometimes skipped patrols and relied on the perimeter light and the surveillance cameras to do their jobs for them. The guards would often stop for a cigarette and the twenty-minute patrol might take twice as long to complete. Once, Dane found a raccoon that had been caught in the fence and electrocuted. It was nearly an hour before the patrol got around to removing the slowly smoldering carcass.

The last patrol had gone out a little after ten and they'd be reluctant now to make another round. Dane had set up three deadfalls along the fence, each within fifty yards of the other. It would take him less than a minute to trip all three and bring down the fence. He had time enough for that and more.

He lay back on the ground and looked up at the sky. The glow from the trees below ascended toward it, like a cloud of silver creatures scattered overhead, slowly changing into stars. He felt the movement of the wolf beside him. The animal turned his head and looked back in the direction of the house. His ears pricked up at some sound, some stirring in the woods behind them that was too slight for Dane to hear. He rested his hand on the wolf's back and closed his eyes. There had never been a time when he felt so calm, when the future seemed so certain to him. The past was only abandoned books and half-forgotten memories.

He heard a howl, high-pitched and strong. The wolf sat up, muscles tense, suddenly alert. The howl wavered quickly and died, only to be answered by another, closer, more distinct. The wolf stared off in its direction and whined quietly. Dane stroked his thick fur to calm him. Eventually the wolf lay down again by his side. He hoped it was only a pair of strays and not the same pack that had attacked Jenny. That would jeopardize everything. He listened again but the trees and the hills and the distance distorted the sound so much that it could have come from anywhere, been almost anything. Dane relaxed. He could easily be mistaken. What he had heard might have been only the echo of a night owl's scream.

He hoped Jenny had gotten away. There'd been one moment, just before he hit her, when he thought of taking her with him. But only for a moment. He saw the anger in her eyes when she reached for the gun. All he could do was pull back at the last second to keep the blow from breaking her jaw. She fought him even as she was going down. Her legs buckled and he caught her. In the basement he kissed her good-bye and fled, afraid that if she woke up he would change his mind.

He'd set the traps to protect her, give her more time if something went wrong. He couldn't even remember where they were from or why he'd kept them. He'd picked the two traps up blindly, no longer repulsed by them. The cold metal had warmed to his touch.

He'd set them carefully. The sheet wound around the first trap like a snowdrift on his bed upstairs. He set the other one downstairs and laid the clothes over it gently. The house was empty, devoid of any life that he might have known there. He waited for some feeling to come but there was nothing; he felt numb, like he had severed a nerve. His past belonged to someone else and there was no reason to go back. The kitchen door closed behind him. It had been a relief to be free of it at last.

He raised himself up. Something was moving in the preserve. He heard the metallic click of the trailer door opening and saw one of the guards move to where the Overland was parked. They had decided on one last patrol before midnight.

It was only a question of a few minutes one way or the other. He could draw them out one at a time now. It was probably easier that way. The guard climbed on the toad-shaped bike and zoomed off around the perimeter.

Dane and the wolf slipped down the hill along the bottom of a dry spring bed. The path was hidden by fallen trees and piles of dead logs as high as his head. It was the same one he had been using since the night he'd first visited the preserve earlier in the spring, a time that seemed so long ago that he had trouble remembering what it was like.

The guard drove by fast. When he'd gone, Dane and the wolf slipped in close to the fence, out of sight of the cameras, and made their way to the first deadfall.

The guard on the Overland was more than ready to get stoned. Karl, the manager, had been on his case all evening, but with a little luck he'd be in bed by now. There was no excuse for Karl. He was a prick. He talked like a prick and acted like a prick, muttering in German and stamping his feet when he got upset. Karl said he was raised in Glassboro, New Jersey, but the guard had him pegged for Wiesbaden and a stint in the Hitler Youth; he enjoyed giving orders too much.

At the north corner of the preserve, the guard parked the Overland and called the trailer on his radio.

"I'm at the north point," he said. "No sign of an invasion here. The Fatherland is safe for another night."

"You made the point in less than three minutes this time," came the reply. "That's a new land speed record. Will you be taking that code seven now?"

"That's a big affirmative on the code seven," he said, and grinned. He pulled out the joint and spun it between his fingers. "Why don't you dim the lights a tad. I need a little atmosphere down here."

The lights went down by half. The forest grew dark. He couldn't see more than twenty feet in any direction.

"That's better," he said, and lit the joint, taking a deep drag.

"Take your time," the voice on the radio said. "See you at the top of the hour."

Ten minutes later the guard was thoroughly stoned, noodling along on the Overland when he heard a crash somewhere behind him. He stopped the bike and looked back but it was too dark to see anything. Seconds later he heard another crash, only this time it was in the darkness *ahead* of him. He grabbed the radio and fumbled for the switch.

"I think we got something out here," he whispered.

In the trailer the guard was looking at the electric wall map of the preserve. On the map, the fence was marked by an outline of tiny white lights. Each light represented an in-ground sensor. Two lights were blinking. That meant the fence was down in two different places, one just past north point, the other halfway between that and the western corner. While the guard watched, a third light began blinking, this one on the southern edge of the preserve. Whoever it was, he thought, they're heading right for my trailer.

The guard locked the trailer door. Then he moved the lights up to full and locked the surveillance cameras on the downed-fence areas. In the monitors they looked basically the same. A dead log had fallen across the fence and knocked each section flat. He called the other guard.

"What's going on out there?" he said.

The other guard didn't respond.

He's gone to take a look, the guard said to himself, and he'll be back in a minute. He counted off thirty seconds and tried again. Still no response. Okay, he thought, the dumb bastard gets one more shot.

"Listen," he said, hearing the desperation in his voice for the first time. "Quit fucking around. Just tell me you're okay." There was nothing. "Come on," he pleaded. "Just let me know you're all right. Tap on the mike, anything." The other guard didn't respond.

There was something on one of the monitors. A shape slipped through the fence and disappeared into the trees. He tried to follow with the camera but it was too fast. The monitor screen suddenly went black. They were going after the goddamn cameras now. Two more figures slipped through the fence.

That did it, he thought, and reached for the phone. He was going to get Karl out here. He punched out the number and prayed that the asshole was still awake.

Karl had just turned off the television when the phone rang. It took him a few seconds to understand what the guard was trying to tell him. When it finally sank in, he said he'd be right there and hung up the phone. Then he got his shotgun and an extra box of shells from the front closet. He opened the door and started down the steps.

Someone was waiting at the bottom of the stairs. The manager was so scared by it that he nearly fell over. He steadied himself and swung the shotgun around.

"Hello, Karl," Van Owen said.

Karl stopped and looked carefully at the figure.

"Van Owen?" Karl asked. "Is that you?"

"Of course," he said.

"You scared the hell out of me," Karl said. "We got some break-in and I thought you were one of them." Karl moved down a few more steps and stopped again. "You okay? How come you got that stuff all over your face?"

Karl moved a few steps closer. The silence was beginning to make him nervous. Van Owen was carrying something odd in his right hand.

"What've you got there?" Karl asked, and pointed with the shotgun.

"This?" Van Owen said, and raised his hand. "Let me show you."

The guard in the trailer felt deaf, dumb, and blind. He kept trying to raise the other guard but there was still no response. If that wasn't enough to terrorize him, he had to sit and watch helplessly while two more monitor screens went blank. That meant there were only five working cameras left.

A figure came down the path from the main lodge building. The guard watched him pass through the gate on one of the remaining monitors. Thank God, it was Karl. The son of a bitch even waved his shotgun at him.

The guard heard a loud knock on the trailer door and flung it open.

"Karl," he said. "I'm sure glad it's you."

It wasn't.

Dane heard the shotgun blast while he ran toward the next camera position, a spot high in the rocks on one of the observation sites a hundred yards north of the largest clearing. Beside him, the wolf slowed in midstride. The sound, sharp and unexpected, rippled through the trees from the direction of the trailer. It seemed to shrink the space around him, pull the night air in tight around his chest.

Something had changed in the preserve. He wasn't certain how it had happened but he knew that Van Owen was inside the preserve. Worse, he was inside the trailer, watching him. Dane ran faster to get out of the way of the remaining cameras.

There were only two more cameras, one in the rocks directly above him, another mounted near a small open area on the other side. He'd taken out the first two cameras after knocking out the guard and wiring his hands to the rear axle of the Overland. There was no skill to dismantling the cameras. They were mounted on metal brackets bolted on the tree trunks. He'd climbed the trees and smashed the lenses with a stone.

Without warning, the lights came on full force.

The sudden glare made him stumble. He knew he had to get off the path but momentum carried him forward. The wolf broke away and cut north through the trees around the rocky base of the observation site. Dane let him go, abandoning what little control he had left.

He slowed to keep from falling and looked up at the camera, almost lost in the glare from the lights on top of the rocks. He saw the camera swing around. It tracked him until he stopped.

Atwood froze in terror at the sound of the shotgun. Until then it had been quiet. They had driven almost a mile past the lodge before they turned off onto what looked to be an abandoned road, grown over with vines and tall weeds. They drove deep into the woods until the car bucked and died. They walked the rest of the way. He followed behind her and kept one hand on the tranquilizer gun in his pocket. She noticed it but said nothing. Atwood was exhausted by the time they reached the preserve. With the lights on, the preserve looked like something from a fairy tale.

Jenny pointed.

To his right, Atwood saw Dane and the wolf running along the perimeter. Something fell across the fence just behind them as they disappeared into the trees. He pulled the gun and one of the sealed darts from his pocket.

"What are you doing with that?" she said. Her voice was sharp and filled with alarm.

"It's for the wolf," Atwood said, and loaded the dart in the chamber. "It won't hurt him."

Jenny ran toward the preserve. She jumped over the broken section of fence and disappeared straight into the heart of the preserve. Atwood followed quickly but already he had lost sight of her.

Then he'd heard the shotgun. It came from his left, at the other end of the preserve. The lights exploded in front of his eyes and he covered them with his hands, the gun grip cold against his forehead.

He uncovered his eyes and ran, hoping he could find Jenny before it was too late. He ran into the trees, away from the lights. Something caught his leg. He fell forward and struck one of the trees. The gun flew from his hand. He crawled across the ground after it.

Jenny ran past him and scooped up the gun. He tried to reach her but the pain in his head was too much. All around him, the lights flared brightly and faded, a starburst of energy that burned white hot and then collapsed into a murky red glow.

In the last few seconds of light, Atwood's vision was clear. He saw the wolf running next to her, an extension of her own shadow. They vanished together.

Van Owen stood on the shooting platform and watched Dane as he crouched by the edge of the clearing. He wanted to see his face but the light was too dim for that. All he could see from the platform was the man's hands and the dull shimmer of the knife blade as he moved cautiously around the clearing.

It was what Van Owen had expected him to do. He escaped from the rocks, just as the wolves in the canyon had tried to do. And ran straight into me, he thought. The man looked up at the shooting platform. Van Owen stayed hidden in the darkness. He wouldn't need the shotgun right now, he thought, and laid it gently on the platform floor. The crossbow would do. He wanted to see his face when he shot him.

He climbed down from the platform quietly. There was no hurry at all now. The man was alone, armed with only a knife. Van Owen came out from beneath the platform. Dane entered the clearing. Van Owen slid a bolt into the bow and locked it in place.

At the noise, Dane stood very still. Van Owen took a few steps forward, just close enough to see his face. What he saw surprised him. There was no fear, no anger, no hate. Dane's expression was of someone who had run out of reasons to live.

He heard something behind him and swung the crossbow around. The girl stood at the edge of the clearing, the wolf crouched by her side. She had a gun aimed at him. He glanced quickly at the man and pointed the crossbow at the wolf.

"You won't make it," he said to her. "I'll kill the wolf, then I'll kill him."

Jenny steadied the gun.

"No," Dane said. "Don't do it."

Van Owen took a step closer to the wolf. "Put the gun down."

Jenny hesitated and then dropped the gun. Van Owen grinned at her, a sharp, hungry grin that frightened her more than the crossbow. It was like a part of her past come to life again. He doesn't want Dane, she thought, he doesn't even want the wolf. He wants me.

"Run," Dane screamed. She ran down the path with the wolf beside her. Van Owen spun around. Dane rushed forward with the knife. The stupid bastard, Van Owen thought. He waited until the last moment and shot him.

The bolt ripped into Dane's thigh and knocked him backward. Van Owen loaded another bolt and walked over to him. Dane had both hands wrapped around his leg. Blood spurted out of the wound into the dirt.

"I aimed for the artery," Van Owen said, and looked at the blood gushing from the leg. "You won't live long."

Dane slashed upward with his knife across the back of Van Owen's right leg. The blade cut through muscle and tendon and scraped along the bone. Van Owen roared in pain. He stepped back and then brought his foot down hard on Dane's arm. The arm snapped and the knife dropped from Dane's hand. Van Owen grinned through the pain and pressed the point of the crossbow against Dane's arm. The bolt speared his wrist and pinned it to the ground.

He picked up Dane's knife and cut a long piece of his shirt away and wound it around his knee several times to slow the bleeding. The pain made it even better. He loaded the bow and went after the girl.

The path led back to the rocks. Van Owen hurried along for a few yards and then ran into the woods to cut them off before they could climb to the top of the observation site. He heard the wolf, the tremendous noise the animal made as it raced through the trees to reach the site.

His leg felt cold and the blood burned hot against his skin. The pain made him run faster. Tree branches whipped across his eyes. He smashed them down with the crossbow.

A low shadow crossed in front of him, a blur of movement as the wolf raced for the safety of the observation site. He broke through the trees and cut off its escape. The wolf was a black shape trapped in the rocks. He caught a glimpse of flat yellow eyes. The animal growled and bared its teeth. This time, he thought, this time.

The woods were suddenly silent. Van Owen looked for the girl but couldn't find her. He knew she was there, he could feel her eyes on him. He raised the crossbow. The animal lunged out of the shadows. He held the crossbow steady and waited until it was only a few yards away. The wolf leaped and he fired. He saw the animal crumple in midair and stepped aside at the last moment to let it land at his feet.

Van Owen dropped the crossbow and took out his knife. He lifted the animal by the scruff of the neck and brought its head up close to his.

He dropped the knife. It fell with barely a sound.

It wasn't the wolf. He looked again. There was no mistake. It wasn't the wolf. The dead animal he held in his hands was a large black dog, a half-breed shepherd with dark yellow eyes. It seemed so impossible that Van Owen began to laugh. He flung the dog aside and looked up. What he saw was the black shape of the wolf as the animal leaped down on him, the last thing he would ever see.

Jenny stood on the rocks and forced herself to watch him die.

When it was finished, the wolf loped away toward the clearing. The lights came up around her. She climbed down and ran after the wolf.

Dane stood in the center of the clearing, balanced unsteadily on one leg, his shattered arm cradled against his chest. The wolf stood beside him, head low, ears flat against his head. The bolts lay in a circle of blood-soaked earth at his feet.

Atwood stood in front of them, only a few feet away.

"Please," she heard him say to Dane. "There's still time."

Dane shook his head. His knee bent and he staggered forward.

"No time left," he whispered.

Atwood moved closer. The wolf dug his paws into the dirt, ready to spring. The veterinarian froze.

"Get the hell out of the way, Atwood."

Atwood looked behind him. Yates walked into the clearing and stopped ten feet from where Atwood stood. He held his gun in both hands and aimed it at the wolf.

"Move," he told Atwood. The veterinarian stepped between Yates and the wolf.

"I won't let you kill him," Atwood said.

Yates edged closer.

"Wait," Jenny said. Dane turned around. She picked up the dart gun and held it up so he could see. She wanted him to move away from the wolf, to let her save him. Instead, he moved closer.

"No," he said to her. "It's too late for that." He held out a hand to her, one sad final gesture, and fell.

Yates stepped to one side and fired.

Atwood threw himself in the way. Yates pulled up at the last second and the shot went wild. The wolf leaped over Atwood and struck Yates in the chest. The gun flew out of his hand.

Yates swung his fist at the wolf's head and missed. The wolf bit down hard on his wrist and shook it. Yates kicked the wolf away, then rolled over and scrambled for the gun, blood streaming down his arm.

The wolf attacked again, tearing at his shoulder and neck. Yates grabbed the wolf by the front legs and threw him off. He grabbed desperately for the gun. His hand struck the handle and it spun out of reach. He was losing strength fast.

Atwood picked up the detective's gun. He looked for Jenny but she was gone. He was the only one left. Yates got to his hands and knees. The wolf tore into his shoulder and neck. Atwood aimed the gun at the wolf's back and fired. The bullet knocked the animal over. The wolf started to get back up. Atwood fired twice more and the animal stayed down.

Yates collapsed on his side, his neck and arm covered with blood. Atwood threw the gun down.

"Pull me up," Yates said. Atwood helped him to sit. He held his shoulders to steady him. "I'm all right," Yates told him, and shook his hands away. To prove it, the detective reached over slowly and picked up his gun and slid it into his pocket. It made him feel better to have it back.

Dane's body lay in the dust a few feet away. He had his hand outstretched, as if he were still waiting for Jenny to take hold of it. Atwood dragged the wolf over and laid him beside Dane. Yates closed his eyes. Atwood walked into the woods after Jenny.

Jenny picked up the crossbow and Van Owen's knife. With her foot, she kicked his body aside and took the bolt case. She saw Atwood at the end of the path. He called her name. She loaded a bolt into the crossbow and pointed it at him.

"Don't come any closer," she said.

Atwood raised his hands and stepped back to show that he understood. She slung the bolt case over her shoulder. He hoped she might say something, acknowledge him in some way. Instead, she turned her back on him and walked away.

When Atwood could no longer hear her, he walked over to Van Owen's body. "Time to join the party," he said. He hooked a foot under each arm and dragged him down the path.

Yates opened his eyes to find Atwood sitting beside him on the ground. There was another body. The veterinarian had laid it at Dane's feet.

"Who's that?"

"Van Owen," Atwood said. "What's left of him."

"Where's the girl?"

"Gone."

Yates looked at the bodies and then at his mangled arm.

"What a fucking mess," he said, mostly to himself.

WINTER/
SOMETIME
LATER

THE PILOT DROPPED the big Lodestar helicopter close to the ridge and swooped along the canyon wall. He didn't much think about his passengers, six geologists on their way back from drilling sites north of Great Bear Lake and anxious to get back to their base camp at Carmacks before nightfall. What other pilot would be willing to make a run this late in the season? They were lucky to get him. Hell, they were lucky to get anybody.

He flew south along the Mackenzie until he was nearly to the Selwyn range. Just above the range, there was a line of narrow, flat-bottomed canyons that he'd never used before to cross the Divide. That's where he was now. It looked like he'd made the right decision. The wind was good, there wasn't any turbulence, and he was having a good time. He had no idea what his passengers were doing.

His passengers were busy talking among themselves, arguing whether or not the offshore sites were going to amount to much of anything and whether going farther north into the Beaufort Sea would do them any good. Only one of the six bothered to look out the window. He'd only been in Carmacks for a year and still got a kick out of the scenery. The other five had been there for years and hated the wilderness. It got in their way.

"Jesus Christ," he said, and turned to the others. "Did you see that?"

"See what?" one of them asked.

"I think he means the trees," another said, and burst out laughing.

"There's a woman down there," he said. "I just saw her. She's standing in the middle of a pack of wolves."

A couple of the other geologists glanced out their windows at the canyon floor.

"I don't see anything," one of them said. "Is she making them do tricks?"

"I'm telling you I saw her," he said, and moved to one of the backseats to get a better view.

"You made a common mistake up here," another geologist said seriously. "That wasn't a woman you just saw, that was Big Foot."

The geologists laughed and patted the new man on the back and returned to their discussion. He stayed at the window and tried to memorize the canyon's topography but it was impossible. It looked like every other one he'd seen so far, the gray rocks and endless forest and the snow-covered mountains beyond. He couldn't find the place again, not in a million years.